# THE
# SECRET
# TO
# BEING
# FRANK

## EVIL BEYOND INSANITY

# JOE LESLIE

Matador
9 Priory Business Park,
Wistow Road, Kibworth Beauchamp,
Leicestershire. LE8 0RX
Tel: (+44) 116 279 2299
Fax: (+44) 116 279 2277
Email: books@troubador.co.uk
Web: www.troubador.co.uk/matador

ISBN 9781 783060 658

British Library Cataloguing in Publication Data.
A catalogue record for this book is available from the British Library.

Typeset by Troubador Publishing Ltd, Leicester, UK
Printed and bound in the UK by TJ International, Padstow, Cornwall

**Matador** is an imprint of Troubador Publishing Ltd

'It seems to be a mode of seeing, added to that which nature generally bestows, and consists of an impression made either by the mind upon the eye, or by the eye upon the mind, by which things distant or future are perceived, and seen as if they were present.'

Dr Samuel Johnson 1709 - 1784

# CHAPTER 1

# CHARLOTTE

Charlotte sat quietly at her desk in the cellar listening to a rat scampering under the floorboard. Behind the marionette lines in the corners of her mouth, she smiled inside. *Is the rat called George?*

Instinctively wrapping a thin cotton nightgown around her skeletal frame, she barely noticed a dull ache from gripping the pen. Charlotte had no room for self-pity. Again, her vivid imagination wandered to atone for her parents' refusal to accept she had any right to exist. Inadequate as she perceived herself to be, Charlotte considered herself more than capable of daydreaming and simultaneously carrying out the task mandated by Father. Looking at her handwriting on all the reams of paper on the desk and with a degree of satisfaction, grasping the pen again in her left hand, she wrote, 'Charlotte needs to come to terms with her perpetual lies, accept the blame for her self worth and comply with the house rules.'

George had given clear instructions to his eleven-year old daughter to write down the lines until she had permission to stop. The subtlety in the parameter governing this task said a great deal about George. He could have stipulated the number of lines, with an open agenda to continue writing; George retained total dominance over his daughter. Concentrating on the finer detail would destroy the very core of her dignity. Charlotte focused on the task in hand. She had no thought of slackening off. Alone in the cellar she could feel his black onyx eyes glaring at her through the wall. Suddenly she turned her swivel chair around to catch the monster. *I know you are hiding somewhere Father, one day I will catch you.*

*Why didn't he tell me the rule I have broken this time?* After giving it serious thought, Charlotte decided worthless individuals always had an excuse to disguise wrongdoing. Life had become unbearable since the death of her three-month-old brother, Charles. However, when she looked back on the incident, she was less certain about that statement. Before his death, she had been a huge disappointment to the family. The object called Charlotte had lost count of the occasions Father had reminded her of how inconsequential girls were, particularly the one called Charlotte. *No for goodness sake, you are missing the point, because of Father; I know how hopeless I am.* The raggedy edges of a grey cloud drifted past the cellar window. Her flaxen blonde hair captured the sunlight as she recalled the day when she found the courage to tell George how useless she was.

Even George, an insipid individual who showed little emotion, raised his large charcoal wispy eyebrows and could not disguise his pleasure from witnessing her meltdown. Why did she have to spoil it all when she asked him to explain the extent of her inadequacy? Like a killer bee defending a disturbed hive, he flew into a rage. 'How dare you, how many times do I have to tell you not to speak without my permission?' Charlotte wiped the droplets of projecting spittle running down her face.

'But Father, please don't be angry with me, I was trying ...'

Intuitively, he lashed out and struck her across the face with the back of his hand. Rebounding off the wall, her brain shuddered against the inside of her skull.

After the incident, George reflected on his reckless behaviour. He could have left a mark and serious consequences could have ensued.

Somewhere in his festering soul, the itch to degrade and hurt her again had to be scratched. With Charlotte standing naked in the corner of the living room, blindfolded, George took out a pair of leather gloves from the drawer and put them on. Without any warning, sporadically he slapped the little girl across the buttocks and thighs. At the end of each spank, pausing, just for a moment, blotchy sagging skin around his high cheekbones tightened as he shouted in her ear. 'Listen GIRL, you are lower than the dog shit under my feet, do you understand me?' She nodded the lesson not to show any sign of anxiety had registered a long time ago.

Behind the curtain of his emotionless face, a victorious, sarcastic smile signalled that, once again he had total control. Charlotte had no idea when the next attack would take place.

George sat on the settee watching her thin arms and legs trembling from the vulnerability of a whack. Then he heard something that he could only describe as music to his ears and, strangely, in tune with his beloved fast scherzo of Beethoven's fifth, her teeth were chattering.

Clenching her teeth, biting the inside of her mouth, she tried to hold back the tears. The clicking noise stopped and tears ran through the blindfold onto pallid cheeks. At ten years of age, Charlotte knew exactly what he wanted. George wanted her to beg for mercy. He would have to wait until hell freezes over before she would do that.

Lying on a bare mattress in her bedroom, Charlotte took comfort in not giving in to the bully. Only a small victory, but at least she had something to hold onto in the afterglow of the dark. Finally closing her eyes, lucid black and white images would soon sever her psychological cord with reality. Darkness and the dread of night would take her to a far safer place. Charlotte made a wish on the dark side of the rainbow that she would die inside; pass to another world, any world where parents love their children. With her eyelids rapidly twitching, citrine-green eyes slithered along the corridor leading to the dark beyond. Charlotte could hear the sound of madness calling. All the fantasies of killing George and Rose pleaded with her to join in with the imagery.

Yet another page finished, glaring at the ceiling Charlotte cursed the dim glow from a small light bulb. It seemed like yesterday when she heard Rose, her mother, howling when she found Charles dead in the cot. *Mother sounded like a mad dog that should be put down. Because of her, they call me horrible names. It is only fair and proper that I should do it.*

*Now stop it, you mustn't think about it, you didn't really mean to do it.* In her daydreaming, she created the image of the anorexic fragile frame of Rose asleep in the bedroom. Charlotte could see herself creeping into her room carrying a carving knife from the kitchen. *Yes the really big one with the sharp pointed edge.* She paused for a moment. *Stabbing Mother in the heart is far too good for her. It would be over too quickly, it must be one where...* The illusion started playing again. Leaning over the bed, slowly raising the knife above her head, and with all the force she could imagine Charlotte stabbed Rose in her right eye. She continually twisted the handle of the knife in the hollow socket of the skull until the eyeball popped out onto the carpet. *Stop rushing it, stop it at once.* Creating a similar picture, she punctured the other eye. *Do not stab her any more or you will kill her. Not yet, wait for her to scream. She's blind now think of something else, more blood think. Right wait and look at Mummy, her cheeks are swollen. Look at all that horrible white hair growing on her face and legs.* Moving the scenario on, gripping the knife, the wakeful dreamer inserted the sharp point of the blade in Rose's nostril. Jerking her hand upwards as if holding a knife, she pushed the imaginary blade further up the nostril. Charlotte could feel the drag of the flesh against the knife as she slit open her nose. *The blood, look at all the blood.*

In the magic of imagination, Charlotte could see her mother sitting up in bed covering her eyes. Her nightgown and bed sheets were saturated in blood. *I will let her scream like Father and call her, what does he call her. Oh please, please remember. That is it, a hysterical, fucking whore. The next thing to do is...* Holding a hand out for Rose to get out of bed, Charlotte visualised the blood spurting from the two bony sockets of her skull. *This way Mother or Father will get to you again.*

Rose reached the top of the staircase. *Quick hurry, Father is on his way.* Taking the next step into mid-air, hitting the far wall, Rose tumbled down the staircase and landed helplessly at the bottom of the stairs. Charlotte made herself busy. She pushed back the rolling shutter of the bureau and found a cigarette lighter. On the canvas of the macabre, bending down, she set fire to her dressing gown. *I lied, it's not Father at all, it's me. What was it again, I know, burn and go to hell you whore.*

Stepping back, watching the nightdress in flames, Charlotte heard the most terrifying scream she could possibly imagine and clapped her hands with glee. *You can die now Mother, I don't mind because I can always kill you again tomorrow.* The girl who idolised the star of *Satan* never tired of the fantasy of killing both parents. In time, the flight of imagination became more elaborate, where Charlotte had control, something she had never experienced in reality.

Daydreaming seemed to be having a profound effect on her writing. *Gosh another page. Now think hard about something else. I know when Mother and I were friends.* After considerable thought, her mind wandered again to Charles's death. In spite of their differences, they seemed to bond together as the result of the tragic loss. *Now I remember Mother allowed me to suck the milk from her breasts.* This adherent experience lasted until the result of the inquest.

The report from the pathologist summarised the circumstances surrounding the death. Rose had placed the baby on his stomach for the midday nap. She looked in on the child two hours later and the baby was lying motionless. There were no marks, choking, bleeding, asphyxiation or anything to suggest foul play. Rose must be the perpetrator.

Under the microscope, Inspector Bright explained that, 'Postnatal depression plays on the mind of these women. She is either a clever bastard or she's stumbled on a foolproof way to kill her child.'

Two interviews later, he was less certain about his prime suspect. Who next? He dismissed George, a local bank manager and county councillor as an option. The bright spark again pointed his team in the right direction. 'A case like this, the type of skulduggery is the hallmark of a female.'

The next suspect had to be Charlotte. Moreover, the motive was again obvious. Bright had finally nailed the culprit. 'Do you know any woman that isn't jealous about something, they are all the same, mood swings the lot?'

Rose did everything she could to transfer the blame onto her daughter. 'Yes, she is a spiteful manipulative creature capable of any mischief, including harming her own flesh and blood.'

Again Bright failed to pin the tail on the donkey called Charlotte and the inquest returned an open verdict.

George and Rose condemned their daughter as woefully guilty. They badly needed a scapegoat. Rose decided to withdraw from the family circle. 'If I am not responsible for killing poor Charles, it must have been that girl. The very sight of her makes my flesh crawl and as for taking her to school, it is simply out of the question.'

Employing part-time staff and hiring a taxi to deal with the domesticity were all in place. 'And the arrangements will continue until my so-called daughter has the decency to confess to murdering our son.'

*How could my own flesh and blood do such a heinous thing? Good lord woman, the next thing you will be thinking is that she is innocent.* A sly grin filled the void between her forehead and neck. *Am I missing the obvious? I have always had suspicions about that birth. It's as plain as the nose on her face. There are ruinous differences in our appearance between my dark, auburn hair and brown eyes and her short curly blonde hair and green eyes.* At last, Rose had finally managed to work out the conundrum. *There must have been a mix-up in the maternity ward. It would not be the first time that some unsuspecting mother had the wrong baby.*

No one realised, not even George, the deep hatred Rose felt towards Charlotte. After a while, the loveless child with a death wish became isolated, alone and confined to the bedroom.

Charlotte never knew what it was like to have friends or any outside interest. That experience, 'Had no place in the life of a child responsible for killing her brother.' As time passed, the sexual aspirations of the husband were also not her concern.

George had difficulty in coping with the death of what he considered his only child. Keeping afloat on his psychological wreck, the bully took comfort in the authority he wielded both inside and outside the family. The position of bank manager gave him an opportunity to crush anyone. He took pleasure from that. At home, he also had the moral obligation to put everyone in their place. He excelled at playing both the short and long game. 'Anyone found talking to Charlotte will be instantly dismissed without any salary.'

The disciplinarian made a fundamental contribution to his long game when he encouraged the rumours suggesting the guilt of his daughter. Tea and sympathy from the public proliferated to hero status when the details of his demise became the subject of gossip. A heart-rending explanation captured his position. 'I can hardly discuss in public the extent of the disorder in my daughter. That, I am afraid, would be letting the side down because of the particular circumstances in the case. I am grateful to the police who decided not to pursue the matter.'

Charlotte, ostracised, had a miserable life. George on the other hand had all the tea and sympathy and an additional slice of Madeira cake with cherries for standing by her. Subjected to ridicule at school, on the domestic scene she doubted her existence. His short and long game had started to close the loop that one day would bring about her degradation and loss of identity. The message, at last, was finally getting home to the little girl who had never experienced affection.

With a glass of whisky, the rotund rat-like grieving frame smothered the leather recliner as he listened to Beethoven's fifth Symphony vibrating throughout the household. He turned up the volume. The masterpiece became progressively louder with every glass. Even the grouse on the label rattled its reddish brown tail and covered its ears to the noise erupting though the floorboards of Charlotte's bedroom.

From the reaction of the bird, she knew the time had arrived to leave her room and sit quietly on the stairs. Looking down the staircase into the lounge, she could see George punching Rose in the stomach. Above the deafening noise, the girl without an essential self could hear the ranting of a crazy incensed alcoholic. Like a diva, agonising shrieks from Rose when her rib snapped only encouraged George on to more violence. Tearing her nightdress to shreds, he forced her jaws apart and pushed the white cotton remnants into her mouth, before sinking his teeth into her breasts.

Through the spindles in the balustrade, Charlotte could see the prominent teeth marks on her breasts and shoulders. George stopped to catch his breath before pursuing his most deviant pleasure. Seizing and pushing her backwards onto the reclining chair, forcing her legs apart, he used a whisky bottle to penetrate his wife. Charlotte sat and watched the humiliation night after night. *What did Father mean when he said,* 'If you stop screaming, you whore, I will get even more violent with you?'

After a while, Charlotte started to wonder what it would be like to be George, always in control, always violent. Longing to take on the role of a violent aggressor, she could almost taste it.

The game of grotesque violence ended when Rose stopped screaming. George used a broken bottle and went way beyond the threshold of humanity.

One night, Charlotte heard a noise coming from the bathroom. Creeping onto the landing, looking through the keyhole, she could see her father sitting on the toilet masturbating. George vigorously used both hands. She could see the relief on his face. Where had she seen that well-being before? Nothing more certain, he had that same refractory expression after violating Rose. For some inexplicable reason, Charlotte knew she would experience that look again. The next time his unshaven harsh threatening face would be against hers. The next time she could touch it.

The 'Peeping Tom', only two steps away from her bedroom door, almost had a heart attack when a floorboard creaked on the landing. Rasping through the toilet keyhole the occupant recognised the noise as betrayal and indiscipline. *That bastard girl has left her room without my permission.*

In a vicious temper, George kicked the bedroom door wide open. Grabbing hold of Charlotte's short fair hair, the dutiful father dragged her down the stairs. Taking the cellar key off the hook, unlocking the door, he pushed her into a dark eerie gloom the rats called home.

George locked the door and waited. He noticed the absence of noise coming from the cellar. *Did she make any noise or attempt to resist? She must have screamed when I punched her on the stairs.* George knew the answer. Was he still in control or had that nocuous child seen something, just something that could have given her hope? In his incestuous brain, Charlotte had made an undeniable statement.

With another page slipping off the conveyor belt, Charlotte stopped, climbed onto the desk and looked around the cellar. She hated rats, particularly two legged ones.

At thirteen, she had reached the age of puberty. Mrs Wallace, a part-time cleaner, explained to Charlotte the magic of womanhood. The cleaner also informed the head of the household. He totally ignored her.

More rumours started to circulate about George and the strange association with his family. Speculation had reached the ear of the chair of the board. George had no alternative other than to take unpaid leave until, as the chair put it, 'Things were seen from a more agreeable perspective by the customers.'

Festering ominously around the house, the dejected manager spent most of the time with a drink in his hand. Sitting on the settee, listening to Beethoven's fifth, George raised his glass. 'To Rose, sexual frustration and boredom, but most of all to that special whore that has put me in this predicament.' His life seemed as empty as the bottle of whisky on the table. Of late, the scapegoat had visibly put on weight around the hips and buttocks. Through the obscure haze of alcohol, George tried to rationalise his need to have sex with his daughter. *She is asking for it, who am I to deny her.*

How would he survive without Beethoven? He listened attentively to the distinctive four-note motif in the opening movement. *Hand on heart, there it is hand on heart, I have tried everything to modify her behaviour, and how has she, and she certainly is a fucking SHE, responded? With total ingratitude. Mrs Wallace was quite right to* point out that the attention seeker had reached maturity. *At least she would now serve some purpose in life.* Taking yet another drink, holding the taste of the single malt in his mouth, he made a mental list of that *bloody girl's felonies. Single-handedly she has destroyed MY, yes MY, family structure, MY sex life, MY job, MY health and the life of MY son.* Pouring another drink, degradation of the human soul sank to the bottom of the glass and incest floated to the top.

The overwhelming compulsion to have intercourse with Charlotte consumed his every thought. *I want sex, but not for its own sake. Penetration of that bitch will be the pinnacle of my dominance.*

The masterpiece had reached the fourth and final movement. The music stopped on a dominant cadence before the final crescendo, his favourite part. Hoffman's critique when he described the masterpiece in dramatic form exploded in his brain. 'We become aware of gigantic shadows, which rocking back and forth, close in on us and destroy all within us except the pain of endless longing, a longing in which every pleasure that rose up amid jubilant tones sinks and succumbs.' With the symphony ending on twenty-nine bars, all in C major, George climbed the stairs leading to hell and the damnation of his soul.

Things improved, her departure to the cellar became less frequent in recognition for the frequent visits to her bedroom. In the mind of the loveless child, Charlotte started to confuse the essence of love and intimacy with violence. *It is only right that I dress up in Mother's clothes and use her makeup. After all, Father uses me like Rose.* Finally, she started to lose her identity.

Sitting upright in bed, Rose watched Charlotte rifling through her wardrobe. George was not the only one trying to justify their behaviour. Despite placing a pillow over her head to drown out the noise, Rose had *a* regrettable experience when she heard Charlotte shrieking, begging, and pleading for mercy on the night moral degeneration took up residence in the dwelling. *Goodness me, surely Charlotte could have shown a little more understanding towards this whole sorry situation. I do not support the immorality of his act. At the same time, I can see his reasoning. I can hardly expect him to take involuntary celibacy for the rest of his life. Whether I like it or not, there is a need that has to be satisfied. He must have decided to keep it in the family. Considering everything, he made the most sensible choice. Besides, if anything came out it will not help my reputation. What would people think,*

*I can hear them gossiping. She failed her husband, and now she has failed in her duty to protect her daughter? Why does the blame always fall on my shoulders, how else am I supposed to react? Has Charlotte approached me or asked me for help? Even if she did, what point is there in telling the local constabulary? What could they do? There were no witnesses, who were they going to believe, a girl of dubious character, or an impeccable member of society? No, the best thing is to leave well alone. If she approaches me on the subject, I will tell her the truth; the best that she can hope for is to end up in a foster home.*

As she watched Charlotte slightly tilting her favourite peach bloom hat to the left, something crawled up inside her chest and held her breath. *Why is she looking in the mirror? She was about eight the last time she did that.* Glancing at the reflection of her daughter, she could feel her heart banging against her rib cage. Licking her lips, she could taste the salt in the sweat from the pores of her skin.

She glanced away as the pallid face turned towards her.

'Look at me Mother, and see what you have done.'

The muscles in her legs started twitching, jerking. The confidence in Charlotte's voice instilled a fear that made her blood freeze. A powerful force that Rose had no control over lifted her head and turned it to face Charlotte.

'Open your eyes Mother or I will hurt you really badly.'

Rose stared into her demonic glare. Black pupils in devilry, hunter-green eyes widened. They seemed to be throwing poisonous darts into the inner recess of her mother's immortality. Rose maintained eye contact, she could feel hatred and revulsion crawling under her flesh. Guilt, self-reproach, replaced what she wanted to believe. The disease in her daughter's eyes had wasted away any vindication.

For the first time Rose admitted failure. In their relationship, she was afraid and incapable of loving her daughter. If honesty had knocked on the door years ago, things could have been different. Pulling away from her gaze, with life ebbing away, she wanted it to end sooner rather than later. 'You can kill me now Charlotte, I promise not to scream.'

'No Mother that would be too easy. I want you to waste and rot in your bed until you die. Will you do that for me?'

'Yes if you want me to.'

'That is exactly what I want Mother. I also want to tell you

everything Father does to me. You must listen to every word I say.'
Rose nodded.

She walked towards the bedroom door, stopped and slowly turned around. 'Oh, and Mother, when you are really weak you must tell me, because I want to smother you with a pillow.'

Charlotte raged towards her fourteenth birthday, dominant fantasies took control. She ached at the thought of what it would be like to have power and control over something in real life.

George had finally started back to work, leaving Charlotte to her own devises.

Curling her frizzy blonde hair around her finger, sitting on the doorstep in the back garden, Charlotte watched the leaves floating onto the lawn. *Why is Father more relaxed with discipline? If I didn't know better, I would think he is showing a gentle side to his nature.* Instinctively, Charlotte put her hand on a cluster of bruises on the inside of the top of her thighs. *He didn't show it last night. I think I like this one, what did he say. I've got to write down a list of all the words I know that read the same backwards and forwards. Why did he give me the word 'DAD' as an example?* The sickly incestuous smell of alcohol on his breath from last night still plundered her nostrils. *That's it, he was drunk when he told me.* Charlotte failed to see any rhyme or reason behind the change and then suspicion gave way to the truth. *Father, you must do better than that. Would you like me to use the forbidden word, MUM so that you can punish me to your heart's content and say it is my fault?*

A tuxedo black cat from next door was busily sharpening its claws at the base of the tree. Running into the kitchen, filling a saucer with milk, Charlotte carried it out into the garden. The cat, smelling the milk, scampered towards her. Carrying the saucer into the garage the feline trailed behind. An excited teenager placed the saucer on the floor, closed the garage door and waited. The curling tongue of the cat almost brushed the surface of the milk. Grabbing the saucer, throwing the milk out of the window, she sat on the bench. The feline's sixth sense must be working overtime, looking up, meowing, a refractory smile broke across her flush face. *I must be hurting the cat or it would not be making that noise. What do I do now?* In the corner of the garage, she glanced at a crowbar propped up against the wall and picked it up. A sensation from holding the cold bar tingled through her frame. In her world of imagining, the object symbolised the despotic power to wield life or death. At last, Charlotte was in control. She looked at the cat again and touched the chilly steel of the crowbar. Charlotte experienced a state of euphoria beyond her wildest dreams. Common sense shouted from the dark half to wait and savour the moment of supreme power. Killing time soon fell away to the strong desire to chase her dream. Not to spook the cat, carefully, unhurriedly, she lifted the iron bar above her head. Brutally she brought the bar down on the cat's back. The sweet sound of a hissing noise, and then the cat squealing in agony, raged through her eardrums. The blow shattered the spine and crashed the cats back against the concrete floor. Her head rocked on her shoulders as she experienced a rush from the blood, pumping, throbbing through her veins. Taking a deep breath, she looked at the white markings on the paws and they were twitching. Mesmerized, Charlotte could hear the silent whisper of the heartbeat of a cat. *Oh thank you, thank you, the cat is still alive.*

If only she could find a way to slow time down. The cat would die soon, leaving her quest to destroy still wanting. In desperation, her hypnotic glare scanned the garage. A pair of garden gloves on the bench caught her eye. Rummaging through a toolbox, she found a small handsaw with a rusty blade. Hurrying, as if the cat's life depended on it, she opened the jaws of a bench vice. She picked up the cat and held it firmly with one hand between the jaws. Then she turned the spindle and closed it. With the cat hanging suspended in the vice, she grabbed hold of the hacksaw. Charlotte started purposely sawing through the white markings around the neck. The rusty teeth of the blade gripped the flesh under the soft fur of the neck and started to cut through the bone. The movement of the hard teeth of the blade cutting deep into the bone vibrated through the handle of the saw. Feeling dizzy, warm spots appeared before her eyes.

From a vantage point above the bench, looking down she could see herself sawing through the cat's neck. A strong pungent musky stench from the friction of the hot steel blade against bone floated into her nostrils. In slow motion, the severed head of the cat tumbled down onto the floor. Charlotte wanted to hold onto that ecstasy forever. Within seconds, feeling a fuzzy whir, she experienced a sinking feeling in her gut. Still in a translucent state of awakening, fusing back into her body, she found herself standing by the bench with the saw in her hand.

With the power and euphoria ebbing away, standing all alone in her shadow, a sense of achievement and control washed over every nerve ending under her skin. The head rush, now lost in the moment, had left something to hold onto. Without any remorse or feeling of wrongdoing, she regarded the cat as an object, not a living creature. She had destroyed the cat, not killed it.

Charlotte dug a hole with the crowbar in the back garden behind the shed and buried the cat.

In all the excitement, Charlotte had overlooked the task. Sitting on the steps, she mulled over the conundrum. *What was it again? I have to make a list of words that read the same backwards and forwards.* She applied her mind. *Gosh, this is not as hard as I thought; let's see there is RACECAR, PUP and PEEP.* The not so obvious palindromes were about to skip into her inspirational bubble when insanity held them hostage. Like news feed at the bottom of a screen, words flashed across her mind. Only sentences could capture the totality of her lunacy.

She recognised her craziness and burst into tears. Leaning forward, gently holding her head in her hands, repressive tears streamed down her pale sullen cheeks. Then, the girl who had never experienced a kindly smile from Rose did something extraordinary. Sinking to her knees on the grass, Charlotte repeatedly shouted and screamed out for her mother. Could this be her last cry for help or was she apologising for the havoc that one day she would bring to the world? Charlotte had crossed the line to insanity. Finally, she came to terms with her predicament. After all, there was little point in crying over spilt milk.

As the sun slowly disappeared below the horizon, Charlotte climbed the stairs to her bedroom. Butterflies, a tingling sensation raged to her throat and shoulders. Still hanging on, excitement gave her little hope of falling sleep and she went to the toilet. Her retreat from experiencing unbelievable pleasure had brought on diarrhoea, the shakes, and a blinding headache. Left with an emotionless shell, how could she recapture that moment again? Opening the bottom drawer of the bedside cabinet, she took out the head of the cat, stared and cradled it with her nightgown. The headache subsided and the tremors stopped. Charlotte was back where she wanted to be, in control, playing God.

George decided to call at the local. He also had an insatiable thirst. Eagerly he picked up Charlotte's task left on the dining room table. Mum's the word was all he needed as an excuse to drag her out of bed. Glancing at the top of the page George could see, **'Was it a cat I saw.'** He read it again only this time backwards, undeniably the same sentence. Another sentence on at the bottom of the page read, **'Dogma I am God.'** Quickly he turned the page. At the top of the next page he could see, **'Evil is a deed as I live.'** Again, the same sentence backwards. This time a sentence in bold capital letters at the bottom caught his eye. **'DAMMIT I'M MAD.'** No **'MUM.'** How disappointing. Was there a subliminal message in the words? Reading the last sentence again, his head started to twitch. That night George decided to leave Charlotte alone.

Wasting away in her skin, Rose's guilty conscience gnawed at the flesh on her skeletal frame. Her mouth was dry. Reaching out for the glass of water on the bedside cabinet, the ache, weakness in her bones left her wanting. She wondered if the cleaner had called it a day. The hands on the clock pointed to time out. Her predicament seemed hopeless. Lacking moral strength, she now lacked the physical strength to reach out for a glass of water. Musing, afraid of everything, Rose had spent her life hiding away from responsibility. *It would have been easier to experience love rather than guilt.*

With the horror and loathing of someone watching, an invisible hand pushed her chin upwards. Charlotte, standing by the bedroom door carrying a transparent plastic bag, walked over to the side of the bed. Rose avoided eye contact. Charlotte pulled up a chair. Tight lipped, a darkly synthetic scowl signalled the moment of truth. 'I have decided you will die now Mother. I intend to end your miserable life. Would you like to beg for mercy, I am more than willing to listen to you?'

Confronted with inevitable death, numbness turned into anxiety and then panic. Despite everything, Rose was more frightened of dying. Licking her dry lips, she pointed at the glass of water. Charlotte obligingly picked up the glass and held it above her head. 'If you have to beg for your life Mother it is only fair that you have to beg for a glass of water.'

Apart from the eventual scream before a preordained death, Rose decided there was little point in saying anything. Painstakingly, Charlotte trickled water from the glass over her head. Slowly the water ran through brittle tangled hair onto her angular hollow face. Rose tried to lick the water running down the side of her mouth. Somehow, she knew the rules of the game. Under no circumstances could she use her hands.

Watching Rose's pathetic attempt to quench her thirst, cunningly, a carving knife appeared from behind her back. Charlotte held it against her throat. 'I can't tell you how much I want to cut off your head Mother. If you don't do what I say, I will. I am afraid I have lost patience with you, just as you lost patience with me from the day I was born.' Very business-like Charlotte held the bag up for Rose to see. 'I am going to put this bag over your head. It really is a good idea because I can see your face through the plastic when you die.' There appeared to be no sense of urgency in her voice to move things on and yet she anxiously wanted to experience that feeling of elation again. Holding the knife against her throat, she used sufficient force not to break the skin. 'Resist Mother. Please try to stop me because if you do I will gouge out your eyes and set you on fire. Would it surprise you, Mother, if I told you I have dreamed about killing you like that?'

Using only her right hand, Charlotte placed the plastic bag over her head. Rose offered no resistance. She tied the string at the bottom around her neck until it was airtight. Within seconds, the plastic pressed hard against her mouth and nose as the muscles in her body tried to get her to inhale. Gasping for air, she urinated in the bedclothes. Rose made one last gesture to remove the plastic bag. Charlotte grabbed her hands and easily held them down by her side. She had experienced palpitations when she entered the bedroom, now she was shaking from a sensation surging though her legs. 'Go on Mother try your hardest, go on or you will die.'

This time the feeling of ecstasy was far more intense than any previous experience. Evil watched intently as her eyes started haemorrhaging. Weirdly, for the first time Charlotte experienced a bond and intimacy with her Mother. Sentiment reached into the blood of her soul and somehow she felt very close to her mother. For the last time, her eyes dropped into the back of the head. Reaching over, Charlotte grabbed a pillow and placed it over her face. Pressing hard, she turned her head to look at her chest.

Rose stopped breathing.

Intoxication rushed into her brain. Charlotte thought her head was going to explode. Multiple zigzagging colours in front of her eyes celebrated the buzz of snatching death from the jaws of purgatory. Sitting down in her mother's favourite chair, self-indulgence explored her madness. At the end, at the very end, Charlotte saw a calm acceptance in her eyes before Rose closed them for the last time. Carefully untying the string from around the neck, she removed the bag. There were no marks on her neck or anywhere else. She wiped the perspiration and blood from the surface of her skin. Apart from a faint discoloration to her nose, Rose looked serene.

*Yes Mother, as you would say, everything is in apple pie order.* Charlotte was about to close the bedroom door when she stopped and made her way back to the bedside. Reaching out, she touched Rose's hand. Her long bony fingers were still warm. Charlotte had always wondered what it would be like to hold her hand. 'I know you can hear me and I know you can see me. Because we are friends now Mother, I would like to tell you my special secret. It was quite easy, I just pressed the back of his head into the pillow and he stopped breathing. Gosh, Mother, I wish you were still alive so I could kill you again.'

Mrs Wallace found the body. The local doctor, a friend of George had no hesitation in signing the death certificate. Without any enquiry, Charlotte was free to kill again. George, took the loss of his wife to heart and grieved for the missed opportunity to put things right. The bank manager questioned his own judgment and professional integrity. How in heaven's name could he have overlooked the obvious? George had forgotten to take out life insurance on his wife.

# CHAPTER 2

# INDOMITABLE SPIRIT

A ghost-like mist lingered at the base of the bleary landscape waiting for the early morning sunlight to penetrate through a sea of grey suspended in the sky. Ink-stained tinges at the edge of the opal shape of the clouds suggested another rainy day in the Monmouthshire valley and another disappointment for at least one of the inhabitants.

Elsie Evans, like most of the residents of Westgate, did not have a pot to piss in. Brazen sinister eyes glared out of a grimy window in despair. She could see the heavy rain dancing along the pavement to the eerie drone of a didgeridoo coming from a blocked drainpipe. Many moons ago, Albert, her dearly departed, had purchased a Black Forest weather house. It took pride of place in the hallway next to a tapestry of 'Crann Bethaoh, the Celtic Tree of Life'. She winced in agony from arthritis that had left her movement to a clicking shuffle. With her nylon stockings rolled down below her knees, the 'neighbourhood witch' entered the hallway and cursed the damp weather. *Someone will have to pay.*

She frowned at the weather house. Again, the figurine of a man, carrying an umbrella had popped out from behind the door with the blood-red knocker. Although she had never experienced it in all the seventeen years of the weather house gathering dust. According to Albert, the figure of a rotund girl with pigtails, wearing a tight-fitting bodice and Bollenhut hat would appear in fine weather. Every day the unwelcome figure heralded another agonising disappointment. He was obviously taking the piss. *You will never fool me, I can see your footprints in the dust.* Elsie balanced precariously on a ladder-back wooden chair rocking back and forth. Finally, she managed to unscrew the motley jester from the front of the weather house. To her astonishment, the umbrella man was wearing a bowler hat.

Now in the twilight of her years, Elsie epitomised the indomitable almost invincible spirit inherent in the valley. The stalwart wondered if the man in the bowler hat and the mysterious woman were married. If they were, it seemed to be a bizarre relationship. Surely, at some stage 'Charlie' had to pop back into the house to indulge in *Faire l'amour*. On reflection, it might have been somewhat remiss to jump to conclusions. After all, Albert had always popped out without her wearing his bowler hat. The opulent crazy design on the kitchen wallpaper seemed to capture his roguish wicked face.

With her mental projector flickering intermittent pictures of Albert onto the screen, Elsie recalled the day when she found him in a brothel in Inkerman Street. In typical fashion, she had jumped to the wrong conclusion. Thankfully, Albert pulled the ripcord and instigated a happy landing when he pointed out the rope burns around his wrist and the set of handcuffs dangling from his arm. Indubitably, so characteristic, in classic Albert fashion he managed to escape before they had time to send a ransom note. What a little trooper. The likelihood of it happening once seemed remote, but twice! Elsie entered into the spirit of the dubious incident when she allowed Albert to tie her to the bedpost to share the trauma of the kidnap. She could feel his breath against hot sweat on her skin. Rough hands pulled and tugged at her dress for the lust of something dirty. Albert could see the ache and anticipation behind her eyes. Dirty long nails scratched the skin on her back and he told her to scream. From somewhere deep inside, raw excitement clawed up her spine and whispered, 'Don't be afraid, go right to the edge, you are not on your own.'

What was Albert doing up in the attic on the day of his tragic accident? Was he playing with his didgeridoo? She had no idea why he had been literally hanging around up there. Musing all day was of little consequence, time and tide waits for no weatherman.

Eventually she found a corkscrew amongst the spoons. With the thought of retribution, Elsie placed a spiral tip against his wooden anus and turned the corkscrew. She could taste and smell his sweat on her cracked lips. *I can feel your pain now feel mine.* After inserting a thermometer into the hole, his silhouette looked decidedly unbalanced. With care, Elsie placed his head in the jaw of a nutcracker, pressed hard and crushed it. *If there is one thing I cannot abide, it is a man wearing his hat in doors.* Like the vast majority of the inhabitants in the valley, Elsie could be extremely hostile to anyone who *prise de la pisse*.

Standing majestically on the edge of the Welsh border, the town of Westgate rubbed shoulders with Gloucestershire to the east and shook hands with Glamorgan to the west. Situated at the head of the valley in Monmouthshire, the county represented an industrial gateway to the west. England and Wales regarded the county with such high esteem, they both refused to lay claim to it. Nineteen seventy-four saw the party that filled every piss pot in England when the government decided the county belonged to Wales.

During the chartist uprising in 1838, Westgate lived up to a rebellious history when thousands from the valley marched on Newport. A plaque at the side of the road leading into the town commemorated a history of violence. Carved in granite stone it read, 'This town helped win the democratic rights for all British people.' At the turn of the twentieth century, a giant steel plant over a mile long at the base of the valley, replaced the smithy at the Victoria Works. Seven tall furnace chimneystacks reached out against the sky, polluting the air with thick black smoke and a gas that guaranteed an early grave. The proud inhabitants, who lived in the coke-stained terrace houses, damned the public corporation who owned their homes, schools and food stores.

Bingham Colliery symbolised the only alternative employment. Situated a mile east from the steel works, coal mining started in Westgate during the middle of the nineteenth Century. From inception, the colliery showed an insatiable appetite to bury any collier who dared to enter the pithead cage. In March 1904, it demonstrated the full extent of its greed. A gas explosion collapsed the roof of tower two and twenty-nine colliers went to an early grave. Kindred spirit and neighbourliness held the community together to face the grief reverberating throughout the town. Management showed a malevolent side to their nature when they decided to open the colliery for 'business as usual' the following day. Seven colliers had the effrontery not to turn up for work. According to the officials, the time for grieving the loss of a brother or father, had nothing to do with the working class. A taste of unemployment and starvation soon broke down their unwillingness to accept that loyalty belonged to the double-decked pit cage.

Nineteen forty-three solely tested the worker's loyalty to the colliery when the majority decided they would rather die on the beaches of Dunkirk than work down the pit. Ernest Bevin, the Minister of Labour had other ideas. He forced them to stay underground with the canary, always the first to die from toxic gas. The system had turned a generation into 'Bevan Boys'. In spite of all the deprivation, the residents laughed in the face of adversity and gave allegiance to the elderly sitting in God's waiting room.

Eventually Elsie had the privilege of meeting the figure in the tight fitting bodice. In the meantime, she took solace in the appearance of a headless 'Chaplin'. During the lonely days waiting for the 'Angel of Death' to touch her on her shoulder, Elsie thought about Albert. She could hear his soft whisper and feel the gentle pull of his teeth. Through the thin veil, that separates this and the other world, Albert looked into her soul and smiled at her handiwork. The lonely widow, brooding for her love lost, daydreaming, listened to the illusionary click of Celtic heels and made a wish. If only she could taste his lips pressing, whispering secrets against her cheek. Then Albert appeared in her wish. Elsie could feel his warm breath on her neck, that manly odour and awareness of feeling safe in his sheltering arms. The pain disappeared. In the light of the full moon, she looked out of the window. A single helpless teardrop, falling, splashed onto the windowsill. She listened to the swing of the pendulum of the grandfather clock. A click of the second hand heralded eight Westminster chimes. Another hour of crazy had drifted away, another day closer to that passionate moment when Albert would take the piss out of her again.

# CHAPTER 3

# TAIBHREARACHD
## Second Vision

Nineteen fifty-four saw the change from austerity to a golden era. Hilary had finally managed to climb Everest, Sinatra found three coins in a fountain and food rationing ended. Even the continual dismal weather had little effect on the inhabitants of Westgate. A brownish grey haze of smog covered the skyline from the stagnant smoke and gas continually bellowing out from the steel plant. That familiar acidic taste of sulphur settled in the back of every throat.

A gleam of sunshine piercing though the low dark clouds kissed the brass neck of the thirteen-year-old sitting on a garden wall waiting for his mother, Aislinn. The teenager glanced down at his short patchy trousers that fell well below the knees. Like all teenagers, Frank had difficulty in coming to terms with puberty. Weird and wonderful things were happening. His voice had changed from tenor to baritone and hair seemed to be sprouting out from the strangest of places. At least it showed the humorous side to God's omnipotence. Other parts of the anatomy also appeared to have a 'will' of its own. Where later in life he accepted that there was no discernible difference between his brain and penis. At thirteen, why was the ever-growing organ standing to attention every morning before he had the chance to open his eyes. Everything was so confusing, it all seemed to make sense.

He gently kicked his heels against the wall and glanced across the road. Through the smog, he could see the three dimensional shadow of Aislinn, on her knees scrubbing the doorstep of Grant's Manor. The white button-down cotton dress and petticoat she wore at her husband's funeral hung from her thin frame. Fading sunset, reflecting from a single point in the sky, ignored the grey landscape and scattered softer shades of Halloween orange into her dress. The lad with strange eyes looked again. Were his eyes playing tricks? No, he could see an aura of pastel colours, like a halo, around

21

the shape of her body. Spectral shades mixed in the aura to form the unique colour of love. The Celtic blue pigment of 'expecting nothing in return' and the caustic red of 'never letting go' reflected in the light. Through the smog, the trailing edge of the light fell in love with Aislinn's strong, thin, sharp features and russet brown hair that fell to her shoulders. Like every woman, in her own way, she looked beautiful.

Holding a scrubbing brush in her hand, she cleaned the last step. The shrill of a siren announcing death from the steelworks crawled into her mouth.

Her employer, Grant the undertaker, had a different reaction towards what he considered music to his ears. Inside his calculating skull, Grant could hear the bell of his cash register, halleluiah another burial, the second this month. The rich ignorant tyrant had little time for the working class. Business arrangements with Benton, the coroner, had exceeded even his greedy expectations. In the interest of hygiene, Benton had issued clear instructions. If anyone wanted to bury their dead, they had to call on the services of the local undertaker.

Grant had plans for the cleaner. With his wife and daughter in London taking in the spectacle of the Coronation, he intended to take full advantage by inviting Aislinn to watch the event on the television. After 'God Save the Queen', no one would save her. *What a loathsome woman. On occasions, I have been obliged, yes obliged, to remind her that she is working class. Why she thinks she is anything else, other than something I can wipe my feet on, is beyond my understanding. Her misplaced sense of pride will give more satisfaction than any prostitute.* Night after night, he wrestled with his pillow and thought about the bitch that always, yes always, miraculously showed her pretty ankles at the very moment he passed. He hoped the self-sanctifying whore would put up a fight. Taking away her self-respect with brute force would make the whole experience even more pleasurable.

Aislinn knew Frank had been watching her for some time. She lifted her head and made eye contact. The single dimple on her right cheek broke out into an ineffable smile. Standing, rubbing her knees, the boy with strange eyes ran across the road and put his arms around her. The chill from the concrete disappeared through the strength in his arms, and yet fear and anxiety seemed to linger on her skin. Something was wrong. A reluctance to release his grip suggested it was serious.

A carpet of dense smog hovered over the pavement as they hurriedly made their way through the drizzle to a one-room bedsit in the council flats. Inside, grudgingly, Frank let go of her arm. No one seemed to notice the cold damp running down the walls. After lighting a coal fire, sitting on an old spring sofa, they faced each other. The glow from the silhouette of deep lava-red flames dancing on the wall lit up the dark gloomy room as the young lad peered into the window of her soul. Aislinn waited.

'Mum I've seen a strange thing in my head again. Something is warning me you're in danger.'

'Is this the same thing you experienced when your father died?'

'Yes, pictures in my head just came and went. I must have fainted because I woke up on the floor.'

Frank explained he was sitting on the sofa reading when he experienced a warm tingling sensation at the back of his eyes. An electric charge connected with the optic nerve behind his right eye and opened his mind to picture thinking. At the front of his brain, he could see Angus Grant dragging Aislinn across the floor by her hair. Grant hurled her onto the bed. He firmly pressed his forearm against her windpipe and rigorously punched her several times in the face. 'I've wanted to do that for some time, you bitch. Nothing, not even your misplaced pride is going to save you now.' Pleading for sanity to come to the rescue, it had no effect. Grant continued to ravage her innocence lost. The undertaker demonstrated the extent of his contempt through the excessive use of violence. His primary motivation sex had taken a back seat. Now he wanted to slowly defile and degrade her through the ultimate expression of anger, rape. Tears ran down the boy's face as he lived through the trauma again.

Aislinn held onto him. 'Frank, now listen to me. I said listen to me, what you saw will never come true. I promise you I will never work for that man again.'

The incident regarding Joe, his father, again exploded in his head. He was twelve when he first experienced the trauma of 'being different'. A glorious summer's day on their rented farm in Bridgewater started like any other, feeding the chickens. He glanced up at the sky and shaded his eyes from dazzling sunlight. Like the finger of God pointing at an observer from outer space, visible light penetrated his eyes and opened a porthole to 'second sight'. At the front of his brain, he could see Joe driving a tractor along the bottom field. The picture on the canvas homed in on Uncle Jack in Royal Navy uniform, running from behind a hedge and climbing onto the back of the tractor. Joe only realised his presence when the sailor started bludgeoning him over the head with a hammer. The noise of the metal base sinking deep into his skull cracked into the air like a whiplash. 'That's for taking Aislinn away from me you bastard.' The blows, raining down with such ferocity, splintered and cracked open his skull. Joe collapsed over the steering wheel. This time the assailant used the V shape claw of the hammer until he was too exhausted to wield it any more.

With the image of Joe fading, Frank ran towards the lower field. In the distance ahead, he could see the gate. Pain, tightening like an iron fist around his chest, moved to his neck and shoulders. In agony, contractions in his muscles surged through his frame. Experiencing an epileptic fit, he fell to the ground and lost consciousness. Rain soaking his thin frame brought the lad to his senses. Still confused, he dragged himself to the field where Joe was lying in a pool of blood. His legs were underneath the tractor, only part of his torso protruded out from under the machine. The injuries caused by the hammer had almost severed his head. Frank could see compressed brain tissue pushing through the open cracks in his skull. Shock waves cut through his gut like a razor blade. He was too late.

A month and more passed before Frank recovered sufficiently to tell Aislinn about the precognition. Courage held her together that day. Somehow, she had to bury the trauma in the back of her mind. The inquest returned a verdict of accidental death two weeks after a judgment of suicide by hanging on Jack. The family had no option; the cottage came with the job of farm labourer. Within a month, they moved to a bedsit in Westgate.

Could Aislinn throw light on this phenomenon? She waited to collect her thoughts. The significance of their Celtic ancestry, could in part answer the question. Aislinn started with their family history and his great, great grandfather, Belenus. He was raised in the Highlands in Arran Village situated at the base of the rugged 'Ghàidhealtachd, the place of the Gaels' mountainside. In his generation of the Macleod clan, Belenus was the seventh son of the seventh son. As such, he inherited the gift of '*An-da-Shealladh,* the two sights'. Through the endless tunnels of second sight, Belenus could see danger yet to take place. The gift was spontaneous and involuntary.

One day through the picture of the *Fey,* in his mind he could see the local church engulfed in flames. Horrific screams echoed through the sanctity of the building as the blaze dragged the congregation into hell's inferno. Belenus ran towards the church to warn his people. In the distance, he could see the majestic dome of the building spiralling into the clouds against the landscape. Families were slowly making their way along the rutted path to the old stone building. It must have been his imagination. He could even see the neatly piled sacks of grain inside the entrance to the church set aside for the hard winter that lay ahead. Realising he still had time to avoid the impending disaster, he warned the villagers and saved them from hell.

Shortly after turning away the congregation, the inferno in his picture thinking became a reality and the church burst into flames. Belenus told the villagers about '*Taibhrearachd,* second vision'. Consequently, he lost the gift. The clan thought the seer would protect them from any danger. They dispensed with the bonfires that encircled the village and stopped making the arrows and dirks made of silver to kill the '*ilchruthach,* shapeshifter werewolf'. The moon eclipsed the sun and held the light. Villagers feasting and drinking, told each other tails about the power of the '*druidh,* sorcerer'. Stealthily, a pack of shapeshifter werewolf's, far stronger than any human, savagely launched an attack killing the clan chief and several villagers. Belenus had failed to raise the alarm. He plummeted from hero to villain. Cast out of the clan as a '*spiorad olc,* evil spirit', Belenus spent the rest of his life as a recluse in the mountains. Like all the others who had acquired the hereditary magic of second sight, he looked upon it as a curse not a gift.

For some inexplicable reason the faculty to see danger had passed to Frank. As far as Aislinn could tell, any precognition would include anything or anyone, except the recipient of the phenomena. Without any warning, he would still be susceptible to imminent danger.

The pupil had already experienced vulnerability without any

warning of the danger. On his first day at Westgate Secondary School, he joined the other new pupils in the playground where four boys confronted him with long hatpins. They held him against the wall as he watched them sharpening the steel point of the hatpins against the granite surface. The gang repeatedly stabbed the pins into his backside and legs to the bone. After a while, a sense of numbness, like local anaesthetic at the top of the legs, replaced severe pain. Still facing the wall, sharp needles continued to penetrate his lean bloody buttocks. The so-called initiation ceremony seemed to last forever. Frank could see malevolence in Lee's eyes, a spectator, three years older, he was undeniably the most sadistic bastard in the school. Lee had orchestrated the assault on the new arrivals. He took pleasure from brutality.

Frank had the pleasure of meeting Lee the week before near the old bakery. A tall lanky frame leaning against the wall cradled his face. Rex, his father, in a foul mood that day, had punched Lee to a standstill. The voice of insolence told Frank to, 'Fuck off or you will get some.' As the echo of pretence ebbed away, Lee allowed the junior to clean his bloody face with a handkerchief.

His legs gave way, the bullyboys dragged Frank off the floor, and frog marched him to the high perimeter wall surrounding the school. As the entourage passed, Lee gave a gladiatorial thumb down, he wanted the new pupil to beg for mercy. Frank clenched his teeth and waited in line for the big drop. This provoked a response from Lee.

'Haven't you got something to say? Right throw the bastard over the wall head first.'

Within seconds, dangling over the wall the victim faced the concrete pavement some twenty metres below. The two holding his ankles gradually released their grip.

'Pull him back. I'm going to kick his head in until he crawls on his knees for mercy.'

Reluctantly they hauled him back over the wall and unceremoniously dumped him on the playground. The short stay of execution ended when Lee used him as a football. The assailant showed an ingenious side to his character. He delivered a range of penalty kicks and at the same time ordered his gorillas to seek out the next sacrificial lamb. Lee declared half time by standing on the victim's hand. 'Listen to me you little piece of shit, if I wanted to fuck you up I'd kick you in the head. Now piss off before I change my mind.'

The swaying foot of Fortuna, the goddess of luck, again kicked Frank in the backside in classroom B when he obligingly sat at a desk directly in front of one of the henchmen. The headmaster, Mr Garfield, announced that, 'Bullying would not be tolerated from anyone unless it's a member of my staff.' His speciality consisted of a heavy leather strap with holes to increase the severity of blistering on a pupil's backside. Instilling a tough sense of unruly discipline, it also achieved a noticeable absence of masturbation amongst the boys.

Garfield encouraged anyone subjected to the initiation ceremony to come forward. An uneasy silence hung in the classroom. Frank could feel the sharp needle of a compass sticking into his back and he looked up at the ceiling.

Aislinn's explanation seemed surreal. Taking a hot bath in front of the fire and listening to the 'Ray's a Laugh' show on the radio brought back the familiar norms in his life. Frank glared at the clock on the mantelpiece. The reality of the sick feeling in his gut told him that the public houses were about to close. John, his brother, would soon be tumbling through the door. Home would no longer be a safe place.

'John the elder', no disciple of brotherly love, had declared war on his younger brother as soon as he could crawl. Jealousy and resentment spurred on the tormentor to the extent he had made bullying an art form. As brothers, they had little in common in temperament or appearance. John, the eldest by five years, with fair hair and pale-blue eyes bore little resemblance to the rest of the family. The similarity between Aislinn and Frank, who both had auburn hair and a dark almost olive complexion, intensified that jealousy. John regarded the boy as a freak. The colour of his left eye was seal brown and the right decidedly aqua blue. *If she likes the freak more that is her funeral. It will be his as well.*

He enjoyed inflicting physical and mental torture. Subtlety, cunning and a twisted imagination all played a part. At every opportunity John teased and taunted Mummy's little freak. As soon as the infant could stand, he deliberately pushed the child over. The bumps and continual bruising made Aislinn wonder if the infant had balancing problems.

One of the jewels in his malicious crown had both imagination and flare. The weather outside had nosedived to below zero. Aislinn had left the two-year-old in the capable hands of his brother. The unsuspecting mother had only left seconds prior to John filling the steel tub with cold water and undressing the infant. *Why is he smiling at me, he won't be smiling for long?* John placed the child in the bath. The freezing temperature of the water had an immediate response. Leaning over the tub, splashing the water, John looked on at the pain and misery he was inflicting. *His colours changed, bloody hell he's feeling it now. Stop screaming. Bollocks, some nosy neighbours outside the door they're not going away, give it a rest.*

The situation changed dramatically with the level of the victim's understanding. Telling the small boy what he was going to do generated a sense of euphoria matched only by the harm.

This torturous episode ended when Frank had reached ten. They were in the kitchen. 'Look at me you little shit. See this rope, I'm going to put it around your scrawny neck. Do you know what that'll do to you?' No response. 'Answer me you bastard if you know what is good for you? The boy nodded, 'When I pull it tight you won't be able to fucking breath. You'll get dizzy, sick, your freaky shitty eyes will pop out and you will DIE. When you start breathing I'm going to cut you bad with my knife.'

Fear, panic pushed hard against his ribs. Gulping, he took a deep breath. *He's bloody stronger than me.*

The predator moved attentively towards his prey with the ends of the rope in each hand. He wanted to see the terror in his eyes.

*He's going to cut me, two can...* Frank seized a bread knife from the kitchen drawer. Lunging, lashing out with deadly accuracy, John instinctively stepped backwards and covered his face with the rope. Frank moved forward, swinging, slashing out with the knife in his left hand. The serrated edge cut the skin on his right forearm.

Frozen to the spot, John gawked at the ragged edges around the long gash for some time. He wrapped a towel around the wound. Petrified, he rubbed the cold sweat from his eyes.

*Now who's bloody frightened?* 'If you ever touch me again, I'll kill you.' Cold piercing breath from the boy seemed to tear apart the jagged edges of his bloody gash. *Was that his voice?*

Staring in horror at the crazy dark expression, raw terror of hardened eyes had replaced the mask of the boy aged ten. With a feeling of revulsion, goose bumps, the hairs on his forearm stood up and he backed away.

John tried to make a joke of the incident in order to salvage some dignity. *It's about time she knew what a vicious little bastard he is. He'll get the bollocking when I tell her I didn't do anything.*

Was this experience a defining moment in Frank's life? Is it all about doing unto others before you give them a chance to do it to you? His 'in your face gutsy attitude' was starting to form.

Aislinn had a problem, the undertaker still owed her a week's wage. Without that pittance, life would be difficult until she found another job. She had no option other than to confront Grant and stand her ground. Then Frank came up with an alternative solution.

Darkness slithered between the cracks in the curtain. Casting a cloak over the last ember, the fire surrendered to the hour when the devil looks back in the mirror. The lad glanced at the last candle flickering in the dark. Somehow, he knew a spirit was passing by. Aislinn wrapped a towel around his thin frame. She could feel his skeletal bones through the blanket. Frank closed his eyes and reached out to the world between reality and unconsciousness. He thought about Grant.

Standing nervously outside the front door of Grant's manor, with both hands in his pockets, Frank rehearsed his script. He rang the doorbell again. Eventually Grant opened the door and glared at the freak with peculiar eyes. Camera, roll them, using a polite and yet subservient voice the actor delivered his lines.

'Sir, my mother's ill and apologises for not coming to work. She's sent me to collect her pay.'

The undertaker glared at the boy and saw the same streak of insolence inherited from his mother. *Hell and damnation, the sheer audacity, that spoiled brat is actually looking me in the eye. Time to take the mongrel to task.* From that moment, Grant walked onto the stage and rehearsed his lines. *Aislinn your boy is lying you have my word on that. I handed him your full salary of three pounds. The only conclusion I can reach is that he has stolen it. I am quite prepared to come to an alternative arrangement that would, I am sure, satisfy both you and I.*

Grant gave thought to his performance in act two. *Her only choice is to let me slide my hands under her cotton skirt and touch the soft thighs. If I stretch my fingers, they will touch her wet...* He had little interest in holding a conversation with a lowlife. At the same time, he felt duty bound to impose his authority. Standing upright, towering over and looking down his nose at the boy, Grant gave act one the propriety it deserved. Taking great pains, making the lad wait, he painstakingly dragged two one-pound notes from a fat wallet and placed them in an eager waiting hand.

Their fingers touched, Grant could feel a tingling sensation running through his fingers to the optic nerve at the front of the brain. Sensory illusion activated pictures in his head and he witnessed his own funeral. Grant could see a glass covered coffin lying in the church he attended. There was no congregation. The image changed to a carriage making its way along a cobbled street to the graveyard. Residents he had cheated opened their bedroom window and spat on the hearse below. Several emptied the content of their piss pot. Tremors vibrated through his arrogant frame. *What in heaven's name is that?* Grant recognised the unmistakable stench of rotting flesh wafting up his hairy nostrils. He pulled his hand away from the boy grinning in front of him.

'Do you want me to show you more or are you going to hand me the money?'

Cut it's a rap, Frank picked up a pound note from the doorstep where Grant had left it. The undertaker stared as he turned the corner. *He knows, somehow the boy knows.* The undertaker ran into the house and locked the door. He was too late.

# CHAPTER 4

## EVIL

The Macleod family expected Christmas to be a little more generous than in previous years. In the autumn, Aislinn had started work at the Astoria Cinema. Her slight increase in salary heralded a more optimistic entry in Santa's diary.

Domestic life in the bedsit had a subtle variation on the 'rule of three'. However, in their fairy tale they only had one bed. John and Aislinn had the luxury of sleeping in the bed. The youngest member had the enviable experience of sleeping across the base of the bed at their feet. John, ever a team player, exposed the vulnerability of his brother by kicking out under the pretext he was experiencing a nightmare.

The boy who invariably started the day with a foot in his mouth peered over the top blanket at a flute-warbling sound coming from outside the window. A Robin, with the blood of Jesus on its breast, was busily pecking away at the old wooden frame. A golden hue of sunlight kissed the grey brush marks on the side of the bird's neck. Standing motionless in what looked like two small brown wellingtons, the waft of Christmas Eve gently lifted the olive tinge on the flycatcher's plumage to give way to the magic whisper of Christmas morning. He strained his neck as if the end of his agonising wait depended on a clean cut from 'Madam Guillotine'. Through a glimmer of light, Frank could make out the outline of a stocking hanging from the mantelpiece. Anxiously biting the inside of his lip, he also saw something on the floor.

An awe-inspiring longing released butterflies in his stomach. The excitement of the day started to make everything fuzzy around the edges. Shadows held the night in the corners of the bedsit. On schooldays, winter sunlight soon tapped on his shoulder, where was it now? Of late, attending Nebo Baptist Chapel on Sunday had taken on a new meaning for Aislinn. Her newfound friendship with Ben, a lay preacher, seemed to have a profound effect on her.

When Aislinn introduced Ben to Frank, their friendship turned into a peach blush on her cheeks that moved to her neck and shoulders. In the coming months, Aislinn graced the world with the sound of felicitous laughter. Something extraordinary had touched her heart.

Finally, the clouds shrouding the sun moved on and sunlight entered the bedsit. The light captured the hue on a spider web hanging in the corner of the room. He glanced at the clock on the mantelpiece. *There is no way it's only seven it's got to be eight, bloody hell its seven.*

Frank started to fidget. Aislinn turned over onto her right side to see his disappointed face.

'How long have you been awake?'

Frank closed his eyes and pretended to be asleep.

'I would be very disappointed if you were still asleep. Don't you believe in Christmas anymore?'

'Then I'd better not disappoint you, I've been awake for hours.' Laughter captured the moment. At last it was their day to believe, their time to experience the spirit of Christmas when hope is always strong.

'Has he been, why don't you find out?' The woman with one dimple knew there would be no consoling him. Aislinn jumped out of bed and wrapped her arms around his thin frame. 'Happy Christmas son!' Hugging, they briskly made their way to where the stockings were hanging.

Ecstatic eyes rested on two presents under the mantelpiece wrapped in tinfoil tied with string. Breathing in the excitement, the fresh bitter smell of sacred Celtic holly tickled the back of his throat. Out of the corner of his eye, he thought he caught the room winking at the homemade decorations held together with tacky glue.

Swallowing a scream, imagination and anticipation turned his attention to the mysterious presents. *Get your hands on them through the tinfoil and you'll have an idea what they are. For Christ's sake, what are you waiting for?* With that thought in mind, bending down he reached out for HIS parcels. He had no doubt whatsoever, someone had even written his name in invisible ink on the tinfoil.

'Will you do me a favour and leave those presents until later. Ben is joining us for dinner, I thought it would be a good idea if we could unwrap our presents together?'

His jaw dropped and nearly collided with the coalscuttle. Another agonising wait before he could open his presents was inconceivable. He glared at the empty sherry glass on the table left by the midnight caller from Lapland. An innocuous impersonation of the man with rosy cheeks gestured his reluctance to play the waiting game.

John rubbed his bleary eyes and rose like Lazarus from the dead. On Christmas Eve, someone had slipped a hangover into his drink. Nevertheless, he still had the good sense to choose his words carefully in front of Aislinn. His jaw hardly moved as he spoke through clenched teeth. 'Can't you be quiet, some people are trying to sleep in this house?'

'I can do quiet if you can do sober.'

*One-way or another I will get that little bastard before I go.*

The ambience in the room changed to a more sombre mood. Frank glared at John, his hands decided to imitate a clenched fist. To defuse any argument, Aislinn approached her eldest son. She leaned over and planted a kiss on his forehead. 'Merry Christmas son, I think it's time to get dressed. We're having company for Christmas dinner.'

John could hear the excitable sizzle in her voice. *Company, is she having a laugh or what? Who would want to visit this fucking pigsty?*

'Before you say anything you might regret Ben is joining us for dinner.'

*That Bible-punching bastard, bullocks to him and his bible, hang about this is my chance.* 'Hey Mum the boys are having a Christmas drink down the club. Is there any chance of a couple of bob so I can join them?'

Her expression, and the fact she never bothered to check her purse, suggested bad news. 'Join them by all means. If you are relying on me you'll be standing at the bar without a drink.'

*She's spent all her money on that bastard.* Aislinn fetched his stocking and placed it on the bed. *You can bet on it no drink. Instead, I'll get a jolly fucking apple or one of those amazing tangerines.* The stocking, akin to a tobacconist, contained shag tobacco and bottles of beer. Other presents included a pair of jeans, shirt and a tie.

Because of his impending conscription to the armed services, Aislinn had spent more on her eldest son. Despite Santa's generosity, she had to pawn her wedding ring to pay for his clothes.

The jolly apple and amazing tangerine made a guest appearance in Frank's stocking. It also contained nuts and a snakes and ladders board game.

With the Yule fire lit and the wisp of white magical smoke wafting from everyone's chimney, Aislinn whisked through the flat. Sitting in front of the mirror brushing her hair, she thought about her favourite preacher. Handsome warm features had awoken an excitement inside her that was more than attraction. As the romance evolved, a deep tender need and connection replaced the bitterness experienced from the loss of Joe. Although it seemed the most natural thing in the world, Aislinn felt special in his company. The thought of his touch heightened a sexual desire within that made her ache.

Ben arrived at eleven o'clock on the dot carrying a chicken and a bottle of red wine. Frank left them on the doorstep holding hands and he ran into the flat to open the presents. Flabbergasted, pinching himself, he marvelled at his first pair of long trousers.

The visitor opened his carrier bag and handed the excitable teenager an old bush hat from his army days fighting the Japanese in Burma. 'I don't know why but I thought you might like to have this?'

Frank snatched the hat out of his hand. Tilting it, he paraded in front of the mirror. 'You're right, thanks.'

John, still not in the reverie of the day, looked on in disgust. *What a load of shit, the bastard is trying to impress her. If he gives me a hat, I'll piss in it.*

As if on cue, Ben glanced in his direction. 'I honestly didn't know what to get you so I thought you could buy something for yourself.' Taking out a pound note from his wallet, Ben handed it to the pretend reluctant recipient.

'Why are you giving me this?'

'Because it's Christmas day!'

'Right, I suppose you'll be telling me next you believe in Santa Claus.'

'Why would I deny the existence of a kind old gentleman who gives presents to children?'

Anxious to continue the confrontation, John decided to wait for a more opportune moment to embarrass the visitor. *Anyway, I can get rat-arsed. If he wants to get inside her knickers, so what, just one more dig.* 'Why aren't you in church with the rest of your Bible-punching mates talking to your so-called God?'

'God is everywhere. It is unfortunate the same can't be said about good manners even on Christmas day.'

John could have sworn he had a 'don't mess with me there's a good little boy' glare from the preacher.

In the blink of an eyelid, they were sitting around the dinner table waiting to start Christmas lunch. Aislinn standing, as if by royal command, blushed and asked Ben to say grace. He did so with sincerity that even impressed John.

Ben picked up his glass of wine from the table. 'I hope this is not intruding but I would like to propose a toast to the memory of Joe. You are always in the thoughts of your family, to Joe.'

Aislinn lifted a glass to her lips and her hand started to shake. 'To my husband, we all miss you so much.' Silence captured the respect for the departed and held it as the world did the same for the reverence of Christ.

John declined the invitation to join in the toast and started to feel uncomfortable. He had to come up with something to shatter the sentiment in the room or his head would explode.

Aislinn wiped a tear from her eye with a handkerchief. John noticed that her wedding ring was missing. Breaking the silence, glaring, he again grinded out his next confrontation. 'Where is Dad's ring? I've never seen you without it until now.' He transferred his hostile glare to Ben. 'She's bloody taken it off because you're here?' *Two for the price of one let them get out of that.* 'Well, I'm waiting for an answer?' A sardonic smirk reflected the persona of someone who enjoyed inflicting pain.

Aislinn burst into tears, she had no option other than to confess to pawning the ring. She was on the brink of breaking the bad news when Ben gestured and interrupted her.

'It is a shame your manner toward your mother is not as good as your observation. My presence has nothing to do with the absence of the wedding ring.' From his waistcoat pocket, like a conjurer, he pulled out the proverbial rabbit and retrieved her wedding ring. 'Aislinn told me some time ago she wanted to have the ring polished. I thought this would be my Christmas present to her.' Ben leaned over the table and handed Aislinn the ring. Her eyes almost popped onto the table.

Slowly and with purpose in his stride, the preacher made his way around the table. Kneeling down by the side of Aislinn, he gently took hold of her hand. 'I was going to leave this until later. Apparently, it appears the father of all children and that includes you John, has chosen this moment. Aislinn I have never known anyone like you. I love you with every fibre of my being. I know I can never replace Joe, but would you consider being my wife? If the answer is yes, if you like please continue to wear Joe's ring. In fact I would consider it an honour.'

Aislinn slumped back into her chair like a rag doll and glanced at Frank beaming from ear to ear. Confused, with Ben still on his knees, she gazed into his eyes. Behind the mysterious steel blue, she could see the transcendent love she longed for. There seemed to be no end to the depth to his affection.

Still in a daze, she gripped the back of the chair with both hands. 'Please don't think I regard you as a replacement for Joe. Somehow, I know we have his blessing. The last thing I want to do is to get carried away. The sensible thing to do is to take my time and consider your proposal.' A Silent pause. 'However, I have no intention of changing the habit of a lifetime. Ben you and I have something in common. I also love you with all my heart and the answer to your question is YES, YES. It would be a privilege to be your wife.'

As if on cue, the old iron bells from the nearby church rang out to join in the roar of approval. John turned his head away, motionless he tried to think of an appropriate response. He grabbed his coat from behind the door. 'Do what you want, I've never felt part of this so-called family. All you are doing is replacing one softie with another. I'm off to the army, as far as I'm concerned you can all go to hell.' John slammed the door and made his way to shake hands with his best friend, demon drink.

With his departure, the remainder of the day took on momentum. The end of the Queen's speech from Auckland heralded the start of a board game. Under the masquerade of that well-known good versus evil game, the first throw of the dice sent the mask of deceit down the snake and out of the house. The day ended, hazy yellow flames from the candles held the light to create a ghostlike effect. Gradually it fell away to the darkness in the bedsit. Ben's departure closed the door to another Christmas past and the rain turned to snow. Aislinn and Frank sat on the sofa reflecting on a day that would breathe in their soul forever.

A noise storming from the flat above shattered the stillness of the night. Rex, Lee's father, had returned from his watering hole in a belligerent mood. An empty wallet was the only reason he had made his way back to the flat of degradation. For that, even on Saint Nicholas day, the family would suffer the consequences. A pitiful scream of impending danger raged through the floorboards and pierced the eardrums of the two in the flat below. 'If you hadn't spent the money on that snivelling bastard, I'd still be in the pub.'

That surreal feeling of a thumb pressed hard into their throat. Almost choking, swallowing hard, they listened with every nerve ending to the brutality of the ghost of Christmas yet to come. The next shriek of pain tumbling through the darkness belonged to Rex.

In an attempt to break Rex's strangle hold from around his mother's neck, Lee picked up the poker and brought it down onto his forearm. Ringing out like a pistol shot, the crack from the shattered bone vibrated against the wall and hung in the air. The harshness in Lee's voice masked the noise of someone in shock. 'Got you now you bastard, now it's my turn.'

'Lee don't be a fool, I'm your father don't…'

Another crack, this time the bone in the same arm splintered, separated, and twisted in the muscles of his forearm. Jagged edges pushed through the surface of his skin. Rex, whining like a dog, pleaded with his son to stop, but Lee was going for best on show. Only the intervention of his mother prevented the world from screaming bloody revenge.

An ambulance arrived and took Rex to hospital. He never ventured over the threshold again. Discipline helped him to carry his suitcase. With Rex out of the way, the inhabitants of Westgate would soon discover what that meant.

In the space between reality and forgotten dreams, Frank and Lee thought about their journey on the road to Damascus. The former revelled in the thought of joining the tribe called Benjamin. He was a good honest man who seemed to take a genuine interest in getting to know him. The teenager tried to recall their conversation. It started when Ben apologised for what he called his 'inappropriate white lie' about the ring. At some stage, the preacher asked Frank what he would like to achieve in life.

*Why did I tell him that I wanted to be liked by everybody? That's not going to cut any ice with someone like Lee.* A softie definitely had a limited 'sell by date' in the valley of hard knocks.

Stretching his legs on the bed, hands behind his head, Lee glared at the figure in the doorway. 'If I want to keep my fucking shoes on, I'll keep them on. Now piss of or you'll get some.' No one would ever push Lee around. The darker side of existence was totally in accord with the way he saw things turning out. Playing through the assault, he readily accepted that violence was more than acceptable if you can get away with it. Nevertheless, had he thought things through? Lee realised the repercussions of his vicious assault. He would be more careful the next time. No conscience had distinct advantages but gross limitations through the bars of a prison cell. Out of the darkness, Lee clearly saw the way ahead and he decided to take the road to damnation. Frank on the other hand thought about taking the road to a lesser good. The rain, flaying against the window frame, had a soothing effect on the young lad as he reached out for the twilight zone.

The harsh wind whistled through a crack in the window frame. From the porthole in his mind, a voice vibrated against his skull. *Know and learn the difference between what is and what ought to be. Darkness is nothing but the absence of light.* In his mind of picture thinking, he saw a ghost-like finger writing the word EVIL at the front of his brain. He saw the same word again, only this time backwards.

# CHAPTER 5

# RAPE OF THE INNOCENT

The players in the tapestry of life had moved on. Golden threads of destiny were clearly visible in the revelation from adolescence to adulthood. Whilst the future is uncertain, destiny would argue that the bullet with Lee's name on it was already in the chamber. Any time soon, fate would pull the trigger. However, Frank still had the opportunity to influence destiny.

In the winter of 56, the wheel of fortune had stacked the chips on Frank's side of the table. It came as no surprise when Ben and Aislinn became soul mates. After a reception in the village hall, the newlyweds moved into a two bedroomed flat situated next to Lee. Rich, warm, exciting patterns promising a new beginning started to replace the images of previous hardship. The family finally bonded when John received his call-up papers to join the army.

Lee continued to excel in brutality. However, he recognised his limitations when it came to inventiveness and common sense. Where could he find a bunch of morons to carry out his dirty work and do the thinking? He came up with the unoriginal idea of arranging a meeting for potential candidates at the Ace Café.

Frank glanced around the cafe to see if he knew anyone. With a swagger and a hint of conceit, almost ski walking, he made his way to the Wurlitzer jukebox. Without inserting any money, he pressed the selection 'Rock around the Clock'. *You never know*. Begrudgingly he paid the 'pied piper' and the tune burst through the two speakers on the wall. Thanks to Aislinn's day job, he first heard the song in the film 'Blackboard Jungle'. He clocked his slim athletic frame in the glass dome of the jukebox. There was a single hair out of place in the sweep of his straight back auburn hair. Smarting about that, hell, he even thought his open neck white shirt deserved a round of applause. He listened intently to the first solo break on the record, the guitar riff. The teenager's in the cafe responded with ravenous shouts to turn up the jukebox. Frank picked up his ears at the next sax solo. *The clever bastards they've changed the solos around. The sax was the first solo break in 'Black Board Jungle'.* Into the new style of music, it had everything, as well it pissed off the grownups.

Hypnotic shimmering eyes glanced through the menu for his final selection. 'That's all right' by Presley, Scotty and Bill had that rockabilly sound. *Don't be a Dumbo, nothing sounds like 'Heartbreak Hotel'. Hang on, someone is bound to play...*

'Who the hell are you?' He turned on his heels and nearly collided with a cute baby-faced girl wearing a light-blue poodle shirt and matching scarf. With ash-blonde hair hanging in a ponytail, her slightly turned-up nose reminded him of Judy Garland. The similarity ended there. At 16, she had an hourglass figure. 'Don't you remember me, I'm the one you just said who the hell are you to.'

'Don't try to be clever with me what's your name?'

Almost diving into her viridian green eyes, a whimsical smile came to the rescue of his wow girl raised eyebrows. 'Anything you want it to be as long as you stick boyfriend after it.'

This time it was her turn to give the sixteen year old the once over. Her smile suggested she liked what she saw. 'Well aren't you a funny guy. Will you still think you're funny when I grab your marbles?'

'If you don't get your fucking arse in here right now I'll be the one grabbing your bollocks.' The crew cut, gaunt lanky frame of Lee glared from the entrance to the back room. Reluctantly he left the girl with the sparkling wit in her eyes to join the usual suspects seated at a coffee table near the window.

Roy Betts, nicknamed 'the weasel' because of his chisel features, long neck and short legs, sitting next to Lee, welcomed the new arrival. 'Why did you invite that freak?'

'Well if it isn't my mate Roy. I see you still haven't gone to out-patients to get rid of that fucking chip on your shoulder.'

Brian Harris looked like a mischievous choirboy with his basin haircut. He tried to hide a smirk behind his hand. The familiar multiple-broken nose and wild ginger curly hair of Dina Thomas sat next to Brian. Small in stature, it bore little resemblance to his violent uncontrollable temper.

The weasel homed in on the two silver rings on both little

fingers of the new arrival. Initially his great grandfather had handed them down to Joe. The rings were a birthday present from Aislinn. Both rings had a mounted head with silver wire twists on either side of the head. One ring had a Celtic Spiral carved into the centre of the mount. The other displayed the symbol of a Celtic sacred cross with a circle superimposed onto the centre of the intersection. The design of the spiral ring was even more unusual. Three spirals moved outwards in a circle from the centre in a counter clockwise direction.

He remembered trying on a ring. Despite piano fingers, the broad band rested on the tip of his little finger. *Try both rings and see what happens*. Again, they balanced precariously on the top of each finger. Without any warning, an electric charge in both little fingers tingled through both hands. The sensation raced through his frame and exploded like a flash bulb at the front of his brain. Dark spots appeared before his eyes. Frank looked at his hands again. Strangely, he saw them in black and white. He glanced around the bedroom. There was no depth or perception in anything.

Both rings slipped to the base and tightened around his little fingers. A sharp stabbing pain down the right side of his face pulled a curtain over his eyes. Suddenly the pain stopped and a nasal yet unthreatening Gaelic accent vibrated in his skull. *Welcome my blood to your manhood. The time has come to thank the god who has brought you to this time in your life. Today on your birth on the eve of the Celtic New Year, your ancestors see you as a man. Through the thin vale between the living and the other world, I will show you the past of your ancestors. A moment at which we know our self is rare. To know who you are you must first know what you are.* Listening intently, the spirit of the ancient Seer told him about the history of the Celtic Nation.

Living close to nature, God and poverty, Celtic civilisation extended throughout most of Europe, across the Alps to the Balkans and into Asia Minor. They were a formidable enemy of the Greeks, Normans and the Roman Empire. From the third millennium, the Celts had fought to preserve the culture still inherent in Ireland, Scotland, Isle of Man, Wales, Cornwell and Brittany. With pride, he gave an account of how the Celts confronted the tyranny and evil of anyone who dared to take their land, particularly the Romans. *Our ancestors welcomed the Romans to Britannia as the Messiah Jesus bid us to do when he came to our shore. Still they killed our blood even*

*though they stood paralysed with fright at the way we defended our right.*
*They drew the first blood that made our young Queen Boudicca ride her*
*chariot in front of her army to destroy the Roman legions in Camulodunum*
*(Colchester) and Londinium (London).*

The curtain in front of his eyes opened. Through pictures in his mind, he could see the image of a tall young woman with titian red hair. She was wearing a multi-coloured tunic under a thick cloak, fastened with a broach. Boudicca a warrior goddess, standing in her chariot, acknowledged her army. The severed head of two Roman soldiers slain in the battle trailed from the neck of her horse. The scene gave way to the bodies of two thousand Roman legionnaires strewn across the battlefield.

In the distance, centurions hanging in chains from wooden gallows on the hillside pleaded with their god to cut the thread of life. With a spear driven through his wrists and ankles, a centurion pushed hard trying to breathe air into his lungs. Exhausted, at the point of death, he raised his head and looked down the line. The last, he knew he was the last Centuria. Again, his right foot pressed against his left in an attempt to push up. Then he remembered, the Celts had broken both his legs. Proudly holding his head up, he pushed out his square jaw and waited for the light without hatred to shine on his face. Battle Ravens, shrieking overhead, watched a fellow forager scavenging the putrid flesh of a soldier's head impaled to the gallows by a spear through his mouth. Frank could see the ultraviolet outline of a bird sinking its claws deep into the victim's chest. *Look, it is the goddess Morrigan, the chooser of the slain.* The rise and fall of its head ripping flesh from his face exposed a white tip on the raven's curved black beak.

The warrior queen had no interest in taking any prisoners. Seventy thousand had already fallen victim to the savage onslaught of her army. Boudicca signalled to a warrior, tattooed, and painted with blue dye. He held up and passed a frail little girl standing next to her chariot. Her army of a hundred thousand included women, children and warriors. The Celts campaigned and rebelled together with a gratuitous violence that demanded respect. The image on the canvas changed to Boudicca now holding both her daughters, one in each arm. She lifted her children into the air in order to see the carnage of a nation that dared to rape the two of them in public in front of their mother. She had a torque made of twisted strands of gold around her neck. Two decorative knobs of a Celtic cross and a spiral were at either end. *Look at the circle within the cross. It is the symbol of Christianity. The shape of the cross represents the four roads created by the omphalos the sacred point at which heaven and earth are connected. The circle shows infinity where the soul will reach enlightenment with no beginning or end. It represents the life-giving properties of the sun and God the greater. To Boudicca and you it is the sacrifice of your life for the good that is your destiny. It is a right death that gives life a purpose. Now look at the spiral. This is the spiritual balance between inner and outer consciousness and has the power to prevent evil and injustice. Use it well or it will turn away from you. Now see the world in the knowledge of what you are and what you must become.*

Colour and perception gradually returned to his world where the Celtic New Year has another name, 'Halloween'. This is the day when the veil between the living and the dead is the thinnest. Frank was born at midnight when the ghosts and souls of the dead mingle with the living. It is a time when the clock strikes thirteen. The world also dresses in costume in the hope that the travelling dead will see them as their own.

Closing the bedroom curtains, the teenager looked up into the sky and saw the vast galaxy of the Milky Way swirling around in space. The extraordinary design of the galaxy looked exactly like the shape of a spiral. The bright star clusters at the centre were the same as the spiral on his ring. In later years, he recognised the symbol as an accurate representation of planetary configuration. Aislinn asked him if he had experienced anything unusual from the rings. Joe had an electric shock when he tried them on. He borrowed one of Ben's white lies.

A drawling voice shattered his daydreaming and the harsh reality of the cafe came into focus. 'I told you he's a nancy boy, look at his rings.'

'Roy don't be a shit all your life, act like a fucking grown up.' Lee's lazy eye homed in on Roy and the other squinted at Frank. 'If you two don't stop squabbling I'll bang your heads together.'

Finally, the self-elected chair moved to the business end and emphasised the ground rules. 'When I tell you lot to jump, you fucking say how high.' Lee wanted them to come up with roguery that had financial gain. Dina knew a scrap metal dealer who would not ask questions if they decided to steal the lead on the chapel roof.

A decent earner with little chance of having their collar felt. 'Dina, talk shit again and I'll fucking punch you to a pulp'

The idea of breaking into Hancock's textile factory rolled from Frank's tongue. With the place alarmed, Brian, who worked at the factory rejected the idea. Lee winced and glared at the entrepreneur. 'You had better come up with something if you want a sex life with that bitch.' He explained the so-called obstacle could work in their favour. He asked Brian if he could switch off the alarm when the factory closed for the day. The answer showed promise, Brian would be the last one to leave. When they made their escape, they could switch it back on again and set the alarm off. Then, the police were unlikely to suspect it was an inside job.

Lee's eyelid twitched again, the involuntary spasm usually signalled he supported an idea. He scowled at the 'know it all'. 'Well is there anything else?'

'Yes, don't stay in the factory too long. When we set off the alarm, it will take the police at least half an hour to get to the factory. We have about fifteen minutes to get the job done. Don't take anything that can be traced stick to cash.'

The plan went off without a hitch, the cash box contained eight pounds. A factory worker had another seven quid in a drawer. Brian kicked the door in again to set the alarm off on the way out. They were in bed by the time the police had arrived. Lee decided to split the proceeds evenly. After his cut, the gang had five pounds between them. Frank had problems sleeping that night. What if the escapade had not gone according to plan? Was this his interpretation of travelling down the road to a lesser good? If so, his journey would probably be short-lived.

Ben called in a favour from a colleague who had pull in the union and Frank started work at the steel plant. The prestige and responsibility of his occupation bore little resemblance to the title, 'Office Boy'. At sixteen years of age, he thought he had gone to heaven working in an office with five delicious typists. All registering on his fantasy list, one in particular, Edna, in her late thirties had taunting heavy breasts to die for.

Morale reached a high in the middle of the week. Edna wore a tight fitting yellow silk blouse that left little to the imagination about the size of her pink nipples. An imaginary finger hit the 'replay button' as the office boy visualised the duo pushing hard against the buttons on her blouse. This time he pressed 'fast forward' and the button-popping scene gave way to another spectacle in the office.

Paul Starkey, the manager, aged early thirties, tall and slim, had an everyman persona. His smouldering looks gave the female staff many a sleepless night. Frank waited outside the manager's office with the mail and mulled over his instructions. 'Knock then wait, don't enter my office until I say ENTER.' His knuckles were inches away from the door, when he heard what sounded like furniture moving around. Something must be wrong the blinds were drawn. He came up with the answer. *The lazy bastard is sleeping it off. He's been on the piss. Hang on, if he's asleep who is making all that bloody noise.* He rejected the idea of bothering Starkey and yet he wanted to avoid the sharp end of his tongue.

The office boy peered through a crack between the blinds to see if sleeping beauty had pricked his finger. He saw a different kind of prick. Edna was sprawled face down over the edge of the desk with her pencil skirt pulled above her shapely waist. Her strawberry blonde shoulder-length hair tumbled around her face. Soft pale breasts rubbed against the polished surface as she gripped the end of the desk. Starkey was standing behind her with both his hands on her shoulders. Taut muscular legs and firm buttocks drove his shaft into Edna with the ferocity of an animal. The rhythm and thrust gained momentum. His testicles bounced against her backside and made a clapping noise. The spectator thought it sounded like a round of applause.

Edna tightened her grip on the desk and eagerly pushed backwards. The excitement of watching them ravaged any rational thought. His penis decided to stand up for masculinity. The sensation took control, animal instinct challenged him to open the office door and join in. More than anything else, Frank wanted to see the expression on her face that would tell him everything he wanted to know. Starkey, pumping, thrusting deep inside her went into overdrive. The teenager could hear voices echoing down the corridor from the typing pool.

Every feeling nailed his legs to the floor and to hell with the consequences. Finally, common sense kicked in. *How is it going to look if they catch me with a hard-on acting like a peeping tom?* With difficulty, he entered a three-legged race taking place along the corridor. Turning the corner, he could see the finishing tape across the door of the gent's toilet. Alone in the toilet, splashing his face with cold water, he tried to cool the sexual urge still pulsating through his veins. Looking in the mirror, the fire flush expression on Starkey must have transferred to his face.

Starkey had satisfied his sexual appetite. However, the office boy was still languishing in the toilet with a hard on. Bemused, Frank entered one of the cubicles and locked the door. Pulling his trousers and pants down, he sat on the toilet seat. 'Mr Motivator', rising to the occasion, launched an e-mail to his brain. *I am waiting for you to touch me, go on, I know you bloody want to.* Frank looked at the ceiling to where his penis was pointing. *You can stand there all pissing day. I'm in work for Christ sake, leave me alone. Come on think about Edna. Think about Starkey shagging her like a stallion did you see her... Piss off, I'm going to think of something else.*

Intense concentration focused on the bumpy texture on the ceiling. *Right, I can make out a pattern on the surface. It looks like a spiral or is it...* The head of his penis had seemingly lost interest. It nosedived under the toilet seat. *Look concentrate, there's another shape!* Two large raised bumps on the surface directly above his head seemed to take on the subliminal shape of popcorn. *Are you losing it, look at the size of them sticking out of the paper? Hell, they're as big as Edna's nipples!*

Starkey's hand cupping, palming her soft smooth breasts, wafted in front of the shape. Tight pointy nipples responded to his fingers gently whisking over them. Something stirred down below. *I don't believe it.* Was that his imagination or did the eye on the head of his shaft actually wink at him. Sweet surrender, catching hold of his penis he pulled back his foreskin. The sensation of his hand moving up and down his shaft heightened as he thought about Edna. Imagination painted a graphic picture of how she looked face down on the desk with suspenders on. Vigorously he started pumping his fist. The office boy fantasised to a point where he was inside her, not Starkey. Yes, he was the one touching her pink nipples, breasts and suspenders. A throbbing, tingling in his testicles moved rapidly through his shaft and he ejaculated into the air.

Moments later, he went into meltdown and guilt replaced sexual chemistry. If the rumours were true, he expected all sorts of repercussions. Was it a sin or an old wives tale spread around by the clergy because they wanted to keep a good thing to themselves?

What about the so-called blind theory? Stealthily, hesitating, he peeped around the toilet door. Frank expected to see lightning, a white stick and a Labrador dog in the corridor. Back in the office, he checked to see if there were any hairs growing on his palms.

Mulling over the changes, he had achieved wanker status in more ways than one. Surely, screwing the factory and watching Starkey screwing Edna, were all part of his learning curve. Would he be the next one screwed by the police? The chances of that were remote. Everything had gone according to plan. What could have gone wrong, his imagination must be working overtime?

The last green ray of sunset gently touched his forehead and entered his eyes. Moving electrons energised the skeletal muscles in his frame. Through the porthole of second sight, he could see Roy sitting at a table with the fuzz. Leaning forward with his elbows on the table, both hands masked his face. Roy looked in serious trouble, shaking his head. An insolent snigger from the officer sitting opposite smarted of a job well done. The image changed and focused on something on the table. He tried to make out the object but the picture ended as abruptly as it began. Annoyed, Frank knew he had no control over the projector. *Roy's been up to something, he'll drop anyone in the shit*. Would he have the opportunity to find out or was it too late?

Lee had organised another meeting, this time at the Liberal Club. Dina's father, the secretary, had nominated Lee for membership. It gave him the opportunity to keep an eye on Dina and *that psychopath* he was going around with. The club, well known for fragrantly breaching the law encouraged underage drinking.

He agreed to meet Brian on the corner of Walcott Street. Of late, they had become close friends. Frank was thankful to Brian for coming to his rescue when they were playing football in the park. Roy was about to deliver a vicious tackle from behind that had hospital food written all over it, when Brian intervened and shoulder-charged Roy out of the way. His gangly thin frame, full of geniality, dutifully looked after his mother, a chronic alcoholic who spent most her day pissing his wages down the toilet.

Frank could see Brian leaning against the wall at the far end of the street. He made a wager with himself that his friend's opening remark would be, 'Hi butt, how's it going you ok?' Jackpot. 'All the better for seeing you mate.' As they strolled down the hill of dreams, a harsh bitter wind carrying the devil's breath hardened against their skin. At the bottom of the hill, the bustle of the steelworks held centre stage against the background of icy mountains dusted with snow. Neither had a coat, the mystical robe of friendship captured the moment. Frank placed his arm on the shoulder of the brother he had always wanted. In the years ahead, he would have given anything to do that again.

Gill the steward, glared at the new arrivals waltzing into his sacred lounge. He made his way from behind the bar. Lee and the rest of the banditos were sitting in the far corner of the smoke-filled lounge. They only had time to marvel at the sharp dark grey double-breasted suit on Lee, when the hefty bald figure of Gill closed in on them. 'Well fuck me who have we got here. Do you know gents this is the first time I've seen shit walking?' Gill glared at Lee. 'Aren't you the snivelling little bastard we made a member?' Cross-eyes gawked in a different direction and he ignored the question. 'It's true isn't it? Greedy bastards like you just can't wait to take advantage of this club. I suppose you're here to see the fight!'

Lee clenched his fists, an angry glare cut through the eyes of the person who had dared to call him a *bastard*. 'What are you talking about, what fight?'

'Don't you know it's the fight between me and you if any of you get out of line?'

Lee grabbed the neck of a beer bottle on the table. 'Before you move a muscle I'd like you to meet someone, he's dying to meet you.'

No one noticed the baseball bat discreetly hidden behind the steward's back until he waved it under Lee's nostril. 'Do I make myself clear or do you want my sweet spot to give you a fucking headache?'

Dina glanced at Gill who was looking for trouble. 'You will have no probs with any of us Mr Evans. My father said to give you respect. We only want to get off the streets for a couple of jars.'

'Gent's you've had your warning, there won't be another one.' Slowly, Gill made his way back to the comfort of the bar.

In a generous mood, Lee ordered five pints of M&B dark beer and told Roy to pay for them. The chair opened the meeting by reminding the delegates of his outstanding contribution to their last escapade.

The mood of the conference changed when Frank challenged that remark. A hostile, incensed look grabbed the edge of the table. 'Why are you always talking through your arse?'

'Why don't you ask us if your plan went well?'

Lee tightened his grip on the table. 'I was in a good mood wasn't I boys. You've changed that, what you are on about.'

Frank glanced in Roy's direction. 'Don't ask me, ask him.'

Everyone looked at Roy. 'Roy tell me now or I'll come over there and give you one.'

Roy had to say something whilst he still had the opportunity. 'He's stirring the shit, listen I did my bit, I found seven quid in the drawer.'

Lee sharpened his vile tongue. 'Right this is your last chance. If you don't tell me now I'm going to drag you out of here and drive my fucking foot in your bollocks.'

Leaning back in the chair Frank thought about his next move. 'Threatening him isn't going to get you anywhere. He'll tell us, if you promise not to hurt him.'

'Ok fair enough, fire away, I won't do anything to you if you tell me.' Everyone knew Lee did not intend to keep his promise.

The instigator crossed his fingers in the hope that Roy would tell all. 'Roy if he touches you we'll walk out. We're not going to stand for someone who can't keep his word.'

With the endgame nowhere in sight, Beth, Roy's girlfriend entered the club. She was about to make her way to the bar when Lee turned around and clocked the curvy, tall seventeen-year-old brunette with pale daisy freckles. 'Frank get the scrubber a drink and leave her in the bar. Beth don't leave the county, if I can't sort out your boyfriend here I'll sort you out.' Wearing a devil green swing skirt, necklace and high heels, she turned her head away and ignored his threat.

Frank deliberately let Beth take the lead. Her long toned curvy legs and charismatic sway, gave the impression she was walking to the swing 'Doo Wop' playing in her head. Sashaying forward, when her foot touched the ground she turned her head and moved her taut shapely backside to the 'Dooooo-wop-wop' harmony.

They were standing at the bar when his left hand accidentally brushed against her swing dress. The contact triggered off a surge that vibrated though his arm. In his mind of picture thinking, he could see Roy handing Beth a wristwatch. It had a distinctive blue jade dial with a white leather strap. The picture faded but the watch remained in focus on her left wrist. *The watch must have been the thing on the table He'd never be able to afford that. He's stolen it from the factory.* 'Beth do me a favour, when no one's looking, hand me your watch.'

'I wouldn't give you the time of day. Now piss off back to your so called mates.'

His tight-lipped 'wrong call' response unsettled her. 'No problem, I was going to tell you that your boyfriend's dropped you in the shit. He stole your watch from Lee. If he finds out, he'll cut your throat.'

Beth could feel something smothering her face. Wheezing, gasping for breath, her hand holding a glass started to shake. 'I knew he'd get me in trouble. Look, I didn't know it was Lee's so help me God. Here, give it back to him it's trash anyway.' She took off the wristwatch and slammed it on the counter, her legs buckled at the thought of Lee. A whistling noise screamed in her ears and she ran into the ladies.

You could cut the atmosphere in the lounge with Lee's knife. Roy, his face still stinging from a slap from the back of a hand was only moments away from serious injury. Frank sat down to face Lee and he placed the wristwatch on the table. 'Roy told me he took this watch from the factory. He was going to tell you until you frightened the crap out of him. Tell him Roy, if we can't be honest, we're fucked.' *How did he know about the watch, he must be screwing Beth?* Roy knew the game was up and he apologised. When he stole the cash in the drawer, he saw the watch and took it. Lee grudgingly accepted the explanation. After all, their adventure had paid dividends. He also liked the fact no one had challenged his cut in the proceeds. Nevertheless, Roy had broken the rules.

Their next venture sweetened the bitter taste in his mouth. Davies the bookies had real potential, particularly if the rumour about Baxter the manager were true. Baxter had a foolproof system. He siphoned off money from the owner by not declaring all the bets taken over the counter. Dina knew the layout. Access via the window, front, and back door would set off the alarm. The plan was simple. Before closing time, Dina would hide in the toilets. When everyone had left, he would place a strip of rubber between the bell and the hammer to stop the alarm ringing.

Lee had good vibes about the burglary. Nevertheless, he still had that misdemeanour to sort out. How could he teach Roy a lesson without inflicting pain? In a moment of inspiration, he found the solution. His promise had nothing to do with his so-called girlfriend. For some reason the poor bastard doted on the slag. In his twisted mind, Lee decided to have sex with Beth in front of her boyfriend.

Frank had the task of explaining to Beth the inevitability of it all. 'You know what he's like, you can either let him fuck you or pick a burial plot.'

Torrential rain, squalling across the car park, had little effect on Beth. Dina and Lee dragged her to a secluded spot behind the club. Lifting, pushing her backwards and holding her down on the bonnet, she took solace in the rain. At least it would disguise the tears swelling in her eyes. Beth decided not to struggle, she would deal with it in her own way. To resist or defy Lee would be his biggest turn-on. Beth did not intend to give him that satisfaction. With her long legs hanging down on either side of the bonnet like a lead weight, the rain, stinging, soaked into her bones.

Lee, standing in front of Beth, viciously grabbed and ravaged her swing skirt. Leaning over the bonnet to see any reaction, he yanked and tore off her knickers. Harsh unshaven bristles continually rasped against her pale freckled face and neck. Eagerly, he waited for her to scream, plead and even beg for mercy. There was no response.

Dina, Brian and Frank strong-armed Roy into the car park to witness the humiliation. *That bitch is trying to make a fool out of me.* Lee slapped and then lashed out with his fist, and again, knuckles cracked hard against her nose.

Beth turned her head and spewed out the blood from her split lip, still no reaction.

'You've been asking for this for ages you bitch. I've seen you moving your fucking arse.'

Lee lifted what was left of her skirt. He forced her legs further apart and grabbed her neck in a stranglehold. Slowly, he climbed on top of Beth still lying motionless on the bonnet. *Give the slag another dig, go on fucking head butt her.* 'This will make you wet you bitch.' It had no effect and with difficulty, Lee used sex as the ultimate weapon to defile her every reason to believe.

Instead of looking away, with her face covered in blood, Beth gazed into his eyes and saw his fanatical hatred and anger. There was no expression or emotion behind her eyes.

With the rain pinging off the car, chinking as it bounced on the tarmac, the bonnet bashing ended abruptly. Beth still splayed, defiled on the bonnet, made no attempt to move. The rain lashed down on her thin frame and tried to wash away the *why, why, why* eating into her soul. Then she remembered that look, the craziness in his eyes that said, *Why not, why, because I fucking want to.* Roy dropped to his knees, a dull vague ache in his stomach, twisting, gushed into his mouth and he threw up.

During the long lonely hours in the dark, shock and disbelief without tears gave way to anger and her profound fear of death. Despite the strong need to run away, Beth remained in Westgate. *Where could I go, no one is interested in anything I have to say?* Apart from the recurring dream about killing Lee, there were no frantic hysterics. Beth had blocked out the trauma to the extent that she could not remember the rape. Continually the pictures flickered and seemed to stop at the point where they dragged her through the car park and lifted her onto the bonnet. Then the silence, that numb feeling, disconnected and alone, the assault again played from the beginning. The affair with Roy had splintered into a thousand nightmares and so did her self worth. Her younger years had been fraught with abuse from the games adolescents play in the toilets. Raped in front of her boyfriend had left her with no hope for the future. *Why, why, why.* Beth eventually drifted back to her previous existence. This time things would be different, anyone who wanted sex would pay in recompense for the shame of her urban tragedy.

The break-in at the bookies had thrown up an unexpected bonus. Baxter had sixty pounds from his nice little earner in a cash box in his drawer. The police checked the cash in the safe against the betting receipts. Everything appeared to be in order. With nothing else stolen, they came to a conclusion that suited their crime rate. It must have been vandalism.

Frank had difficulty in fathoming out why luck always seemed to be on the side of those who least deserved it. Beth deserved a break, any break. He refused to believe that everything happens for a purpose. Is it the throw of a dice that determines your fate or can something be done about it? Guilt questioned the path he had chosen. Fortune favours the brave. When it knocked on his door, he turned out to be a coward and allowed a monster to rape the innocent. The more Frank thought about it the more he realised he had no control over his destiny. Lee blamed the so-called gang for leaving the safe in the bookies. Would he accept their limitations or move on? How could Frank outmanoeuvre fate? Would things work out or was it all down to the will of Allah?

He took off his shirt and neatly folded it on the bed. The rings fell from his fingers onto the floor. Disorientated, with his knees buckling he sank to the floor. An electric shock buzzed like the needle teeth of insects burrowing under his flesh and he lost consciousness. When he recovered, he tried on the rings again. This time they balanced on the tip of both fingers and stayed there. Apparently, he was not the only one disappointed.

# CHAPTER 6

# THE RITUAL

The only thing certain in life is the inevitability of death. In the years between 1957 and 1964, the mystical reaper would hand out his calling card to both the innocent and guilty. As the tiny grains of sand passed through the hourglass, the future seemed to hold promise for Westgate. A new expansion at the steelworks had made unemployment virtually a thing of the past.

Nineteen fifty-eight saw the grand opening of a new tinplate mill that made the plant one of the most modern in Europe. Co-operative stores replaced the miserable corner shop that reminded everyone of food rationing. With a spring in their step, a strong sense of identity and money in the back pocket, the inhabitants moved forward together. New or renovated youth clubs and community halls gave promise to the future as well as tackling the poverty still prevalent amongst the elderly. Working hard, playing hard, continued as a way of life. Alcohol and gambling had reached a unique level of addiction. The golden age of the club had finally arrived. Social drinking left by the back door and alcoholism sat down on a stool in the bar.

Every Sunday at precisely noon, the doors in the council flat's and Letchworth Road simultaneously opened like passengers alighting from a train. The travellers had one thing in mind as they made their pilgrimage to the club. Unhurriedly, Gill, behind the bar, served the customers in order of seniority. Frank and Brian rested their elbows on the bar and waited for him to serve 'Dylan the Poet'. As usual, it took time, the appointed bard only spoke in verse. Gill kicked the bottom of the bar in despair. *Why the Scottish accent?*

The poet, undaunted, continued. 'Let other poets raise a fracas...' In desperation, Gill looked at the bottles on the shelf. 'I'll take it you'll be wanting your usual glass of whisky?'

Dylan had the facade of a poet. With long grey curly hair falling to the shoulder, he always wore a buttonhole in the lapel of his tweed jacket. During the Great War, Dylan's life had changed forever. Five hundred yards away from the trenches, his field artillery opened up with mortar and shrapnel. The salvo cut down fifty and more of his unit. Still moving forward, looking to his right, he could see a headless colleague still standing. Blood, pumping from his neck, spurted into the air. Despite the shrapnel in his side, Dylan shouldered a crippled 'Borderer' and he made his way back to safety. His next attempt never came to fruition. The butt of a corporal's rifle crashed into the back of his skull as he tried to leave. In shock, feeling in constant danger, he reached out for normality and turned to poetry to erase the painful memory. Mentioned in dispatches, Dylan refused the Distinguished Conduct Medal when someone told him the citation read, 'Courage under enemy fire'.

Seating arrangements were also prearranged. The committee sat next to the bar. Blue and his warriors occupied the next table. Jehovah, Dylan and Sid faced the motley crew from the other side of the bar. The new members had to be content with a table at the far end of the room. Frank could hear the hand on the clock behind the bar clicking as it moved to one o'clock. Within an hour the majority were pissed, most of them were topping up from the night before. A male voice choir burst into four-part harmony from the lounge to herald the threshold of drunkenness with a traditional Welsh hymn. '*Calon lân yn llawn daioni, Tecach yw na'r lili dlos,* a pure heart is full of goodness, more lovely than the pretty lily.'

Mischievous roguish behaviour from Blue set the standard in the bar. With an open neck shirt, showing his lean strong physique and silver medallion, standing, he banged the table to get everyone's attention. 'Gill, put your teeth back in your gob there's a good lad. Start a raffle, collect a shilling from everybody in the bar, winner takes all. To get this handsome prize all you've got to do is to guess who is going down on Sid's wife.'

A studious Gill came from behind the bar licking his biro, he looked straight at Blue. 'Right, we'll start with you, what's your guess?'

'Well my money is on the first battalion of the Grenadier Guards.'

Jehovah's soft gaze settled on Blue. 'Why don't you leave the man alone and get on with your drinking?'

'Why don't you go and tell Sid's wife to stop shagging everything that came out of the Ark with trousers on. I was going to ask you to tell her that Jehovah hates nymphomaniacs, but you can't fucking spell that can you.'

Sid picked up his glass of whisky and pretended to be oblivious to the slurs coming from the table opposite.

'Sid old mate, I'm only joking. Look, I've brought you a present out of the kindness of my heart.'

Taking his shirt off, Sid flaunted the reason why he had no chance of seeing his penis without bending over. He picked up and with great difficulty, Sid put on the grossly undersized tee shirt. 'Thanks for nothing. Do you know, I'll spill more down this tee shirt in the next hour than you'll drink in a fortnight?'

With the gauntlet thrown down and the challenge on, they agreed to drink each other under the table. The last man standing declared the winner. A referee in the guise of Gill tossed a coin. Winning the toss, Sid dispensed with the tobacco he was chewing and decided on whisky as the lethal weapon to restore his honour. The duel started with a round of two large whiskies. Sid stayed focused despite the innuendos coming from his opponent.

Gill declared half time when Dylan's wife entered the bar. Carrying a dinner plate brimming over with Sunday lunch, Sally marched through the bar and slammed the plate down on the table in front of Dylan. The smell of freshly cooked lamb and vegetables wafted through the bar. 'You live in this club, you might as well eat here.'

The poet glanced at the dinner and then at his wife. A warm smile broke across his thin etched face. In a distinctive theatrical voice, reminiscent of Richard Burton and with an actuarial whimsical look, Dylan burst into poetry. 'I surely never hope to view a lamb more luscious than you do. Exuding warm ambrosial fumes but sad to see no mint from you.'

Dylan had fallen for his wife's mint trap. 'Your wish is my command, husband dear.' Before he had time to take action, unscrewing the top off a bottle of mint sauce secreted in her apron, Sally steadily poured the content over his head. By a quirk of fate, the mint sauce ran down his face and dropped onto his plate.

Twisting his tongue, he continually licked the mint from the side of his mouth. Standing, he glanced at his lapel. 'He wears a red rose in his button-hole, a poor clerk on Sunday dining out. To taste black lamb that frolicked in the snow. But must protest the mint for sugar it has nowt.'

Sally was furious. 'You are as mad as a Hatter. I am sick of you and I am sick of your poetry.' She scowled at the audience. 'Your so-called friends might think you're funny, they don't have to suffer like I do. Last night I was in bed with my knickers down and where was this one. I will tell you where this nutter was. He was standing by the bed with a hard-on reciting act one, scene one to three from Romeo and Juliet.' Before Dylan had chance to reply, Sally marched out of the bar and slammed the door.

Her departure sounded the whistle for the second half. Sid decided to go for the jugular. He consumed three large whiskies within half an hour. Of the two, his opponent looked decidedly the worst for wear. After another two rounds, leaning heavily towards the starboard bow, Blue gave up any hope of reaching the toilet. He literally had his back against the wall. His eyes had already moved to a more comfortable location. Sid had no problem in walking to the bar and ordering another two large whiskies. Making a gesture in triumph, Sid lifted his glass and slowly swallowed his drink down in one. Blue had difficulty in raising his head let alone a glass. Both hands gripped the table to stop him from falling over. Minutes passed in silence. With no sign of movement from Blue, Sid's chunky bold-headed frame, wearing a ripped tee shirt, leaned across the table. He placed his hands on either side of the opponent's face and gently lifted his head.

'Can you hear me mate, I am fucked. You're too good for me, you win.'

Blue nodded and fell over the table onto the floor.

A sullen dark expression moved forward. 'Leave him be, I SAID leave him be.' Sid dragged him to his feet. Standing motionless in the aisle, they put their arms around each other. 'Blue, listen to me you bastard, remember the day when the roof fell in and you were stupid enough to came back and get me?' Blue could just make out his blurry, fuzzy reflection in the mirror. The scars on his forehead and right cheekbone were still prominent.

The last fading light held the silence in the bar. Memory and nostalgia recalled a time when serious problems had knocked on every door. Jehovah remembered when no one employed him because of his religious belief. Hard times, a scarcity in basic rations did not thwart the hungry love of his neighbours from putting food on the table for his children. Dylan thought about the tragedy that had taken his only son and the humiliation of not being able to afford a decent burial. A collection paid for the funeral. Wearing a new suit, standing proudly at the altar, with sincerity he delivered Shakespeare's sonnet, 'Friendship'.

Glancing around the bar, the true test of friendship had bonded them together. He could taste and feel the kindred spirit in the room. Through the equality of trust, loyalty and friendship, Frank experienced that rare moment when thought and feeling mix to create the spirit of camaraderie.

A bittersweet longing recalled his schooldays and that sinking feeling when he had to say farewell to his classmates. His last day in school had finally arrived. The teacher, Mr Holland held with tradition. He brought in a cake decorated with twenty-eight candles, one for each of the pupils. The class linked arms as Holland placed the cake in the centre of the table. At a given signal, they deliberately sang 'Auld Lang Syne' out of tune, followed by a minutes silence as a mark of respect for each other. Frank, standing next to Brian, could see the tears rolling down his face.

Bug-eyed, Brian looked at his friend. 'Hey, we'll always be mates won't we?'

'You try and stop me.'

Signifying their last act together, they blew out the candles. United through industrial hardship and without an allegiance to any country, affinity inherent in the valley always blew out their candles together.

Brian placed his arm on Frank's shoulder. Like everyone else in the bar, the youngsters would always be there for each other. No one would dare break that code, not even Frank. Eventually the resolute, unsteady swaying figure of Blue left the bar. Sid followed behind everyone knew that would happen.

# CHAPTER 7

# MONSTER

Another defining moment came when the gang of five decided to go their separate ways. Lee summed up the situation. 'Big fish swim in a big pool. Useless tadpoles stay where they are and get to be frogs.' One of the gang had the inclination to tell him that if you kiss enough frogs one of them could turn into a prince. The sentiment would have been lost on him.

Andy Gardner on the other hand had already achieved the status Lee wanted to aspire to. Gardner was doing very nicely thank you with his life of crime. He had a finger in more pies than Sweeny Todd. The time had arrived to give Gardner a visit. Finding him would not be a problem. He virtually lived in the Stags Head. No, the problem would be trying to catch him without his so-called henchmen. Lee came up with a proposition, the trade-off left his bunch of morons with little alternative. 'Help me with this last one. If you don't, I swear one night you will all wake up and smell something burning.'

The plan, again like the architect, was simple. Brian would be the first to enter the Stag's Head. When he spotted Gardner on his own, he would throw a toilet roll out of the window as a signal for the rest to enter the pub.

As insurance, everyone tooled up. Dina carried a knife knuckleduster. Frank had a sheath knife strapped to his forearm. From a discreet distance, Brian could see his muscular target accompanied by two mates enter the Stag's Head. After a while, he followed them into the pub. It was virtually empty, Gardner and the two minders were busy playing cards. Gardner clocked him straight away and Brian started to feel uncomfortable. In an attempt to look less conspicuous, he asked the barman how much it would cost to hire the upstairs room for a party. Their conversation wafted over to the card table. They continued to play. Brian, with his back to their table, looked in the mirror behind the bar. He could see one of the henchmen leaving the pub. Gardner decided to use the phone behind the bar. Nicotine teeth and scaly red skin sneered at Brian. 'Fuck off for a piss, this is a private conversation.'

Brian locked the door, opened the window and threw out a toilet roll.

When he returned to the bar, Gardner made it obvious that his presence was annoying him. 'Are you back already? Finish your drink and piss off as soon as.'

'I'm waiting for my mate, we're scouting for somewhere to hold a do.'

Gardner's large frame and shovel hands moved in on Brian. A threatening shaven head literally pushed the youngster hard against the wall. 'Don't outstay your welcome, there's a good boy.'

Ten minutes passed before Lee, Dina and Roy entered the bar under the pretence of a stag night. Later, Frank joined Brian at the bar. Lee glanced in Gardner's direction. 'Boy's, luck's on my side, best week of my life.'

Roy and Lee casually waltzed over to the table where they were playing cards. 'Any chance of joining in?'

Gardner flexed the dragon tattoo on his right forearm. His sullen leer gave little hope. 'This is a man's game we don't play for pocket money, piss off.'

Lee controlled his temper. *We'll soon see who is the man around here you bastard.* Taking out a wad of notes, he waved them in front of Gardner. 'Does this look like pocket money?'

'Ok sunny Jim; don't go crying to your slag when you lose.'

Gardner excelled as a barefaced cheat. He had already polished the picture face of the aces in the pack. Carefully watching the dealer, when he saw a card leaving his hand a little more quickly than the other cards, he knew who had an ace. Aces were high in three-card brag.

Lee soon found out what it was like to play against a stacked deck. Every time he had a king, Gardner had an ace. Within no time, the money dwindled down to his last note. Gardner dealt the next hand and the soft touch threw his last fiver into the pot.

The dealer's brazen glare gave the sad loser the once over. 'I hope you shag better than you play cards. I'll do you a favour, I'll go and fuck your girl after this hand. What have you cunt got, I mean got cunt?'

'I've got this you bastard.' Lee jumped to his feet, smashed his pint glass against the edge of the iron table and rammed it straight into Gardner's face. The jagged edges of the glass pierced his eye. Gardner tried to stand as Lee repeatedly forced, jabbed and twisted the glass into his face. He fell backwards onto the floor. Roy pulled a knife, lashed out and slashed Gardner's mate across the face. Despite the injury, he tried to get to his feet. Dina repeatedly slammed a knuckleduster into the small of his back and he fell, rolling around in agony. There was blood everywhere. Gardener's eyeball was out of its socket, dangling from the muscles at the back of his eye. It rested on his cheekbone. Lee and Roy grabbed hold of his feet and dragged him into the lounge. 'Who's the kiddie now? Who's doing the fucking now?' Lee acted like a crazy. 'Want more, do you want more, you bastard? Roy pass me your knife, I'll cut his fucking head off.' Gardner was still on the floor in a state of shock. 'Not saying a lot now are you, you clever bastard. I'm going to cut your ugly face if I don't get a cut of your business. It's your choice. If you've got objections say so and we'll finish you here and now.'

Still in a daze, Gardner nodded. Everything seemed surreal. He could feel a strange presence in the room. Where was he and why did everything appear trancelike. Then the horror and fear of the unbelievable, unthinkable stuck in his throat. *I can't fucking see. I can't fucking see anything!* He tried to work out his insanity. Fright, twisting a knife had ripped his nervous system to shreds. Something crawled out of his anus and he shit himself. Dina fetched a towel from the toilet and hurled it at Gardner. No one called the police, he refused to go to hospital. With a towel around his head, oblivious to the foul smell of urine and faeces from his trousers, he sat at the bar smoking, drinking whisky, trembling like a leaf.

Lee had earned his reputation. His cards were well and truly on the table. Nothing was beyond his capability. He had no shame, empathy for the victim or true recognition of the difference between right and wrong.

A month after the incident Frank saw Gardner walking down the road like a zombie. Wearing a patch over his eye, deep scars were still visible under his left cheekbone and around his nose. The card shark had lost the sight in one eye and his bottle. Lee had accomplished everything; at last, his new gang had credibility. Brian and Frank were superfluous to requirements, Dina and Roy joined the gang. Nothing was beyond their resume, they even screwed the bookies again. This time Lee employed a more sophisticated approach.

To obtain the keys to the safe he held the Baxter family hostage in their home. Lee took his favourite hammer along. Baxter was willing to hand over the keys, however, the crazy wanted to impress on the family the consequences if they grassed him up to the police. Two henchmen held Baxter's wife down on the bedroom floor and Lee drove a nail straight though the palm of her hand. Every hammer blow hitting, banging the head of the steel nail further into the palm, gave him an intense state of euphoria of going beyond. The thug sat on the bed and watched her struggling to free her hand nailed to the floorboard. He even shouted words of encouragement, 'Come on you bitch, GO ON, FREE IT. If you don't I'll nail your other hand to the floor.' Crying, begging to the point of hysteria, it made no difference. *If she thinks she is rocking my boat she has another thing coming.* Chronic pain sinking its teeth, gnawed at her spine. After a while, like a cancer eating away, it turned into a dull, dull ache.

The gang left the keys in the lock after opening the safe. Baxter told the police he must have accidentally left them in the office. Lee, not for the first time thought about the different ways and how long it would take to kill someone. That moment would arrive sooner rather than later.

He had not entirely severed ties with the past. Using his individual style of persuasion, he enticed Beth to join his money-spinning prostitution racket. The more lucrative prostitutes moved off the street into a semi-detached house equipped with a bar upstairs. The gang added to their portfolio and entered the world of insurance. They provided protection to those too terrified to refuse. This lucrative pastime appealed to Lee, with little effort the money kept rolling in. Roberts, the owner of the local brewery, made the wrong decision and he declined the offer. Lee shattered both his kneecaps. News about the offer spiralled throughout the valley. You either paid or ended up on crutches. Lee felt cheated when the majority decided to take up the healthy option.

Lee visited Bristol in order to learn new skills from Howard Joyce, a notorious gangster who ruled the city with an iron fist. Anything new, including drugs, had his trademark stamped all over it. Joyce introduced Lee to drug trafficking. The variety of drugs was endless. A relatively new yet old recreational drug, marihuana, had huge potential. Joyce agreed to supply samples of 'rush drugs' and barbiturates for a substantial cut in the valley market. All Lee had to do was to target the vulnerable, hook them on drugs and reap the reward.

Joyce made the point that he usually supplied drugs in bulk to clientele with far more financial influence than Lee. Could Lee achieve that criterion? Brutality was about to tap on the shoulder of anyone with real money

Things were moving on at a pace. Then he became involved in the Annie Walcott incident.

Annie an elderly spinster lived alone in a mansion surrounded by acres of land on the outskirts of town. Her estate that included stables and a courtyard had been in the family for generations. Since the death of her husband, Annie spent most of the time involved in charitable work. Every day she grieved for her loving husband Harry. Forty years was a long time and she missed him dearly. In the lonely hollow mansion at night, she would lose herself in remembering. The album of their wedding was never far away from her gaze.

Like most of her generation, she mistrusted the banks. A solicitor had tried to persuade her otherwise but she declined. Mistrust was not the only reason. Somehow, with the money hidden safely behind a false cove in the pantry, it made her feel closer to Harry.

Annie retired to her bed clutching his photograph. His serene face had a more calming influence than any pill prescribed by a doctor.

Three intruders broke into the mansion. They walked in, Annie had forgotten to lock the conservatory door.

A creaking noise on the wooden staircase hardly registered. Turning over in bed, she could vaguely remember hearing a thud from downstairs. The gracious lady rubbed her eyes. Was she still dreaming? Rubbing again, no, Annie was not mistaken. Three men were standing around her bed. Confused, half-asleep, trying to focus, she could make out the balaclavas, gloves and jogging suits. *For pity sake, why are they here dressed like that?*

'Where is the money you old hag?'

She looked away and pretended not to hear. Again, the same question, only this time with far more aggression. 'I don't know what you are referring to.' Annie could hear the quiver in her voice.

Leaning over, Lee grabbed the top of her nightdress, pulled Annie towards him and punched her in the face. A hard fist inside the glove snapped her nose like a twig and it started to bleed.

Annie was a proud individual. *I am not going to hand over my money. I will not be bullied.* Despite the overwhelming fear rasping her thin frame, she refused to let Harry down.

Lee and Roy grabbed her arms and dragged her out of bed. 'I don't think you heard what I said. Drowning you in the bath will clear your ears out.' Roy filled the bath with cold water. Lee shouted obscenities and tore the nightgown from her thin fragile body. He clocked the stark ashen horror on her gaunt face. It was only a matter of time before Annie would tell him what he wanted to know.

Unceremoniously, they picked her up and lowered her into the bath. Roy, holding both her feet at one end of the bath, lifted them in the air. Lee grabbed her long silver-grey hair and pulled her head under the water. When she surfaced, gasping for breath, spewing out water, he punched her in the stomach. Every time Annie surfaced, Lee asked her the same question. She refused to answer and he pushed her under the water.

Roy could see that his boss was holding her under the water for long periods. If Lee continued, he would end up drowning her. 'She's no good to us if she's dead is she boss.'

With a hysterical pitch in his voice, he glowered at his victim. 'Search the house. Find it then I'll do her, did you hear what I said witch. You're going to die, you're going to fucking die.'

After ransacking the mansion, apart from Annie's jewellery, they found little of value. Lee's anger had now moved on to loathing. It was time to resort to more torturous methods. 'Fucking sit on her and hold her fingers out one at a time.' Using pliers, placing the top of her nail in the jaw, closing it, he paused and slowly ripped her nail out of its cuticle. With a frenzied smirk on his face, after tearing each nail from her finger, he stopped and asked the same question, 'Now tell me where the money is if you know what's good for you, you fucking hag?' Annie remained silent. 'Roy, come on, get a grip, open her mouth and hold her nose.' He pushed the fingernails into her mouth and made her swallow. Changing to a more macabre approach, Lee started forcing needles into the flesh left under her nails. She screamed in agony from the raw pain burrowing into her fingers. Carrying her, grabbing both wrists, he plunged her hands into the bedroom sink. Roy held her hands in the sink as Lee poured vinegar and rubbed salt into the open wounds around her fingers. Annie stopped screaming and she lost consciousness.

An irritating smell of ammonia playing on her nerve endings started to bring her around. Semi-conscious, hallucinating, Annie focused her thoughts on Harry. She wanted to join him. In agony, she pictured his handsome almost saintly face on their wedding day. Defiantly, and with a distinct motion in her hands and head, she closed her palm and grasped a hair slide. With the needles still in her fingers, Annie raised her chin and pinned back her hair. She glanced at her hands. The bloody folds of the loose skin on either side of the vacant nails were in shreds. Shocked to the very core, every single second of every minute she had to endure would bring her closer to Harry.

This was now personal. Lee intended to have one last attempt. Annie coughed, or she croaked. He attached two bare wires from an electric socket to the index finger on both her hands. After switching it on, he watched as the electric current travelled along the nerve and blood vessels in her thin frame. The corners of her mouth on the right side of her face contracted, and pulled her jaw to one side. After a minute or so, Lee switched off the current. He asked the question one last time.

The current had left tissue burns on unprotected skin and she lost control of her bladder. Digging down into the depth of her soul, somehow, she found an inner strength. Annie again lifted her proud head and looked at the ceiling. 'Harry, bless, I knew you would come for me. Please make it better, there's a love.'

Finally, like a red-hot poker burning into her chest, the electric current surged through her heart muscles. Annie closed her eyes for the last time and finally passed into the other world where there is no pain.

*Through the continuum of brilliant light, she could see Harry in the distance. Annie looked into the alluring light and yet for some strange reason it always seemed to be behind her. She instantly recognised Harry, it had little to do with his appearance. She approached Harry without moving her legs. Somehow, she could stretch and move like a rubber band. With the sheer joy of raw emotion washing through her soul, she entered the bright light into infinity. Then and only then and forever Annie could see his face.*

Lee went berserk. In a crazy frenzy, he pulled a carving knife from his belt. Systematically he cut off her ears and nose before finally decapitating her. Still in an uncontrollable rage, Lee continued to cut lumps of flesh from her body. The pathologist who carried out the post mortem concluded that the injuries had little to do with crime. It had everything to do with the sadistic gratification of the killer. In the report and for the only time in her career, the pathologist used the word MONSTER to describe the offender. There was little forensic evidence left at the scene, Joyce had taught his pupil well.

Terror like a deadly virus hung in the air. Although no one could see, touch or smell it, everyone knew the chronic parasite was out there. Several greenhorn attempts on Lee's life were unsuccessful. The odds were stacking against him. One day some amateur could get lucky.

Would Annie's grandson, Jeremy Walcott, be the lucky one? He had been unlucky enough to find her body parts strewn around the mansion. From that moment, swearing revenge, his initial attempt to finish off the monster failed, but that only made him more determined. Shortly after her funeral, clearing out the attic, he came across his grandfather's double-barrelled shotgun and a belt of cartridges.

Hiding behind a hedge near the Boar's Head, Walcott could feel wave-like spasms of cramp in his stomach. Lee had recently moved into Dina's bedsit around the corner. Night, dressed in a long black shroud, smothered the circles of light coming from the street lamps. From his position, Walcott still had a clear view of the flat. At around 2.00 a.m. the lights went out in the flat. The time had arrived to make his move. Walcott knew the layout. The bedroom was the first on the right from the passageway. He checked his shotgun and the safety catch was off. Without making a sound, in the stillness of the night, he crossed the road and quietly made his way up the stairs to the flat. He had to move fast, there would be no second chance. Silent whispers in the dark started to cast doubt over the outcome. *I'm going to die, it's going to be me not that bastard.*

*Please god please let it be that fucker. His* eyes were stinging from sweat and he wiped his brow. *If I have to, I'll kill everyone in the flat.*

Kicking in the front door, on the second attempt it burst open. Hurrying down the passageway, Walcott entered the bedroom. 'Got you at last you bastard.' At close range, firing both barrels, the flame from the discharge lit up the room. The pellets and gas had no time to spread. In a mass, they tore through the blankets. Disintegrating his skull, fragments splattered against the back wall. Thick, warm, sooty blood containing small pieces of bone and brain trickled down the side of the wall. Reloading, suddenly, he heard the noise of someone hurrying into the street. From the window, he could see Lee disappearing around the corner. Dina was the headless victim in the bed.

With the luck of the devil on his back, Lee kept on running until he reached the outskirts of Westgate. He had outgrown the valley, there were lucrative pickings waiting for him in Bristol.

Joyce welcomed him with open arms, a partnership and more would be in the offing when he decided to retire.

Walcott still refused to accept defeat. He tried to find Lee in the big city. This time Lee found him.

Shackled to the railway line on the outskirts of the city, Walcott only had time to curse Lee before the train sliced his torso in two.

Joyce sent his own kind of message to Westgate, Lee was now under his protection. The same thing would happen to anyone foolish enough to make a move on his protégé.

A cardboard box delivered to Walcott's home emphasised the message. His wife carried it into the kitchen and opened the box. Looking inside at the unreal horror, she recognised the wedding ring on the finger of a severed hand clutching a note. It read, 'Your children will be next.'

# CHAPTER 8

## ILLEGITIMUS NON CARBORUNDUM

With Lee and Gardner starting their partnership, another career opportunity as junior clerk at the west of the plant had also loomed for the ambitious office boy. At the same time, Davies, the turf accountant, wanted a part-time bookies runner to take care of the business at the west side of the plant. Candidates had to be honest and trustworthy. Frank thought his portfolio ticked all the boxes. Starkey had other ideas, he had already promised the vacancy to Sheila. He wanted a one-off no strings attached shag with the redhead for employing her son. Starkey made it clear to the prospective runner, he had no chance of realising his expectation. Would it do any harm if he reminded Starkey about his extracurricular activity with Edna?

The manager recognised blackmail, especially when it was standing in front of him with a smirk. 'Don't try to blackmail me or you will end up without a job and little prospect of you getting another.'

Frank touched his favourite table and stood his ground. 'Mr Starkey, think about it, if I don't get it I'm going to phone your wife, Rachel isn't it, and you'll be in the shit. As well is shagging allowed in work?'

'Grow up. Who do you think is going to take your word against mine?'

'Rachel will when I tell her you've got a mole and a butterfly tattoo on the left cheek of your arse.' Attention to detail generally pays dividends, and it did. Within a week, Frank started in the admin department at the Bessemer under a new manager, Ivor Llewellyn.

In a former life, Llewellyn had attained the rank of colonel in the Borderers before leaving under dubious circumstances. His ability to stagger pissed as a newt from the main gate to his office usually held an audience. Aloof, he had one friend, the pink elephant who followed him around. During the junior clerk's third week, a racing pigeon suffering from a bad case of diarrhoea, homed in and discharged the unwanted mess over Llewellyn's bowler hat. Answering a muted cry, the junior clerk opened the office door. Llewellyn, leaning against it covered in bird shit, fell into the office. With skill, Frank shunted the manager into his office. He gently lowered him into his seat and then made his way to the kitchen. Llewellyn had given clear instructions. Daily, two raw eggs whisked in milk had to be 'Ready in short order or you will be on a damn well fizzer.' Frank cracked the last egg against the side of the cup. It nosedived onto the floor. On his knees, scooping up particles of red dust and the odd yolk he placed it back in the cup.

Tiptoeing into Llewellyn's office with the lethal concoction, blurry eyes attempted to focus under a bowler hat. 'Hello sir reporting as instructed. I've got your drink but I don't think… '

A pompous, guttural voice roared disapproval. 'Hello sir, are my ears deceiving me or did YOU have the bloody audacity to say HELLO SIR. What is the army coming to?' With a grand gesture of dismissal, he snatched the cup out of the clerk's hand and drank it. 'At last you're getting the hang of it, smart drink.'

The junior clerk attempted an about-turn, marching towards the door, standing at attention, he saluted with the wrong hand and closed the door behind him.

The affable broad smile of the head clerk, Adrian Small, greeted him in the main office. Behind NHS spectacles, his crystal-blue eyes were the windows to his soul. With long spidery legs, Adrian stood head and shoulders above a generation who refused to accept gays. The phone rang, a security guard at the west gate gave them the warning to expect an unannounced visit from Richard Lewis, the plant manager. Lewis, a dedicated serial bully, permeated his dysfunctional behaviour through the plant. He held a deep prejudice towards gays. Adrian's previous encounter with the manager had been confrontational.

'Frank, please don't get involved, he wants to sack me. I'm afraid I have given him the chance, the registers are not up to date.'

The junior clerk ran to the front door, locked it, retrieved the cooling register from the cabinet and handed it to Adrian. 'Read the thing out loud to the boss in his office.'

'I can't, he's asleep. Anyway, it's not up to date. I'm sorry but I think it's dishonest!'

Frank listened to the subtle tones of honesty from his colleague. Placing a hand on his shoulder, he looked into the integrity behind his eyes. 'Adrian please hear me out. I believe in you, I don't believe in bullies. Llewellyn will get the sack as well. If you think I'm going to just stand here, think again.' Adrian nodded and he reluctantly made his way to the manager's office.

Within minutes, Frank popped his head around the door of the manager's office. Llewellyn was still wearing a bowler hat. Fast asleep in the chair, he looked serene under an orange blanket that Adrian had brought in. Back in the main office, the junior clerk waited for Adrian to begin. The head clerk cleared his throat and there was a loud bang on the front door.

Opening the door, Lewis barged passed. 'Why is this door locked?'

'Instructions from Adrian sir, he's going through the weekly cooling report with Mr Llewellyn. He doesn't want to be disturbed.'

'It's about time that queer got his act together.' Lewis had one assignment he intended to sack Adrian. Ignoring the junior clerk, he stood outside Llewellyn's door. With his ear against the door, Lewis could hear Adrian's voice.

'The maintenance of C Sector cooling system is pencilled in for next Tuesday, it will take a month.'

Without knocking, Lewis partially opened the door. With his vision obscured, he could not see the manager.

'Morning Ivor, Small get your arse in here.'

Adrian walked to his desk with his shoulders back and head held high.

'Did I ask you to sit down?'

'No but I thought!'

'I don't pay you to think, I do all the thinking around here.'

Adrian waited for the inevitable bollocking. 'Small, I don't like you, I don't like what your sort get up to, do I make myself clear?' Adrian looked straight ahead. 'Ponce's have no right on my plant, I didn't hire you but I can fire you.' The manager glared at the head clerk still holding the file in his hand. Adrian turned to face the vindictive, insulting figure that every bully looks like. To Lewis's astonishment, the clerk made non-threatening eye contact. There was no shame, fear or subservient guilt in his eyes. Lewis seemed to be drowning in the moral hue of his honesty. He looked away and started to feel uncomfortable. An awkward silence seemed to hang in the air forever.

'Although you're a worthless piece of shit I've got to admit you're doing your job. Don't get me wrong, give me an excuse and you're out of here.' The emotional vampire left the office in the knowledge that he could always come back and suck the fear out of Adrian again.

Frank smiled at the head clerk. 'Was that a compliment?'

'Well as you can see, he doesn't like me.'

Why did everyone dislike homosexuals? If Adrian wanted a relationship with men, surely that was his choice. Curiosity joined in with the conversation and asked about homosexuality.

Adrian said he was standing up for what he believed in. Nothing could alter the fact, he was gay, true to his identity and proud of his sexual orientation. 'You see Frank they see me as a threat. I think they are more of a threat to me than I'll ever be to them.' Adrian described the hate and violence he had to endure. At eight years of age, Father Jones had subjected him to a brutal sexual assault. In the years to follow, he told Adrian that homosexuals were no longer welcome in the house of the Lord. Despite everything, he refused to give in to the recurrent oppression.

Ridicule whirred around in the junior clerk's gut. He made an excuse and collected his bookies bag from the kitchen and left. Standing outside the office, Frank glanced up at the mass of grey storm clouds in the shape of an anvil hovering overhead. *How did that bastard Father Jones get away with it?*

A flash of zigzag lightning travelled through a gap in the clouds at the bottom of the anvil. Purple fuzzy edges, at the front of the fork, splintered into several yellow and blood red pencil shapes before hitting the ground. Instinctively, Frank knew they were marking out a target. Like the thundering feet of a horse pulling a chariot across the sky, the rumbling noise gave way to a cluster of sharp booming thunderclaps. The afterglow of an electrical jade aurora in the shape of a spiral lit up the entire sky. This time, a rotating blue sphere the size of a basketball with a trail, moved through the burning path hurtling towards the ground. He looked again, the explosion on impact seemed to be in the same area as the lightning. The fireball must have landed near the vicarage or the Catholic Church.

In the coming months, the congregation concluded that the replacement for Father Jones seemed to be far closer to their God. With crystals of rain bouncing off the hard surface, Frank made no attempt to shelter from the thunderstorm. Maybe just maybe he could help a friend.

★★★

For Adrian, hell on earth had arrived in the guise of his neighbour, Hue Morgan. In his crazy world, the cruel tyrant felt safer if he hated someone. To relieve the humdrum, he hammered and wrote slogans on the clerk's front door. After a while, Morgan took hostility to a new level and Adrian found his cat hanging from his letterbox. The message in red paint on the door read, 'You next you queer.' Distraught, he contemplated suicide. The cat had brought something special into his life. That gift was now lost forever. Hatred towards the culprit had never entered his head. Adrian refused to acknowledge the disease.

The sunset, fading behind the box house hills, scattered the last light on Brian hiding behind the hedge. Armed with the butt of a snooker cue, he watched his friend strolling along the path to the front door. Brian could hear Frank's voice. 'Don't worry about me hit that bastard and give it everything.' Frank placed a tin of red paint on the doorstep and he retrieved a brush from his back pocket. With all the time in the world, he scrawled on the door in paint, 'You next you bastard, try me for size.'

He hammered on the door, within seconds, Morgan, in his fifties, as thin as a toothpick stood in the doorway. 'What do you want?'

'I've got a message for the shithead living in this pig sty.'

Morgan glared in the direction to where he was pointing and read the message. Confused, the muscles in his jaw tightened, as he looked the teenager up and down. 'Are you out of your mind, what's this all about?'

'Good question, YOU LUMP OF SHIT. I'm going to make you suffer, just like you made Adrian's poor cat suffer.'

Morgan could see the uncontrollable anger behind cold eyes. He did not intend to mix it with someone capable of fighting back. 'Delyth, bring Rebel out here now.'

Delyth appeared in the doorway with a vicious pit bull barking and pulling on the leash. Frank, only seconds away from bowel movement, stepped back onto the path. *Adrian didn't tell me about the dog.*

Morgan grabbed the leash and dragged the dog towards him. Growling, opening massive jaws, the terrier showed its scissor-like teeth. He started to release the steel link of the choke chain around the dog's neck and whacked it several times with the leash. 'He went through the paper boy's shoe last week. Now he's going to bite your fucking head off.' Slowly he released the dog. Lowering its ugly head, steadily it ran towards the intruder.

A prickly warm sensation from the last light wafted through the cells at the back of his right eye. Instinctively he knelt down and looked straight at the dog charging towards him. Not threatened by the dog, he licked his lips and spoke with a rich Gaelic dialect. *'Mo chara nach bhfuil feicthe agam agat ó réimse an shábháil tú dom as an tarbh,* my friend I have not seen you since the field when you saved me from the bull.' The pit bull terrier stopped and sniffed his hand. *'Ní mór duit a lorg anois amach an ceann a rinne tú feargach amhlaidh,* you must seek out the one who has made you so angry.' The terrier turned its head, looked at Morgan and ran back towards him.

Within striking distance, the dog, lunging, bowled his master over. Sinking long fangs into his neck, closing locking muscular jaws, biting, the pit bull started to shake him like a rag doll. Morgan screamed and he begged the dog to stop. The dog refused to let go and mauled him on the ground. A taste of blood seemed to increase the tenacity of the attack.

Frank attempted to intervene but the dialect had faded. He thought about his own safety. As they ran from the scene, they could hear the siren of the ambulance in the distance.

After months in surgery, wearing a surgical collar, Morgan eventually left hospital. For the rest of his short life, the victim never spoke about the incident or anything else. His voice box and windpipe had been torn from his neck. Without a satisfactory explanation, Brian decided to forget about the incident.

# CHAPTER 9

## ADDICTION

Frank had no idea that bad habits were forming part of his addictive pattern. The pilgrimage to the club had changed to a daily ritual. He came to regard the watering hole as the font of all knowledge. There was always someone hanging around the bar with 'the done that got the tee shirt' attitude. Blue, his nickname synonymous with his attitude towards sex, typified this mind-set. The seventeen-year-old had to replenish his glass if he wanted the benefit of his encyclopaedic knowledge. He regarded it as an investment. It certainly paid dividends when Blue told him that women probably liked sex and certainly thought about it more than their male counterpart. With the alcohol taking effect, pissing his inhibitions against the wall, the conversation turned to Blue's version of the Karma Sutra.

The teenager blushed and cleared his throat, 'What about all that love thing?'

'Listen, love has ruined more lives than black suspender belts. The best you can hope for is a divorce. Look after your dick lad because that is all you'll walk away with after a divorce.' It was time to put his newfound knowledge into practice.

Huddling in a shop doorway out of the rain, he almost had an erection thinking about kissing Marian in the back row of the cinema. Conversation with Marian was easy. Confident with a gentle way, she bore little resemblance to the girl he had met in the cafe.

Already on their third date, the last one had shown promise. In the late autumn sunlight, they decided to walk in the park. Strolling arm in arm between the lines of oak trees on either side of the path, sunlight reflected off the rustic leaves floating down in front of them. The grass verge, cloaked in a wealth of golden and green seemed to take on a magical look. The rustle of dry leaves crumbling, crunching beneath their feet, turned on a million flashing lights in his head. His right eye homed in on a single brittle leaf falling from a branch. If he wanted luck, he had to catch the leaf before it touched the ground. He ran forward. The wind juggled with the leaf and it fell on the path. Was that a sign of bad luck? Still longing for sexual intimacy, at that moment, walking along the path, he experienced something far stronger than the desire of the flesh. An unbridled feeling to put his arms around Marian surged through the blood of his soul. Everything seemed to be moving in slow motion and in a higher resolution. He watched as the fern leaves slowly changed to yellow and then vibrant brown. A train full of love had run over him on the path, he wanted to hold onto that feeling.

At the entrance to the pond, with his arms around her neck, their lips brushed and tasted each other. Her eyelashes whisked against his cheek and the sensation hurried over his skin. She seemed to be whispering with her mouth. The kiss lingered and he experienced that familiar stir in his groin. A red squirrel ran across their path and scampered up a nearby tree.

Marian kissed him on the cheek. 'I think you had better cool it, or that squirrel will stick your nuts where the sun doesn't shine.'

'Very funny, look if this sort of thing carries on I will be writing to that bloody agony aunt about you.'

'Will you post my letter as well? It'll save me the cost of a postage stamp. Frank I feel the same as you, but we've got to be sensible about it.'

'Who the hell's this guy called sensible?'

'Oh him, he's the one standing between the right moment and the right time.'

'Can't I just!' Frank gently palmed her backside.

'What difficulty do you have in understanding the word No?'

'Well it's the opposite to yes for a start.'

'Right, let me try and clear up any misunderstanding in our relationship. You would like to get into my knickers, is that right? The only way you will get your hands on my knickers is rummaging through my cabinet.'

'What drawer are they in, describe them to me?'

A chilly autumn wind whistled through the branches and touched their cheeks. Holding hands, fingers touching, flirting, arms swinging, gliding along the path they kicked the leaves underneath their feet. Eventually they reached a park bench.

The sun, with an Ebenezer Scrooge nightcap, climbed down the ladder behind the landscape. Softer light changed the red and yellow foliage to a dark rustic colour.

Frank plunged a hand into his jacket pocket, wrong one. From the next, he salvaged what looked like tissue paper. 'I've bought you a present.'

'If it's a condom, put it back in your pocket.'

Clumsily, he unravelled the paper and handed Marian a silver Saint Christopher pendant hanging from a snake chain.

Marian looked at it for what seemed like an eternity. 'I never expected this, I love it thank you.'

In their colourful world of adolescence, again he experienced that desperate urge to get physical. Without rushing the intro, lazily, he started sliding over to her side of the bench. 'I was wondering if…'

'Don't tell me, let me guess. You were wondering if you could warm your cold hands on my breasts, perhaps under my jumper. Better still, WHAT ABOUT under my skirt?'

'Marian there's more to a relationship than sex. I was going to ask you if you would like to sit on my knee.'

Confused and dumfounded, Marian jumped to her feet. 'You were going to ask me what, you liar, you made that up.'

'Sit down FOR Christ's sake people are watching. Your thing with sex, sex and nothing but sex is starting to piss me off.'

Marian was speechless. Staring at each other, they burst out laughing. Grabbing her arm, pulling, tugging, she sat on his lap. They held onto the fascination of love before it eventually gave way to intimacy. Then they spoke with their eyes above an intimate smile that never fades. Holding each other close, without saying anything, they wanted the same thing. With no ulterior motive, the only thing left was the phenomenon of that special moment, that inimitable feeling, when you experience something extraordinary for the first time. Endless hours of talking about the irrelevance of everything ended when they arrived at her front door.

'Right, do you think there'll be a time when you know?'

Marian looked at him in exasperation. 'If we keep using up your favourite word, there won't be any left for anyone else.'

★★★

As usual Marian was late and as usual, she would have a plausible excuse. Half an hour passed before she made an appearance. Her father owned the lucrative ironmongers shop, and it showed in the way she dressed. The teenager's heart paused and took his pulse as she walked towards him wearing a powder-blue dress, gothic black leather jacket, and white socks rolled down to her ankles. Approving raised eyebrows fell away to the revelation of her touch.

'Sorry I am late but I had to...'

'Would you like me to fill in the blanks with bullshit?' Another genial smile broke out on her 'got me' face.

As they walked to the cinema, Frank gently caught hold of her hand. Fingers exploring, entwined, touching silk skin, intermingled with the revelry of a teasing glance.

The lights of the cinema dimmed as they made their way to the back row. It was nearly empty. *Hello, this is frustration here with a capital F, when are you going to make a move?* Wasting no time, he gently sucked and tugged on her lower lip. Knuckles pushed softly against the inside of her silk blouse. Stretching his fingers, he touched her breast. Through the cup of the bra, her nipple responded to his touch. Frank hardly noticed the pinkish sex flush on his face and neck spreading to his back and arms. He had an overwhelming compulsion to jump out of his seat and announce, *I've touched her breast, see these two fingers they've touched, I said TOUCHED her nipple.* This time with her earlobe between his lips, hesitating, hovering, sliding he touched the outside of her dress between her legs. The look on Marian's face suggested things were going well. She grabbed his wrist and pulled it away.

His brain went numb, pulse racing, the arteries at the side of his neck were about to explode. With a dull sickly ache, he attempted to sit upright and a thousand butterflies nervously tickled his stomach. Blue's voice yanked on his belt and shouted down his trousers, 'Don't forget, when the lady says NO, respect it.' That was all he needed, two hard nipples seemed to be waving at him through her blouse.

Leaning, still eyeing the best duo act he had ever seen, he kissed Marian on the cheek. 'Fancy an ice cream during the interval.'

She glanced down at his groin. 'I'd love one, but I don't think you can stand.'

Outside the cinema with the rain falling, oblivious to the shower, Marian jumped on his back and he carried her to the front door. The young lady knew what she wanted out of life. Bath College had already accepted her application to join them next term. 'Frank have you ever, you know done it with anyone else?'

'Ye loads of times with these two.' Holding out both his arms, he pretended to play the piano. 'Because of you I'm now ambidextrous.'

'I have as well, but get this one Frank, I'd give my right arm to be able to say I am ambidextrous.'

Not strictly true, Frank had encountered one sexual experience he would rather forget. It happened when he was sixteen years of age. Wales were playing rugby at Cardiff and Brian had managed to get tickets. Touched by the drunken fairy after the game, they made their way back to the hotel. His recollection was somewhat hazy. He had a convenient memory. Both crashed out on the bed. During the night, Frank could feel an arm around his waist. Still intoxicated, something hard touched his backside. Brian had an erection. A hand slipped inside his pants and touched his penis. The stimulation and excitement of someone touching his penis for the first time raged through every nerve ending. Within seconds of Brian coming, Frank ejaculated. In the morning, acting like strangers, the refusal to make eye contact spoke volumes about their insecurity.

Confused and scared, Frank started to question his sexuality. What frightened him was the fact he had liked it. Consumed by guilt and with something to prove, sex with Marian would erase any lingering doubt about his heterosexuality.

Flirting, gazing at his mouth, Marian put her arms around his waist. 'Frank please just give it time. I'd just like to pick the right moment for us that's all. I know I'm going to sound as silly as you, but I even thought how things will eventually turn out the other day when I used my typewriter.'

'I'm trying my best. All you can talk about is your bloody typewriter.'

'So am I, look at the top row of letters and focus on the letter 'U'. You are pretty good at doing that.'

The frustrated teenager splashed most of the puddles on his way home. *For Christ's sake why can't it bloody well rain. She's driving me crazy, what was all that typewriter bollocks about.*

Alcohol had the answer. After calling in at the Old Oak, a buzzing intoxication seemed to dull and shrink the capital F.

'Well if it isn't my knight in shining armour. What's wrong Lancelot, lost your horse.'

He cursed under his breath, he should have caught that leaf. The last person he wanted to see was standing on the opposite side of the road waiting for prospective punters. Frank still had a hang-up about Beth. As he crossed the road, he could see the ladder runs in her stocking. Gaunt prominent cheekbones had dramatically changed her face. 'Hi Beth, how's it with you?'

'What, you mean since you and the rest of your so-called friends fucked up my life.'

'Look, I'm sorry for what happened.'

'Right and that is going to make everything okay is it, you saying you are sorry.'

'If there is anything I can do let me know.'

'Well there is something you can do. Put business my way and use your prick for something else besides pissing through.' He handed her his last pound note. 'And what can I do you for? I'll tell you now fucking me is going to cost more than a measly pound.'

'I don't want anything Beth.'

'If you think I'm taking charity from you, you can forget it.'

Beth put her arms around his neck. Thrusting, pushing, he could feel the shape of her well-formed breasts and long shapely legs through his clothing. The blood in his veins ignited as her tongue searched for his mouth.

'Come on baby I know you want it.'

With his scrotum tightening, in the moment he lost self-control.

'Look I'll give you a blow job, you'll love it.' Touching his penis through his trousers, she dragged him down the alleyway. Pushing him against the wall, with one yank she undid his belt and his trousers fell to the ground. Kneeling on the pavement, she untied the bow of the halter-top around her neck. Beth caught hold of the shoulder straps and gently pulled her cotton blouse down to her waist. She placed his hard penis in her mouth. Blue steel eyes looked up at the glare transfixed on her beautifully formed small breasts. Within seconds, his first experience of deep throat ended with a crescendo.

An enlightened smirk danced on his pillow as he stretched out on his bed and thought about Beth and Marian. They had different standards. Marian had a conscience and the strength to stand up for what she thought was right. Beth had no scruples. One was definitely in the right, the other could do no wrong. In their different way, they both made him feel good. Frank saw his role as the innocent bystander. He decided to play the waiting game with Marian, and occasionally call on the services of Beth. What else did Beth have in her magical box called sex? Her illusions were probably endless.

Trying to stir from his slumber, his dream about Beth whirled around in his head. They were in Starkey's office, bending over, she had her right leg up on the desk. He vigorously ravaged her from behind. Edna decided to join them. Naked to the waist, standing behind him, he could feel the surging peak of her breasts and hard pulsing nipples pushing against the strong lean muscle planes in his back. Arching, driving, jerking, the sexual act seemed to last forever before he climaxed. With the fantasy still playing, he pulled back the sheets. His dream had been a wet one.

Straining every fibre, with her stomach sticking in her throat, Marian tried not to throw up. What started out as an innocent conversation in the street had turned into her worst nightmare? Beth vividly described the sordid details with her so-called boyfriend.

'Do you know he was that frustrated he couldn't get enough? Hell, he was that excited, I thought he would never stop coming.'

A whirling sensation dragged her to the ground and her legs gave way. She grabbed onto the garden wall and almost fainted. 'It's not my Frank, I'm telling you now it must be someone else.'

But it was and for good measure, Beth told her about the incident in the car park with Lee.

Waiting a lost lifetime to get even, Beth showed no mercy. Marian was a physical wreck by the time she had finished. Sitting on the pavement, head bowed, there were no tears or anger. Still in a state of shock, with puffy eyes and a swollen face, she had difficulty in breathing. Beth looked at the agonising figure sprawled on the floor. Kneeling down in front of Marian, she held her tight as the tears ran down the prostitute's face. *What a mess, I had no right to do that. Those bastards drove me to it.*

Catching her breath and driving air into her lungs, she dug in deep. Marian thought about that magical day in the park, and gradually the blood started to flow back into her brain. Caring for someone, more than anything else, does it have to end in anguish and betrayal? 'Why, please tell me, why did you do this to me?' As Beth held onto her, she repeated the question.

'They might as well have killed me that day in the car park. They killed any feeling I can ever have for anything or anyone. I'm like a sleepwalker walking around this planet. I wanted to hurt you to get even. Say you're going to be all right.' Marian's day of remembering choked on the hard edge of deceit sticking in her throat. Were they very different or just two people paying lip service to deceit and hypocrisy?

Marian took time to recover. Bath College would finally test whether she had turned the page to a new beginning. Did she have the courage to forgive, that would be her biggest challenge? The season of new life replaced the harsh winter. With the days getting longer, so did self-belief. Hurt and vulnerability changed to a newfound confidence. Closure could only happen through true forgiveness.

A blush of warm sunlight touched Marian's cheek. She saw Beth in the distance turning the corner into Bridge Street. It had been a while since their last encounter. Without thinking, running she called out her name. Beth looked around to see who it was. Marian caught up and instinctively put her arms around her neck. In the middle of the street, they hugged like long lost friends. 'Hi, are you ok?'

'What do you think, what are you looking so pleased about?'

'I can't wait for next week, I'm off to Bath University. I thought I'd say goodbye hope things turn out for you.'

The sincerity in her smile startled Beth. She looked away and started to feel uncomfortable.

Marian gently touched her arm. 'Take care.' Walking away, a shamefaced gaze followed her.

'Go for it kid, make it for the two of us. God I'm sorry, please forgive me.'

Marian's next move would be even more challenging. Did she have the courage to forgive Frank? She had not returned any phone calls.

Brian broke the news that all hell had broken loose. He reacted in his usual chauvinistic way, 'Look Bri, I don't give a shit, it's her loss not mine.' Changing his usual route to work to avoid Marian, his loss of appetite and regularly on the piss, said more about his true feeling. In the dead of night, the devil whispered in his ear. The nightmare of Marian crawled into his bed and burrowed into his conscience. Her voice, swimming around in the alcohol in his stomach, regularly surfaced to remind him of his two-timing. Long dark days turned over the pages of the calendar, and Frank started to come to terms with his guilt. Dragging himself out of bed after another night of looking at the world through an empty glass, he wondered if his three o'clock alarm would ever end. He was almost through the door when he stepped on a letter in the hallway. It was from Marian. It read:

*Hi Frank, I am off to college. Sorry I did not have the courage to face you. I wanted to remember us as we were. I was frightened that we might meet in the street and have one of those horrible strange moments. Thank you for all the fun we had together, you made me feel so special when I was with you. I hope you find what you are looking for. I will never forget you. I have already posted my letter to the agony aunt and she has told me that it is time to move on. I thought I would share that with you and save you a postage stamp. Do not forget the typewriter. God bless, Marian.*

The letter said nothing about being a selfish, self-centred bastard or his failure to act responsibly. *NO, all it says is that I fucking well made her feel special.* Reading between the lines, Frank recognised the true meaning of the letter. Marian believed that she was not the only person who mattered. She would not have written the letter unless she had good reason. Despite everything, from somewhere, she had the courage to forgive. She also wanted him to forgive himself. Unsurprisingly he missed work that day. Frank had to fathom out what it all meant. Running through the episode, he blamed the demon drink. He would never have gone with Beth if he had been sober. Then he remembered the honesty in her letter. If he wanted to turn things around was there any point in lying? In truth, he had sex because he wanted to. With the best will in the world, no one could change that.

The junior clerk hauled himself into work the following day. This time he took the usual route and arrived ahead of Adrian. Sitting at his desk, he pondered over the top row of letters on the typewriter and focused on the letter U. What was Marian driving at? About to throw in the towel, he noticed the letter I was next to the U. Marian's words bored into his brain. 'I thought how things would turn out between us when I looked at the typewriter.' Sinking back into his chair, Frank had worked out the conundrum. *Like the letters on the typewriter, U and I will always be together.* Marian had already made a decision to move to a stage where she was more than happy to make a commitment.

★★★

From the far end of the railway station, Frank looked down the platform. He could see Marian saying goodbye to her parents. Boarding the train, she made her way down the aisle to a first-class carriage. Through the partially steamed window of the compartment, he could see Marian struggling to lift her suitcase up onto the rack. He was thinking about his next move when a signalman, waving a flag, blew his whistle and shouted, 'All aboard this train is now leaving for Bristol Parkway.' The train slowly rocking jerked forward as it started to build up a head of steam.

Running down the platform, he stopped outside the compartment. Marian stood up, pressed her face against the window and smiled. Frank responded and bowed his head. He did not have the courage to look her in the eye. The train started to move out. Running alongside the carriage, he wrote, 'God bless you' with his finger in the gritty steam on the window. With a huge cloud of steam, the train pulled out of the station. Stepping back onto the platform, with his head still bowed he waved goodbye to his future. In the years to come, the man with strange eyes played the scene out again. Imagination visualised a different scenario. This time he had the courage to hold his head up. This time his soul bathed in the deep green wash of her emerald eyes. Her lips were moving, eyelids wisped his cheek, she was whispering with her mouth again. In his daydreams of remembering, the train never left the station. All he had to do was close his eyes. God only knows how much he missed the girl with the crystal eyes and a smile that never tells a lie. Forgetting everyone's birthday was one of his lesser misdemeanours. On that rare occasion when he remembered, he signed the card, 'God bless you' and thought of Marian. There are things in life that you never forget.

The years and Marian faded into obscurity. His sex drive had taken on marathon status. A distinct pattern now emerged in his lifestyle. Apart from sex and alcohol, he had little interest in anything. Even his friendship with Brian had taken a down turn. Withdrawing from the family circle to pursue his addiction, any addiction, had Aislinn on his case. One day Aislinn finally managed to corner him. Jokingly she mentioned that if the rumours were true he might as well take up smoking. It was about the only dependency missing in his life.

Take a bow the new nineteen-year-old smoker on twenty a day. Self-indulgence with sex left him wanting more. The habit kicked in shortly after Marian announced her engagement to another graduate. Both were on campus studying pharmacy. Andrew, the heir apparent to a good hiding if they ever met, graced Westgate when he visited Marian's parents. The dejected ex spent many an adulatory hour outside the house waiting to wish Andrew health and prosperity in another life. *Blue was right, fuck them and then forget them. Who does she think she is and me with my head bowed. Bollocks to that, I'll never ever bow my head again to any bastard.* Then the heavens opened up and droplets of on-going anxiety and suppressed anger drenched the dark side of his soul. There would be no more 'people pleasing', the lethal combination would see to that.

Malcolm, his new soul mate had wheels. He readily accepted the offer to sow his seed in pastures new. Brecon, Tiger Bay, Blackpool all in the pursuit of sex confirmed the inevitable. Frank had no control over his addiction. The fixation reached a degrading high on a visit to the red-light district in Tiger Bay.

As they entered the bar of the Jolly Tar, eyes rolled at the sight of a young Jamaican in a G-string and suspenders performing on the stage. Simulating well-known sexual positions, charcoal eyes above senile freckles scanned the room. Psychologically she had intercourse with everyone in the bar. The rhythm changed to ska music and the lights came on in the bar. With a 'Sapphire' attitude, the Jamaican walked down the steps from the stage. Slowly making her way amongst the tables in the bar, she invited the customers, mostly merchant seamen, to rub oil over her body.

Finally, she arrived at their table. Leaning over, showing the shape of her well-formed breasts, she placed a collection box on the table and handed them a jar of oil. Frank gently palmed the oil onto her breasts until both nipples were rock hard. White glistening teeth captured the light in the room.

'You fuck Holley on stage, buy condom for five pound.'

Malcolm's five-pound spring boarded from his wallet and dived into the collection box. Holley smiled an eloquent thank you and made her way to the next table. Her back was now towards them. They could see the outline of her firm buttocks and the full extent of her shapely legs. The next turn-on came when two sailors at the next table gently rubbed oil into the cheeks of her backside. Frank's five pound joined the collection.

With the lights dimming, music changing, she made her way back to the stage. Holley removed her white G-string. Lying back on a mattress, a single spotlight caught her shimmering curly raven hair as she waited for the patrons to make their way to the stage. The first customer in the line stepped forward. On hands and knees, Holly fervently turned her back on him. In the spotlight at the centre of the stage, driving his penis into her, the audience clapped to the aggressive rhythm of the sexual act.

Then the valley boys stepped forward. Malcolm suddenly realised everyone was watching and he could not get an erection. Howls of laughter came from the crowd as he tried to put a condom on. Frank, on the other hand, experienced an adrenalin rush. His craving for sex, any sexual act, went way beyond intercourse. Holley moved onto her back and opened her long legs. With help, he eased himself into her. She beckoned to Malcolm to kneel down at the side of the mattress. Holly stimulated his penis and at the same time, she had intercourse with Frank.

'Look at him, he fuck me nice, look he ride me good you too.' Her wet pouting lips and the depth of the pool in her eyes fascinated Frank. With excitement beyond belief, he ejaculated inside her. Malcolm watched his mate impersonating a new born colt attempting to stand. He then moved onto the mattress, this time he had an erection. Holley forced him onto his back, astride and standing, she enthusiastically lowered herself onto his shaft. The last candidate moved forward to the ridicule of the crowd. Frank could see his own tragedy acting out in front of him on the stage. Alcohol stimulated his brain and the coil in his groin tightened. He wanted more. In a trancelike state of arousal, sexual craving and need walked to the stage. Edgy, waiting, he vigorously entered her again. This time he carried the act out in silence. Raw animalistic eyes watched intently as the drama unfolded. They were all inside her, this time they were all acting crazy. A crowd made their way towards the stage.

★★★

Frank asked Malcolm to drop him off near the Hope and Anchor under the pretext that he wanted to walk home. With the exception of a milkman, the street was deserted. He walked up the path leading to a terraced house with a red door and rang the bell. Irene, the keeper of the brothel opened the door. He asked for the services of Beth.

An hour passed before she appeared at the top of the staircase. 'Well look who it is, bad pennies always turn up.'

'Beth, are you alright for the rest of the night?'

'If you've got the money Lancelot, you can shag me till the walls of Camelot fall down.'

Frank closed the bedroom door and glanced at the bed in the centre of the room. He could taste the smell and stink of sweat and semen wafting from the bedclothes.

A glimmer of light from a shade less bulb hanging in the middle of the room touched her emotionless face. 'And what can I do you for my nightmare?'

'Will you do anything I tell you?'

A matter of fact voice delivered a similar line she had already used that night. 'Your wish is my command, but it will cost you.'

He placed a five-pound note on the cabinet table next to the bed. 'Is that enough for the night?'

An unexpected smirk almost revealed her teeth. 'That'll do nicely, you randy bastard.'

He undressed, got into bed and told her to do the same. 'Put the light out.'

'Well, well are you getting shy in our old age?'

Turning towards each other, he placed his hands around her neck. 'Do the same and hold me.' The prostitute responded and her client fell asleep.

Awake, he still had his arms around Beth. She pretended to be asleep. His lips brushed her forehead, he dressed and made his way towards the door.

'Frank, you're a bloody softy aren't you? Are you still missing that girl in Bath?'

'I don't need a lecture.' For the first time, he looked into her fresh pool-blue eyes and saw the woman that might have been. There was an awkward silence.

Beth turned her head to one side and her face took on a childlike quality. 'If you leave this godforsaken hole will you take me with you?'

'I'll be back for you one day, I promise.' He opened the door and left.

For some inexplicable reason Beth could feel a pearl-shaped teardrop running down her cheek. One day, no matter how long she had to wait, that bastard would be true to his word. She had to hold onto that dream.

Months rolled around the universe. In pissed oblivion, Frank moved on from one conquest to the next. Without realising it, he had lost contact with Brian. The end of Jeremy and Annie Walcott saw their transition to another experience. Through the light, everyone they wanted to see from their earthly life was there to greet them. Dina never had the opportunity to transcend through the bright tunnel to beyond. So many emotions, love, deceit, addiction, and friendship had all filtered through the hourglass of time into the bottom of the bulb. Soon every grain of sand would pass through the neck, and there was nothing Westgate or anyone else could do to turn the glass upside down.

# CHAPTER 10

## EXTINCT

The earthquake named Doris, continued to shake the foundations of her family to the very core. Any reduction in her daily binge drinking inevitably resulted in violent mood swings. The children had to rely on hand-me-downs in order to satisfy her insatiable thirst. Her daily fix fluctuated from the real thing to surgical and methylated spirits watered down with cider. Eventually, alcohol pulled her eyelids down and turned out the light. A drowsy, uneasy peace descended on a household that prayed she would never see the light of day. With his world, closing in, anxiety kidnapped Brian's soul and held it in the dark half.

He made one last desperate attempt to break out of his miserable existence and joined the committee. Excursions organised by the club were free. Every list started with his family.

The annual outing to Barry Island came as a source of relief for the children. This year two would have to stay behind. Hayley, aged six, pulled her big brother down the corridor to the nearest empty compartment. Brian could see their reflection in the glass panel. Hayley seemed to add a magical charm to the tear in his tartan jacket. Glaring out of the window, bright eyes bulging with excitement, announced her first weather forecast.

'Bri I can see all the cows standing up, the sun is out. It's going to be a sunny day.' Round pale-blue eyes popped out of her head as she literally launched herself at Brian, and put her arms around his neck. Her tattered shabby dress had noticeable signs of wear. As if on cue, the sun appeared from behind the dark clouds. A glint from a sunbeam glancing off the window kissed and danced on the golden hue of her frizzy hair. From a parallel universe, a warm finger made a euphoric curve on her mouth that lit up the compartment and the rainbow colours in her dress. She looked as cute as hell.

'Hayley, the sun is always shining when you're around.'

She tightened her grip. 'Bri, I do the best I can. I'm not a naughty girl am I?'

'No, you are the best sister anyone could wish for.'

'Why does Mummy hate me so much?'

'I've told you before, she's very ill. Anyway guess what she said to me last night?' With her head on his shoulder, Hayley gave him another bear hug. 'Mummy told me that I mustn't buy you an ice cream, I've got to buy you two for being such a good girl.'

She screamed with delight. The little girl was experiencing just that one day without rejection. She jumped off his lap. 'And a candy floss Bri, and a candy floss as well.' Suddenly she realised the implications of her request. 'Bri I don't need to have all those things honest. I don't mind as long as I'm with you.'

Brian gave her a quizzical look. 'Thanks, but I'm still going to buy them and guess what, I can have them all to myself.' His serious expression slowly turned into a 'got you' look. 'Brian stop teasing me.'

The train chugged past the Barry Island sign. She ran to the nearest exit door leaving Brian still in his seat. At last, the train came to a standstill. Hayley, the first onto the platform, landed in the middle of the rotating twister. Excitedly, she looked up and down the platform trying to find the yellow brick road to Barry sands. Brian, alighting from the train, bumped into Maxi Brown, one of the girls working in the factory. Maxi had been carrying a torch for Brian for some time. 'Would you like another girl to look after you as well, or am I being a bit pushy?'

'Maxi, I'd be upset if you hadn't asked me.' Walking along the platform towards the exit, Brian held hands with his two favourite girls.

Expectantly, it turned out to be a perfect day. Brian's endearing moment came at the fairground. Adept at darts, his last six pence whispered there would be no second chance. With the accuracy of a true professional, he lifted the grand prize, a rag doll with pigtails dressed in a kilt. Brian handed it to Hayley.

Hugging the doll with both hands, she proudly announced to the world that, 'I've got the best brother in the world. I don't mind about anything else do I Bri, because I've got you.'

The day had gone in the pause of a single heartbeat, and they reluctantly boarded the train for the journey home. Maxi decided to join them. As the train pulled out of the station, Hayley thought about the recurring nightmare waiting at home. The excitement was all too much. Cuddling her new doll, the motion from the train rocked her to sleep.

'Why haven't you asked me out Bri? I think you and I would be great together'

'I wanted to hundreds of times Max, but you know the problem I've got with Mum. I think too much of you to get you involved in all that stuff.'

Maxi leaned over and left a lipstick smear as she brushed her lips against his cheek, 'I think you know how I feel don't you Bri?'

'I hope so Max.' Despite the marvel of her long titian red hair, a shy look gently lassoed his eyes and softly tugged them down.

'Well I'm going to say it straight out. I've loved every second with you Bri. You are the sort of person I'd spend the rest of my life with. Look, when the time is right, I'll come running.'

Brian kissed the cluster of light chocolate freckles on her petite nose and under her eyes. He made a wish on every one of them that the circumstances were different. Catching hold of Hayley, he gently placed her on the seat opposite. For the first and last time, Brian and Maxi held each other close as the train made its way through the fog and drizzle towards Westgate.

★★★

In his immaculate pinstriped suit, Mal Bevan looked out of the office window in time to see another double-decker bus packed with steelworkers. Two cigars appeared from the silver box on his desk. He handed one to Louis Chapman, a steel consultant from Chicago. Bevan had spent most of his life in politics as a local councillor and then a 'Member of Parliament'. The politician reached the epitome of his career as 'Minister for Labour' in the shadow cabinet. He claimed to speak for the common people. However, like the majority that pass through the gates of Westminster, Bevan practiced the age-old tradition of bribery and corruption.

Chapman, holding the cigar with his chubby nicotine fingers, cut off the cap and placed it in his glutinous mouth. 'Have any of those unfortunate bastards any idea of their fate?'

Bevan swirled the whisky in his tulip glass, raised it to his lips and stretched out his stumpy legs under the desk. 'I have kept them in the dark for the last decade and fed them bullshit. When things come to a head I intend to do the same.'

Chapman looked mildly interested. 'How many people are going to the wall?'

'The last figure I have suggests something in the region of about ten thousand.'

The number even surprised the steel consultant. 'So you're going to turn your birthplace into a ghost town. If you have any doubt, for Christ's sake say so?'

Bevan inhaled and allowed the smoke to waft around in his mouth. 'My friend, why are you looking for remorse on my part that simply isn't there? Did I have any conscience when I increased the price of coal to make steel in this country uncompetitive? Did I show any hesitation in making certain that Westgate remained the only steel plant in the country under state ownership? And will I give a FUCK when the cessation of steel making in this town ends. The answer to that my friend is no.' Tiny muscles around his black eyes tightened to dispel any doubt his colleague had.

Chapman raised his glass. 'My colleagues in Japan and the good old USA will show their appreciation. You're going to be an extremely wealthy guy, here's to you.'

'My pleasure. By the way, if you want to continue doing business I suggest you swallow your scepticism.'

Bevan, true to his word, behind the scenes played a critical role in the government steel modernisation and expansion program. The politician gave the impression that he supported the union. Fervently, he made a stand against the closure insisting the plant had a future. Any name threatening the program found its way to his opposite number in the cabinet, also on the take. The blast furnace finally closed after producing sixteen million tons of iron. A new tinplate built on the east side of the works salvaged four hundred jobs. The rest received generous redundancy money, thanks to the hard work of the shadow minister of labour.

Anger gave way to demonstration and violence as the valley fought for its livelihood. The government held firm, there would be no investment in new technology to save the plant. Negotiations with the union had broken down. Strike action would only bring forward the inevitable closure of the plant. The steelworkers were determined to make one last desperate stand. At the entrance that once held stage to Llewellyn and his pink elephant. Wave upon wave of unruly demonstrators, armed with anything they could get their hands on, charged forward to challenge the strong arm of the law.

The police had extensive training to deal with the confrontation. They also had clear instructions not to show mercy to any demonstrator. Initially the police used water cannon to disperse the crowd. When that failed two hundred police officers moved forward in a V shaped formation. The continual clash of truncheons against the riot shields sent a message of impending violence to the crowd. Undisciplined, the crowd held their ground hurling bricks and bottles as the police closed in. Less than a hundred yards away from the rebellious mob, a whistle sounded and the formation charged forward. Within seconds, four police officers at the leading apex of the V broke through the crowd. In a flying wedge, using shields and truncheons, the police cordon pushed the demonstrators back. Thunderous cracks fused with shrieks of pain rang out as the lead-based staff hit hard against brittle bones. The police wedge pushed further into the crowd. Like skittles, the injured fell to the ground from the solid impact of brutality. Bodies started to pile up on the floor against the outline of the wedge where it had made contact with the demonstrators.

From the roof of a security building, a leggiero tenor's voice, bursting into song, soared above the gore and misery. *'Mae hen wlad fy nhadau yn anwyl i mi,* the land of my fathers is dear unto me.' The Welsh National Anthem, temporarily brought sanity back to the trauma. Aching arms and shoulders from wheeling out the punishment relaxed. Battered and bruised, the crowd started to disperse or pulled back carrying the injured. An inspector moved forward. 'You've got ten minutes to disperse. You know what to expect if you don't.' At a given signal, the police cordon turned left and marched away from the crowd.

Injured stragglers exceeded the ten minutes. This time the police formed a straight line and waited. Blue, at the front of the crowd, attempted to grab Sid before he fell. After wiping the blood from around his eyes, Blue pulled him back to safety. Sid deliberately dragged his heels against the concrete. Breaking free, he tried to get to his feet.

'What the fuck are you doing Blue? You're going the wrong way. Those bastards are lined up over there.'

'Don't be a dumb arse all your life Sid. What are you playing at, you can't even walk?'

'I can, well just about. I'm telling you now there is no way I'm running scared of that shit.'

Blue grabbed hold and pulled Sid to his feet. He held on as the police cordon moved forward. Blue tried to remonstrate, but to no avail. 'I can't talk you out of this one can I?'

'In your dreams. Look you know what's at stake here. It's about jobs, but it's about being proud of who you are and what this valley stands for. Are you going to take this bollocks or are you coming with me?' Sid broke eye contact, knowing he was about to die. It showed in the rattle of his voice. 'Mate I'm afraid of dying, but I'm more afraid of facing you lot in the bar. You know bloody well what we have to do.'

Blue glanced in the direction of the police cordon. 'You stupid, stupid bastard.' With his shoulders back, Blue thought about what he would miss the most in his world. 'Fuck it, I can't think of a better way to go. Anyway we outnumber the bastards.' He picked up the bricks strewn around the floor and handed Sid a piece of wood with nails driven through the end. Turning, they walked towards the police line. A hundred yards away, the past and the present seemed to fuse into the single continuum in time.

Within striking distance, Blue launched a brick, and another. Travelling in a closed timeline forever, they collided against a helmet behind a riot shield. Ambling, Sid dragged his right leg towards the blue line and brought his makeshift weapon down on the nearest uniform. With all the strength he had left, Sid repeatedly hit out until the constable fell to the ground.

Forming a circle around the two, the police moved in. The circle started to close. With their backs to each other, punching, pushing, they kicked out at anyone within striking distance. They were only moments away from their demise. The dull thud of the staff cracking, splintering and crushing bone exploded into the air. The blows rained down, Blue fell to the ground. Two riot shields pushed hard against and deliberately held Sid in a standing position. Batons, sinking into his head and upper torso, fractured every bone. The blows dehumanised his face and shoulders. Only then did they allow him to fall to the ground. Hobnail boots and steel toecaps kicked out against human muscle and the circle closed. The repression of madness held in the rank. They remained in the circle until the inspector decided any hope of recovery for the victims they were standing on had ebbed away. Sid died from multiple fractures. Blue bled to death from his injuries. Blood, running down the gutter into the drain signalled the end of a way of life in the valley.

Elsie Evans looked at her weather clock. A girl wearing a bodice and apron had popped out when she was in the garden listening to the noise coming from the plant. From her disconsolate heart, she screamed out a eulogy and waved her stick at the weather girl. 'It's too late now, it's all too fucking late now.'

Townsfolk in their thousands emigrated to take up employment at the new steel plant on the west coast. Factories closed and Bevan planned his next closure. In the years that followed, Dylan the poet had what he considered a meaningless life. He spent long lonely days reminiscing about his comrade in arms. Holding onto his small bunch of flowers, in a wheelchair, Dylan made his way to the far end of the west gate.

'Grandpa, why do you visit this place every year, there is nothing left of the old steelworks.'

The poet smiled at the volunteer pushing the chair. 'I've got news for you lad, this could well be the last time that you'll help me out of my chair.' Dylan used his grandson's shoulder as a crutch.

'Are you going to say that poem again?'

'Got it in one. Only this time listen to the words. It's about living your life to the full. It's about two people who had the courage not to accept a meaningless one.' Dylan cleared his throat and recited Dylan Thomas's poem, 'Do not go gentle into that good night'. 'Though wise men at their end know dark is right, because their words had forked no lightning they do not go gentle into that good night…' Half way through the words lifted his festering soul. Standing upright, straightening his shoulders, he deliberately dropped his stick and looked up to where heaven and earth are connected.

'Finished Gramps?'

'Yes lad, I think life is about to finish with me.' Slowly falling back into his wheelchair, he filled his lungs with air for the last time.

Two pairs of hands caught hold and gently lifted him up into the welcoming light of the world beyond.

★★★

Brian had lost his job at the factory and he ended up on the dole. Financially he was even worse off than the steelworkers. They had redundancy money. Gradually depression and the hopelessness of it all started to tighten around his skull like an iron fist. Doris's aggressive mood had reached a stage where he was fearful for the safety of the children. After weeks of torment, the whistling inside his head stopped, and gave way to the rattle of the devil incarnate urging him on to kill. *You know what you have to do, kill her and everything will get better. KILL her now, before she kills Hayley.* Invisible fingers probed under his skin to reinforce the message. With nowhere to hide, the recurrent nightmare of Doris harming Hayley pushed him into free fall.

One night the elastic band holding his sanity together snapped. He climbed the wooden stairs and crept into her bedroom. Doris, awake glaring at the ceiling, had waited for this moment since the death of her husband. Brian sat quietly on the edge of the bed and reached out for a pillow. Black psychotic eyes stared at her son. She knew why he was there. Without any emotion, rejection, or refusal, she accepted the inevitability of death. In her last living moment, she could see herself sitting in bed in a maternity ward with a baby boy in her arms. Moving the blanket back, she gazed into his innocent eyes.

The next image was different. It showed the incident of her nightmare that only faded through alcohol. Her husband Jacob was lying in the bath after slashing his wrists and throat. From that day, she saw the world through the tinted colour of blood. Angrily, Doris recalled the useless bastard. Then she remembered the reality of who he was. A gentle, loving man without hatred or malice who worshipped the very ground she walked on. Brian reminded her of Jacob, his features, mannerisms, even his voice. Her gaunt frown changed to a synthetic smile as he placed the pillow over her head. A single thought held, she was going to be with Jacob, her precious and dearest husband. There would be no more blood, insanity or blame, no more alcohol. Then Jacob appeared and for the first time the tinted colour fell away from her gaze. She could clearly see Jacob holding her hand.

Brian used bodily pressure against the pillow. He watched his mother kicking out violently in one last automated attempt to cling onto life. After a while, her heart stopped and she put her arms around Jacob. The voice in Brian's head also stopped.

★★★

How long would the redundancy money last? How dependant was his addiction? A new generation had joined the ranks of prostitution. Respectable women desperate to put food on the table offered their service. Ellen was one of the new breed. Her husband and his redundancy money had mysteriously disappeared to pastures new. With the sun still high in the sky, Frank took a leisurely stroll to Ellen's cottage, situated on the outskirts of town. Timing his arrival to perfection, at exactly six o'clock, he looked through the front window and saw Ellen filling a jug with cool cider. As he sat in the living room with a glass of cider, he wondered about the prospect of the sexual encounter ahead.

His imagination was taking his fantasy to the edge. Strong sunlight, shining through the window, bounced off the windowsill into his eyes and he sneezed. Suddenly Frank started to feel uncomfortable. Hysteria, paranoia, craziness oozed into his nervous system. He experienced a warm feeling at the back of his eyes from alpha particles changing to personal impulses in the cortex in his brain. Suddenly he heard a voice. *All you have to do is finish the job, there is nothing left for you here. What is going to happen when they find your Mother. The children, how are they going to cope? Why don't you take them with you? It is for the best you can all be together.* In the lobe between his eyes, he could see Brian in Hayley's bedroom. He then ran down the stairs into the back garden. *Douse the house with petrol and set it alight. Go on douse the house.* A light bulb exploded inside Frank's skull. His mental reaction to the trauma hit the cells at the back of his eyes. Somewhere between reality and the other world, his thinking process changed to impulses and connected with the life source in Brian's brain.

Frank ran from the cottage, jumped the garden fence, and made his way towards the main road. As he sprinted along the pavement towards Westgate, he pleaded with Brian not to set fire to the house. Suddenly he stopped. 'In that case listen to me mate, do it for Hayley, do it for her.' In his mind of picture thinking, he could see Brian outside the garden shed carrying a can of petrol. His crazy fanatical eyes were transfixed on his sister's bedroom window. A dutiful smile washed over his face. Brian knelt down on the path and unscrewed the top off a plastic can. He poured the petrol over his head and waited for it to soak into his clothing. Methodically, he did the same thing again until he saturated his clothes with petrol. A sincere affectionate glance peered in the direction of Hayley's bedroom. Striking a match, he set his clothing alight. Instantly, the dominant orange in the flames reached into the air as the petrol ignited. The flames, burning through his flesh, changed colour to a hint of blue. Bodily fat gradually seeped into his clothing and acted like the wick in a candle. The fire sustained its heat for several minutes. Huge quantities of soot filtered into the air. Finally, the flames engulfed his almost skeleton frame. *CRACK, CRACK,* the noise from his bones exposed to the heat, wafted into the air towards the bedroom of a little girl still asleep. Something gently touched her curly hair and whispered, 'You're the best sister anyone could wish for.'

A hunched, grieving frame, walked along the garden path. Ashes and the strong smell of burning flesh settled on him like a blanket. He could see the black charred body of Brian near the garden shed.

'Hey, sad bastard what the hell do you think you're playing at?'

He turned to face a fire officer standing behind him. 'I'm his mate?'

'If I was you, I'd be a bit more careful about choosing your so called mates. It looks as if he's douched himself in petrol. God, what a way to go. Have you got any idea why he would do something like that?'

Seemingly, in a trance, Frank looked away from the smouldering carcass. 'I told him to do it. It was the only thing he'd accept, I had to stop him from setting fire to the house with the children in it.'

'Are you lot all nuts around here or what. When did you tell him to do that?'

'About twenty minutes ago.'

'You're a liar. Our fire engine passed you running like hell along the main road at around that time. Look at your shoes, you haven't been near him.'

Guilt-ridden, almost suicidal, he looked away from the gaze of the fire officer. 'Was he holding anything?'

'There is nothing left of him. Hang on, I found something on the path in front of the poor bastard.' They walked over to the fire engine and the officer opened a brown envelope.

'Do you know what this is?'

'Yes, he was holding his sisters rag doll. It gave him the courage to do what he did.'

Unimaginable emotion and shock traumatised his soul. Nausea raged in the pit of his stomach. Confused, almost trancelike, he walked over and placed the doll against the charred remains of his body. 'Hey mate, I'm so sorry I've let you down. Keep a place for me will you, I can't wait to see you.' He could also hear the spirit of the seer rumbling in his gut. *Féach ar na treoracha ar an anamacha iad ag taispeáint gluaiseacht shábháilte do chara chuig an otherworld,* look the guides of the soul are showing safe passage of your kin to the otherworld. Overhead a flock of ravens, in formation, were flying towards the horizon.

Like Cronos, who castrated Uranus on the orders of mother earth, Bevan succeeded in the emasculation of the spirit in the valley. Gala, the goddess who personifies the changing seasons, whispered in Frank's ear that it was time to move on. He had already pissed his redundancy money against the wall months ago. *No problem, they will be queuing up.* Then he fell to earth. He compared his synthetic CV against the vacancy ads. Would anyone employ a criminal with an addiction to sex, cigarettes and alcohol? Surely, his business acumen of not giving a shit and his dubious gift must score some brownie points. What value would he have placed on to the bruising and soft scar tissue now forming on his brain from the guilt and remorse about Brian? The scar, hardening over time, could affect the wiring to his brain.

For the first time in ages a fake grin broke into a sneer across his face, the answer was simple. Frank decided to join the boys in blue.

# CHAPTER 11

# WISHFUL THINKING

Frank had finally moved on. At twenty-two years of age he realised that time was passing him by. Eager, impatient to get his hands on an application form, he hit a snag.

A counter clerk at the local station was more than happy to deal with his request. 'You've got to be fucking joking. Do me a favour and piss off back to that hovel where all the other rats live.'

Undaunted, Frank refused to let an off-the-cuff remark from Jenkins act as an obstacle. The time had arrived to rein in all that anger, negativity and dubious character. Trying to create a favourable impression would not go amiss. Aislinn had a saying for everything, the one befitting this occasion was the infamous, 'actions speak louder than words' maxim. Jenkins had a reputation as a gardener. Surely, he could do something to help him achieve any unfulfilled ambition.

To promote his tomatoes to medallion status, the Good Samaritan purchased a fertiliser, mistakenly with the words 'Weed Killer' on the box. The egotistical young man experienced that rare occasion where he wanted to take on a simple yet self-rewarding task to help his fellow brethren. His benevolence went even further; any credit for the unselfish task would remain his little secret. Bearing that in mind and with everyone hitting the home run to slumber land, surreptitiously he made his way to the greenhouse and meticulously emptied the undiluted chemical into every pot. On that fateful night, Jenkins thought he heard screams for help coming from the greenhouse. Devastated at the demise of the plants, Frank showed another exemplary side when he sent a RIP condolence card through the post.

The murder mystery took on an unusual twist. Colonel Mustard and Mrs Peacock, cleverly disguised as an undertaker and a florist, turned up unexpectedly on the doorstep to offer their services. Curiously, Jenkins wondered if some rat was taking the piss.

Two weeks later, an application form to join the Monmouthshire Police arrived in the post. Duly completed and returned, a second letter hit the carpet inviting the applicant to the local station to take the entrance exam comprising of general knowledge, English and Maths.

'Look Macleod, I don't seem to have your name here on the bail list. Who arrested you?'

Frank explained to the duty sergeant that he was not there to answer bail. 'Are you Sam Miles's father?'

'Yes that's right son, do I know you?' Miles took a long hard look at Macleod. The young man had intervened to prevent his son having a hammering from some crazy called Lee.

Two officers, namely Sgt Miles and DC Wilson who excelled at geography and arithmetic, volunteered to help the candidate with the examination paper.

Miles placed the exam paper in an envelope and sealed it. 'We are even Macleod, the rest is up to you.'

Frank wondered if the sergeant had an interest in gardening.

The local inspector waited patiently for Frank to step off the bus in Abergavenny. He congratulated the candidate on his excellent pass mark, one of the highest from any applicant. The bad news came when the officer mentioned an eyesight test. Frank would have little difficulty using both eyes. However, an examination of only his right eye could cause problems. Thirty years as an optician and Trevor Richards had yet to examine someone with a different pigment in each eye. The right eye seemed to have a mind of its own. When the optician gently tilted his head from side to side, the eye should have moved. Instead, it looked straight ahead.

From twenty-five feet the examinee read the chart with both eyes. Taking a step forward, he covered the right eye with his palm and easily read the chart with only his left eye. Richards nodded approval. Instead of testing the right eye next, the candidate stepped forward. Keeping his palm over the right eye, he read the chart again with the left eye. The examination was almost at an end when the optician caught him out.

'No, I said cover your left eye so I can test your right.'

'No problem, B A C.'

'Sorry, is anything wrong Macleod?'

Typically, his right eye looked at the letters through a thick filter. He had to wait until the letters eventually came into focus. In desperation, he had to think of something. 'The light from the window is in my eye. It's stopping me from reading the chart.'

Richards, not as gullible as he looked, examined the right eye again. Using a magnifying glass, he could see the lens in the eye focusing on the letters. However, there was a delay of about a minute before Macleod could interpret the chart. His nervous system started to play Ping-Pong. Looking anxiously at the examiner, the non-verbal on the opticians face suggested bad news.

'I don't know lad, there seems to be something strange going on, I can't fathom it out.'

The honesty in the examiners voice gave little hope. 'Look, I really need this job. The only thing wrong is that sometimes my right eye takes longer before I see the picture in my head.'

'I'm sorry but I haven't got a clue what you're talking about.'

*Hell, I'm back on the bus unless I come up with something.* 'Well it's sort of hard to explain, I think my eye's got a blind spot.' He appeared to be genuine. There was nothing genuine about his explanation.

Unknown to the optician, the retina and ganglion cells at the back of his right eye continuously scanned the light. Acting as a transducer, after a short delay, it changed electro impulses in the light into audio or visual images in his brain. In desperation, Frank wished that he had control over his so-called gift.

Incredible spiritual strength shuddered through his frame and opened the phenomena of second sight. On a canvas at the front of his brain, he saw a child playing with a ball in the garden. Instinctively he touched Richards on the forearm. From that point, simultaneously, they saw a little girl chasing after a ball rolling into the path of an oncoming van. The front of the van collided with the child. Bouncing off the bonnet, she landed in the roadway. The image faded and Richards stared at his patient in disbelief.

'No please God, say this isn't happening. She's my granddaughter.'

'Phone her parents straight away. Tell them to look after her until you get there.'

Hurrying from the room, minutes later a more relaxed Richards returned with the good news. 'She's safe, my daughter is not going to let her out of her sight.'

The unsuccessful candidate breathed a sigh of relief. At least the day had not been a total waste of time. Richards demanded an explanation.

'If I could answer that I'd tell you. All I can say is that I mean no harm to anyone.' His attention span was starting to close down. He vaguely remembered the optician saying something about following his career with interest. The good news hardly registered. A sharp pain used his brain for target practice, before settling in the pit of his stomach. After exchanging pleasantries, leaving, the successful candidate had grave doubts that he was capable of reaching the Angel Hotel around the corner.

As he ran through the foyer, an unpleasant stale alcohol smell oozed from the pores of his skin. He used the lift, a seizure was only moments away. Within seconds of reaching the hotel room his muscles contracted, convulsions kicked in, and he fell to his knees.

The following day he had no recollection of where or who he was. Still confused, exhausted, his memory gradually filtered back. A severe headache, pins and needles in his neck and back, brought him to the verge of vomiting. The incident with Richards must have triggered an epileptic fit. He decided to stay at the hotel to recover. In that monstrous space between reality and the other world, he could hear the voice of the seer. *My blood I beg of you, be careful of what you wish for or the day will come when it will destroy you.*

Three months later, Frank started basic training at Bridgend with the other recruits from Wales. Slightly overawed about wearing a uniform, he also felt uneasy about the strict discipline at the training centre. Sgt Bosom, the class instructor, also from Monmouthshire, re-enforced every minuscule rule. Most of the class were ex-army squaddies, including the class leader, Richard John Jones, an ex-grenadier guard, born within the sound of Bow bells.

His first day in paradise started at 7.00 a.m. sharp with a uniform inspection carried out in the pouring rain. Scurrying from the parade ground, the class only had time to change into dry clothes before boarding a bus to the local swimming pool. *Why did that bloody sergeant tell me to get my haircut, he couldn't even see it under my helmet.*

Bosom marched the class into the changing room and bawled out instructions to be poolside in less than ten minutes. The instructor ignored the ten-minute rule. The class could see something hovering, sliding suspiciously above the top of the door. It looked like a snake. Bosom turned on the hosepipe and soaked their number two uniform.

Apart from smarting about his haircut, Frank was off to a cracking start. Standing in the pool, the water gently washed against his genitals as he thought about the receptionist. *She would make a good shag, she reminds me of Edna.* Sexual dreamlike musing changed to fantasy. Unexpectedly, his brain started skipping up and down inside his skull. The lush fantasy must have triggered something. Frizzy, fire engine flashing lights, and more bounced around at the back of his eyes. At the same time, a woozy warm feeling sat down on the top of his brain. A last flash of brilliance posted a cautionary note through his letterbox. How ridiculous was he going to look standing in the pool with a hard-on in the company of his fellow male students? *Sorry to interrupt, but this body is closing down until further notice, sweet dreams.*

It had nothing to do with the receptionist. Bosom had whacked him over the head with a hefty wooden safety poll almost cracking his skull. When he regained consciousness, Bosom gave the recruit words of advice. 'When I tell you to dive and catch the side of the pool do it.' The warning more than compensated for the bruising on his skull.

Jones showed signs of leadership when it came to pilfering from his classmates and breaking the midnight curfew. To impress Bosom, the scrawny shaven-headed figure volunteered to grass on the rest of the class.

A month slipped by before the new recruit noticed there were only a handful of policewomen on campus. Frank thought about banging the receptionist. For some reason, it brought on a migraine. He decided to break the curfew with Jones.

On their only escapade in Bridgend, Jones tried to get off with a local girl. Instead, showing bad taste, she ended up with his colleague.

The class leader's response was predictable. After a quiet word in Bosom's ear, Frank had guard duty for the rest of the course. A rather incensed recruit cursed his naivety. There had to be a get-out clause.

One night, patrolling the centre, he stumbled across damage to one of the lockers. His genitals twisted like a corkscrew when he saw the name BOSOM on the locker. Some bastard had forced the locker with a sharp instrument, probably a screwdriver. A single groove close to the lock smarted of a culprit with know-how. With the standard definition of a constable ringing between the ears, he focused on his responsibility to protect property. Frank placed the screwdriver back in his pocket. Diligently searching the locker, he homed in on a photograph. The rugged complexion and receding hairline of a male in a compromising position with a girl half his age was unmistakable. The culprit must have written the definition in the dust on the locker. Duty-bound, he took possession of the photograph.

Despite the bewitching hour, he knocked on the sergeant's door. Eventually, a permanent sardonic smirk stood in the doorway with a huge stick of dynamite in his pants.

'Sorry to bother you sergeant, can I have a word?'

'You can Macleod, but the answer is no.'

'I was wondering if you've given any thought about taking me off guard duty.'

'I told you the answer is no, now fuck off.'

'Bloody hell, Ann said you'd say yes. You're always saying yes to her.'

Bosom rubbed his eyes and looked around for the exit door in the flying saucer. 'Who the hell is Ann?'

'She's the one sexing your tonsils in this. Nice sentiments written on the back as well.' The instructor squinted at the photograph pushed right under his nose, 'It looks as if you've been giving her English lessons.'

Bosom hit the pause button. 'I cannot believe I'm hearing this.'

'Look on the back of the photo. Nice sentiments, but there is only one G in DOGGY and the H is missing in FASHION.'

The sergeant again glanced at the photograph. 'You bastard, where did you get that?'

'In your locker hidden next to your marriage certificate.' The word bastard registered. Frank was more than capable of holding his own when it came to using bad language. However, a derogatory remark about Aislinn was another matter. 'Let's get this straight, you've been the bastard since the start.' The recruit had lost it.

Finger prodding signalled that fisticuffs were moments away. 'Now I've tried to be civil, this time I am telling you I'm off guard duty and Jones is on. If you pick on me or any of the class for the rest of the course, I'll shop you.'

Bosom scowled, his thick neck disappeared into his shoulders. 'I will get you for this, mark my words Macleod.'

'With all due respect, and please don't take this the wrong way sergeant, but go fuck yourself.'

Apart from watching his back, things settled down, Frank teamed up with Reg Wallis, also from Monmouthshire. Wallis had joined using the fast-track entry system. Within five years, promotion to inspector would be a formality. One morning, during the tea break, Wallis decided to stretch his legs. As he passed the sleeping quarters, through the window, he could see Jones hiding a small bottle of gin under Frank's bed. The punishment for possessing alcohol was instant dismissal.

At the bewitching hour of midnight, an inspector and sergeant entered the sleeping quarters and made their way to Frank's bed. Without saying anything, the inspector methodically searched under his bed, cabinet, wardrobe, and found nothing. A drowsy recruit standing by the bed watched the bespectacled inspector with interest. 'Sir, if you tell me what you're looking for, I'll help you find it.'

'You're the one called Macleod aren't you?'

'Yes sir.'

'Looks like I've got the right one, but the wrong information.'

Standing to attention, the recruit leaned over and whispered in the inspector's ear.

'No sir, right information but the wrong one, try the class leader.'

Like a bloodhound sniffing scent, the inspector thoroughly searched under his bed and opened his cabinet. It came as no surprise to someone that it contained the bottle of gin.

'Sir, I tell you now it's a bleeding set-up, someone is having a laugh.'

'Jones, think, there's a good lad before you talk bollocks. How could someone have planted it, your cabinet was locked?' Jones sat down on the side of the bed. Bosom's plan had backfired.

Frank decided to join in. 'Sir the class leader could be right, someone's playing silly buggers. I thought he was stitching me up but it could be anyone. Fingerprint the bottle. If Jones's prints are on it, he's lying. If you find someone else's prints, you've got the culprit.'

The burly officer scratched his full beard. 'Boys, don't try to mess about with an old shoe like me. I'm warning you now, if your prints are on it you will get the sack.' The inspector carefully placed the bottle in a plastic bag, switched off the lights and left. Jones had problems sleeping that night; his prints were on the bottle.

During a cigarette break behind the canteen, Jones gave serious thought about resigning. His favourite classmate decided to join him.

'You owe me big time Jones, don't you forget it.'

'I owe you alright, what about a .22 in the back of your fucking skull.'

'Is that any way to speak to someone who's saved your job?'

'Fuck off Macleod, you know my dabs are on that bottle.'

'How can they be, I wiped them off before I stuck the bottle in your cabinet?'

'You what?'

'You heard.'

'How did you plant the bottle it in my cabinet? It was locked.'

'The brass screws at the back aren't.' Frank took a cigarette and left the class leader to work it out for himself. Jones was not the only one confused. Bosom had difficulty in understanding the ruse. From that moment on, he had an uneasy feeling about Macleod.

At the end of the course, Wallis collected the accolade for the most promising student. Another recruit from Monmouthshire walked away with the mythical survivor's cup. The final day heralded the traditional passing out parade. 'The British Grenadiers', a traditional marching song, blasted through the loudspeakers on the wall. In quick time, Jones marched the class onto the square. Halfway down the parade ground he snarled, 'eyes right' and saluted the senior officer taking the parade. Frank could see Aislinn and Ben amongst the crowd. He could hardly miss them. They were standing next to a fuzzy transparent manifestation of pure energy. The recruit closed his eyes and opened them again, and the ghostly figure started to fade. Then he remembered, the parade was taking place on his birthday, the beginning of the Celtic New Year known as Halloween. This is the only time that the spirits can reach back through the thin veil that separates this and the other world.

# CHAPTER 12

## THE GAMES PEOPLE PLAY

Turned out to immaculate training standards, the new recruit arrived at Abergavenny Police Station at 9.00 a.m. sharp to start his first day. With no one in the foyer, he waited at the counter. A rather distinguished looking gentleman, sporting a handlebar moustache, entered the foyer. He glared at Frank with contempt.

'Why isn't an officer on the cross to look after the children going to school?'

'I'm afraid we only do the cross on a Good Friday, sir.'

'Are you trying to be funny with me young man?'

'No sir, leave it with me, when I see the sergeant, I'll resurrect what you said.'

Obviously upset, the visitor showed his displeasure by nearly taking the front door off its hinges on his way out.

Finally, the counter clerk and duty sergeant arrived. For the first time Frank walked through the sanctity of the police station. Sergeant Paine, an experienced officer, sitting at his desk stared across the table at the new recruit with strange eyes. His 6ft 5in burly stature easily carried an impressive broad moustache and West Country accent with a distinct Bristolian lilt. The telephone rang on his desk. 'Good mornen, yes sir, yes sir tha's right.' The conversation was one-way, Paine had little to say in the exchange.

'Congratulations Macleod, I'm thinken you've set a record this mornen. You've ended a career before it's started. The person you've been speaken to at tha desk a short whil ago is none otherr than tha chief constable. E has just said e's goen to sack you.'

The recruit stressed that he had made the comment in the excitement of the day and unreservedly apologised. It would not happen again. Paine quizzed him for the next half hour trying to establish if the recruit was worth saving. He then left to join the chief constable.

Paine made it abundantly clear there would be no second

warning. The probationer would spend a week in the sergeant's company. After that, his career or otherwise, would be determined.

Standing with Sergeant Paine under the clock in the square, the young constable still had that uncomfortable feeling in uniform. Aislinn must have put too much starch in his shirt. He placed a finger inside the back of his collar and he tried to stretch it.

'Stop fidgeten lad, tha public will think yo got ants in yorr pants. If yo don't stand up straight, I'll make yo walk around this yer town with a broom andle up your backside.'

The recruit glanced and thought he could see a semblance of a smile under the moustache.

'What arr you Macleod?'

'I'm a fidgety bugger who can't stand up straight, sergeant.'

'I did't ask yo who yo arr I asked yo what you arr. To save the greying matter in yorr head lad, I'll answer tha question. You arr a policeman and proud to wear tha Queen's uniform. Now I want yo to say tha aloud. When yo do, yo will show pride in what yo arr in yorr stature and bearen.'

Paine took two steps onto the pavement. Remembering the sentiment, halfway through his recitation, Frank pulled his shoulders back and stood up straight.

'Neverr forget it lad, neverr forget what yo arr and what tha uniform stands for.'

At closing time, the pubs turned out. The presence of the sergeant had a sobering effect on the drunks. One or two even said goodnight to the giant of a man standing next to him. Paine knew everyone he gave a running commentary of their family history. A fight broke out on the opposite side of the street. 'Walk at a steady pace lad, they'll see us ar coming an they'll be knackered by tha time we get there.'

Paine grabbed the first drunk within his reach. At the same time, he lashed out at the second with his cape. 'What's it goen ta be boys, tha highway orr my way?' Both of them decided on the highway, Paine issued a stern warning and continued to impart basic knowledge to the new recruit. 'Walk on the outside of tha pavement duren the day lad when yo want to be seen, and on tha inside duren tha night when yo don't. Neverr give way orr step around anyone except for tha elderly, females and children. As a rule of thumb if yo see someone committen an offence, first warn, then bollock and then book them. Do not forget lad, tha person yo book for somethen trivial could in tha future be tha very same person who could solve yourr crime.'

'Paine's Law' and his bookmark were sitting in the sergeant's office the following morning. The counter clerk informed them that the two culprits from the night before had asked to see the sergeant. Paine noticed the shorter of the two sporting a black eye.

'Ow did yo get tha eye son?'

'My father gave it me after our neighbour told him about last night.'

'Isn't yorr father Harry Merchant?'

'Yes that's right, he sends his regards and he's sent us down to apologise.'

'Apology accepted, nex time lads yorr in the cells is tha understood?'

Frank tried to understand the relevance of it all. In Westgate, the public regarded the police as the enemy. This appeared to be about the respect for one individual. A debrief ended the shift and the probationer completed a pocket book entry. After inspecting it, Paine added his signature.

'Last thing lad, yorr a public servant, don't yo everr forget it'. For the next seven days, the shift ended with the sergeant reminding the new recruit that he was a public servant.

During the week, they dealt with a domestic incident. Wearing cape issue, the dynamic duo walked towards a semi-detached house. Paine stopped, pulled his truncheon out from his trouser pocket, and placed it handle-first up the sleeve of his uniform jacket.

'Do tha same lad, andle first, when yo punch someone, put tha bottom of tha staff in tha palm of yorr hand. Nicholls lives here, es a wrong un.' The wrong un opened the front door. He was drunk. 'Where's yorr wife George?' Paine pushed passed and entered the hallway. She was sitting in the living room with her face covered in blood.

'He was hitting our lad sergeant. I tried to stop him and he butted me in the face.'

Paine had his back towards Nicholls. He seized the opportunity and grabbed a knife from the kitchen table. Nicholls was about to stab Paine in the back, suddenly he stopped to listen to the festive sound of a Christmas cracker being pulled. Then he experienced excruciating pain. The constable had punched him with the staff held in the palm of his hand fracturing his rib cage. He dropped to his knees, rolling around on the floor in agony.

After handcuffing both hands behind his back, the recruit made his way to the bedroom. Andrew aged seven, shaking, peered from under the bed. The constable wrapped a blanket around the small boy's thin frame and he noticed swelling to the right side of his face. Through the blanket, he touched what appeared to be cuts or holes on his back.

'Hey sunny Jim, do you mind if I look at your back. I promise I won't hurt you.' Gently he lifted Andrew's pyjama top and winced at the mass of gruesome circular cigarette burns and cuts over his back. Red streaks radiated from the seat of the burns. A foul smell of pus from a burst blister collided with his nostril. Skin tissue, at different stages of healing, confirmed that someone had inflicted the injuries on separate occasions. A pattern seemed to be emerging in the marks. The constable also noticed fingertip bruising on his right upper arm and ear.

The fair-headed freckled lad hugged the constable around his neck. He started to realise the significance of his role. 'Mister, please don't let them hurt me will you.' *He said THEM.*

'Don't worry son, no one's ever going to hurt you again. Look, this happened to me at your age. My brother did the same to me. But hey look at me now Andy, I'm great.' He pretended to flex his muscles. 'Do you know I'm that strong I can even crush a grape.' Frank's broad grin waited for a response. Gradually, the corners of Andrew's small mouth turned up to show the most innocent smile imaginable.

'Mister, did your brother wake you up when you were sleeping?'

'Ye, all the time, I bet you could even tell me what he did to me.'

Andrew lifted his head and wiped his eyes on the top sleeve of his pyjama, eager to continue with the guessing game. 'Did he hurt you playing games on your back?'

'Afraid so, the game was, now let me think it…' He waited for Andrew to fill in the blanks. 'Draughts, it was draughts mister.'

'Andy, did your Mummy try to stop daddy hurting you?'

Andrew hesitated. 'No, Mummy gets drunk. She gets mad if Daddy starts to win.' The story unfolded, both parents were systematically torturing their son.

'Hey I've got to go. Look I've just moved to Abergavenny, I thought you and I could be mates.'

'You bet, I don't know anyone who's got a copper for a mate.'

'Don't jump the gun Andy. You don't get to be my mate until you pass the test.'

The word 'test' seemed to drain the enthusiasm from the lad's face. 'I knew there'd be a catch mister, what have I got to do?'

'Well it's not easy, I'll tell you that.' He paused for effect. 'Can you crush a grape?'

★★★

The probationer quietly briefed Paine about his conversation with Andrew.

'Arrest both of them fo cruelty to children, make certain yo get tha caution right.'

Happy to oblige, Frank was even more elated when he locked the cell doors behind them. Both were pissed. A doctor attended to Nicholls, they were not in a fit state for interview until the following day.

DC Neal Walsh would interview the suspects. He reluctantly agreed to allow the probationer to sit in with a watching brief.

'Your job, Macleod is to say and do fuck all. Don't even fart, unless I tell you to.'

The detective went straight for the throat. Even the constable thought his bullying tactics were over the top. After telling the prisoners they were wasting valuable drinking time, he concluded both interviews with the same subtle approach. 'If that's the way you want it, you can rot in the cells until you're ready to talk.' Walsh frogmarched them back to their respective cells and stripped the blankets from the bed.

The interviewer glanced across at the new recruit. Smiling, he took another sip from his mug of tea. Frank nearly vomited on his shiny shoes at the thought of his colleague's performance.

Half-heartedly, Walsh provided an explanation. 'Have you ever heard of the good cop, bad cop sting?'

'No, but I've just witnessed a crap interview.'

Walsh ignored the remark. 'Well it goes something like this. I'm the bastard who scares the shit out of them and you're the nice guy they're going to confess to.'

'How are you going to pull that off? They won't say bugger all to me after your bullying.'

'That's where you are wrong Macleod.'

They spent the next hour or so rehearsing the script. The constable unbuttoned his tunic and took off his tie. Entering the cells, he could see Lyn Nicholls crouching in the corner shivering from the cold. Her knuckles were raw from continually banging on the cell door. He placed the blankets on the mattress and handed her a mug of hot tea.

'It's all right love, he's gone. Walsh won't be back until he's good and pissed. Here, this will kill the pain.'

Lyn grabbed the two tablets out of his hand.

'Fancy a cigarette?' He tossed Lyn the packet.

'Thanks, your mate's a nutcase. He's the bastard who should be banged up in here, not me.'

'You haven't seen anything yet. Wait until he gets back, you'll see how crazy he is.'

The prisoner took a drag from her cigarette as if she was about to face a firing squad.

'Do you want me to ask your husband to get you a packet when he's released?'

If looks could kill. 'How is he being released and I'm not?'

'Well I shouldn't tell you but I think he's cut a deal with Walsh. Don't say you had it from me, he's told the DC that the draughts game was down to you. That's why he hit you.'

'That's a load of bollocks. We were both pissed, what's that draughts thing all about?'

Frank gave her his favourite 'don't be stupid all your life' look. 'Your husband has told the DC everything. He's even said what a bad loser you were.' The constable could see he had touched a nerve. 'Get real Mrs Nicholls if you want to get out of here. Even I couldn't make that up.'

She glared at the floor and then the constable. 'I'm in the shit aren't I? I'm not going anywhere except Swansea Prison?'

'If I was you I'd put my thinking cap on. How are you going to explain away the injuries on his back to the social services? Whether you like it or not you're going to get charged.'

'And that bastard is walking out of here, and I'm left taking all the blame?'

'Well you can still do something about that. Get your statement in first. That'll go down well in court, especially if you say you made it to save Andrew giving evidence.'

'I suppose I've got no choice have I.'

'It's up to you, look love I have to go. The sergeant wants me to type out your husband's release papers.'

Lyn, accompanied by the young recruit waited impatiently for the custody sergeant to acknowledge her presence.

'Mrs Nicholls, please tell the sergeant what you just told me.'

'I want to make a statement about you know, for the sake of my kid.'

The custody sergeant continued writing. 'Walsh is not here, you will have to wait until he comes back.'

Nicholls started to panic when she heard the word Walsh. 'It's now or never, I've got to get it off my chest. I'm not making any statement to that nutter. I'll make it to this one here.'

Frank, undecided, was that a compliment?

She made a detailed statement. After reading it, George also decided to co-operate.

The constable rubbed the teeth marks on the top of his thumb. He had to do something or he would have lost his temper. Sergeant Paine examined his pocket book and signed it.

'Just one orr two points Macleod. Before we went into tha house, we shoulda established who were in there. It cuts down tha element of surprise. I shouldn have turned my back on Nicholls. When I saw tha injuries to his wife, we should have cuffed im straight away. Eliminate tha one yo knows is goen to give yo trouble. Don't ferget lad, yo can de-arrest someone if tha circumstances change. Has Walsh de-briefed yo?'

'Yes sergeant, he told me I can go back on the beat with the rest of the prostitutes.'

'Did e mention to yo ow important tha confessions were?'

'I asked about the 'good cop bad cop' routine. He told me that was the only way we could get a result. He also said that you could not compel married couples to give evidence against each other in court. If we hadn't got both their statements, they could have walked away.'

'Wha have yo learnt from this Macleod?'

'Well if I'm honest, I shouldn't jump to conclusions about anyone.'

'Arr you referren ta Walsh?'

'Yes, with your permission sergeant, I think I'll buy the detective a pint.'

'Arr yo aware lad if it wasn't for yo they would still be torturen their son?'

'If it wasn't for you, I'd be on the dole.'

Paine lifted his eyebrows. Behind a reverential smile, he looked the constable straight in the eye. 'Wha arr you constable?'

'I'm a public servant Sergeant. I'll never let you down.'

Walsh practically lived in The Lanark pub situated off Bridge Street. The recruit glanced around as he entered the bar. Definitely, love at first sight, the place had character. Soft tinkling on a piano wafted from the lounge. The most endearing quality had to be the female customers in the bar. Narrow, dark, piercing black eyes glared at the new arrival. Walsh turned his stool at the bar to confront the recruit. 'Did I ask you to sit next to me?'

'I didn't see your name above the door when I walked in?'

'Observant shit aren't you, its cost me a fortune to sit at this end of the bar. If you think you can just waltz in here and park your backside on the stool next to me, you can think again. If you want that stool, you have to earn it. If you don't, you can piss off.'

Frank gave the unshaven small skinny frame a quizzical look. 'If I pass, will you piss off?'

'Right clever dick, when you entered the bar who was sitting at the first table on your left?'

'Easy, David Lean, he must have been talking to you before I came in because he had his head up his arse.'

'Macleod, go and annoy some other poor unsuspecting bastard.'

'I'll have a guess, there's a male in his early forties. Long dark curly hair, what a hooter. He's wearing an open neck shirt, black waistcoat, and rimmed glasses. Wrong colour frame. The hooter was talking to a woman, peroxide hair, ponytail, with ringlets down the side of her face covering her spots. About early thirties, she's wearing jeans and a white tank top. For the wrong reason, she's wearing one earring. For the right reason she looks like a good shag. The good shag is holding a cigarette in her left hand. Her glass on a tablemat is to her left and the earring is in her left ear. So guess what, it's a shot in the dark, but I'm going to say she's left handed.'

'Full marks you little shit.'

'No, sorry I've got it wrong.'

'Not from where I'm standing.'

'I forgot to mention, her black bra strap is showing on her left shoulder and her backside is as big as your ego.'

'I've got it wrong as well. You're a randy little shit.'

Before long, they were talking as if they had known each other for years. At one point, the proprietor, Brendon Cairn, joined them. He looked younger than his middle sixties. With a white silk cravat, blue stickpin, blazer and long grey hair, he looked the spitting image of a tailor's dummy.

'This is Macleod, he has just joined us. You two should get on like a house on fire, he's nearly as randy as you are.'

'Welcome, a thousand welcomes to you my friend. Tell me, what do you like the most about the female anatomy?' His infectious Irish accent originated from Cork.

'I used to be a leg guy until I saw the designer breasts on that woman at the bar.'

'I see, you mean the delicious Sadie, she really is a fine half is she not laddie.' Cairn placed his hand on the young man's shoulder. 'You look a happy go lucky individual, can I be taken it you are still single?'

'Yes that's right, I'm allergic to wedding cake.'

'Horrible stuff the old wedding cake, I've had problems as well. Do you know the cake has an effect on a woman's sex drive? It did just that to my darling sensuous wife after our wedding.'

*Did I ask him to put his arm on my shoulder he's pissing me off?* 'Well she was like a bitch on heat last night when we were in bed.'

Frank wondered if there were any Gall wasps around. By the expression on Cairn's face, one must have stung him on the nose.

'Good, did you make her wet down below, young man?'

'Yes I told her that you had an accident and she pissed herself laughing.' There must be a nest in the loft. A wasp must have stung his hand. He removed it from his shoulder. The stinger left in the skin seemed to trigger off a cynical reaction.

'I'm so glad you were able to entertain her. You are a big joke to me as well.'

There was a hint of sincerity in the constable's voice. 'My pleasure, but in fairness I fall below your standard in that department.'

'What are you like, tell me more?'

'Well she said you brought entertainment back into the bedroom. She can't stop laughing every time you take your clothes off. Your wife's been married before hasn't she?'

'And how did you deduce that, my young randy friend?'

'The rice has played hell with her looks.' His direct in your face attitude had unsettled the Irishman. Cairn decided to teach him a lesson.

Whisky chaser joined his friend lager at the bar. Cairn mesmerised the female audience with his dexterity as a pianist. Before long, the young officer took centre stage and gave a rendition of, 'That certain smile'. Walsh popped his head around the door. 'Careful, an old friend of yours walked into the bar about an hour ago.'

Through the serving hatch, he could see the snobbish, fit frame of Sergeant Max Bosom in conversation with Inspector Hughes.

At around midnight, the crowd started to drift away. Frank decided to say goodnight to the soft lilting Cork accent coming from the lounge. Cairn and Sadie were standing at the bar facing each other. After unbuttoning her white blouse at the front, long piano fingers gently caressed her breasts.

'Come on in and join us, there's a fine fellow. Sadie has something to show you, don't you my darling.'

In her late thirties, with a slim figure, long brown straight hair and clear topaz eyes, she practiced the 'anything goes philosophy'. Sadie turned around to face the new arrival and she opened her blouse. Cheekily licking her soft pouting lips, she looked down at her breasts. Cairn, standing behind, kissed the side of her neck and cupped the side of her taut heavy breasts. Hypnotised by the raw sexuality in her eyes, Frank could have sworn she was imagining that his hands were fondling her.

'Let me introduce you to Sadie. She is a posh tart who loves to play games, especially the one where she does anything I tell her. Let me illustrate what I mean. Sadie would you kindly lift your dress up and show our fine young policeman fellow what you are wearing.'

The temptress leaned forward, and slowly pulled up her pleated dress and petticoat from her knees to the waistline, to show devil-red suspenders and knickers. Again, Sadie gazed in the officer's eyes to see his reaction.

'Now then my young Sherlock, I'll ask you again, what part of her body do you admire the most. Whatever your choice, I am sure Sadie will only be too happy for you to touch it.'

With his brain smouldering at the thought of touching her creamy flesh, Frank realised how pissed he was. Cairn seemed to be playing a game. Without saying anything, Sadie searched for his lips and pressed hard. Taking hold of his hand, she gently slid it under her knickers between damp thighs.

'Do you think you will be able to make her come my bow street runner? Already from the look on her face, I think the answer is in the affirmative.'

She placed her hand on top of his. Large almond shaped eyes rolled back and her breathing quickened. He could feel her hips rotating, gyrating against his hand. Suddenly Sadie stopped. With her body rigid, she yelled out and reached an orgasm.

'There my lovely lass, I knew you could do it lad. But look here Sadie, he has a hard-on. See the huge bulge in his pants Sadie. I think he wants to come inside you. Would you like to see to her over the stool, my randy fellow?'

Sexual yearning had reached the point of no return. He pulled on the zip fastener at the back of her skirt and it fell to the ground. Frantically in the process of taking off his belt, Cairns stepped between them.

'Unfortunately this is where I have to say all good things must come to an end. Sadie, step back from our randy policeman, our game for tonight is over.'

Through the mist of alcohol, Frank realised he had been duped. 'Are you insane or what?'

'No my bow runner I am not and I hope neither are you. If you touch her again I am afraid you will have to suffer the consequences because you will be doing so without her consent.'

Sadie somewhat disappointedly, glanced at him. 'I am sorry but Brendon is right. You see the fun in our game is to stick strictly to his rules. Touch me again and I will make a complaint to your sergeant.'

Reeling from frustration, his skin on fire, he pretended not to react. 'Don't worry lady, I wouldn't touch you with his. What's the next rule in your little game?'

'The next rule my friend is that you will now leave my establishment sexually frustrated like a buck who cannot find a doe, and when you do, I will have my way with Sadie.'

A touch of irony helped the constable with his next remark. 'I know this might sound a bit Irish, but aren't you mixing yourself up with somebody else. The girl behind the bar told me you can't get a hard on. Sadie will be drawing her old age pension before your little limp shillelagh rises to the occasion.'

A surly expression on Cairn's face captured the moment. 'Time to leave my friend, I think you have outstayed your welcome.'

Verbal confrontation was about to turn to physical contact. Frank decided to get up close and personal with Cairn. 'Good night to you my little Irish leprechaun. My mother told me there are two things to avoid. One is never outstay your welcome. The other is never outlive your sex life.'

'Are you going, or shall I throw you out?'

'Sadie, would you tie one of my hands behind my back. I think our mischievous little Irish bloody fairy here wants to have a fucking pop at me.'

The dejected suitor leisurely made his way up the hill leading from the Lanark. He could sense cold eyes penetrating his back. Turning the corner, glancing back, he saw movement behind the curtains. Things were starting to get interesting. It had nothing to do with his vocation.

★★★

Walsh waited for him to sign the duty register. 'Well you tart, did you fall for Cairn's trap?'

'Yes, hook line and sinker. Hang on what do you mean trap?'

'He does it to all the new recruits. He says he's interested in human behaviour and all that bollocks. I get the feeling he has some sort of perverted pleasure from screwing with your mind. What did he rig up for you?'

'Well he wanted me to shag Bosom over the bar, I couldn't turn that down.'

'Isn't that a coincidence, he's going to do the same thing to you in his office. He wants to see you pronto!'

Bosom, a relief sergeant, carried out the role as a requisite to promotion. With an impressive CV and the support of the local lodge, the next rank to inspector seemed a formality. Nothing would hinder his progress, not even the new recruit. Bosom made it clear he would not tolerate any maverick behaviour. The probationer responded with a 'yes sir no sir three bags full sir' routine. The lazy dishevelled corpulent frame of PC Dick, 'Wanker' Walters, introduced himself as his tutor constable and guardian angel assigned to look after Frank during his probationary period. Curiously, he had a small pink angel kiss birthmark on his right eyelid.

Walters drove the Anglia van out of the station. His passenger had yet to learn the art of driving. After a rundown on the residents living on the Gurnos Estate, he turned into a back lane and pulled alongside a Mini. 'Like that little beauty Macleod?'

'Is that your car?'

'Yes, goes like a dream.'

The recruit was busy with the conversation going on in his head. *Having a good day? Had worse, my tutor's a bit of a dickhead. Anyway, what do you want? What do I always want, I'd like you to take the piss out of your new colleague? Look, you nearly got me into serious trouble in the Lanark. I know what you're up to, you're trying to drop me in the shit again. Now look here, if you wanted a sober conscience you should have said so years ago. No, your choice was good old mischievous in your face me. I get you to do what you do best, that's annoying everyone. Piss off, you're annoying me now. Go on you know you will like it. Are there any Gall wasps around today? Oh, yes look there's one right on the end of his nose.*

'Macleod, dream in your own time.'

'Sorry, I was thinking about what my mate said the other day. He's a head shrink, anyway, he said something interesting about cars. I hope you don't mind me asking, but have you got a small prick, Dick?'

'What the hell brought that on?'

'According to the shrink, cars are a phallic symbol. You know, small car, small prick. Now if I was buying a car I'd have to go for something like a Bentley.'

'Stop taking the piss, any more bollocks like that and you'll walk back to the station.'

'By the way, what size shoes do you take?' *Buzz Buzz*.

Walters, ranted obscenities, alighted from the van and slammed the door. He opened the boot of the mini and took out an empty can with a long plastic tube. Through the wing mirror Frank could see Walters siphoning petrol out of the police van into the can and then into his Mini. *Brainless, why isn't he siphoning the petrol from the van directly into his mini with the tube.*

He placed the equipment back in the boot. Walters could see a young woman watching his every move from the house opposite. 'Nosey bastards around here aren't they? Follow me Macleod.'

A young girl, about twenty carrying a baby in a shawl answered the door.

'Don't stick your nose in where it's not wanted, this is a reminder.' Walters pushed her in the face. His ring caught the inside of her nose and it started to bleed.

Frank grabbed him by the lapels and held him against the wall. 'Touch her again and I'll down you.'

'Look Macleod, you've got to show these people who the law is around here.'

'Then act like the law.'

Walters made his way back to the van. The new recruit held the baby as she wiped the blood from her face.

'You're new around here aren't you?'

'Frank pleased to meet you.'

'Will you get into trouble, you know for siding with me?'

The recruit gently lifted the baby into the air. 'Don't worry this isn't the first time that I've been left holding the baby.' Corny, but it worked.

'I shouldn't tell you this, but watch your step. People on this estate have had enough of you lot bullying them.'

'With your help I can get on their good side. We've had complaints from this estate. Someone's stealing knickers off the clotheslines. Any ideas?' Her expression suggested she knew something, but she seemed reluctant to tell all. 'Sorry, forget it, I just thought I'd catch that silly bastard before he does something serious.'

Hesitating, she broke the silence. 'I lived on the Morse Estate. There's a pervert over there called Ian West, it could be him.'

Surprisingly the police van was still waiting for the recruit. He knew there would be an uneasy silence for the remainder of the shift. The conspiracy of silence ended on the outskirts of town. Under a street lamp, Frank could make out the silhouette of a gorilla pissing on the lawn.

'As much as I'd like to see you get a good kicking, that's Willy Rush. He's a nutcase, let sleeping dogs lie.'

'Pull over.' The recruit opened the passenger's door. 'No harm in having a word is there you coming?'

'I'll stay here, when he pulls your head off I'll call for assistance.'

Rush finished christening the flowerbed. His huge frame towered over the constable.

'Evening Rush, sorry to bother you from your well-earned piss but I have a message for you.'

Rush looked puzzled. 'Who the fuck's it from?'

'It's from God. He's asked me to tell you that he's invented rain to make his flowers grow, so you can stop pissing all over his planet.'

'And what are you going to do about it copper?'

His burly muscular frame showed definite signs of physical strength.

'Good question, you look a decent sort, hell if I had a sister I'd point her in your direction. But, and it's only a small but, you've been caught pissing in a public place. I'll toss a coin, you call, if you call right end of. If you get it wrong, I'll book you for pissing.' The constable showed Rush the coin before tossing it in the air. 'Call.' Without realising it, Rush called tails. The constable picked up the coin. 'Heads, congratulations mate, your summons will be in the post. What about double or quits?'

'What the fuck for?'

'For swearing in a public fucking place, that's what for. I've got a feeling in my water, excuse the pun, that your luck is going to change, here goes.' He tossed the coin into the air again. 'Call.' Reluctantly, Rush called tails. The coin dropped, it was heads. 'I told you, you lucky bastard, that's your second summons in the post.'

Rush looked bemused. 'What's going on here with this coin tossing?'

'It's getting interesting mate, get this one wrong, three strike and you're out. You're calling this time not to get done for insulting words, conduct and behaviour. You are going to piss this one, think about your call. Are you sure you want to stay with tails?'

He was about to toss the coin when Rush turned and ambled down the road. 'I'm off; I've never seen piss all like this. Is this what justice is coming to?' Rush continued to glance back over his shoulder. Frank yelled. 'It's bloody good news. I put you down for tails and guess what you lucky git. Your third summons is in the post.'

★★★

Days after he had pissed off the gorilla, the young recruit attended a disturbance outside the local fish shop. As Frank turned the corner he recognised the unmistakable figure of Rush glaring in his direction.

'There's that nutter I was telling you about.'

The gang of three, like model citizens, walked quietly down the road in the opposite direction.

# CHAPTER 13

# FRIENDLY PERSUASION

Despite the occasional reminder on the daily incident state, Frank had forgotten all about the tip off. Pursuits that were far more interesting required his attention at the Lanark. Months later, he saw another entry about stolen knickers on the daily incident sheet. With that, 'nothing ventured nothing gained' attitude, he decided to visit the Morse Estate and have a word with West. The police van pulled up outside twenty Park Lane, his last known address. West answered the door. The constable recognised the occupant from a photograph album at the station. He reluctantly acknowledged that he was out of his league. West had gone through the system before. A PNC check had shown previous convictions for indecent assault. *What am I going to say? Don't ask me you always engage your mouth before your brain.*

'Morning Mr West.'

'And what can I do you for constable?'

Was that a tinge of insolence from the late-thirties, long necked individual with glasses standing in the half-open doorway? Frank thought West was more than capable of making a fortune modelling as a pervert.

'I don't know if you're aware of it Mr West, but the police and other services are helping each other to save petrol.'

'No I didn't know that, what has it got to do with me?'

'Well this week the police are helping 'Per Vert' the local dry cleaners. I'm here on their behalf to collect all the knickers you've stolen from clothes lines.'

West, somewhat taken aback remained calm. 'Constable, I have no idea what you are talking about.'

'Then let me enlighten you, you're a pervert and I'm a policeman. It's my job to catch perverts like you. In your little world, you steal knickers from people you know so that you can put a face to your fantasy. You sniff them, wank off, or if you've really got a good hard-on, you put the knickers on, stand in front of the mirror and masturbate. Now in my world as an officer of the law, it is my duty to incriminate you by planting false evidence.' He had his own individual way of asking questions. 'Question: where have you hidden them?'

'You tell me officer, you have all the answers.'

'Question: do you live alone?'

'Yes.'

'The answer to the first question then is they're probably stuffed under your pillow, or in your bedside cabinet with your other cock books. If you're a pro, and congrats, Mr West you are, you've hidden them somewhere else. West I am arresting you for theft and anything else I can think of on the way to the station. I must caution you that if you don't tell me what I want to know, I'm going to fucking make it up.' The prisoner still looked confident. He gave the impression that he had nothing to hide. As they walked towards the van West nonchalantly waved at a neighbour, and the constable did the same.

During interview, West said nothing and the constable found exactly that when he searched his flat. The only thing of interest was the burnt remnant of what could have been a pair of knickers in the rubbish bin. *Clever bastard, he's stashed the knickers somewhere, brings them in the house one, two at a time and when he's finished he burns them. John Long used to do that.* The probationer had definitely taken on more than he could handle. He decided to involve Walsh.

The DC's nose hovered precariously above the stink of the conversation with his detective sergeant.

'Are you sure this is a crime, Walsh? It won't be the first time you've dropped a clanger.' DS Williams was a life member of the Magic Circle owing of his trickery to cuff crime. Real crime mysteriously disappeared up his sleeve. This brought about a handsome reduction in recorded offences committed on his patch. 'Neal, I'm having doubts about you. Did you have to record the crime as a burglary? At best, you should have put the broken window down as damage and not burglary.'

The DC shook his head and had a *Hiroshima* moment. 'But there were size eleven prints on the windowsill inside where someone had climbed in. They trailed all the way to the desk where the money was nicked.'

'Your attitude is getting in the way of promotion. The chief constable has confidence in me to keep the detection rate high and the crime rate down. I very much doubt if he has the same opinion about you.' Williams glared at the constable standing by the door. CID invariably treated uniformed officers as inferior. 'And what do you want?'

'I'd like advice from Detective Walsh, sergeant.'

'You're not recording anything as a crime are you?'

Frank noticed the nervous twitch in his upper lip. 'Good Lord no sergeant, first I'd have to be certain it's a crime before doing that.'

'Look and learn Walsh, look and learn.'

Apart from the 'why don't you plant knickers' suggestion Walsh came up with zero. A search through the crime register showed three similar offences recorded over the past two months. Walsh put the record straight and handed over a list of thirty other complaints not recorded as crime. In the second interview, West denied everything put to him. Without a confession or recovery of the stolen property, there was no case to answer. Annoyed, with steam coming from his ears, the constable left the interview room.

He returned some twenty minutes later dragging his mouth along the floor.

'West you're free to go.'

An insolent smirk pushed his glasses to the end of his nose. 'Thanks for nothing constable, now I suppose you'll keep me under observations. You'll be wasting your time.'

'The world is full of clever bastards like you. Let me put you straight on something. I don't have the stomach to keep you under observation. Doctors are more qualified to do that.'

West nervously pushed his glasses back and squinted. *Was that a threat?* 'I see, as a last resort you're going to beat the shit out of me.'

'No Mr West I'm not, but they are.'

The prisoner seemed confused. The constable pulled the cord on the venetian blind. As the slats opened, they both looked out of the window. Three men all with thuggery tattooed on their forehead were standing at a bus stop on the opposite side of the road.

'I'm sure you know them, they're the boyfriend or husband of the women you've terrorised with your perverted sad little habit.

126

Hang on, sorry I've given you duff gen. You know Rees Williams don't you, the one built like a brick shit house. He's just done a stretch for grievous bodily harm. It wasn't his wife's knickers you stole it was his little girls. The bad news is she is wetting the bed. He's made it clear what he intends to do to the bastard responsible.'

'What are they doing out there?'

'They're waiting for you Mr West, that's what they're bloody doing out there. I phoned or got a message to them that I was going to release the pervert responsible for terrifying their family. I said there was nothing I could do to stop you doing it again. Here's the funny bit, I've got to tell you this. When we told Williams, he picked up his kitchen chair and smashed it against the wall.'

A whiter shade of pale pushed his smirk right down the chart. 'You can't do that, it's your job to protect me. I'm not going out there.'

'I can't remember it saying anything in the oath that I'm supposed to protect perverts.' Frank grabbed his arm twisted it behind his back and marched the prisoner towards the door. A sharp knife-like pain shot into his shoulder. 'The only thing that will save you from being beaten to a pulp is to cough. Because you've messed me about, I don't really give a fuck either way.' As they approached the front entrance, the three amigos saw them through the window and crossed the road. 'I'll see you in hell.' The constable partially opened the door.

West sunk to his knees and grabbed his legs. 'For God's sake officer, those bastards will kill me. Look, I'll tell you everything. I'm begging you, for pity sake.' West forced air into his lungs and yelled out a sorrowful shriek nearly shattering the glass in the front window.

'I don't want to, but I'll give you one more chance you bastard and that's it.'

Several minutes passed in the interview room before the prisoner managed to compose himself. 'Question: where have you hidden them?'

The thought of not saying anything crossed his mind. Silence. The constable grabbed the phone. 'Angie, there are three men outside, one of them is Williams. Would you show them into the waiting room? I'll be down shortly with Mr West. Question: where have you hidden THEM?'

'Down by the bridge canal on the Abergavenny side under stones near the feed pipe.'

'Question: how many knickers are still there?'

'About twenty eight.'

'Question: how many knickers have you stolen altogether?'

'About sixty.' The interview lasted an hour. Reluctantly, West made a statement under caution. His memory was phenomenal. He recollected the times, dates, even the locations of most of his roguery.

In the second interview, West again fell in love with the items recovered from the bridge canal. He had no difficulty in identifying and matching each pair to the respective owner.

The constable appeared to be in a generous mood. 'I'm willing to put in a decent report. I'll say you told me, you wanted to get it off your chest. But like everything, it comes at a cost.'

'I've already told you everything.'

'No you haven't, give me a name of someone else that's been up to mischief.'

'If I do, will you get my belongings from my flat?'

Frank nodded,

'Samuel John, I think he's from the Cardiff area, he bothers with schoolgirls. That's all I know. He's got a caravan down by the canal, I saw children going in there.'

West had bail on the understanding he attended therapy sessions. The new recruit looked forward to his next enquiry concerning Samuel John.

# CHAPTER 14

## STAIRWAY TO PARADISE

This time there would be a more systematic approach to the investigation. Walsh would be involved from the outset.

'I hear you were a lucky bastard with the knickers snatcher.'

Frank glared at Walters, 'I won't be a lucky bastard much longer if you don't keep your eye on the road.' The mischievous leprechaun scratched his brain with a pickaxe. He decided to test the gullibility of the man sitting next to him. Stillness crawled through the top of the window as they sat eating their sandwiches. *Hello, I said hello, when are you going to take the piss.* 'Sorry if I'm a bit edgy, I was out on the piss with my mate last night. He paid for all the booze.'

Walters held the sandwich to his mouth. 'You lucky bastard, why was that?'

'Well I met up with him at the Lanark. When I got there, I hardly recognised him. I couldn't believe my eyes, his hair had grown back. I've known him since we were kids, he was about sixteen when he started going bald. Anyway, when I saw him, he looked like a guard with a Busby on his head.'

The driver instinctively touched the top of his head. At thirty-two, the best part of his hair had fallen onto the pillow years ago. 'He must have been wearing a toupee?'

'That's what I thought, he wasn't. One of his mates back from Cuba told him to rub chicken shit into his skull. He did and hair started to grow. You've got to rub it in twice a day and leave it there.'

He seemed more than curious. 'I've never heard of that, are you having me on.'

'Look, I couldn't give a shit if you don't believe me. I'm chuffed about how different he looks, you know more confident.' The rest of the shift passed without any conversation. Walters was obviously deep in thought about something.

The vice president of 'taking the mickey bliss' sat at the bar in the Lanark wallowing in his daily fix. As if on a high from marihuana, he burst out laughing. He visualised the tutor constable sitting in front of the mirror rubbing chicken shit into his skull. Surely, even Walters was not dumb enough to fall for that! Walsh had touched on the tutor's gullibility when he mentioned a so-called initiation ceremony held at the Lanark. Three new arrivals paraded in front of a crowd and listened intently to the rules. To pass the initiation ceremony the prospective candidates had to masturbate and ejaculate over a line from a standing position. Cairn blindfolded the contestants. Anyone who failed would have to resign. Walters the last of the three, looked slightly hesitant when he heard his name called out from the lounge. In reality he was the first, the other two were decoys. Sadie escorted the blindfolded contestant to the spot marked gullible. She pulled his trousers and pants down around his ankles. Despite the unusual predicament, Walters had little difficulty in getting a hard-on. Squeezing his second finger and thumb, he played a 'middle c'. Applause from an audience encouraged the cellist to perform the whole range of octaves. The applause changed to hilarity when the contestant reached a crescendo and ejaculated over the line. Walters realised the con when he saw the photographs of the ceremony.

'We are closing on time tonight Frank, you know that don't you?' The disappointing news came from Sue behind the bar.

'If this place ever closes on time, you can slap my arse and call me Nancy.'

'No I mean it, my father has taken mum off to an antiques sale in Ireland so I'm on my own.'

'What do you think he'll get for her?'

'Less of your cheek or I will stop tap on you now.' Sue, the landlord's daughter, usually spent her holidays from college serving behind the bar. With long raven-black hair, full cherry lips and an hourglass figure, at eighteen she looked stunning. 'Time gentlemen please. Frank could you stay behind until they all go?'

Eventually all the customers had left. 'Want one for the road?'

'Can we do plural?' Sue poured a pint of lager and a large glass of wine.

Both conversation and alcohol were going down well. After the third glass of wine, Sue decided to sit on the stool next to her only customer. The gentle waft of her perfume crawled up his nostrils and yanked on his groin. Sitting on a stool, with her legs on the high rest, a captivated audience watched her tight black and white check skirt lifting above her knee boots. He could see the shape of her suspender buttons under her skirt. Leaning over, with a hand on her knee, he gently ran his tongue along her lips. She caught her breath and started to flirt with his eyes. Frank pulled her closer by the nape of her neck. She could feel the sensation of his soft moist breath on her neck and inside her ear. A hand lingered outside her grey jumper before gently touching her honey soft breasts. Sue responded with a passionate kiss and tongues touched. Standing up together, he whisked her backside. Frank touched her sensitive breasts again. With her nipples hard, breathing uneven, leisurely he put his hand down the front of her silk knickers.

'Please don't stop what you're doing.' Catching hold, almost tugging his hand, Sue led him through the door marked private. They were halfway up the stairs when he pulled her back, and she sat on the stairs.

'Pull your skirt up, leave your knickers and boots on.' One-step above, the tingle of anticipation, desire for intimate contact, opened her thighs and he placed his head between her legs. Kissing the apex of the thighs, he gently put a finger in the moistness between her legs.

'Oh my god you're going to make me...' Moving like a predator, he pulled her legs apart and pushed into her as she was about to climax. Still experiencing an orgasm, sinking, thrusting, quickening his rhythm, he ejaculated.

Without saying anything, they both knew the stairs episode was only a prelude. Later they had sex in the bedroom and the shower. Finally, he left the pub exhausted as daylight broke through the magic of what had been. The incredible experience of sex ached in his legs. What started as frivolous laughter had ended with a permanent grin.

★★★

Apart from someone reporting a prowler near the chicken shed there was little in the previous day's incident log. Frank approached the van, he could see his enthusiastic partner waiting patiently behind the wheel. He opened the passenger door and instantly collided with a strong smell of rotten vegetables that almost bowled him over. 'What is that smell?'

'Quick, get in Macleod before anybody hears you.'

A repulsive stench from inside the van brought the recruit to the verge of throwing up. 'Well what is it?'

'I've done it, taken your advice, you know about my hair and rubbed it in.'

'Are you telling me you've come to work with chicken shit rubbed into your nut?'

'Yes, I've got this little tin here full of the stuff to rub in later on.'

'I can't work in this stink. Bloody hell it smells like rotting shit from a sewer.'

'I'm the boss, what I say goes. You're not going to believe it, but I can feel my hair growing. I looked in the mirror through a magnifying glass, I could see bristles coming on my skull.'

'I don't care if you've got hair growing wild out of your arse. I can't work in this cesspit.' The recruit dived out of the van. Fresh air rather than any enthusiasm to check the lock ups was decidedly his motivating factor. Hurrying to the telephone kiosk, wrestling with the door, he picked up the phone and dialled. The image of Colonel Ivor Llewellyn flashed across his brain.

'Abergavenny Police Station!' Angie the receptionist answered the phone.

'Put me through to the assistant chief constable.'

'And who shall I say wants him?'

'My good lady, the phrase, 'and who shall I say wants him', shatters all the basic rules of prescriptive grammar. In God's name, is this force capable of getting anything right? My name and title madam is Major Wainwright. My purpose is to give Windy a piece of my mind.'

A moment's silence. 'Good evening, Sergeant Bosom.'

'Look Bosom I don't want to speak to you, is Windy Hill there?'

The distinctive tone, intonation and articulation in the voice started alarm bells ringing in Bosom's head. 'Sorry Windy who, sir?'

'That, sergeant, is the straw that has broken the camel's back. Ineptitude in this force has just hit rock bottom. Good lord man don't you know the name of your assistant chief constable, Windy Hill?'

Bosom nervously caught his breath. 'I apologise but he is not available, can I help?'

'Not available hey, there is a reunion next month, I will have a word with old Windy about his non-availability. Look Buxom just a word, why in the interest of human decency have you failed to scrub up that mangy Alsatian dog before sending the poor little bugger on patrol?'

'I'm sorry sir but I don't...'

'Look hear Braxton, don't play the innocent with me, I've had this one right from the horse's mouth. As we speak, you sir have had the audacity to send a van out with a dog on board, smelling like a woman's fanny that has been left out in the Sahara desert for a month.'

'Major, I'm sorry but you have...'

'This is no time to be sorry Buxom. This is time for action, call the van in before the skunks in the park get an inferiority complex. Any shilly-shallying and I will be calling in the RSPCA.'

He returned to the van just in time to catch the message to return to the station.

Bosom jumped down his throat. 'Macleod, have you been carrying animals in that van?'

'Only Walters, sergeant.'

'Where is that lazy bastard?'

'He's staying in the van sergeant, in case there are any messages.'

'All the messages, as you well know, are sent to you from this station for Christ's sake.'

Frank volunteered to get the tutor constable, who in his dubious wisdom decided to shout at the sergeant from the entrance of the station.

Sincerity from Walters joined in the conversation. 'Anything wrong, sergeant?'

'No, to be honest with you I was just feeling a little lonely. GET YOUR BACKSIDE in here straight away you're causing a draft.'

'If it's all right with you I'd prefer to...'

In exasperation, Bosom jumped up and down on the spot. Sex off the menu usually attributed to his sarcastic mood. 'If you don't get in here right now, I'LL FUCKING DRAG you in here!'

Walters reluctantly entered the control room.

'Right what have you two...?' Bosom failed to finish his verbal onslaught. An obnoxious smell wafted up the nostrils and tried to strangle his tonsils. 'What is that smell?'

Beads of perspiration popped out on his forehead. 'I can't smell anything, can you Frank?'

Bosom, holding a handkerchief to his mouth, approached Walters. 'It's you, you walking dung heap. What is it? Tell me now or you're on a charge.' The relief sergeant looked at the ceiling for divine intervention.

'It's chicken shit, sergeant.'

A mocking cynical tone signalled the prelude to someone about to lose his temper. 'Isn't that funny, do you know lads, I was going to say it was chicken shit? HOW IS IT CHICKEN SHIT?'

Frank intervened. 'Sergeant, PC Walters was checking the allotment, there's a message in the daily state about prowlers. He slipped in the shed and he's covered in chicken shit.'

Bosom's flush face did an 'excuse me' with the floaters in front of his eyes. 'I can't trust you pair to do anything properly, can I. Walters take a shower, Macleod clean the van out, when you've done that you can both walk the beat until further notice. By the way Macleod, I've booked an appointment for you with the doctor. There's something wrong with your hearing.'

'Sorry sergeant, I didn't get that, I think I've got something wrong with my ears.'

'Then read my lips you cocky bastard, where were you last night. I called you over the radio at nine, and at ten?'

'I was dealing with Mr Zapanski the polish gentleman on the Gurnos Estate.'

'Are you two having an affair or what? This is the third time I know of you've dealt with him.'

'No sergeant, we're not making any announcement yet. He's depressed, suicidal, after a while I can talk him around.'

Overstated self-pity grabbed the next line. 'He's depressed, he's bloody depressed, what has he got to be depressed about. He should be in my shoes with you two bloody idiots. Walters, you bloody numbskull, what have you been teaching Macleod here? I don't know if you've noticed it lads, look take your time, but you are fucking policemen not a bunch of psychiatrists.' Bosom gave the next remark serious thought. 'Look, I can see where you're coming from Macleod, this sort of thing can be a bit delicate. I'm aware of your inability to deal with this or anything else for that matter. Bring Zapanski to the station the next time we are on days, I'll have a chat with him.'

Zapanski sat in the passenger's seat. During the journey, the constable questioned his attitude towards Bosom. Had their encounter at the training centre clouded his judgment? Even he had to admit the gesture to help Zapanski exposed a caring side to his nature.

After pleasantries, Bosom suggested that they retire to the courtroom attached to the police station. Coffee and biscuits were on the table waiting for them. Initially his approach religiously followed Freud's 'The Aetiology of Hysteria'. Gently, Bosom probed around his anxiety to unravel the core of self-destructive behaviour. Then came that unique moment when Bosom actually smiled at Zapanski.

'My friend, I think I have the answer to our problem.'

A tremulous grin broke across Zapanski's face. 'You sergeant and me like you know best friend I ever had.'

Bosom stood up and walked towards the curtain cordoning off the magistrate's bench from the dwell of the court. Slowly he pulled back the curtain. A hangman's rope hung suspended from a beam. The noose hovered menacingly six feet above a chair directly underneath it. Frank and Zapanski, sitting at the table, looked at the rope in disbelief.

Bosom broke the eerie silence. 'Mr Zapanski, I'm here my friend to grant you your wish. It appears to me that you want to kill yourself. I'm going to see that you do it.'

A hesitant and somewhat nervous voice joined the exchange. 'No, I feel how you say, good to me, I live for future.'

'Perhaps, you know best friend I ever fucking had, I had better clear up any understanding. You have wasted the time of this officer by your silly nonsense and I'm having no more of it. Consider me a Polish fairy granting your wish. We are going to lift you onto the chair, place the noose around your scrawny little neck and hang you as they say, until you are dead.'

Legs started knocking against the table. Breaking into a sweat, Zapanski stumbled out the next words. 'I go now to see my...'

'The only place you're going is on that chair. Macleod, grab the little bastard and bring him over here.'

For some inexplicable reason, Frank grabbed the 'little bastard'.

Sinking to the ground, he pleaded for mercy. Bosom ordered the constable to fetch a Bible from the witness box. He was in the process of handing it over when Zapanski jumped up off the floor and ran into the street.

★★★

The calls stopped. A month later, the probationer patrolling the town centre, saw his favourite immigrant coming out of the local chemist. Zapanski, in the process of boarding a bus, looked in the direction of the officer. They made eye contact. Frank could see a tint of red in the etheric aura around his skeletal frame. Any self-recharging process in his body had stopped. He had lost the will to live. Looking again at his frame, fear, sadness, and a crazy longing penetrated the constable's heart. Somehow, Zapanski had glanced into the other world and he liked what he saw. From images of normal phenomena, his right eye started to stretch time. Everything seemed to be moving in slow motion. Like a three dimensional statue, Zapanski had his right hand on the safety rail and one leg on the platform. Frank closed his eyes and opened them again. The scene reverted to normality and the bus pulled away.

Concerned, he called on the Polish family the next day, but no one answered the door. Shortly after that, they reported him missing. A month later the constable with thirteen on his epaulettes found his body in the corner of a derelict barn. Walking through the stench of dead flesh, with a handkerchief over his mouth, he approached the body. Footsteps disturbed the unacceptable. A huge rat that had gnawed into his cheek scampered out from the side of his face. A history of depression, brought about by his experience in the Second World War, had finally claimed its victim. The atrocities carried out by the SAS on his parents were never far away from his thoughts.

The sun settled on the horizon like a fireball. Above, the entire sky turned to a hue of violet blue. From the dividing line in the atmosphere that separates life and death, a scattering of light entered his eyes. Pictures from the past flashed onto a canvas in his mind. He could see a small boy with Zapanski's kindly way looking down at his parents lying on the ground. The boy watched as Filip, his father, stretched out to hold his mother's hand. Filip's eyes seemed to reflect the inexplicable, only felt with the heart. '*Moje serce jest pełne miło ci dla Ciebie,* my heart is full of love for you.' The voice fell away, a shot rang out and shattered her skull. The proud elder stumbled to his feet. Instinctively, he brushed the dirt off his raincoat and glared down the barrel of a Lugar pistol. '*Ich woul mag sterben aufstehend,* I would like to die standing up.' The toggle locking action of a semi-automatic granted his request

Bosom must have triggered off an unbearable sense of alienation and longing in Zapanski for his parents. His soul departed from the old world and transcended to one of untainted spiritual affinity. Zapanski looked beyond the consuming light and he could see his parents coming towards him. They were holding hands.

# CHAPTER 15

# THE SPONSOR

The freedom of foot patrol appealed to Frank. It gave him the opportunity to indulge in sex in the firm's time. Every night shift followed the same routine. Walters slept in a carriage at the railway station. That left the probationer to shake hands with the door handles in the town centre. The Angel Hotel, standing ornately next to the market hall, welcomed a visit from the local police officer. A crowd on the dance hall were twisting the night away despite the inability of the singer to stay in tune. Torrential rain raged against the front of the building. It had little effect on the constable in the foyer drinking coffee with the desk clerk, Kelly, a strikingly tall attractive blue-eyed bottle blonde. She had an endearing quality not always apparent in mere mortals. Like all sins, the noise from hell faded into purgatory and the crowd started to disperse. Reluctantly he dragged himself away to stand outside the entrance to the hotel.

Apart from one or two stragglers, the crowd quickly disappeared through the drizzle. As usual, Paine was right, rain is a policeman's best friend.

'Can you help me officer. I think someone's stolen my amplifier?' Frank recognised the young lad with the slicked-back ducktail hairstyle as the singer from the group.

A search of the stage and ballroom failed to track down the illusive amplifier. 'Kelly, have you seen anyone carrying a black plastic box with a speaker?'

'I saw the gent from room twenty-three carrying something. To be honest it could have been anything.'

'Who is he?'

Kelly checked the register. A Mark Benson had signed in. She used the room intercom, big Zs rumbled through the speaker.

As they climbed the stairs, Frank signalled to Kelly to pass the keys to the room. Quietly turning the key in the lock, opening the door, the constable crept into the bedroom. Benson was sprawled on the bed asleep. He made a cursory search of the room. His luck changed when he opened the wardrobe, and saw an amplifier hidden away on the bottom shelf. Surreptitiously, he closed the door behind him. *The last time I dealt with theft, I messed it up big time. This time prove the offender didn't intend to give the property back.*

Finally, after continually banging on the door, Benson, a beer-gut portly individual in his forties, masked the visitor's face with alcohol fumes.

'What do you want?'

The constable brushed passed two bleary red eyes trying to focus. 'Sorry to wake you Mr Benson, but this lad's had his amplifier stolen.'

'So what?' Benson had a slight lisp. He had difficulty in pronouncing the letter 'r'.

'So, have you seen anyone with a black plastic speaker box?'

'Aww you taking the piss, aww you telling me you've waken me up at this houw to ask me about an amplifiw.'

'I was just wondering if…'

'It's two o'clock in the mowning, no I have not seen anyone with an amplifiw. Furthew mowe, I could not caw less. Now piss off and let me get some sleep.'

Kelly's jaw dropped, she hardly recognised her favourite 'in your face' constable.

'Perhaps you've come across it and you were going to return it…'

'Aww you hawd of heawing, no I haven't seen it. I know nothing about it. I can tell you now, I'll be seeing youw sewgeant fiwst thing in the mowning. Close the door behind you when you leave.'

Frank had already closed all the evidential doors that Benson could have used to provide a rational explanation. The mood of the conversation changed.

'Mr Benson, sorry, look I'm prepared at my expense to offer you an overnight stay in our luxurious cell down the station. By the way, you won't be the only fucking rat occupying the cell.' Benson rubbed his eyes and wondered if he was still in the twilight zone. 'Good, I've got your attention. My guess is you've hidden the amplifier in the wardrobe. Am I hot or cold?'

'You can't seawth that wadwobe without a wawant.'

'Benson you're starting to annoy me, the receptionist, she's the one with the badge saying 'Weceptionist' has given me permission. I take it I could be hot then shall I?'

Opening the wardrobe, he retrieved the amplifier and he placed it on the bed. The slight speech impediment seems to be contagious. 'Benson, you're nicked and I don't give a shit what you say or how you say it. Put your hands behind your back, and face the wall so I can put the cuffs on. I'm wawning you, I'm not vewy good at it. The last time I put the cuffs on a snivelling bastawd like you. I accidentally on puwpose tore the skin away from his wwist.' Gobsmacked, in next to no time Benson was sitting in the back of a traffic car on route to the station.

'Can I have your details, Michael?'

'I didn't know you lot operate like that?'

'Don't lose sleep over it, you've got your amplifier back. Benson will get his day in court.'

'I can't wait to tell my father, look I'll put in a good word for you.'

'Who's your dad?'

'He's your new superintendent, we've just moved here from Cardiff.'

The constable rocked back on his heels from the nest of Gaelic wasps stinging his genitals. 'Let's keep it a secret, if you have to, just stick to the basic facts.'

★★★

Bosom looked impressed. 'Are you psychic or what, I haven't circulated the bastard yet.'

'I'm doing my best to keep that a secret, sergeant.'

'If you are there's no need to tell you that Benson, or Bennett, that's his real name, is wanted in Hereford for ripping off one of the hotels last night.'

'What did he steal?'

'Three thousand pounds.'

They found the money in his suitcase. This break would certainly get him noticed for the right reasons.

Amongst all the excitement, he had forgotten about Walters. Warm sunlight, flickering through the dirty carriage window, tickled the hairs up his nose. He sat up blurry eyed and stretched

140

his long neck. Looking down the platform, he realised his worst nightmare. The sign read 'Bristol Parkway'.

★★★

Frank was fantasising about his two favourite pillows after a long night shift, when a car pulled alongside him. Sadie opened the passenger door. Obligingly he accepted the offer. Her perfume continually danced the Cha Cha Cha on his testicles as he clocked the little black strapless number she was almost wearing. 'That must cost a couple of bob.'

'The car unfortunately belongs to daddy.'

'I'm not talking about the car. I'm talking about the lead around your neck stretching all the way to the Lanark.' Her hypnotic mind-blowing silky legs seemed to be sending him into a trance. 'Tell me, playing games with that Irish leprechaun, does it turn you on?'

'Yes, I have to say I find it intriguing.' He loved the way she spoke with a 'plum in her mouth'.

'Would you do anything, I mean anything?'

'I would have no choice, this is the exciting part about it.'

'Has he ever, you know?'

'Yes, a long time ago darling but as you rightly pointed out, old age has caught up with him. Although I have to say tonight, he actually ejaculated.'

'What did you do to him?' Edna's red flush, climbed his rock hard face and rested on his cheeks.

'To be honest, he masturbated.' Sadie opened her legs and lightly splashed illusionary droplets of sexual magic onto his eyelids. 'Which brings me nicely to why I stopped? I was wondering would you be a darling and make horny old me come the way you did the other night?'

'It'll be my pleasure, are you wearing suspenders?'

'Of course darling I wear nothing else. They turn men on like you and that turns me on.' Sadie took his hand and placed it on her knee. 'Can we go somewhere straight away, I really need to have you inside me?'

He could see that distinct excitable sizzling pop in her eyes. 'What happened down the Lanark to turn you on? Tell me, and I'll make you come all night.'

'Do I have to? Look, let us not waste time shall we.' The conversation was definitely making Frank rise to the occasion. She looked down and saw his erection bulging inside his trousers. 'I know the old ones are the best, well except for Cairns, but is that a truncheon in your pocket or are you pleased to see me?'

Still intrigued, sliding his hand under her dress, his fingers hardly brushed the hairs on her thigh. Gently opening her legs, he touched her knickers and they were wet. 'Tell me what happened and I'll make you come while you're telling me.'

The thought of sexual intercourse in a public place under the street lamp had an appeal. 'It was another one of those games that fortunately got out of hand. Two nurses were in the bar pissed. They were supposed to be on a hen party. Somehow, they separated from the rest of the hens. Anyway by pissed, I really mean they were pissed. Brendon, as usual on the lookout for some kind of sexual pleasure, noticed it straight away. By the way they were touching each other they had obviously slept together.'

'You mean they were lesbians?'

'Darling, please don't show your ignorance. I am living proof, so to speak, that not all women who sleep together are lesbians. Anyway, Brendon invited them to play cards, strip jack naked in every sense of the word. He told me to deliberately lose and take my clothes off to turn them on. I was down to my bra and knickers, they did not attempt to disguise the fact they were staring at me. The younger one, Jane, pretty, very long legs, blonde ponytail, only wearing her skirt and high heels, looked sexually frustrated. In all honesty, she was touching herself under the table. Brendon called me a cheat and I had to pay a forfeit. He asked Jane to remove my bra and kiss me on the lips.'

The lady with an Oscar for a submissive role opened her legs wider. 'Darling would you put your hand inside my knickers and touch me. Only this time, put your finger inside me.'

He needed no second invitation. 'Go on.'

'The taste of her lips was simply delicious. As she kissed me, she softly touched my breasts. Then that bastard Brendon stopped her.' Sadie's short sharp gasps started to affect her speech. 'Anyway he told Jane not to touch me anymore. He suggested that she could touch her friend instead. Oh my God, just keep doing that s-l-o-w-l-y. They started kissing, Jane had her fingers inside her friend and she came in no time. The older one kissed Jane on the side of the neck and caressed her nipples. She started groaning like an animal, she pleaded with her to make her come. Jane then took her knickers off and sat on the chair. The other one, I think her name was Margaret, knelt down in front of her and put her head between her legs. Within seconds, she screamed and had an orgasm. However, that didn't stop Margaret, she put her fingers inside her and she came again. Jane was screaming, God I wish it was me her mouth…' Sadie stopped, 'Faster, go faster.' She pushed against his hand, he bent over and brushed her hardened pulsating nipples inside her bra. Her body straightened, Sadie gave a huge gasp and she had an orgasm.

Both of them, vaulting the car seats, dived into the back. Frank turned her around to face the door. He pulled up her knee-length skirt. Tugging her knickers to one side, he buried his shaft deep inside her. Arching, bending, pulling her back, he whispered in her ear. 'Think of her tongue touching your clit, think what it would feel like…' Going into overdrive, Sadie had another orgasm. With one hand lifting her hips and the other pulling on her suspenders, his incessant vigorous rhythm continued until she pushed back. Moving her backside, with an agonising gasp, he ejaculated. Rolling back into their seat, Sadie adjusted her knickers and straightened her dress. He immediately responded placing his hand between her legs.

'Let me help, can you remember how she tasted when she kissed you. Tell me again how she managed to put her long legs on Margaret's shoulders, when she had her head between her legs.'

This time Sadie went into a trance. Playing out the animalistic craving for raw sex, she never wanted it to end and she showed it again and again.

After several entries on the daily state regarding good police work and with the support of the local superintendent, his dream became a reality. At last, an attachment to CID, quite an achievement for someone with less than three-year's experience. He had a three-month window of opportunity to impress. If he succeeded, a CID course could be in the offing. DS Williams read out the riot act before he had chance to sit at his desk. With his retirement imminent, anything untoward and Frank would go straight back into uniform.

The phone rang three times. On each occasion, Williams answered it. Reading between the lines, the last call from the local antique shop, seemed to be reporting a theft. He rejected the detective's offer to help. Williams would deal with it. An hour or so passed before the DS returned to the office, there had been no theft. Frank decided to play his get out of jail card. During the lunch break, he visited the antique Shop.

Mademoiselle Marseille was in no doubt at all, an 18th century Spinazzi bird branch sculpture made of porcelain, valued at least a thousand pounds, had disappeared. She last saw the porcelain in the display cabinet early that morning. By lunchtime, it had vanished. As she recalled they were busy. The only one Marseille had suspicions about introduced himself as a rep from Aitkin and Co. Antiques in Bristol. His calling card gave his name as Phillip Dance.

The next day followed the same pattern. Again, the detective stayed in the office reading the CID manual, and again Williams made himself conspicuous by his absence. From sheer boredom more than anything else, Frank placed the calling card on the desk. If this continued, he had little chance of impressing the guy who cleans out the shithouse latrines in Glasgow, let alone the chief constable.

After giving the dilemma some thought, writing notes on a pad he placed them by the side of the telephone and dialled the number. 'Good morning, 'Aitkin and Co.'

He decided to use his ex-class leader's cockney accent. 'Morning is you the punters who cover Wales as well as the west.'

'You could say that, can I ask who is calling.'

'Ye, I'm Dave and I'm doing a ring around for Silstar Antiques, Chancery Lane, to see if anyone's got a couple of bits and pieces we're interested in.'

'What exactly are you looking for?'

'First up, a pair of English Victorian maiden candelabras.'

'Sorry but I cannot help you. There is a sale on next week, I will let you know.'

'Great, you are?'

'My name is Phillip, is there anything else?'

'Yes we know there's a porcelain Spinazzi branch sculpture 18th C out your way. Give us a bell if you come across it.' Silence, 'Phil, are you still with me mate?'

'Yes still here, I may be able to help you there. How much are you willing to go to?'

'One thousand two if you've got the right one and it's in good nick. Look one of our buyers is in your manor, we could close the deal today.'

'I can probably get it for you by four. One sticking point, would it be asking too much if you could possibly pay me in cash.'

'That's a bit unusual Phil, we don't generally deal in 'Nelson Eddies' only cheques.'

'To be honest, I take on occasional work for another dealer friend of mine. He has the sculpture, at least I think he does. Unfortunately, I cannot put it though Aitkin's books. And if I am being perfectly honest, he prefers cash.'

'Wait a moment Mr...'

'Dance, the name's Dance.'

'I'll have to check with one of our purchasers about this. I'm putting you on hold.'

The trainee detective looked at his watch, waited five minutes and then continued the conversation. 'Phil, you still there?'

'Yes.'

'Well the purchaser gave the green light, but for reddies he's only willing to go to a grand; you know, no receipt all that.'

'Under the circumstances I am sure my friend will accept your offer.'

'Right, nice doing business with you chief. Larry our buyer will call at the shop at four.' Frank put down the phone, collected his thoughts, and then phoned Bristol Central. He spoke to Detective Sergeant Wallis who seemed enthusiastic about the dupe. Because of something untoward in the Bristol area, he would personally visit Aitkin's under the guise of Larry at four o'clock. It worked like a charm, an hour or so later the sergeant phoned him back. Dance had his next meal in the cells and the sculpture was safely locked away in the property room.

Wallis had put his hand into a hornet's nest. A syndicate were using Aitkin as a front to ship stolen antiques abroad. Packed in cases containing the genuine article, they left Bristol port for China and then onto Eastern Europe before entering the West by the back door. Every time Wallis organised a raid, the syndicate knew about it. That 'something untoward' had more than one officer on their payroll. He asked for the assistance of the specialised Metropolitan squad that deals with antiques. Within a week of his request, they transferred him to another division.

★★★

A distinct knock on the door brought on the rare experience of panic in his gut. *Fuck them they can shove their business. If they want a war, they've come to the right place.* Wiping his sticky sweaty palms on a handkerchief, he sat upright behind his desk and counted to five. 'Don't stand on ceremony, come on in.' Cahill entered the office and stopped at the entrance, cold grey eyes scanned the room. Unhurriedly, long strides made their way to the desk. He sat down, winced from a bullet lodged near his spine, and looked at the person sitting opposite. 'What's your poison?'

Cahill ignored him. 'I'll get to the point, in good faith we decided to do business with you. We believed you to be a person who would deliver.' The tailing off soft tone placed his accent from Dublin.

'I've always delivered what the...'

'If you interrupt me again I will be showing you what we mean by the word deliver. Everything in this hovel called Bristol will be brought to the ground in ruins and you will be standing right in the middle of it. '

*Threaten me again you bastard and I will cut off your Irish prick and shove it down your throat.*

Cahill's threatening eyes looked straight through his adversary. 'The Aitkin incident, it is yourself that's cast a shadow over your own ability. Your failure could well be the death of you.'

The handkerchief was now working overtime. 'Look Cahill everything's water tight, I've sorted it, the copper wasn't on our payroll.'

The clarity in his Irish middle class accent continued to stamp its authority on the conversation. 'That is talking utter bollocks, you told me before that everything was water tight. Tell me how did you develop a leak the size of the titanic?'

'Don't blow things out of all proportion, I'm dealing with it.'

'The truth of this matter is there is a breakdown in the system, your system, what's the story, someone's responsible.'

A shaking hand reached out for the glass on his table. 'Why won't you listen to…?'

'No, it is you that will be listening to me, your life depends on it. We now have the finance to go to war and change the mainland forever. This will start when someone is released from prison. I am a messenger boy, my organisation will not be putting up with your amateur ways. Either you sort this out NOW or you will suffer. I want you to deal with whoever has let you down, is that understood?' *Threatening me now, he's telling me how to do my job.* Lee put his hand under the desk and touched the cold mother of pearl handle of the Browning semi-automatic taped to the drawer.

'Learn before it is too late, you have ten, we are an army. Do what I say or you will die by the end of next week.' Gingerly, Cahill walked towards the door without taking his eyes off his colleague for one second.

A discreet warehouse belonging to Aitkin and Co on the west side of the harbour welcomed the prompt arrival of the henchmen. They handed in their weapons at the door. The agenda had one item, Aitkin, the investigation had seriously jeopardised long-term arrangements. Cooper's podgy, bald-headed frame stretched his expensive single-breasted suite as his ambled forward to take centre stage. A glare from Lee seemed to drain the saliva from his mouth. Gasping, the person responsible for the hand-outs to the good men in blue, licked his lips and explained there was no loophole in their set up. Dance, one of Aitkin's staff had stolen an antique. An officer from Gwent, pretending to be an antique dealer, phoned Dance under the pretence that he wanted to purchase the antique. Wallis, a local officer, not on their payroll, visited the shop and the rest history.

Lee had to find a scapegoat. Cahill was a man of his word. Slowly but surely he could feel his life ebbing away. 'Why didn't we get a tip off from Wales? We're paying some bastard to do fuck all?'

'Yer he tried, but this clever prick gone and done it behind his back.'

'Who is he?'

'Some basdurd called Macleod?'

Lee flared his nostrils. For several seconds his mouth moved without any words coming out. 'Did, did you say Macleod?'

'Yer, I think he's from your neck of the woods.'

'Why didn't we stop this nonsense our end?'

'I told you, Wallis is not on the payroll.'

Lee could still hear a buzzing noise from the word Macleod boring into his backside. 'I know he's not one of US, his fucking DI is.'

'Yer, but he wasn't in the office or he'd have stopped it.'

'Where was he?'

No reply. 'If you don't answer me, I'll fucking shoot you in the head here and now?'

'Stop doggen up, him and me was at the...' Cooper choked on his new status as a fall guy and his farmer drawl fell away.

Crazy psycho kicked in. Drooling from the anticipation of a kill, two bullies grabbed Cooper, tied his legs together and handcuffed his hands behind his back. From the moment of his last word, an overwhelming fear had entered Cooper's vicious world. Muddled, confused, in his whirring hum of mental numbness, he had escaped, run away from the warehouse. *Why am I still here*? Unable to move, paralyzed with fear, he made no attempt to resist. At the second attempt, the end of the rope cleared the beam and dropped down. *Why are they tying the other end around my legs?* It took the burly muscle of three of them to lift his heavy frame into the air. They left Cooper dangling upside down by his legs. With his chin almost touching the ground, he could feel his legs shaking, heart thumping, as it forced the blood to his lower limbs. Lee's crazy was typically spontaneous. There was no spur of the moment about his next move. Lee picked up a petrol chainsaw hidden under a blanket. Standing next to Cooper, to a man the syndicate looked anywhere except at their boss.

'If I see any of you lot looking away, even for a split second, you'll be next, and I don't give a fuck who it is.' The presence of a maleficent buzz in his head put the devil in his eyes. He switched the ignition on and pulled the starter cord. It provoked a snivel and a desperate attempt from Cooper to break free. Two of the entourage held onto a leg each. Lee waited patiently for the blood in Cooper's body to gather into pools in his head and lungs. He wanted him to stay alive for as long as possible, until the saw had reached his heart.

Above the sound of the chainsaw, a soft almost breathless

whining noise from Cooper reached the ears of the audience. Tearing the shirt off his back, Lee turned the dial to full throttle and paused. 'Fucking hold his legs apart or I'll cut you.' Forcing the chain between Copper's legs, he started to cut through his scrotum. Applying more pressure, the teeth carved through his pelvis bone. More pressure. This time the chainsaw cut through the muscles in his rectum. Lee stopped to see if everyone was looking at Cooper squealing like a pig. Endless whining from pain, begging for mercy, forgiveness, to die, entered every black heart except one. He pressed hard again. The teeth gripping against the bone made a rough grinding noise. Slowly the chain continued to saw through his abdomen, spine, and nervous system. At the start, there was little blood. It was now pumping spurting out of Cooper. Halfway down his lower torso, Lee stopped. Wiping the blood spatter from his eyes, he stepped back leaving the saw still running wedged in Cooper's ribcage. He walked around the back of the audience in a half circle. Lee wanted the gory scene to have maximum impact. Cooper closed his eyes, still conscious. With only the sound of the saw running, they all screamed inside and pleaded with him to die. Lee watched the rise and fall in his chest. *The bastard's not breathing.* Cheated out of his final cut, he pulled out his revolver and pushed the barrel against Cooper's forehead. The Browning hardly made a sound as he shot Cooper in the head. Lee continued to pull the trigger after the magazine had emptied.

★★★

Tentatively he picked up the phone. 'We are thinking of placing business your way. One thing, there must be no further loose ends. See to it that Dance's funeral takes place before he appears at court.' The phone went dead before he had an opportunity to reply to the soft Irish accent.

★★★

Despite the clear up, his attitude towards the new detective changed from one of tolerance to gross dislike. By the end of the third week, Williams broke out in a rash and reported sick. Moreover, why was there a 'For Sale' notice on his lawn? Williams had finally lost it.

# CHAPTER 16

## EL CID

Frank looked decidedly at home with his feet up on the desk. The detective glanced out of the window. As long as he came up with results, he did not expect any hassle from Walsh. The DC had a network of informants. He had already set standards in detection that were hard to sustain. The DS also had his own agenda, he wanted his temporary rank made substantive. Walsh considered the partnership as a means of achieving that goal. That was the main reason why he tolerated the detective's 'in your face' attitude.

Mary Ball, one of his informants, thrived on her newfound role. She seemed more than happy to mix business with pleasure. Within minutes of clocking the late-twenties lady with short rich-brown hair standing at the bar, they were deep in conversation. Roger, her husband, aptly nicknamed 'Fagin' had a busy life pilfering despite the diagnoses of cancer to his throat.

Several drinks mingled with a meaningless conversation.

'I've been told tha your officially a dick, is tha right?'

Alcohol had unashamedly made a pass at her nervous system. A pinkish flush appeared on her spotless complexion. He moved his stool closer to the lady slurring her speech as if he was about to reveal some unholy secret.

'To be honest, I've always been a dick. All I've done is to drop the word 'head' after it.'

'Tell me, d'you spell yu dick with a big D or a tiny whimsy little one?'

'It's that big, it's plural.'

'If I messured it how long would it bee...?'

'The last woman to do that said the satisfaction she got from it was immeasurable. As for the size of the honourable member, it's longer under the new metric system.'

Through the window, tiny pockets of scattering light from the edge of the sunset kissed her soft copper hair above smoky greyish-blue eyes trying to focus.

'When was the last time you measured something?'

'Don't ask, Roggers got tha big C so I get FA.'

'Well Foxtrot Oscar, R U having M on.'

The colour in her eyes changed to a darker blue as Mary realised the stupidity of the conversation.

For some pissed reason they decided to make quirky faces. Frank started with a typical gurney expression when he pushed out his lower jaw to cover his upper lip. With the corners of her mouth starting to quirk upwards, Mary clenched her teeth not to laugh. The lady's competitive edge came into play. Pushing her tongue out of the side of her mouth, in true 'Ben Turpin' fashion, Mary crossed her eyes and raised thin arching eyebrows. A charge of laughter was about to rattle his vocal cord, he had to do something. He pushed a finger up his nose under the pretext that it was lifting him. An astonishing grimace started to rise leisurely out of the chair. Gawking into each other eyes, like two mischievous monkeys, giggling turned into howls of laughter. Standing with their arms around each other, hanging on for dear life, they hit the uncontrollable whining stage. Noise finally gave way to the physical sensation of touch. Through her white wispy button-down blouse, he could feel goose pimples on her back. Reluctantly they sat down.

'God knows I needed tha, I've gor ago for a pee.'

The DC was enthralled at the sight of her elegant petite frame disappearing through the door. In true gentlemanly fashion, he decided to follow her into the toilet.

Mary dragged him into the cubicle. Leaning over the toilet seat, she pressed both her hands against the back wall. He tucked the back of her silk green knee length pleated dress under her black belt. Pulling her knickers down, she grabbed his shaft and eased him inside her. Suddenly Mary turned around, grabbed his shoulders, and pushed him onto the toilet seat. Straddling him, holding onto the system pipe, Mary pushed her cute red ballet pumps against the wall in order to gain momentum. Increasing her tempo, a sensual rhythm moved relentlessly to the passion of a woman who had not indulged in the pleasures of the flesh for some time. With the energy of a kangaroo on speed, she continually lifted her hips to his thrust. Frank placed one hand around her waist and the other over her mouth to stop her moaning. Agonising short gasps and a frantic noise, wafted into the bar. The faint sound of footsteps, closing in on the toilet, lost out miserably to the raw scream of hallelujah celebrating the intense pleasure exploding inside. At some stage during the simultaneous explosion, Mary had wrenched the system pipe from the wall. In true burglar tradition, Frank scrambled out of the toilet window and made his escape.

Leisurely, he strolled through the car park and made his grand entrance just in time to see Bosom and Cairn disappearing into the toilet. A dishevelled Mary appeared from the toilet escorted by the two guardian angels. Cairns whispered the tragic circumstances in the detective's ear. Apparently, they found her in the toilet sobbing her heart out. Her husband's illness had taken her right to the edge. Apart from a dig that the detective was again conspicuous by his absence, Bosom flushed the incident down the toilet.

★★★

The phone rang in the CID office. Frank looked at his watch, nearly nine o'clock.

'He's just left in the Morris van heading for the Gurnos Estate by the back lane.'

The DC grabbed the keys to the police car and ran down the stairs. Within minutes, he was waiting at the far end of the lane. Through the drizzle, in the distance, he could see the lights of a vehicle approaching. When the van was about two hundred yards away, he turned on the blue flashing light and waved the vehicle down with his torch. The Morris stopped only yards away. He approached the vehicle, and the driver rolled down the window. 'Anything I can help you with officer?'

Frank noticed the bandage around his throat. Thrusting a hand inside the window, he snatched the ignition keys.

'Why did you do that?'

'To stop you driving away, you'd be wasting your time the lanes cordoned off. '

'Is your name Macleod?'

'That's right, and your name must be 'stupid' for thieving in your condition.' The detective opened the driver's door. 'Leave your hands where they are.' Frank handcuffed his hand to the steering wheel and searched the back of the van. He found four chainsaws under a tarpaulin sheet. 'I'm probably wasting my time, where did you steal the saws from?'

'I'm saying nothing.'

'You don't have to, the serial numbers will tell me where you've nicked them from. You're that clever you didn't have the sense to file them off. If I was you, I'd give it some thought, you scratch my back and I'll scratch yours. In your condition, even with your record, you could get bail.'

'I'll do you a deal. I'll tell you what you want to know, if you tell me who set me up.'

'You can Foxtrot Oscar.'

During the next twenty-four hours, the detective started to get to know the lovable rogue. The thief was genuinely a nice guy. Roger turned down any deal that involved informing on someone. If he had to, he would spend his last remaining days in prison. He managed to get bail, the bottles of whisky on the doorstep helped to kill the pain. Roger never lived to hear his name called out in court.

★★★

Frank glanced in the direction of the cemetery as Mary and the other mourners made their way to a freshly dug grave. He could see her gurney face in a puffy shaped cloud above the cemetery. This time no one was laughing, this time he felt ashamed. Rifling through his pockets, at twenty-four years of age, the occasional cigarette had turned into a chain smoking habit. Lighting another cigarette, leaning against the wall, he thought about his situation. Why was there something crazy always going on inside driving him on? Nothing mattered as long as he had his way. Underneath the surface, anger and impulse rather than common sense ruled his behaviour. At every opportunity, he could not resist the temptation of being in someone's face, regardless of whom or what the circumstances were. Lighting another, he again glanced in the direction of the cemetery as they lowered the coffin into the grave.

Like a phoenix rising from the ashes, would this experience

rekindle the essential character of who he really is? Unique, apparently the mythical bird had strange eyes and a cry reminiscent of a choir singing in the lounge. Unfortunately, the phoenix like all birds of prey, had a natural tendency to get in your face.

# CHAPTER 17

# THE STOOL PIGEON

Probably as an afterthought more than anything else, the detective renewed his interest in the West tip off. The river Usk flows through the heart of Abergavenny. At a point where Gawain pushed his uncle, King Arthur in the river, it backs onto the Morse Estate. Frank casually made his way along the riverbank. In the distance, he could see the houses overlooking a caravan on the river edge. A semi-detached in the far corner with a pigeon loft looked ideal for observations. After continually rattling his knuckles on the front door of number twenty-nine, he used a side gate leading to the back garden. Finally, he fixed his eyes on the broader than long frame of Ryan Gregory cleaning out the loft. Intelligence logs on the spitting image of Lon Chaney, included markers for violence and assault on police.

He intended to play this one straight. After showing Gregory his warrant card, it was time for polite conversation.

'Morning Gregory, I'm DC Macleod, can I have a word?' The detective expected a grunt or at least a hoot from the primate.

'Have you got a search warrant?'

*Cheeky bastard.* 'No, do you want me to go and get one?'

'In that case you can have two words. Fuck off.'

*Fucking me about, two can play silly buggers.* 'It will only take five minutes of your time. It's up to you, do you want to spend the night in the cells and court the following morning?'

'You've got nothing on me, piss off.'

'Gregory I don't know if you noticed, but I'm the one with the warrant card. This is what is in store for you if I don't get any fucking co-operation.'

The visitor stepped back to create more space between him and his aggressor. Taking out his pocket book, opening it to a blank page and without taking his eyes off Gregory, he pretended to read his evidence in court. 'Your worships, at 3 p.m. on the 6th of April I was on duty in that cesspit laughingly called the Morse Estate, when I had occasion to speak to that well-known gorilla called Gregory. I entered his rubbish dump at the back and showed him my warrant card. He said, 'Fuck off copper, I hate you bastards'. I asked him to watch his language or he'd find himself in front of the magistrates. He replied. 'Those tossers, they can fuck off for all I care.' This time he used a more authoritative voice. 'Officer are my ears deceiving me, or did the defendant make a derogatory remark against this bench? I'm afraid he did your worship. I shall take that into account when sentencing him. Carry on with your evidence officer.'

Gregory's large jaw muscles dropped as he glared at the detective.

'Thank you your worship. Without provocation, the nonce grabbed me by the throat. To affect my escape, I had no alternative but to hit him with my truncheon. I cautioned him when we were in the ambulance. He was unable to reply because of his fractured jaw.' He paused for effect, opened his jacket and touched the handle of a small truncheon inside his pocket.

The smouldering tension on Gregory's face suggested his head was about to explode.

'Do you get my drift, you either co-operate or it's the cooler?'

Gregory decided not to bang his chest and he sat down on the steps. Frank's roving eye settled on the pigeon loft. 'Good, that's settled, how many pigeons do you keep in the loft?'

'Thirty-eight.'

'I'm having second thoughts about you. I think you'd be better off in prison. At least there they would teach you to count.'

'I know how many pigeons I've got.'

'The answer Gregory is zero. Null or as we say in the 'Land of My Fathers', fucking naught. You see my feather plucker you will not be keeping any of your vermin in that shed because of... ' He pointed at the four heavy sleepers supporting the shed. 'You and I know, don't we Mr Gregory, you nicked those sleepers from the railway yard. If I went right up close, I bet you a pound to a ton of pigeon shit, I'll be able to see the brand mark burnt into the sleepers. They're stolen property. As someone who bends the law to suit himself, it's my duty to tear down your pigeon loft and take the sleepers and you down the nick.'

A strong breeze wafted against the back of his neck. Glancing towards the horizon, a strange bird with a broad powerful wingspan and gold scarlet tail feathers disappeared over the skyline.

'Give us a break will you, I live for those poor little bastards.'

'Then I hope those poor little bastards won't be in the shed when I tie the rope to that sleeper and the other end to a land rover.'

'Look, I'll do anything. What's this all about?'

The officer pretended to consider his options. 'Well I suppose I could caution you and leave the sleepers where they are.'

'If you do, I'm telling you Macleod, I won't forget you for this.'

'Done, now that you've joined the neighbourhood watch, I'd like to present you with a brand new biro with our motto, 'bollocks to safeguarding the community' on it. See the caravan down there by the canal? For the next seven days, I want you to keep a record of who goes in and out with your pen. Put down the time, description or names if you know them.' Gregory nodded. 'Do you know who owns the caravan?'

'No, I've seen someone going in. I haven't taken much notice.'

'Well take notice of what's going on. I'll be back with a rope next week, same time to look at your notes.'

'What if I don't see anything worth jotting down?'

'Look if one of your pigeons shits on the roof of that caravan you had better JOT it down. If you do a good job, you and your vermin will live happily ever after. If you withhold anything, I swear on your pigeon's lives, this estate will be eating pigeon pie until it's coming out of their ears.' Frank made his way to the side entrance, stopped and turned around with a devil of a smirk on his face. 'I've just thought of something. Have you got any idea what I'm going to call you as a result of our new relationship?' The pigeon fancier, not for the first time, had no idea what the detective was talking about. 'You're my stool pigeon Gregory, think about it.'

*Can I rely on Gregory? Can I hell.* Keeping observations for hours on end waiting for something to happen was never his favourite chore. In this case, Frank had little alternative. As he sat in the CID car parked on wasteland at the far end of the estate, the word 'why' shouted in his ear. Gregory had never bothered to ask the reason why. Hardly the best of locations, he looked at his watch again, 6.40 p.m. If anyone intended to turn up, surely it would be around this time. Another hour passed. To his left, in the distance, he could see the outline of a male walking along the bank towards the caravan.

He cursed under his breath, he had left his binoculars on his desk. The new arrival looked reasonably well dressed in a blazer and slacks. The athletic figure of a man, relatively tall in stature with brushed jet-black hair, approached the caravan. Frank made a note in his journal. The visitor unlocked the caravan and went inside. Half an hour passed, seemingly an eternity, he lost count of the times he had glanced at his watch. Pissed off to the point of anger, he thought about having a quiet word with the mystery caller. What quiet word, and to what purpose? Had experience finally taught him the significance of gathering key evidence before approaching a suspect? With his eyes fixed on the caravan, he mulled over what he already knew about John.

According to West, John originated from Cardiff. He made enquiries. In 1946, at twenty-one, the suspect had received a caution for indecent exposure. A detective from Cardiff Central confirmed there was a file on John. He posted it on the understanding that he shared the content with no one. The MO had little in the way of originality. John, an exhibitionist, flashed to two people as they walked along a bridle path in Roath Park. The summary captured the essence of the incident. 'The offender was some distance away from the two victims. He did not attempt to approach them when he exposed himself.' The narrative clearly pointed to a misdemeanour. Later, both victims withdrew their complaint and John received a caution. A summary written by Inspector Jenkins on the face sheet concluded, 'This person is more of a danger to himself than anyone else. He has apologised and there was no sexual motive.'

A brown envelope attached to the file contained a statement from one of the victims, sixteen-year-old, Alice Worrell. It bore little resemblance to that on file. Alice was walking on the path when John suddenly appeared from behind a tree less than ten feet away, Alice went on to say. 'He was naked from the waist down. He touched his thing up and down and it was hard.' John told her to 'touch my prick.' When she refused, he got very angry and became hostile. He grabbed Alice, pulled her towards him, and slipped on the wet grass. She managed to break free and ran away. The last line of the statement read. 'This has upset me, I cannot sleep at night, I can see that horrible cruel look in his eyes.' The inspector must have got it wrong. The file mentioned two victims, there was no evidence to suggest that in the statement or anywhere else. Someone had gone to great lengths to cross out the last sentence in her statement.

Two hours later the mysterious caller left the caravan and made his way back along the riverbank before entering a lane to the estate. Frank reversed the car, drove up the hill, and parked some distance away from the lane. Within minutes, a male entered the Morse Estate. Surprisingly, he turned left and started to walk towards the CID car. The detective crouched under the steering wheel and waited for the pedestrian to pass. Facing towards the driver's door, suddenly the intensity of the street lighting created an almost daytime effect. Constantly flickering on and off and then dimming to a softer muted glow, the lights appeared to be experiencing a rapid sag and swell in electricity. The temperature inside the car plummeted down, a cold-blooded chill penetrated his skin and crawled up his spine. Moist air from his mouth changed to condensation on the inside of the windscreen. Crystal ice pellets formed at the bottom of the screen. He could hear the click and track of leather shoes hitting the concrete passing the car. Every hair was standing on the back of the neck.

Waiting, he looked in the rear view mirror. The figure was now walking up the garden path of number twenty-nine. Gregory answered the door, after a brief conversation, the visitor drove off in a Bentley towards the town centre. Following at a discreet distance, the car arrived and parked on the driveway of 16 Pennant Crescent, the John residence. *Gregory must have given the game away. Why would he do that?*

★★★

Still seething from Gregory's treachery, Frank pushed open the office door and literally walked straight into his detective sergeant. Walsh seemed less than impressed about the progress of the investigation. Rudimentary information about the suspect, critical evidence of criminality, had yet to be established. The detective appeared to be going through the motions without carrying out a thorough investigation. The wasp sting came when the DS reminded Frank that he could not expect every case to fall into his lap.

That morale-boosting exchange resulted in a far more structured approach to the enquiry. Another phone call to Cardiff Central gleaned nothing. The detective regretted sending him the file in the first place. Frank could also forget about crossing the border to carry out his own enquiries. PC Dan Archer, the local plod responsible for the Pennant area, knew John. He was not aware of anything to his detriment. The suspect lived with his sister Carla. They were well respected and as far as he could tell, socially acceptable. John took up the teaching vacancy at the local secondary modern school some three years ago when they moved into the area. Archer and John were both members of the model-building club. Once a month the enthusiasts met at the school. John's expertise in the arts, particularly stagecraft and scenery, had brought a new dimension to the club. The schoolteacher's enthusiasm seemed infectious. In his own time, he encouraged the pupils to show an interest in the theatre.

The detective loathed his next task. As usual, he found Gregory in the pigeon loft. Without prompting, the pigeon fancier handed over the observation log. The only visitor to the caravan had been a male, the time and description were all authentic. With a dull ache, he apologised to Gregory for wasting his time. He had been mistaken about the owner of the caravan. Incensed, he was fuming to the point that he wanted to hurt someone. On the way to his car, he deliberately scraped the knuckles of his clenched fist against the side of the garden wall. Sitting in the driver's seat, he watched hallucinatory steam coming out of his ears settling on the windscreen. With an imaginary finger, he made a mental note. When the law had finished with John, Gregory and his bloody pigeons would get what they deserved.

Two weeks surveillance on the John household revealed little of consequence. However, observations outside the school had a more promising result. For the first time Frank could put a face to the name Samuel John. Almond-shaped piercing eyes smouldering above a plastic smile gave way to the prominent bridge of his aquiline nose. Looking through binoculars, he focused on his eyes. They seemed devoid of any pigment except for a tint of azure. Frank could also see a mark in the middle of his jaw line on the right hand side of his face. Adjusting the zoom, he focused on the clear image of a dark birthmark shaped like a thumbprint. Frank could just make out the friction ridges in the '*cló ordóg diabhal*, mark of the devil'.

John was popular with the pupils, particularly the girls. The detective put down his binoculars and stared across the road. John placed a sympathetic arm on the shoulder of one of the girls. Taking out a handkerchief, gently and with great care, he wiped the tears from her eyes. They maintained eye contact. The girl seemed mesmerised under his spell. A taut gut feeling in his stomach told him that something was wrong. That look in their eyes, anticipating smile, subtle gestures, and intuitive crush reminded the detective of his early encounter with girls. Now they were standing very close, almost touching each other. Was he watching someone who had a skill in the manipulation of vulnerable children? Although there was no logical explanation to justify that belief, the feeling overwhelmed him.

The school bell brought a strange sense of relief as the pupils made their way to the classroom. What did he really witness in the playground? More to the point, what experience did he have in dealing with child abuse? Any so-called action plan needed more than just fine-tuning. To improve his knowledge base he decided to tap into the experience of the social services. Something else had merit, he decided to open an offender profile on John. Minute holes at the roots of his hair started to tingle and itch as if they were alive. Instinctively scratching his head, dandruff landed in his eye and he brushed it away. *Hell, I was looking at that bastard for ages, he didn't blink once.*

Walsh seemed impressed when his partner handed him a template profile on John. The headings contained all the significant features of a suspect, background, physical appearance, characteristics, associates, type of victim, and MO. Hard work would soon fill in the blanks under each heading. The sergeant was even more astounded when Frank asked to borrow his hand-outs from the initial CID Course.

On the Saturday of the second week, the detective followed the suspect into the town centre. John stopped outside Cantonis' Café, looked through the window, waved at somebody, and entered the cafe. Waiting in the car on the opposite side of the road, an hour passed before the teacher re-appeared. At the last moment, Frank decided not to follow him.

Ten minutes elapsed before someone else left the café. He recognised the girl from the schoolyard, aged about twelve years, very pretty with long auburn hair. Again, she appeared distressed about something. Gravity seemingly pulled her head and shoulders down to demonstrate her mood. He decided to follow her. Eventually, Susan Rees arrived at her home address on the Winch Hill estate.

After a while, Frank started to have doubts about John's implication in devious behaviour. He should have questioned West more thoroughly. Good news, apparently the pervert was back in circulation, time for another quiet word in his ear. Sitting at his desk, he opened the file again. Why the absence of any family background regarding John? Again, he concentrated on Alice Worrell's statement. She must have written it, the signature at the bottom of the page and the narrative appeared to be the same handwriting. He decided to see if he could make sense of the sentence crossed out using his desk lamp.

Holding the statement, needles and pins started to ripple through his fingers from the spiritual signature on the paper. An electrical charge, like ants crawling under his skin, washed through his frame. He clenched his teeth, his muscles contracted as energy raged up his arm to form an image. A canvas between his eyes showed the horrific rape of a teenage girl with distinct red hair. Intermittent and without any warning, pictures changed from scene to scene. The girl, lying naked face down on the bed, had her hands tied behind her back. Razor sharp edges of barbed wire tight around her waist penetrated and punctured her skin. Frank could see a pool of blood on the mattress. The girl glanced to one side, she appeared to be looking at someone. A horrific shriek, like the yowling cry of a vixen torn to pieces by the pack, exploded in his skull. Instinctively he placed his hands over his ears to block out the noise. This would be no quick kill, the figure at the side of the bed seemed to be enjoying the cruelty of the chase. A lavender gypsy skirt with a white belt, hanging on the back of a chair, flickered across the screen. The picture now focused on a bible and candle on the bedside cabinet. It rapidly changed again to a shadowy figure tying heavy black adhesive tape around the girl's mouth and nostrils.

This time the outline, kneeling on the bed behind the victim, picked up a silk stocking and used it as a tourniquet. Taunting her, repeatedly tightening and releasing a stranglehold, the aggressor forced a knee between her shoulder blades. Violently pulling the victim back with the stocking, powerfully holding on, her neck snapped. Time seemed to phase into obscurity as her body went limp. The figure, wearing gloves, released the stranglehold and gripped the barbed wire around her waist pulling her backwards. Like a ravaging animal, the assailant subjected her to a vicious anal assault. Frank looked at her motionless frame. Was she already dead?

Without realising it, he grabbed a pen. Dizzy, lightheaded, Frank slumped onto his desk and passed out. He was still lying face down on the desk gripping the pen when he regained consciousness. Confused, sitting upright, he tried to clear his head to write down the experience still fresh in his head. Cursing, searching for paper, he glanced at the blotting paper on the desk covered in his handwriting. At the top of the paper, he could see the rough sketch of a crucifix hanging from a string of beads. Under the drawing, there were two distinct passages, the first read. 'O blessed Virgin Mother of God, look down in mercy upon me, a miserable sinner, to atone for the offences that are done to thee by impious and blasphemous tongues. O Virgin, holy and merciful, obtain for all who offend the grace of repentance, and graciously accept this poor act of homage from me thy servant. Obtaining likewise for me from thy divine son the pardon and remission of all my sins, Amen.'

The next read. 'O Jesus it is for the love of you, in reparation for the offences committed against the Immaculate Heart of Mary, and for the conversion of poor sinners, that I pray do this.' At the bottom, he recognised the drawing of two mortise keys. Crossing each other in the middle, the insignia belonged to the Catholic Church.

Disorientated, trying to focus, he wrote everything down on another sheet of paper. Hurriedly, he made his way to the basement and rummaged through the Police Gazettes circulated by Cardiff on serious crime. Nineteen forty-six, the year when John had a caution, seemed the most appropriate place to start. After hours of searching and finding nothing of interest, he wondered if the local police had already caught the offender. On the other hand, Frank could have missed something. He had no alternative other than to go through the circulations again, only this time more thoroughly. Turning the page, in a supplement dated October nineteen forty six, under the 'Missing person section', Frank found what he was looking for. 'Missing from her home at 16 North Folk Terrace, Roach, since the 19th September, Alice Jane Worrell B.2.9.1930 5ft 3ins in height, slim build with shoulder-length red hair and brown eyes. Believed to be accompanied by male associate, no further details are available.' In horror, gobsmacked, the name Alice Worrell jumped from the page and continually thumped him in the gut.

Splashing his face with water, he looked in the mirror again and saw the rape unfolding. Her distinctive red hair and general appearance fitted the description in the supplement. The detective thought about his next move. At this stage, he saw little point in informing Walsh. On the other hand travelling to Roach had a sense of urgency about it. His body had other ideas. Pain and contractions in his leg muscles brought him to his knees. Eventually, he passed out from the acute ache in his neck and shoulders. Something the size of a long piece of spaghetti wiggled inside his stomach.

For the next day or so, Frank kept a low profile. His usual sufferance bore little resemblance to this agonising pain that showed little sign of relenting. Psychic energy from Alice's signature had opened his gift to a past dimension. Had he crossed the threshold of unacceptability?

The detective rang the doorbell for a third time, patience was never one of his virtues. Painkillers had little effect, every muscle in his body ached. His head was still whirring, there were times when he lost concentration. David Worrell opened the door. His sunken face, grey hair and skeleton-like frame, gave him a look way beyond his sixties.

After showing his warrant card, Frank apologised for calling unannounced. Under the pretext that Alice's case was under review, he asked Worrell to provide an update regarding her disappearance. The situation had not changed, after all those years they had not made contact. Worrell had no idea of her whereabouts. 'When she went missing your lot didn't want to know.'

'Why do you think that Mr Worrell?'

'Because it's true, nobody gave a shit, that's why. Look, I told your lot from the outset she was in danger. Nobody took any notice, we all know why that was.'

'Sorry, are you saying we didn't take her case seriously?' Fidgeting, he moved his weight onto the left leg to relieve the pain.

'Look, don't play silly buggers with me. Before she went missing, she made a complaint about Detective Chief Inspector John's son. That was the reason why everybody turned their back on us.'

Rapidly approaching the concentration span of a goldfish, the news about the high-ranking officer hardly registered. 'Excuse me are you talking about the flashing incident?'

'How dare you call it a flashing incident? He scared the living daylights out of my little girl. After your so-called flashing incident, she started wetting the bed. And what was done about it, nothing? Look, I think you had better leave, before I do something I'll regret.'

Chronic ache had dragged him to a lonely place. The journey home seemed imminent. Inhaling, taking a deep breath and filling his lungs, with one last desperate attempt he moved on. 'Mr Worrell I'm on your side, I wasn't involved in the early enquiry, but I am now. I know how you feel, I'd be the same if it were my daughter. I swear I won't let you down.' He waited anxiously in the last chance saloon for a response.

Worrell reluctantly approached the settee and sat down. 'What do you want from me?'

'Please start from the beginning, and tell me everything.'

'The wife and I went on holiday to Cornwell, we left Alice to carry on with her studies. We arrived back on the Saturday. She was gone, clothes and all. She left a note saying she had fallen for someone and had gone away. We didn't believe it for one second.'

'Was the note in her handwriting?'

'Yes, and it was the biggest load of lies I have ever read. I know my daughter officer she was already seeing someone. She wouldn't go off with him or anyone else. Nothing made sense, are we supposed to believe that she'd take clothes she had outgrown. I know this is going to sound barmy, for the first time in her life, she left her room in a tidy condition. It was spotless, she must have spent hours cleaning it. Can you tell me why she has not drawn any money from her account? What is she living on, fresh air? She has never contacted us. We worship the ground she walks on. We know, no matter what, she wouldn't do that to us.'

'Was there anyone else in the park with your daughter?' *I'm losing it, just keep going.*

'No, she was on her own when she saw that pervert. Her

boyfriend had to run on ahead, late for work, serves part time at the Rose and Crown.'

'So her boyfriend was with her before John came on the scene.'

'Yes, they were, you know, cuddling and that. She told her mother they were under a tree. All the time she felt that someone was spying on them.' Worrell finished the story.

'Can I see her bedroom?'

As they climbed the stairs, Frank could feel his heart skipping, racing in his throat. Worrell opened the door to her bedroom. 'I was going to say it's as she left it, but it's not.'

The detective entered the bedroom and he instantaneously felt a drop in ambient temperature. The bedroom was the same as the one in his precognition. He approached the bed and walked through a cold spot, the temperature plummeted even further. Shaking from the extreme drop, he glanced at Worrell who seemed unconcerned.

Wavy lines appeared in front of his eyes. Lightheaded, intense fear and anxiety had launched the DC to the top of his psychological roller coaster. Hanging on to an emotional handrail, with sweaty palms and his heart racing, he braced himself for the ride dragging him to hell. The putrid stench from Zapanski's rotting flesh settled on the roof of his mouth. Instinctively, he walked back towards the door. With one hand on the doorknob, he changed his mind and turned around. The colour process in the retina of his right eye started to break down the sunlight in the room into traces of demonic ether. He could see a ghost like trail of millions of micro red cold particles hanging in the air, left by the magnetic field of an unclean spirit. Was he moments away from another seizure?

His next attempt sounded garbled. 'Did the police take anything?'

'Very little, they just went through the motions, took a photograph and Alice's letter, that's all.'

Frank noticed the absence of a bible and candle on the bedside cabinet. 'Is your daughter religious Mr Worrell?'

'No more than anyone else, she went to the Baptist chapel.'

'Does she have a Bible or anything?'

'No and neither do I, what sort of stupid question is that?'

'Did she take any jewellery with her?'

'Yes and her jewellery box, the one with roses on the side. A ballerina pops up and dances to Swan Lake.'

'Did you find anything in her room that didn't belong to her?'

'No my wife would have noticed, as I said before, it was spotless.'

'Have you changed the bed linen? '

'Yes, thrown it out even the mattress. We repainted everything, the wife didn't want it smelling with pee where, you know.'

The detective made a cursory search of the bedroom and found nothing of relevance. In view of the gravity of the situation, he told Worrell the truth and suggested they call in the local police. South Wales would re-open the case and forensically examine the potential crime scene. Worrell strongly objected to the suggestion. He would rather set fire to the place than, 'Let those bastards through the door again.' Frank thought about not giving him the option. Spiralling down, he was in no fit state to argue.

Worrell answered the question the detective should have asked. When Alice left, she was probably wearing her favourite lavender skirt and white belt.

They shook hands at the gate. 'Thanks for sticking by me and not calling in the local mob.'

'I can live with that, you and your wife have lived through enough hell over the years. It's about time someone listened to you.'

'She is dead, isn't she Macleod?'

'She's alive in your heart and I know she is in mine.'

'Dead or alive, please find her, that is all I'm asking. Bring her home. None of my family will rest until you do.'

Gerard Walk was his next port of call. The ex-boyfriend Ross Davies still had a deep affection for Alice. The police had not approached him about the John incident or for that matter her disappearance. At the time she went missing, Ross was visiting his stepbrother in Manchester. He confirmed everything David Worrell had said. He also described the feeling of being watched when they were under the tree. Their last conversation had taken place the week or so before her disappearance. Alice seemed to be in good spirits. When he left, Frank noticed a picture of the Holy Mary hanging in the hallway.

During the journey home, the detective cursed his own ineptitude. *Hello is there any brain cell with an ounce of common sense.*

*You've messed up big time sunny Jim, you didn't even follow basic procedure. Piss off, I can still call it in anytime soon. Ding a ling, pull the other leg, it has bells on it.*

Everything seemed to be fragmenting because of his lack of experience and cavalier approach. What else could go wrong? Frank answered the question and pulled into a lay-by. He should have taken statements from both Worrell and Davies. At least South Wales would not be able to instigate another cover up. Another gratifying thought crawled in one ear and out the other. At least Rees John had kissed goodbye to his chief inspector rank. He was now the assistant chief constable administration for South Wales.

Newley, in excellent voice that day, sang 'What kind of fool am I' under the vacant sign in the rookie's head.

# CHAPTER 18

# THE APPARITION OF FATHER GRAHAM

Father Graham's Irish accent echoed against the walls of his beloved church. 'Well if it isn't detective Macleod. Do you know, seeing you standing in my church only confirms my belief in miracles.'

'It looks as if my reputation has gone before me, Father.'

'Only the bit about fornication, adultery, and alcohol.'

He smiled at the mischievous looking face in front of him. 'With those credentials, I'd be a natural for the Vatican. Has someone been speaking out of turn in confession?'

'The only thing I can tell you about confession is that it is good for the soul.'

'If you've got a moment, would you hear mine?'

'I'm afraid a moment would only leave us with enough time to touch upon your early years, as for the present, what can I do for you?' With pride in every stride, the priest past the font and made his way down the aisle towards the marble alter. Light, peering through the stain glass window, seemed to cast a ghost-like shadow over the lectern. Graham beckoned to his escort to enter a small anteroom situated at the side of the pulpit. A kettle miraculously appeared from nowhere, and so did the tea and biscuits.

Opening the envelope, he placed the blotting paper containing the sketch and his handwriting on the table. 'Father, I wonder if you'd be good enough to look at this for me.'

The priest nodded and examined the drawing. 'And whose handiwork is this?'

'It's something that was left at the scene of a crime in South Wales, can you help?'

Raised expressive thick eyebrows looked even more prominent against his baldhead and arched back. The expression on his face said something was very wrong. 'I can also help you with good manners lad. Do not dip your biscuits in the tea it looks unseemly. Right you are, the drawing represents a rosary which consists of a set of prayer beads, and the devotional rosary prayer.'

'Is there any reason why the sizes of the beads are different?'

'All the reason in the world lad, you see the rosary prayer is full of repeated sequences. If the truth be known, the beads are a physical check to make certain that we get all the prayer right. The small beads represent the sequence in the rosary prayer when we say 'Hail Mary'. The large beads are when we say 'Glory be to the father'. Moving your fingers along the beads when you recite the prayer, will let you know exactly what comes next. And you can take that smirk off your face. Before you jump to conclusions about the ability or otherwise of a catholic congregation to count properly. There is a perfectly good reason for it all. You see, instead of the congregation keeping count of where they are in their head, we would like them to concentrate on the meditation of the mysteries.' Father Graham continued before the detective had the opportunity to interrupt. 'I am ahead of you Macleod. The mysteries of the rosary are the important events in the lives of Jesus and the Blessed Virgin Mary. There are fifteen altogether. They are grouped into three sets, Joyful, Sorrowful and Glorious Mysteries.'

'Can you give me an example of one of them?'

The priest was less than impressed. 'Look at the stain glass windows on the way out and you will see everything from the crucifixion to the coronation of the Blessed Virgin Mary.'

'It's all going on at the same time, is it?'

'Correct. Unfortunately, the same cannot be said about our conversation.'

'Is there anything unusual about the drawing?'

'No, in fact although it is no Michelangelo, it does pay attention to the detail.'

The man of the cloth easily parried the next interrupting lunge. 'Please do not even think about interrupting me. It is only at the point where a large bead is followed by the ten smaller ones that we ask the congregation to meditate on an announced mystery. I'm going to try to pre-empt your questions to save time. The significance of the rosary cannot be over- emphasised. It symbolises the road to God from the Father to the Son, to the Blessed Virgin Mary, and from Mary to the human race. History tells us Mary gave the rosary to Saint Dominic in an apparition in 1214. This is why we call Mary, 'Our Lady of the Rosary'. The rosary has experienced resurgence in popularity in recent years because of the vision of the Blessed Virgin Mary in Fatima, Portugal in 1917. Mary identified herself as the Lady of the Rosary and told the children to say the rosary prayer every day.'

'You say children, Father?'

'Well at least it shows you are concentrating lad. Yes, she presented herself to three shepherd children and confided to them the three secrets of Fatima. Mary also presented them and a new set of prayers said at the end of the rosary prayer. I have a book on the subject to lend you but I would like it returned. Now, let's plough on or there will be no rosary prayers or anything else for that matter in this church on Sunday.'

The detective mimed closing an imaginary zip across his mouth.

'Where the drawing accurately represents the rosary, the prayers that are written below do not.'

'Why is that father?'

'Macleod, I thought so, you are not listening at all are you? Did I not say only a moment ago that the actual rosary prayer contains numerous repeated sequences of 'Hail Mary' and 'Glory be to the Father'? Now tell me how many of those phrases can you see on your paper?'

'Well to be honest with...'

'That's right constable, the answer is none. Now let me carry on please, for ONE last time. I am sure it will come as no surprise when I say that the prayer that starts with, 'O Blessed Virgin Mother of God', is a specific prayer to Mary, aimed at repairing the sins of others against her. This prayer is, in fact, one of many called acts of reparation to Mary. Other prayers are also specific to repair the sins against Jesus and the trinity. Now then, even you will appreciate, the first prayer ends on your paper after Amen. The second one begins at, 'O Jesus it is for the love of you'. The second prayer also has a direct association with the Blessed Virgin Mary. When she appeared before the children at Fatima she emphasised the importance of the prayers carried out as Acts of Reparation, the rosary prayer, and the importance of penance and sacrifice.' The detective's next attempt at riposte ended even before 'advance'. 'Don't worry lad I am getting to where you want me to go. Mary told them that when you make a sacrifice you should add the, 'O Jesus' prayer at the end of the rosary prayer.'

The priest acknowledged his 'Appel'. 'Go on ask a question Macleod, or you will explode all over my church.'

'What is the name of the second prayer?'

'It is called, '*The Sacrifice Prayer.*'

'Can I ask you about the end of the first prayer?'

'Have I got any choice in the matter?'

'The prayer ends using words, 'For me from thy Divine son the pardon and remission of all my sins'. Isn't the person praying, asking for absolution for his or her sins?'

'You are dead right. Now why don't you go while you are ahead?'

Taking a book from the shelf the priest handed it to his new pupil. 'Read the part about the promises made to those who pray. You will find that saying the rosary prayer is the remedy against all manner of evil and a way of redemption for everyone.'

Frank placed the envelope containing the drawing in the book and he gave his mentor an inquisitive gaze. 'Father, why did you mention that?'

Graham tried to straighten his back, as he looked him straight in the eye. 'Because it is what you have been waiting to hear me say lad.'

'Just one more question, what is the thread holding the beads together made of?'

'It's made of silk, does that help you with your puzzle?'

'Thank you for being patient with me Father, I'll leave you to get on.'

'Hail Mary' and 'Glory be to the Father' for that. By the way, are you looking after yourself lad, you appear to be looking a little on the pale side? '

★★★

Walsh leaned over his shoulder and was somewhat taken aback when he saw his partner's reading material. His research had already thrown up a number of interesting factors relevant to his investigation. Mary presented herself to the children of Fatima. She told them to make sacrifices to save sinners and wear a tight cord around the waist that would cause them pain. Another aspect emerged. Primarily she appeared before children at Fatima and the sacred apparitions at La Salette in 1846 and at Lourdes in 1858. All had similarities, on each occasion Mary gave the same message, the world had to turn away from sin or suffer the consequences.

In La Salette, Mary referred to the 'impiety and sinfulness of Man'. Turning the page over the heading read, 'The Power of the Rosary'. Through Saint Dominic, Mary made fifteen promises to Christians who pray the rosary. They ranged from protection to forgiveness and 'a high degree of glory in heaven'. Graham said that the rosary was the way to redemption through the divine grace of the Blessed Virgin Mary. Had John sacrificed Alice in order to atone for his sins and receive redemption through the power of the rosary? At one point, he considered asking Graham if John was a member of the church.

The detective thought Alice was dead. Who had killed her was another matter. Had other children suffered the same fate? Dialling Scotland Yard, the National Gazette Section agreed to send the details of any homicide with a similar MO. He glanced at his calendar on the desk. He should have visited the reformed pervert yesterday.

# CHAPTER 19

# THE STING

His partner in crime seemed reluctant to have anything to do with him. After locking the front door, West peered out of the letterbox and shouted, 'Leave me alone you bastard, I've got nothing to say to you.'

Rejection, yes that personal rebuff, prompted Frank to lift his foot. Aiming several well-directed blows at the lock, the door splintered and burst open. Inside the detective gave serious thought of phoning the psychological hotline. Too late. He gripped the doorframe with both hands and systematically kicked in the wooden panels. West, standing half-naked in the hallway, started to worry about his safety.

'Talk to me now you bastard because I've got two things to say to you. First thing, you need a new door. Second thing, you're nicked.'

Frank grabbed his arm and applied the handcuffs. Before you could say 'Justice for all' West found he was in familiar surroundings trying to avoid eye contact with the custody sergeant. 'This is Mr West sergeant, he's been arrested for fucking up my enquiries.'

Sergeant Barry glared at West. 'I don't need an introduction. Will we be having the pleasure of his company for long?'

'That depends on what he has to say, it's all…' An unholy Interruption by West shattered the sanctity of the custody area. 'I have plenty to say, why…'

This time an interjection from Barry. 'Has the world gone mad, did I hear someone speaking in MY custody area without MY permission?'

'No sergeant, I think it was coming from the toilet. Someone's taking the piss.'

West stared at the ceiling in disbelief. The lift called justice had sunk to the bottom of the shaft, and he was looking at the bellhop.

Unwittingly, West had played into the detective's hands by not letting him in the flat. His so-called arrest, designed to put him on the back foot, had done just that.

The prisoner tried to show indifference about his fate. However, his non-verbal told another story. In the interview room, his defensive posture, sitting rigidly upright, arms folded, indicated that his nervous system had kicked in. Frank waited for the full impact of the loss of his freedom to play on his mind. *Start with open-ended questions.* 'Well, I am waiting for you to tell me. I don't want to be here all night.'

West shrugged his shoulders. 'I've no idea what you're talking about, get on with it.'

*Impatient bastard. Rehearsed reply, background questions to get him talking.* 'Why do we always have to start off on the wrong foot?'

'Why did you kick my door in, you tell me?'

'If I'm not mistaken, didn't I see you right the last time? Look it's about give and take, you help me, and I'll help you to get out of this mess.'

'The last time I nearly had my head kicked in.'

*Encouraging. Short guarded responses, now crank it up.* 'You're really in deep shit. If you don't play ball you're going down for a long time my friend. I can't help you then.'

He glared across the table. 'What are you accusing me of this time? Didn't I tell you everything the last time? Search my flat, go on you have my permission.'

*Hell, we've already got to the denial stage.* 'John will implicate you, he'll drag you down with him, people like that always do. You're looking at conspiracy. There is only one court that deals with that, crown court and that means a fair stretch.'

The detective looked closely at his facial expression to capture any response. West adjusted his glasses and deliberately broke eye contact. He had not expected John's name to enter the conversation. 'What he does has got nothing to do with me.'

*Pupils increasing in size, slowing down his speech, covering his mouth, push him further.* 'Look tell me about John and I'll save your arse. The other alternative is you will go down for conspiracy or child molesting.' *Jackpot. Bottom lip twitching,* it's *sweatbox time.*

'I swear to God, I've never touched anyone.'

The DC leaned over the table to intimidate the prisoner. 'Come on, you can't help yourself. Are you telling me the children's knickers you stole were taken by mistake?'

'I've never touched a child in my life. I can control myself, not like some.'

*Nervous finger tapping, legs crossed, no eye contact at all. He's deciding whether to tell me or not.* 'Listen for Christ's sake, in court he'll say you're involved. I'll give evidence saying you have pre-cons for stealing children's knickers and indecent assault. How's that going to sound to the judge? Last chance. Tell me, I'll cover for you, otherwise I'll lock you up and throw away the key.'

West bowed his head.

*He's deciding whether to say all or fuck all. He wants to end this, TAKE CONTROL.* 'How can I help you if you won't help me? A statement before they drop you in the shit will put you on easy street. The worst thing that can happen is you go Queen's evidence. No one is going to put you away for that.'

*Don't give him any time to think it through, go at him.* 'Time to lock you up. Don't say I didn't give you a chance.'

'Hey, hang on a minute will you?'

*DOMINATE him push him to the edge.* 'No you've had your chance, on your feet, it's time to lock you up.'

A panic-stricken West licked his dry lips. 'Ok, ok, look if I tell you what I know, do I get out of here?'

'Guaranteed.'

'Someone told me that John photograph's girls in his caravan. He gets them to dress up, lipstick and everything, and that's it.'

'What do you mean that's it. You had better start talking or your feet won't touch the ground.'

'That's all I know, except he told me John's got a real fixation with children. You know a real pro. You get your picture taken with them, not real sex, he is too clever for that, just touching, but it costs you. He gets, you know, aroused by watching other people touching children.'

'Who told you all this?'

'I can't say.'

'No problem. Look I'll piss off down the pub, you can rot in the cell and I'll see you sometime tomorrow, the next day, or never.'

'He's called Gregory, Ryan Gregory.'

*Pinch me I'm dreaming, the pigeon has come home to roost.* 'Go on.'

177

'He told me that John is good at enticing girls to his caravan, they trust him. He gives them a drink to get them relaxed. After a couple of visits, he shows them a photograph of an adult touching a young girl to get used to the idea there isn't anything wrong with it. After giving them a present or two, he gains their trust. They let John touch them and bingo they are hooked in.'

'And?'

'Then, they do what he says. If they feel guilty after, they're too frightened to say no. He's got this thing down to a fine art. He even blackmails them to let other people touch them. He's so clever, when there's another adult there with him and a girl he wears a mask.'

*Fire quick questions so that he does not have time to think up a lie.*
'Question: what sort of mask?'

'It's got the face of a clown.'

'Question: how do the customers get to know about the caravan in the first place?'

'Gregory arranges it all, no one deals with John direct.'

'Question: have you ever been in the caravan?'

'No.'

'Wrong answer to the question. I'll ask you again, have you ever been in that bloody caravan.'

'No, and that is the truth.'

'Question: have you ever seen any photographs?'

'Yeah once, there was this girl about thirteen posing naked from the waist up wearing a hat and necklace.'

'Do you know her?'

'No.'

'Who else was in the photograph with the girl?'

'She was on her own.'

'What sort of necklace was it?'

'Pearl, or was it a string of beads. It was beads with a cross.'

'Who showed you the picture?'

'Gregory did, he's got more as well.'

'You seem very friendly with Mr Gregory. Why is he telling you all about John and showing you photographs?'

West ignored the question. 'DC Macleod to Mr Fucking West are you receiving me over. If you are answer the question.'

'He asked me if I was interested in buying photographs or going to the caravan. I was going to buy a photograph, but he was asking too much.'

'Who else is doing business with Gregory?'

'As if he's going to tell me.'

'Question: do you know anybody else involved in this set up?'

'No, Gregory said it was pretty exclusive, he didn't mention names.'

'Where does Gregory keep his photographs?'

'They are not in his house if that is what you are thinking. He's got them hidden away somewhere.'

'Can you get hold of any of these photographs?'

'Ya, I could tell him I've got cash this time.'

'Right, I want you to set up Gregory and John for me. Get as much information as you can, especially about John.'

'He'll kill me if he finds out.'

'You don't need to worry about that because I'll kill you if you don't.'

After going through it all again and summarising, West made a statement. He had twenty-four hours to obtain the photographs and information. In the meantime, the detective would keep John under twenty-four-hour surveillance and apply to a magistrate for two warrants to search the suspect's premises and school. West would contact 'his brother in arms' if anything untoward cropped up. Feeling dirty and bastardised, he stayed under the shower for some time. The belligerence aroused by the wrongdoing had gone way beyond anger.

★★★

A dark figure, lurking in the shadows near the garage, watched as the light from the bedroom went out. Lighting another cigarette, leaning against the wall, he glared at the flame of the lighter. He seemed mesmerised, fixated, by the colour and the shape of the flame. Anger, impulse and need, even the compulsion to destroy, called out to him through the flame. Self-control dragged his memory back to when he had experienced agonising pain, triggered off by fire. *No, stop wait, one day.*

Nancy Rees opened the front door to the well-groomed young detective in his usual black suit with slim lapels, narrow white tie, and winkle-picker's.

She examined his card. 'Aren't you the one who arrested that prowler at the hospital?'

'Yes and the one who had coffee and biscuits. That's why I've put on weight.'

Frank recalled the sexual turn on when he first saw the ash-blonde slim figure in front of him in uniform. *The suspenders, they were all wearing suspenders.*

'Come in, you must be here for some reason.'

The detective asked Nancy if she could keep Susan under close supervision for the next day or so until he had concluded his enquiries.

Nancy took objection to the less than satisfactory explanation about her daughter's implication in his so-called enquiries. Then unexpectedly she came up with a solution. She intended to visit her mother in Swansea with Susan on Saturday. Nancy could easily bring the overnight stay forward.

He glanced at Susan's photograph on the kitchen cabinet. 'How old is Susan?'

'She's just turned twelve. Look, don't take me for a fool. The truth is I've been expecting something like this.'

'Why?'

'To be honest I can't give you an explanation, but I've known for some time that something is wrong. My husband and I are trying to make a go of it after his affair. All the arguments finished months ago, but Susan is still having nightmares, and she's still wetting the bed.'

'Is there anything else that's made you suspicious?'

'Yes, soon she will be approaching a critical stage in every girl's life. I appreciate girls of her age talk about, you know, sex and that. In the last couple of months she has shown awareness beyond a girl of her age.'

The mood of the conversation changed. 'I hate to admit it, but I think I've missed something going on right under my nose.'

'I'm certain things will sort itself out. Do me one more favour, give Susan a hug from me?'

As he made his way to the car, the mental picture of her suspender stud pressing against the inside of her knee length uniform, played continually.

With Susan, out of the way the pressure eased. West would soon come up with the evidence to nail John and Gregory. The pervert was definitely the weak link in the chain, but surely, he had the savvy to watch his step.

The fax machine must have been working overtime from the amount of paper generated in the tray. The 'National Gazette', Scotland Yard, had found one similar match with the MO. A footnote attached to the paperwork asked the enquirer to phone Chief Inspector Roberts, the lead in the case at Gloucester ASAP.

After reading the short transcript, Frank phoned Gloucester Central. Roberts wanted to know why he was interested in the Rachel Morris case. The detective told him he had information about an incident with religious undertones. There seemed little credence to it, but he felt obliged to contact the Gazette. Roberts demanded an update. He reluctantly agreed to fax a summary of the case. Both summary and circulation were brief. Rachel Morris, aged thirteen, lived with her mother on the outskirts of Gloucester. On the 10th February 1958, the schoolgirl had left home to spend the weekend with her father in Stroud. She never arrived on the train. On the 16th February, the local police found her body in the bedroom of a rented country cottage in Painswick, Gloucestershire. Information left at the scene had strong religious connotations.

Frank grabbed his jacket and parachuted down the stairs when he finally remembered his appointment with Bernard Jones, the headmaster. Jones ignored any apology. He expected nothing less from so-called guardians of the law. His fictitious story about the chief constable's new guidelines regarding security checks also brought an uninspiring response. As a preliminary step, the detective had instructions to scrutinise personnel files held at all schools. Jones had no objections. As far as he was concerned, once again, the police were simply wasting their time examining inconsequential information.

The desk in the school library was stacked with files. Frank only had interest in the one named John. The content crawled into his gut. In 1957, John a devout Catholic had taken up employment as a teacher at the Cheltenham Ladies School for girls. After travelling extensively, he then moved to Abergavenny. For the first time Frank could tie the suspect into a real-life murder and not something going on inside his head? A comprehensive PNC check on John returned a no trace marker. He expected to see a record of his caution on the computer. After phoning Walsh on his rest day, he contacted Chief Inspector Roberts and pointed his car in the direction of Gloucester to find out the answers in the Rachel Morris file.

From the outset, Roberts had scepticism tattooed on his tongue. He saw little point in travelling all the way down the M50 to examine a file. Yet, after all that time, the Morris investigation still languished in the abyss. Any tangible lead had taken place during the early enquiry regarding the rental cottage in Painswick. According to the estate agent in Cheltenham, around that time, they had several enquiries to rent the property. No one took up the option. Genuine interest stemmed from two nameless male applicants and a woman. Further investigation, even an appeal for them to come forward for elimination purposes, drew a blank.

Forensically, the depth of the void was infinite. The whole episode seemed bizarre. Someone had meticulously cleaned the cottage. Roberts thought he was dealing with an amateur. Why bother to clean the cottage, the offender could have burnt it to the ground? A psychologist report answered his query. The type of offender capable of such atrocities usually leaves a calling card at the scene. The report stressed the culprit had probably killed before using a similar MO, and would almost certainly kill again.

Roberts glanced at the new arrival reading the file. Raising his heavy cheeks, they ran into the furrow lines under his eyes. Gwent were renowned for issuing parking tickets. He was clutching at straws if he thought for one moment Macleod would add any impetuous to his investigation. This time, contemptuous eyebrows almost disappeared into the lines on his forehead.

'I will leave you to it Macleod. Back in an hour or so, got to wet the whistle.'

Conversation at the bar between Roberts and his DS rounded on taking the piss out of their visitor. The ridicule of the new kid in town took a serious turn. The DS pointed out that the joke could well backfire if their visitor made progress where they had failed miserably.

The DC looked at the photographs of Rachel lying on a bed

facing the ceiling with her hands tied behind her back. Adhesive tape wrapped around her face and a blue halter belt fastened tightly around her waist, showed a similar *modus operandi* to the Worrell case. A rosary hung around her neck, with two yellow roses placed at the base of her feet. A shoulder length picture captured the marks left by a tourniquet around her neck. At post mortem, the number and depth of the cuts revealed that garrotting had taken place on at least a dozen occasions. There were other significant discoveries. A knife, inserted into her vagina, had cut through the lower part of her abdomen. Although less certain, the offender had attempted to remove the uterus from the pelvic cavity.

Photographs showed extensive burns on the palms of her hands. The exposure of both hands to a flame over a prolonged period had destroyed the nerve endings and both layers of skin. Wax, found on the palm and base of the thumb, appeared consistent with a picture of burnt-out candles. The offender had left a personalised card containing a picture of the Virgin Mary. The card read, 'I promise to make you happy, not in this world but in the next'. Using the reference section of a book, he found the index marked Lourdes 11th February 1858.

The day after her disappearance had been the centenary of the apparition at Lourdes. He turned to the chapter dealing with the sacred appearance and it confirmed his suspicion. Mary appeared to Bernadette, a thirteen-year-old girl, wearing a blue belt fastened around her waist. She also had two yellow roses lying at her feet. The Holy Mother asked them to pray. She also said the words written on the prayer card. At some stage in her life, Bernadette held her hands over a lit candle without experiencing any pain or burns. Systematically, he checked the reference section again. In 1917, Mary appeared at Fatima. Another significant apparition had taken place at La Salette on the 19th September 1846. The date jumped off the page and stuck in his throat. Catching his breath, in a daze, the significance of the date attacked his spine like a mallet playing a xylophone. Alice Worrell had disappeared exactly a hundred years after the apparition at La Salette.

Intrinsically woven into the key features of both murders were the Fatima apparition, rosary, penance, redemption from sin and sacrificial prayer. At least he could take comfort that there was no centennial anniversary for Fatima on the horizon. Mary first appeared to Lucia Santos and two other children on the 13th May 1917. His blood cells seemed to crystallise and freeze in his veins. The fiftieth anniversary of the apparition would take place in two weeks. John must have already devised some sickening sacrifice to celebrate the most significant appearance of the Blessed Virgin Mary. A clue to the extent of his madness must be somewhere in the pages of Fatima. He probably intended to kill at least one child Susan.

The saying, 'if you want to know the time ask a policeman' did not necessarily have a ring of truth about it when it came to Roberts. His 'back in an hour' had enveloped into at least three before he eventually returned to the office. With the assistance of the detective sergeant, the rotund frame of the senior officer stumbled into his chair. Spontaneous binges were the best, particularly when the cocktail included cracking jokes about another police force. The caller had already crossed the border into Wales. *Piss trous dans la neige* eyes focused on a letter propped up against the telephone. Macleod had left a note. Roberts read the letter, snorted, doubled-up, and almost fell out of the chair.

'Roger, you've got to listen to what that tosser has written.'

'*Chief Inspector, as you guessed, I am out of my depth.*'

His expression gloated superiority. 'Too royal sunny Jim.'

He continued reading the letter. '*I cannot help you all I do know is…*' There was absolute silence for the next ten minutes until he had finished. Fumbling for his glasses, Roberts read the letter again.

The detective sergeant reacted to the concerning scowl on his governor's face. 'Is everything all right Guv?'

Roberts looked at the ceiling in disgust as he handed the DS the letter. Frank had itemised and linked all the exhibits found at the scene to Mary's appearance at Lourdes. Each exhibit had a reference number of the appropriate page in the book. The letter also contained a page on the rosary, Fatima and the other apparitions. This time the DS inhaled laughing gas when he read the last paragraph. '*Chief Inspector, the offender was right under your nose and you let him go. If he was up your arse, your head might have noticed him, but you were doing what you do best, tossing yourself off in the bog.*'

# CHAPTER 20

# DEVIL'S ALPHABET

The sentiment, 'old habits die hard' certainly applied to Samuel John. After experiencing one of his lesser stressful days in school, he looked forward to another evening in his smoking jacket. No rest for the wicked, thank goodness, his final entry in the profit and loss modelling club register. Archer was obviously incapable of doing the job. The dunce must have persuaded him to take on the role as treasurer. Self-indulgence in the intellectual part of the brain placed his hand under his chin. He glanced at his reflection in the mirror, the pose resembled Rodin's famous sculpture, 'The Thinker'. There were other similarities. In sober meditation, he also continually battled with internal strife.

A slight protrusion in his lips went into pouting mode. Yes, standards had improved at the club. In saying that, the club was seemingly not the only place where standards had fallen short of the mark. John peered at a glass cabinet in the corner of the room. Narrow eyes focused on a bottle of sherry on the shelf. Again, Carla had shown a total disregard for propriety when she had the audacity to purchase a cheap bottle of sherry. At least she had the grace to follow his explicit instructions, not to pour the sherry into the decanter until he had examined the new bottle. With precision, John placed two sherry glasses on their respective pimpernel placemats, and scrutinised the label. 'Cadiz Fine Spanish Wine', he opened the bottle and poured the sherry into a glass. Although not a gambling man, he was willing to wager that the sherry in the glass registered exactly 50ml. Holding it to the light, he tasted it. At last, finally the genuine article.

Like his precise bowel movement, John had planned the evening down to the last detail. In his illustrious silk smoking jacket, he made his way to the cabinet and switched on the radio tuned to the third programme. The feast of intellectual stimuli had already started. A discussion between Sybil Thorndike and Lewis Casson on the 'Recollections of Harley Granville Barker' would follow the current programme, Dylan's unfinished poem 'In Country Heaven'.

The perceived intellectual sat back in his recliner and sipped a second sherry. Nothing, absolutely nothing in this world is sacred. The BBC had reduced airtime and they were planning more cuts. Even the 'Third Programme Defence Society', in the guise of no less than TS Eliot and Larry Olivier, had failed to save the programme. John lit up a Du Maurier cigarette. Holding the smoke in his mouth, forming a precise O with his lips, he blew a flawless smoke ring into the air. How could anyone compare the wireless to other forms of home entertainment, particularly the so-called television? Even the degenerates inhabiting this planet were capable of performing a menial chore and listening to the radio at the same time. That certainly did not apply to the television.

Moreover, and to prove that very point, he moved the painting by Gwen John to one side and opened the safe. The teacher retrieved his most treasured possession, his project album. As soon as his fingers touched the red leather-bound cover, fulfilment pulled up a chair and sat down next to self-indulgence. Could anything possibly measure up to listening to his favourite programme and simultaneously breezing through the delights of his album? The content had taken him a lifetime. Although, he had no intention of admitting it, not even to Carla. The fact was undeniable, John preferred browsing through the gilded pages of his treasure than the Holy Bible.

Holding that thought, his face took on the persona of a little boy caught peering at a schoolgirl's knees. What pray would Grandmother have said about his preference? Granny John, yes, the very person who had shown him the road to salvation. God only knows the hours they had spent reading the bible. John's attention span wandered to a conversation that had taken place in the rest room. As usual, Roger, the history teacher, was in his usual belligerent mood regarding standards of morality. He had the audacity to suggest that moral excellence originates from society, the rule of government, and individual norms. In all honesty, he was not looking for an argument, but he felt obliged to correct him on that score. Where was religion in his so-called conceptual model? Ethical norms had little to do with a system of do's or don'ts that reflect society's so-called standards or conscience. No, it had everything to do with a loving relationship with God through Jesus and the Blessed Virgin Mary. Christian moral values went way beyond the standards and selfish norms of society. Oh yes, religion represented an absolute standard. Not unexpectedly, the historian made an off-the-cuff remark about the authenticity of the Bible. Once again, obligingly, he pointed out to Roger that he was only explaining away God in order to sin. John gave himself a psychological pat on the back. His comprehensive explanation was indubitably an ace on the line. Roger never came back for the final set and theologically limped off the court. Yes, Grandmother would have been proud of him that day.

His ears picked up the quirky voice of Sybil Thorndike talking about Barker's production of 'Midsummer Night's Dream', in which she played Titania, Queen of the fairies. Her performance, to say the least, had been disappointing. Barker and his despicable crowd should realise that in order to retain the core essence of Shakespeare's authenticity, a male had to play the role. How many females were on the stage in the early sixteen hundreds? He doubted if there were any.

Another sherry introduced that magical time to look at his album. John opened it to the first page, the knuckles in his left hand turned white as he gripped the book. Both eyes disappeared into the back of his head, leaving only a white outer window. He felt as if he was standing outside himself. With intoxication pumping through his nervous system, he described his experience as crossing over to death and then being reborn. To *Mens sana in corpora sana, a healthy mind in a healthy body'*, it embodies that inexplicable horror of accepting evil lurking in the dark corners of your mind. This was no ordinary album. The content represented his innermost fantasies and real-life projects.

In his opinion, 'Midsummer Night's Dream' captured the evil inherent in all women from Adam and Eve. Because of Eve, sin had descended on humanity consuming his mortal soul. He recognised this as the truth. The play may be a comedy, but it had strong thematic undertones built into the plot. Although he agreed with Bevington's interpretation when he called the plot 'the dark side of love', he simply had not gone far enough. Hermia sleeping in the wood with the innocent Lysander steeped in sexuality. Was he the only one who could see the mastery in the subliminal message? Magical juice placed on the eyelids of the two Athenians to make them fall in love, had to be the sexual blood of the virgin Hermia. Blood from her first sexual encounter, represented the power that all women have over the opposite sex. John considered the part where the young men had finally lost self-control. At this point, the play merged with reality. Sexual gratification with a virgin had to be the ultimate personification of weakness of the flesh.

His eyes gazed at a photograph taken with Grandmother when he was seven. They were sitting on a bench in the garden in front of a blossom tree. He recalled the golden hue of sunlight softly touching his cheek. Pink petals floated on the breeze on that momentous day when Father had taken his photograph. Pater's time was far too valuable to waste on Samuel. His very existence seemed insignificant in comparison with policing, and golf in particular. Nettles, their lazy Labrador, almost asleep, rested at the feet of someone cut out of the photo. John remembered, as a small boy, defiling the image with a razor blade. On reflection, he would have given anything to erase the part of his brain infected by that bitch.

At eighteen, Alex married Rees John. Although not *virgine,* she lacked sexual experience. Rees joined the police. Ambitious from the off, it turned out to be an illustrious career. Two years later, she gave birth to Samuel. Around that time, Rees had promotion to sergeant. Consequently, he was even more conspicuous by his absence. Alex spent little time with what she lovingly called her 'ugly brat'. Naivety had induced her to bear the unsightly offspring. In order to relieve perpetual boredom, Alex took a part- time job with a local publishing firm. One day in the print room, her boss introduced her to the hard sell of publishing when they had intercourse on top of the photocopier. From that point, she became infatuated with sex.

Alex had an innocent almost vulnerable quality. With a Monroe hairstyle and slender figure, there was no shortage of suitors. After working her way through the staff, promiscuity indulged in something that really turned her on, casual sex with strangers. The thought of someone watching her having sex also played a significant part in her pursuit of the soulless shag. Although hardly original, Alex had sex with the gardener. Facing the kitchen wall,

Alex removed her high heels and frantically lifted her black Pan Collar dress to above her waist. Slightly bending both knees, the gardener grabbed her waist as the good lady helped him to penetrate her. Alex could feel the sensation of his penetration. Continually she pushed back to repel his oncoming thrust. Deep and then shorter, his shaft found her zone. With his hand between her moist legs, the gardener vigorously brought her to an intense climax. She opened her mouth to scream, but nothing came out.

Samuel peered at his mother between a gap in the living room door. At seven years of age, he felt emotionally numb and yet he wanted to burst into tears. Treachery and betrayal tightened like a noose around his throat. *What was Mummy doing, why isn't she doing it with Pater?* He also remembered experiencing something raw and animalistic. Original sin. Confused, Samuel had to see it again, he missed school in the hope of catching them. Alex did not disappoint him. This time, Samuel looked through the patio window and saw his mother lying naked on the kitchen table with a small pillow under her buttocks. The gardener, standing in front, gestured to Alex to place her legs on his shoulders. The executor of the soulless shag turned her head and glanced in the direction of the patio. She could see Samuel watching her through the window. Without any emotion, their eyes met. Every rational bone in his body told him to run away, and yet an uncontrollable urge compelled him to stay and watch. The message in her eyes, that dominant smile was unmistakable. The whore of all damnation was beckoning him to join them. Eventually, after an Olympian career as an adulterer, Alex carrying a torch for her latest knee trembler left the matrimonial home. Within a year, she died from a heart attack brought about by prolonged secondary syphilis, and finally meningitis. Granny John, now responsible for bringing up the children, seized the opportunity to equate sexuality with sin, death and damnation. Any sexual contact was undeniably sinful, corrupt and caused disease.

More real than remembering, a hiss on the radio brought John back from his mental dredging. Without realising it, his hands were covering his eyes. Loosening his smoking jacket, he recognised the evil inherent in all women past puberty. In his mother's eyes, Samuel had seen the power she had through debauchery and pervasion. Her degradation was nothing short of being unfaithful to God. John conceded that she was a harlot. Moreover, through no fault on his part, that made him the son of a whore, a morally unprincipled individual. Because of that bitch, he was destined to damnation without any hope of salvation.

However, he found salvation in the saintly face sitting next to him in the photograph. He could hear the wisdom escalating from her tongue. 'Samuel do you want to end up like your mother or do you want salvation through the Blessed Virgin Mary?'

The conception of the Virgin Mary through the Holy Spirit and the birth of Jesus personified the remission of sin. With no sexual intercourse, no male seed, the fascination of this miracle captured the simplicity of his make-believe morality. Moreover, through the power of the rosary and prayer, Mary captured the essence of saving sinners from damnation.

How comforting, in all the apparitions she looked upon the children with special affection. Pure and undefiled, they had yet to reach an age corrupted with sin. *Why does no one realise what this means?* Children had to be saved from the sinful gratification of the flesh.

John Wayne, his empathy buddy, reached out from the page and placed a hand on his shoulder. In his delusion of mutual acceptance, John could see the resemblance. Both of them were fighting against inordinate lust and sinful pleasure. Divine intervention took centre stage. He decided to offer the ultimate sacrifice to the Blessed Virgin Mary to commemorate the anniversaries of La Salette and Lourdes. The first two projects were pre-ordained. He turned the page, the euphoria of looking through the album took on a dramatic change.

From the dark side of his moral emptiness he gazed at the photograph of Lolita. The twelve-year-old girl was sunbathing on the lawn in a skimpy two-piece bikini, heart-shaped sunglasses, and a straw hat. Like James Mason in the film, Lolita had shaken him to his very core when she appeared on the screen. John acknowledged his obsession with children. Why not, there was nothing wrong with it. He did not intend to apologise for his enlightened opinion on the subject. Through ignorance, the public were only fooling themselves. The vast majority had the same opinion, only he had the courage to admit it. Although a little-known fact amongst the sorry masses, he knew, yes, he knew that Nabokov had sold more novels about the seductive nymphet than

*Lady Chatterley's Lover*. Moreover, as obscure as it may seem to the uneducated, one-day, society would accept or ignore the obvious. A dull ache gripped his mortal soul as he bathed in the ocean-blue innocent eyes of the blonde. John could hear the nymphet soundtrack of the film playing in the background.

With his mother's departure, Granny John subjected him to a psychological dripping tap, that sex was sinful and degrading. The rejection of any relationship condemned him to a history of solo sex. At thirteen, Samuel masturbated at least four times a day. The more he masturbated the more obsessive it became. Intense, degrading sexual fantasies were solely about children. The 'control freak' and dominant element in the fantasy meant that the children had to be younger than John.

At fifteen, drawn by the chemistry of adolescence, he found the courage to approach a girl of the same age. That made him very angry. As they sat on the park bench, he could feel the power she had over him. Straight away, he knew the harlot wanted to send him to purgatory. Yes, she wanted to be the dominant one, the one in control. He could see it in her smile, eyes, even the innocence in her voice. But most of all, yes most of all, he could see it in the way she crossed her scrawny legs. Frustration turned to anger, he had to gain the higher ground. If only he could hypnotise or cast a spell over her. Anger gave way to the destructive side of his nature and he wanted to hurt her really, really badly.

During his transition to adulthood, obsessed with children, John decided to become a teacher. A school environment in order to pursue his obscenity was far more preferable than hanging around schoolyards in the hope of catching a glimpse of a real life Lolita.

Turning the page, the clock in the hall chimed to herald Carla's footsteps coming down the stairs. Halfway down, John glanced in her direction, and again, his heart skipped a beat. Standing at the bottom of the stairs, her tall skeletal frame posed in fashion mode at the end of the catwalk. Dizzy, with blood rushing to his head, he felt unconnected with the space around him. Carla had control and he hated her for that. Despite the smear of Russian red lipstick on her thin dry lips, she looked positively radiant wearing a gypsy lavender skirt with a white belt.

'As usual my darling, your timing is immaculate. I was about to turn to the La Salette Project.'

'Do you like it?'

'What is there to dislike. You look far more exquisite in the dress than Alice could ever have dreamed of.'

She held her pose. 'This is my little treat to say sorry about the sherry. I will not make that mistake again.'

'You have more than compensated for that darling.'

Carla poured herself a large glass of sherry as he recalled the project with affection. A sly satanic smile acknowledged the only time when he was thankful to be the offspring of a high-ranking officer. The self-professed hero brought himself to heal. If he intended to reminisce, the logical thing would be to think about the incident as the event unfolded.

John, a university student, first cast his eyes on the evil known as Alice sitting on a park bench holding hands with her boyfriend. Her features and distinctive red hair, reminded him of the girl who had tried to send him to purgatory. Acting on impulse, he followed the couple as they made their way towards the bandstand. Samuel hid in the bushes and watched them sitting on the grass under the tree. They kissed, and then the personification of the devil's hand touched her breasts. Cursing under his breath, he was too far away to see the sexual immorality in her eyes. The scene moved on to sexual intercourse. In his fantasies, John had total control. However, in reality things were different. He watched and listened to the evil spectacle that he had no control over. It pushed him to the very edge.

An unbelievable surge of energy from an adrenalin rush pumped through his blood. Then it registered and he realised the obvious, they knew, yes they knew, he was watching them. The sordid escapade was just an act to make him feel inferior about his masculinity. Anger seethed into rage and he lost his way to sanity. The dirty vile act ended in a matter of minutes. The boyfriend whispered in her ear and left. John intended to take the high ground, he would show her who was in control. If she wanted stereotypical manliness, she had come to the right place. In a frenzy, he hid behind a tree near the pathway leading to the exit. Alice started walking towards him. He dropped his trousers and masturbated. Getting nearer, fantasising, he could almost taste what it would be like to hurt the whore. Surely, the disappearance of the boyfriend was a sign to treat her like one. Appearing from behind the tree, he saw the sheer panic on her face, in her eyes, now who was in control? In a state of intoxication, John grabbed her arm and Alice managed to break free. Even then, he had total control, he had made her run away.

That day, Satan unleashed the evil inside Pandora's Box. Hope for the victim stayed inside. He posed a question, what would have happened if she had not broken free?

John had to admit that losing control could have had serious consequences. Yes, further progress would require serious thought, if he intended to make his aggressive fantasy a reality. Surely, that must be the ultimate fantasy. Planning everything from the aura stage to the emotional high gave him as much satisfaction as the closure. After all, ultimate control is only achievable when you finally destroy an object. Alice had passed puberty, but the fact remained, she needed saving from her sinful way. The final piece of the miracle fell into place when he recalled the date of Mary's appearance at La Salette, the 19th September 1846. The significance of the date brought into fruition the project known as, 'La Salette'. Her sacrifice would take place exactly a hundred years from the date of the appearance to atone for her degradation.

He had little problem in discovering where Alice lived. After the incident in the park, John had reservations about keeping his emotions under control. How would he react under clinical conditions in a real scenario, however small? Every Thursday, Alice left home at around ten and took her usual route to the library. Carefully, he placed a rosary, prayer book, silk stocking, and other paraphernalia for the project in a cardboard box and sealed it with brown tape. After carrying the box, he left it on the pavement opposite 'Cathy's Café'. He checked his pulse and surprisingly his heartbeat was normal. Thinking clearly through every phase, he even acknowledged a passer-by. Leisurely John crossed the road, entered the café, sat at a window facing the box, and waited. Half an hour or so passed and then Alice came into view walking along the pavement towards the box. This time he was not disappointed. As she passed the box, adrenaline kicked in. He could smell the salt from the sweat underneath his armpits. A humming, drowning noise coming from inside the walls of the café lasted for several minutes. John gulped and held his breath as the object of his first project walked passed her destiny. Less than six no five feet away from her fate, *The next time would be her last, the next time would be his first*. Still in control despite the euphoria raging in every nerve ending, John collected the box and returned to campus. The student could now fantasise about a real-life incident based on personal experience. The next day he missed college, stayed in bed and masturbated until it hurt.

Divine intervention again took a hand when her parents went on holiday. At the bottom of the page, John could see a photograph of Alice on her knees with her hands tied behind her back. When he took the photograph, she pleaded with him to save her pathetic miserable life. Initially he told the 'corrupt whore' that he did not intend to hurt her. The next close-up captured her pale botox scowl. At this point, Alice started to realise she was going to die. Facing her demise, instinct kicked in. Then the whining bitch from the park, the one with a demonic hand down her knickers, had the effrontery to ask him to have sex. To Alice, the terror of dying seemed so final. The word DEATH repeatedly flashed in front of her eyes. She could smell it.

In all the years that followed, John regarded the next stage with the utmost reverence. It epitomised ultimate control, where the victim would do or say anything to stay alive. Even for one more second, one more breath. Then the abhorrent slut lost any hope of survival. The strumpet had finally lost everything. Still on her knees, he placed a rosary around her neck and led in prayer. Alice repeated each phrase and looked up at the evil beyond insanity. John had crossed into his world of mayhem and depravity.

The next picture, his favourite, showed a close-up of her face seconds before he strangled her. It captured that euphoric moment of total dominance, when he was winning over death, when he was still alive, and that whore was dead. The choice of where to dispose of her body was another inspiration, reticent throughout the whole project. Spending time at the family home would never be the same again. Looking out of his bedroom window, he could see her grave in the far reaches of the back garden. *Alice had the courage to die with what is but not the why of understanding. Then she knew herself, at the end of her last heartbeat she found immortality.*

The document, 'Post Implementation Review' on the next page brought memories flooding back. He remembered writing the document in a state of depression brought about by closure. Yes, the project had achieved all the objectives, but in all honesty, it had not lived up to his high expectation. The paper contained a series of 'lessons learnt' bullet points. The first one, 'Failing to plan is planning to fail' was undoubtedly the most significant statement in the album. Bullet point two, 'Never leave an audit trail of association with the object'. If perchance, someone had stumbled on her body, he had to be the obvious suspect. John directed his gaze at Carla in the lavender dress and held it before drawing his eyes back down the page to the heading 'Lourdes Project 1958'.

And there they all were, bless them, his class at Cheltenham Ladies School in 1957. Rachel sat next to him in the front row. Debbie Bury had been his first choice, the Lolita of the class. At thirteen, Debbie showed a sense of maturity way beyond her years. Rachel, on the other hand, lacked confidence. Vulnerable and naïve she seemed the obvious choice. This time he intended to plan everything down to the last detail. Finally making his choice, he set about the subtle art of seduction. Despite the age difference, John played out the scenario in true classic boy and girlfriend fashion. He lavished her with gifts. A visit to a theme park, even a restaurant rendezvous, all sent the right signals to Rachel.

Again, he rested his chin as he recalled his greatest theatrical moment. What a performance, certainly on a par with Irving's portrayal of Becket in Tennyson's play. The masterpiece took place when he informed Rachel that weekends without her were unbearable. With tears saturating both cheeks, John posed the question. *Was there any chance of a stolen weekend together?* Rachel had no hesitation in saying yes to the master of manipulation. Carla phoned an estate agent and they provided the name of three properties available on the anniversary of Lourdes. On the morning of their departure, she physically checked all three to ensure they were still unoccupied. Surprisingly, Carla found the keys to one of the cottages under the doormat. Samuel recalled Carla's pathetic attempt to persuade him that she should take on a more formidable role in the actual destruction of Rachel. Of course, he refused.

John glanced at the photograph of Rachel lying naked on the bed. A neglected Carla glared at her brother. His eyes were still transfixed on the photograph. Again, things had gone according to plan until Rachel realised her demise. *Why oh why did she refuse to accept her destiny?* In an attempt to save her miserable, useless life, she told John about her first period.

'If you want to, you could be the first to cuddle me.'

Why did she think for one minute, one second, that he wanted to have sex with that innocuous bitch? It was always his intention to kill her. That intent, now fuelled by an explosion of anger, spiralled out of control. John knew he was more than capable of dealing with her perverted offer. Her feeble attempt to control him had failed miserably, and for that, Rachel would suffer. Reminiscing, he could feel his hand gripping the sweaty, smelly rubber handle on the carving knife as he plunged it deep inside her vagina. Forcing the knife ever so slowly upwards, John felt the weight of her body standing firm against the lacerated blade as he used considerable force to cut through her flesh. Once again, he held the power of death in his hand. Then the teacher stopped and panicked. He had to carry out the ritual before killing Rachel or face hell and damnation forever.

'Darling, have you reached the Lourdes part yet?'

John raised his head. Carla could see the rage of madness in his eyes.

'Do you mind if we play the tape? In fairness Samuel I helped you with this one, and to be honest, this is not the first time I feel left out of the whole thing.'

He nodded, Carla walked over to the safe and retrieved the tape.

'Play side two.' Switching the cassette to play, she sat back in the leather chair.

'Would you like a top-up darling?'

John could feel the intrusion of her long fingernails scratching the soft outer surface of his brain. A high-pitched shriek burst through both loudspeakers. John described it as the pitiful squeal of a pig after drenching it with hot pig scalder to remove its hairs.

'Is that when you forced her hands over the flame darling?'

He nodded suddenly everything went quiet.

Calm shattered into a thousand pieces of craziness from the explosion of his dramatic voice. 'Go to her, you who are cursed by misery, defenceless against the hardships of life and the indifference of men.'

Once again, another interruption from Carla. 'I know you have mentioned this before but where is that from?' Her query seemed to add more lunacy in his eyes.

John glared, raised his finger to his lips, and listened intently to his own voice. He remembered looking down at Rachel. Rage had brought an early closure to the project. The dirty whore was now bleeding to death. Through the speaker, a sound barely audible through the static, called to him from beyond the grave. John recognised it as the voice of horror, excruciating pain and suffering.

'Sam, Sam, if you have any feeling for me please kill me, I beg you.'

Why would he have any feeling at all for that bitch? He turned the knife inside her again. John could see, hear, and feel her last subjection to pain before he finally destroyed the object called Rachel. *Then the never-ending experience of fear faded from her eyes. Rachel never had the chance to walk through the maze of life. A soft courageous light, flickering, went out and then a million light bulbs lit up the universe. The self is never lost, the princess became a queen in the place called everlasting life.*

The ending always disappointed the woman with the stain on her soul. There was no shrill cry, only the crazy voice of someone living on a razor's edge reciting the sacrificial prayer. When they first played the tape, John tried to console her frustration by pointing out the stages in the prayer where he tightened the garrotte and then released it. As if subjected to flash photography, with her eyes shining like crazy, he handed Carla the crucifix he used to tighten the silk stocking. The design, a hammer and pincer on the crucifix, was identical to that worn by the Virgin Mary when she appeared before the children.

The next two pages in the album contained newspaper cuttings of Rachel's murder from every paper running the story. Notoriety appealed to John. Deliberately, he had made the police look a fool. He touched the revered funeral service at the bottom of the page. John and the rest of the pupils had played a prominent part in the service. The teacher had no hesitation in his choice of reading, Mark 10.13. When he came to the part, 'He was much displeased and said unto them suffer the little children to come unto me', he looked directly at Inspector Roberts. Yes, the second project had professional expertise and moralistic standards etched on every stage. He felt obliged to leave his calling card.

Within months of the closure, John started planning the next the 'Fatima Project'. Needing a new canvas to develop his skills, he decided to leave Cheltenham when the opportunity presented itself.

'Fatima' had now reached a significant milestone. With the fiftieth anniversary only weeks away, he had already groomed the pathetic slut called Susan. Again, he intended to introduce a subtle variation based on the Fatima apparition. Mary appeared before three children, Lucia Sabtos and her cousins, Jacinta and Franciso Mart. She confided in them the three secrets of Fatima. Lucia asked Mary if all three were going to heaven? She replied, 'Yes I shall take Francisco and Jacinta soon but you will remain a little while longer since Jesus wishes to make me known and loved on earth.' Both of them died from a flu epidemic the following year.

When they carried Jacinta's body into the ceremony at Lisbon Church, with the tower door locked and no one holding the ropes, the bells still rang out.

In 1935, exhumation of their bodies took place in Portugal. The skeleton frame of Francisco had decomposed to hair and bone. There were no physical signs of decay on Jacinta's body and a closer examination failed to reveal any red streaks along her veins. A sweet and pleasant aroma of sanctity emanated from Jacinta. The church proclaimed her a saint.

John looked at his note against Jacinta's date of birth, born 1910 to 1920. He revelled in the significance that she had not reached puberty. Like the Virgin Mary, Jacinta remained pure, incorruptible and without sin.

He was astounded when Rachel mentioned she had reached her breeding age. All those years of preparation and planning, he had every right to lose his temper and plunge the knife into her. Susan, on the other hand, will not have reached puberty. This time, on the fiftieth anniversary, there would be two sacrificial lambs delivered up in praise of the 'Lady of Fatima'. John intended to bury them like Jacinta and Francisco. When exhumed, the whole world would see the incorruptible innocence and redemption of Susan, free from original sin. The whole world would see that once again, yes, once again, they were wrong and he was right.

Harry Jones would take the part of Francisco. He carried a torch for Susan. They were inseparable, soon they would be inseparable in death. The last bullet point described the reverence in the climax. 'They kiss their first and last kiss (Photograph) destroy objects simultaneously, they can watch each other die, (Photographs).'

Moreover, like any masterful painter, the best of his artistry had yet to come into fruition, the 'Three Secrets Project.' In her appearance at La Salette, Mary told Melanie the third secret but she did not want it divulged at the time. However, in 1858 Mary gave her permission to make the secret known. Melanie wrote down the text of the secret and sent it by courier to Pope Pius IX. Never revealed, apparently the text was lost somewhere in the Vatican. That did not stop Melanie from revealing the third secret. From that point, she had the mark of stigmata in both her hands and wrists.

Carla glared at John. He was about to confront her when she had the audacity to interrupt him. 'Forgive me Samuel, but am I expected to simply sit here and do nothing while you and you alone fantasise about the past?'

'Would you like another sherry?'

'What I would like brother, is a little more consideration about my role.'

'Carla whilst your concern had a ring of truth about it in the past, you are heavily involved in the Fatima project.'

'Yes, but this is only because there are two objects to take care of. Otherwise once again, I would have been left out of the whole thing.'

There was a short fuse attached to John's dark side. 'If that is the case, why have I taken the time and trouble to read the research you carried out in respect of the Secrets Project?'

'Research yes darling, but you have never discussed or included me in the planning stage. Why for heaven's sake can't we do it now?'

As soon as the words 'heaven's sake' fell from her lips, Carla knew it was definitely the wrong choice of words. The unfortunate turn of phrase triggered a reaction. The white sclera of his eyes turned a grisaille grey. Black pupils at the centre of the amber pigment changed to a devil red. Carla could see her reflection in his eyes. An evil contemptuous sneer contorted his upper lip. Through the window of his eyes, she looked into his dark soul. Carla could see the demonic possession of Salpson, the son of Satan. Was there also a glimpse of the devil incarnate that fell from Attila's face when he drowned in his own blood on his wedding night?

Carla stumbled out an apology and waited for his reaction.

'Be careful Carla, or you will be lost forever. As for the project, there are issues I have to deal with.'

'Brother, please, I might as well go home to Father for all the use I am around here.'

If he wanted her involvement in the next project, John had to appease her in some way. 'Go and collect your notes on the Secrets Project.'

Running up the staircase, Carla retrieved her notes from the bedroom. She tried to conceal her excitement. He had finally agreed to discuss the project instead of treating her like his secretary.

'Would you like to start with the La Salette secret from the point where the Vatican conveniently lost Melanie's text?' John went into listening mode.

At last, Carla had centre stage. 'By all means, Melanie made her secret known despite strong disapproval by the Church. Not surprisingly, the content is a strong condemnation of Rome. Through Melanie, Mary predicted death, destruction, the coming of the Antichrist, even the end of the world. The wrath of God would consume humanity including the Catholic Church.'

John had to take control. 'Show me your research.'

Carla turned to the section in her file marked, 'First Element of the Secret'. 'This transcript adequately covers what Mary said. On the Catholic Church, she said quote, 'The priests, by their bad life by their irreverence's and their impiety have become cesspools of impurity.'

She continued her thesis. 'There is more condemnation; the Catholic Church is linked to the devil that is identified as the Antichrist. Mary said that the devil and the Catholic Church would be as one.

John was tired with his listening role. He tried to move things on. 'What about Fatima?'

Carla continued. 'Like La Salette the third secret of Fatima has caused controversy. Whilst we know the text from La Salette, the third secret she told to Lucia has remained just that, a secret. Those in the know say the secret is too frightening to reveal. Some say it's the same as the La Salette text.'

John glanced at the empty bottle of sherry and then at Carla. 'Have we another in reserve?'

'No darling, but I can get one in the morning.'

His superior knowledge now held centre stage. 'How many times do I have to tell you, failing to plan is planning to fail? The true artistry in planning is to include a fall-back solution. I suggest you do the same when it comes to your menial duties, particularly the simple task of ordering sherry.'

Tonight, was another example of her mood swings? How dare she challenge the extent of her part in anything? John made a note on his mythical pad. After the next project, he would dispense with the services of the object called Carla.

'How do you see it developing, Carla?'

'My immediate reaction is that it is going nowhere.'

A theatrical shake of his head introduced his interpretation. 'Then let me enlighten you about the text you were reading. Does it not also say that Mary asked true believers to fight in God's name against the evil of the church and mankind?'

Carla, somewhat taken aback, glanced down at her notes. 'I don't think I recall reading that.'

Boredom was starting to seethe into anger. 'Pass me your research.'

John plundered her notes. 'Here it is in your very own handwriting.'

He threw the notes in Carla's face. 'I will interpret it in a way that even you can understand. Quite simply, Mary is asking her followers to fight the evil within the church.'

'Yes, but I do not see how this particular...'

John jumped down her throat. 'Unfortunately this is the problem with you Carla. You fail to see the essence of the third secret or anything else for that matter.'

Suddenly the fear of dying crawled into her stomach and saliva stuck in her throat. For the first time Carla could smell the stench of death on her dress. She decided not to engage with her incensed brother.

'What is the matter Carla? Have you conveniently overlooked something? Let me remind you. In the first secret of Fatima revealed, it says that our lady showed the children a sea of fire. Plunged in the fire were demons and souls in human form, like transparent burning embers. When I asked you all you could say was that it was GOING NOWHERE. What is your reaction now? If you say nothing, I will treat it as a personal insult and an invitation to cause you serious pain. AND BY SERIOUS PAIN, I mean just that.'

Minute streaks of red washed over the grey and Carla gasped for breath. On the verge of a panic attack, she had to deliver.

A diffident unobtrusive tone rattled against her teeth. 'Samuel, I have neither the skills nor the ability to present the issues you have brought into the equation. Now that you have clarified my humble attempt, I can see potential in this project.' Carla gave herself time to think, her life depended on it. 'I think you may be taking this project to a level where multiple lives will be destroyed through fire.'

John lunged forward in the chair. His eyebrows almost touched his eyelids. 'Surely you mean the mass DESTRUCTION OF WORTHLESS OBJECTS who deface God by breaching the sanctity of his dwelling? Why I even tolerate your presence in this house is BEYOND ME.' The pitch and volume in his voice paused for dramatic effect.

Saved by the bell, the phone rang and John snatched the handset.

'Samuel, I'm afraid I've got bad news. DC Macleod is poking his nose where it's not wanted. He's all over the place. He visited Gloucester to dig up God knows what.'

Instead of the call and the unfortunate choice of words sending him into an uncontrollable rage, John remained detached, focused and totally in control. 'Go on.'

'Well he's been down to your school asking questions. He asked Father Graham about the Virgin Mary and Fatima.'

'Go on.'

'He's arrested West. When the DC kicked him out, they were the best of mates. I know you hate swearing but Macleod's a bastard, he is cooking something up with West, I'm sure of it.' Another dramatic pause. 'Look Samuel you're not going to like this but if you have anything that's going to incriminate you, get rid of it now. Destroy it ,don't hide it, he'll be knocking at your door any day soon.'

John remained undaunted. 'I think you may have jumped to conclusions. Why does this specifically, I repeat specifically, implicate me?' John could hear shallow breathing on the other end of the phone. 'Take your time. Perhaps it would be in everyone's interest, particularly yours, if you called on me now.'

The voice hesitated and cleared his throat. 'No I don't think that's necessary, the truth is he's been asking me questions about you. I thought it would blow over, but he's still at it.'

'Is there anything else you have conveniently overlooked?'

'No that's it. Except, well you know, I don't want to be dragged into whatever is going on.'

'All you have to do is tell me exactly what Macleod is up to. I am quite capable of taking care of him or anyone else for that matter. Thank you for phoning, I look forward to continuing our conversation.'

Carla could see the apprehension on her brother's face. 'Is something wrong darling?'

'You could say that. The police are making tentative enquiries about me. Unfortunately, we have no alternative other than to dispose of everything that has any association with the projects or other misdemeanours. The reason why we have to take such drastic action is that a visit from the police is imminent. Can I clarify one thing before we begin Carla? By dispose I mean destroy and by everything I mean just that.'

'What about your album darling? All that memorabilia from your projects. Surely you are not going to destroy the album are you?'

'Sad to say the answer is yes. But I can assure you my album is not the only thing I intend to destroy. I strongly suggest that the emergency services invest in body bags.'

She looked at the cold-blooded killer and recognised him for what he was. His dysfunctional upbringing had turned him into a dominant psychopath, a mental monster who killed lesser beings because he wanted to.

John only heard one voice in his head, his own. He considered himself fearless and unstoppable. In truth, he was really killing himself but, in essence, the victim died. In his opinion, he participated in the natural desire within us all. Only he had the courage to cross the line. It was all so senseless, his insanity made sense. Like everyone who thrives on riding the scream machine at the fair ground, John was a thrill seeker. His psychopathic brain functioned at a lower threshold of arousal. Only extreme brutality could give him the euphoria he craved for.

John contacted Gregory from a nearby telephone kiosk. West had been asking questions. The cheapskate also expressed an interest in buying photographs. Gregory seemed curious about his newfound wealth. The facts all led to one inevitable conclusion, he must have turned 'Queens Evidence'. His reaction characterised his anxiety to kill. West would be the next sacrificial lamb. He told Gregory to arrange a meeting at the traitor's gate under the pretext of delivering photographs.

Calmly, John opened a stand-alone cabinet safe in his bedroom and retrieved a file. He then joined Carla in the living room engrossed in throwing incriminating evidence onto the fire.

'Stop what you are doing and have the common courtesy to listen without INTERUPTION. This is a contingency plan. There are actions under your name in addition to the one you are already undertaking.' In order to emphasise the existence of the document, John placed it in the centre of the table. In silence, they looked at it for some time. What started as a smirk changed to a scowl as the teacher transferred his glare to Carla.

'What, pray, have you learnt tonight Carla?'

Life if anything is a gamble. The time had arrived to place her demise on black or red. She thought about the consequences of getting it wrong. The inquisitive rattle in her voice suggested the uncertainty in her choice. 'Failing to plan is planning to fail?'

'Eureka, at last the proverbial penny has dropped. Kindly remember that during your miserable existence, especially when it comes to purchasing sherry.'

# CHAPTER 21

## AN DA SHEALLACH
## THE TWO SIGHTS

Drowsy, half-asleep at the wheel, the driver turned the corner into Tudor Street. Peering through heavy-laden eyelids and drizzle, he could just make out a light flickering from the CID office. Walsh had a strategy. It included putting in overtime for the Queen or anything else to create a good impression. Moreover, leaving the sergeant to cope with all the workload had not exactly helped matters. Frank parked the CID car at the rear of the station and used the side entrance. Although in its infancy, their partnership showed signs of real promise. Their association had that distinctive mix where Walsh had the experience and expertise and Frank had Walsh. There were shades of Bogart and Bergman in Casablanca emerging in the partnership. Especially where Bergman turns to the hero and says, 'You must do the thinking for the both of us.'

Walsh bore a striking resemblance to Bogart. He certainly had the stature of the film star. Frank knew little about his illustrious partner except that his previous marriage to a childhood sweetheart had ended in an irretrievable breakdown in height.

The DS definitely had a 'Napoleon Complex', also known in the valley as 'small dog syndrome'. The detective acknowledged that he had the minor role of Watson in comparison to his arrogant, methodical Holmes. The DC entered the office, how was 'Sherlock' going to react to the news that he had a serial killer on his patch? Would he say, 'Elementary my dear Watson'? No and neither did Holmes. What about, 'Play it again Sam'? Again no and neither did Bogart.

The detective sergeant threw his pen on the desk and cracked his knuckles. 'At last the wanderer has returned. If you haven't got a good explanation I suggest you fuck off until I'm in a better mood.'

Frank ignored his irate remark. He decided to light that sarcastic fuse in his mouth. 'Sit down Sarge, sorry I didn't know you were sitting down. I've got something serious to tell you. There is a psycho on our patch. He's killed two schoolgirls and it looks as if he's going to kill again. Shit is going to hit the fan big time.' The contorting muscles in his face, dry mouth, and glazed eyes suggested he was serious.

'Look, calm down Frank, for Christ's sake.'

'There's something else I've got to tell you, this sounds crazy but ...'

A warm sensation lurking behind his right eye released a charge and exploded. Walsh jumped out of his seat and said something; Frank had no idea what it was. The pain, like a kick in the back of the head, triggered temporary blindness. Out of the dark, pictures flickered onto a canvas. He could see Sergeant Paine walking towards a building holding a flashlight. As he approached the steps leading to the entrance, the door burst open and a figure appeared carrying a double-barrelled shotgun. Without any warning, the occupant placed the butt to his shoulder, cocked the hammer, and fired both barrels at the officer. From that point, Frank could see a single mass of pellets travelling through the air in slow motion. The spread of the round lead slugs, ripping through his tunic, crushed his skin and penetrated his right leg. Paine fell to the ground. Without any sense of urgency, at normal speed, the gunman walked towards the victim and reloaded the shotgun.

Paine looked up at the assassin and waited for death to touch him on the shoulder. He knew the silent curtain was about to fall. The scene again reverted to slow motion. This time he discharged both barrels at close range. Hardened pellets moved slowly in a tightly knit mass. Reaching their destination, the pellets and explosive effect of the gas punched a sharp cavity hole straight through the top of his skull. Blackened fragments of brain and tissue lifted into the air and a stretch tear formed around his eyes. Gradually the image faded. With his eyes sensitive to the light, through blind spots the detective recognised Walsh standing in front of him.

'What the hell happened, did you have a fit or what?'

Frank fell back into his chair. 'Phone the desk and find out where Paine is.'

'I haven't got time to explain, Paine is in danger. Ask control to contact him. If he's on patrol tell them to get him back to the station pronto.'

Walsh picked up the phone and dialled control. 'He's gone to Gower Farm on the Monmouth Road. Control received a 999 call about ten minutes ago. They can't get hold of him.'

Frank staggered towards the door. 'I'll take Alfa 21, ask control to give me directions, call an ambulance and call out firearms.'

'I can't do that they'll want to know…'

'You can and you fucking will.'

Frank disappeared down the staircase. Alfa 21 screeched out of the car park narrowly missing a wall and turned right in the direction of Monmouth Road. His head buzzed like an electric light bulb. Trying to concentrate, the driver had forgotten to turn on the headlights. The incident when he was too late came alive again. The re-occurring nightmare of Brian plagued his sanity. Every ache signalled that another epileptic fit was imminent.

Gripping the steering wheel, he turned into the farm entrance. In the headlights, he could see a police van parked two hundred yards or so away from the building. The burly figure and familiar stride of Paine unhurriedly made his way towards the cottage. Frank put the siren and blue flashing lights on to attract his attention. The cottage door opened. Through the darkness, the silhouette of a man carrying a shotgun was visible against the light emanating from the open door. Both the victim and aggressor looked in the direction of the rapidly approaching car. Paine was the first to react, he half-turned in an attempt to escape. Panicking, he fired his shotgun from the hip and the officer fell to his knees. Closing, only two hundred yards away, the driver could see the gunman loading another cartridge into the chamber. The figure raised the shotgun to his shoulder and aimed at the car. With both hammers cocked, the detective drove straight at the gunman standing on the porch. The front of the car lifted, mounted the gantry and two blasts rang out. Spherical pellets, spreading, shattered the windscreen. The front of the car collided with the offender's legs, pinning them against the wall of the cottage. Before impact, Frank ducked under the dashboard and he hit his head on the steering column. Before losing consciousness, he managed to keep his foot firmly on the accelerator.

The detective opened his eyes as they lifted him from the car. He could see a pattern of lead buckshot embedded in the circular holes at the top of the driver's seat.

The 999 call had been a trap to lure anyone into the web of a crazed farmer who blamed the world for his own misfortune. Chronic aggressive pain, attacking his brain, had more sting than the minor injury sustained from the incident. Paine had pellets successfully removed from his left shoulder. He had every chance of making a recovery. Tears ran down the detective's face when he heard the good news.

Despite his injury, Paine phoned the detective before his body decided to go into meltdown for the next thirty-six hours. 'Listen lad, stop maken a habit of saven my life.'

'Fair enough, are you going to quit the sort of policeman ship that leaves us all bloody standing?'

'One more thin, how did yo know I wa in danger?'

'When I got back to the station I received a tip-off that some crazy was going to go berserk. We checked with control, they said you were on your way to deal with an incident. You must have been in a black spot, control couldn't contact you.'

'Yourr lyen to me aren't yo lad?'

'I'm afraid so sergeant.' An uneasy pause interrupted the exchange. 'Are you still there sergeant?'

'Yes, look somethen's been playen on my mind. I'd like yo to clear it up for me. I wa lyen on tha ground and I saw yo racen pass me headen toward him. I had a clear view, I saw tha front end of yourr car chargen up them steps. He pointed tha gun and fired both barrels. I could see tha flame from tha discharge and tha spiral grooves on tha shot travellen, spreaden like a mushroom through tha air towards yo in slow motion. I even ha time ta look at yo. I'm sure yo saw tha same thin because yo bent down under tha dashboard normal like to avoid being shot. When I looked again, tha pellets still travellen ata slow speed, hit and shattered tha windscreen. Before yo say anythen, don't attempt ta hoodwink me in sayen this wa because I must have had a bang on ma head.' Another lengthy pause.

Frank cleared his throat. 'I'm not going to lie to you again about what you saw, I saw the same thing. I'm not lying when I say that I haven't got a clue how it happened.'

Paine wished the DC a speedy recovery and ended the conversation. From that day, he never discussed the incident at Gower Farm with anyone.

★★★

How could he convince Walsh that he was not a psycho? On the way back from Gloucester, he had decided to tell all. In future, if he experienced anything unusual, Walsh would be the first to know. As a prelude to their conversation, he decided to write a letter to him. Frank closed his eyes. His body ached for the obscure world between reality and the subconscious where emotion and pain were beyond the spirit of his ancestors. At least, that is what he assumed.

# CHAPTER 22

## KING LEAR AND THE TRAITOR

Gregory picked up John and Carla at the bottom of their driveway. He was not even curious about the large cardboard box they had placed in the boot. Turning on the ignition, his next stop was the West abode. Carla's presence started to annoy him. *Why is that evil bitch tagging along? Looking like Cruella, she'll stick out like a sore thumb.* The two passengers were not the only ones organised. His trusty baseball bat was already in the boot. Gregory, hardly an emotive individual, glanced at Carla again in the rear view mirror. No, something else seemed to be bothering him. He soon realised the cause of that uneasy feeling. John, sitting in the front passenger seat, had the devil raging in his eyes.

Continuing the journey, a blunt constant pain of dread started gnawing at his spine. Someone, something, was glaring at him. He glanced to his left and saw the piercing reptilian eyes of his passenger. Gregory glared into the intense eyes of moral insanity and held contact until he realised that he was staring death in the face. Experiencing the presence of evil, hallucinating, irritating mites seemed to be alive on the pores of his skin. Even in the roots of his eyelashes. He gripped the steering wheel and the car mounted the pavement. The vehicle came to a halt outside the flat. Short of breath, with his testicles shrivelling, moving up into his body, he still gripped the steering wheel and looked straight ahead. That empty sick guttural feeling, paralytic, unable to move and helpless, were all part of his personal experience of fear. The horror brought on by the presence of John seemed to heighten his senses. Gregory could smell the distinctive sickening odour of death hanging on his breath. His brain decided it was time to dissolve in his veins.

John made a cutting remark about not having the courage to see things through. After unloading the cardboard box and baseball bat from the boot, he told Carla to drive Gregory home.

West could hear a hissing noise as he regained consciousness.

Curiously, it sounded like air escaping through his head. A sharp pain at the base of his skull exploded into his jaw and teeth. Slowly his brain started to function. He remembered opening the front door, but he had no recollection of John or the whack with a baseball bat. Blinking, he tried to sharpen the fuzzy images and floaters and they started to disappear. Now he seemed to be picking up strange objects in his living room. Inhaling fumes of ammonia from smelling salts, the oxygen cleared his brain. Distorted images came into focus. He was definitely standing in the middle of his living room. Yet he could not feel his feet touching the cold concrete floor. Almost on tiptoe in order to relieve the pressure stretching his neck, he looked up at the ceiling. A taut rope hanging from a beam tightened. West could feel the knot behind his right ear. This time the force applied to the rope tugged and jerked his head up. He was almost dangling from the rope. Something released the pressure to allow him to put his feet on a wooden chair. Both hands were behind and touching the back of his head. With his fingers locked together, he attempted to release his hands. Shooting pains ripping through his spinal cord, vibrated against the back of his skull.

'I would refrain from that if I were you. Both your hands are nailed to the back of your skull. Any movement could be your last.'

West looked at the grim figure securing the end of the rope to the locking mechanism of a pulley fixed to the floor.

John included scarfing and terminal sex as part of his deviant behaviour. From the age of eighteen, he carried out the dangerous practice of erotic asphyxiation. Hanging from a rope to heighten his erection, cutting off the oxygen, nearly had dire consequences when he had difficulty in releasing the pressure around his neck. From that moment, he used a mountaineering brake and ratchet pulley. A confident expressive voice articulated the rules of the game.

'If you have a preference of how you would like to die I suggest you enlighten me on the conversation you had with the police.'

Excruciating pain at the base of his skull was more unbearable when he tried to speak. 'Are you insane? Get me down from here.'

'I am only going to ask you one more time.'

'I said nothing to the police. Now I'm begging you, fucking cut me down.'

'It is too early to introduce begging into our little game. I will only listen to BEGGING when you fully appreciate the fact that you are going to die. That can only be encapsulated through pain and suffering.'

Anxiety showed in the victim's speech. 'I swear I'm telling the truth.'

Leisurely, John walked over to a cardboard box and he retrieved a Burdizzo steel clamping device used to castrate animals. 'West, you really are so predictable.' With a distinct swagger, he walked towards the victim and lifted the device by the long metal handles into the air. West realised he was naked. Insanity opened the device and placed the steel jaws of the clamp around his scrotum. He closed the jaws by releasing pressure on the spring handles until he could feel the skin in the clamp. Gradually, carefully, John released more pressure. The clamp tightened cutting off the blood supply to West's testicles. He held the handles steady to prevent the jaws severing the flesh around the scrotum. 'Excellent news comrade, it is my intention to make you my trusty slave. Are you familiar with the words trustworthy and dependable, I think not. Unfortunately, for you history relates that the most loyal slaves are eunuchs. Putting it so that even a simpleton like you can understand, mate, I am going to castrate you.'

Within minutes, a nauseating dull throbbing ache between his penis and anus turned into an aggressive pain. His testicles were shrinking, softening. Soon they would dissolve into his sperm bag. The eunuch could feel every fibre in every muscle tearing apart from the dire pain twisting in his body. West looked down from the chair. With one eyelid closed, a fainter image of the schoolteacher took on a ghostlike appearance. Then his other eye closed and he lost consciousness. John coughed up saliva. Holding it in his mouth, he forcefully aimed spittle at the Eunuch. The suffering all the endless suffering, and then West would tell all. Closing the handles, the clamp opened and released its grip from around his scrotum.

West regained consciousness and cursed under his breath. His wish to join the other world had not come to fruition. Time had no relevance, past or future, only an eternity of indefinite gratuitous pain. His time had almost run out. All he had left was the time to be very afraid, to shed blood, to tell all, and then it would be killing time. He opened one eye, through the blurry haze he could see a hypnotic glare.

'Nice of you to join me my castrato. As you can see, there again perhaps not, I have been extremely busy during your little siesta.' With a theatrical gesture, John pointed to an oak kitchen table covered with a polythene sheet in close proximity to the cooker. West gawped at the rosary, bible, and silver coins neatly placed in a line on the table. 'You must be anxious to know your fate. If you tell me what I want to know, things will go more favourably for you.'

The eloquent tone rasped against the victim's brain without entering his ears. West recognised the voice. It belonged to the master of hell. He hardly recognised his own whimpering voice. Biting the inside of his mouth, he forced out the words. 'Are you going to kill me?'

'My slave, my master of whispers, you are already dead.'

'For pity sake, that bastard forced me to set you up, he forced me.'

John was on the verge of losing control. He could feel a high from the strength in his muscles reacting to an adrenalin rush. Before long, he would become detached from reality, just an observer in a fast-moving drama, and not actually taking part. The last thing he wanted was to face months of dejection after the destruction of the object called West. Reality would never be as good as his fantasy. He had to move things on before misery brought about the helplessness of it all. This time the authority in his voice belonged to the one who had ordered the genocide of six million Jews. This time, the rage of non-compos mentis polluted the air.

'You have only confirmed what I know. Like all the sons of Simon, you have betrayed the trust I placed in you. And like the first son of Simon, Judas Iscariot who betrayed Christ, you have had the audacity to breach my confidence. In order to save your miserable skin you conspired with the police to harm me. Now it is your turn to experience the TRAGIC loss of your miserable life.'

The thought of the lonely intellect attempting to do him harm heightened his predatory instinct. Craving for the murderous act, it was now insatiable. In the dark recess of his twisted mind, John had to destroy the fool in order to save himself.

Madness and lunacy prompted him to think about his predicament. West, was he the fool or Edmond the traitor in this Shakespearian play? Obviously taking the part of King Lear, the sentiments expressed in Act three totally rationalised his tragedy. John sneered at the victim with an appealing, almost mischievous crazy expression. With the mad ranting of the 'Celtic King', a dramatic somewhat emotional voice delivered the famous quote. 'I am a man more sinned against than sinning.' The line, eloquently put, had little impact on West.

This time it was the voice of the devil on his back. 'Judas has already chosen your punishment in this world and your damnation in the next. He hung himself as a sign of divine punishment for all traitors.' Strutting to the sink, he placed a cloth under the tap and turned it on. Like a proud mother dealing with the white pasty substance on a new born, gently, caringly, he wiped the victim's face. The fresh cold water on the pores of the skin skated down his cheek. Moreover, like any Florence Nightingale, he dutifully placed a wet rag in the victim's mouth.

'It is important that you listen carefully to what I have to say. The way in which you are going to die will also be the eternal punishment you will experience in hell. Your pain and suffering will not end when you die. It will continue in the same manner beyond the grave because of your treachery. The parts of your body that will suffer are the same that you used to betray me. As you can see, hanging is a choice because you used your treacherous voice to betray me. Unfortunately, for you it does not end there. Matthew and the Act of the Apostles explain the full extent of Judas's death. *Recess it et abiens se suspendit*, he went away and hanged himself with a noose. The Apostles illustrate the full extent of Judas's agony. His body burst open, and his inner organs hang out. I hope you understand what this means, because shortly you will experience what it means.'

John glanced at his wristwatch. It was killing time.

West, paralysed, screamed inside and glared at the last human being he would ever see. The time had arrived for him to grieve for the loss of his life.

'Welcome to the road to hell. *Terra ubi umbra mortis et nullus ordo*, the land of gloom and chaos.'

John kicked the chair from under his feet. The noose gripped and tightened around his neck. Hanging suspended from the rope, West stretched out his legs. His feet were almost touching the floor. This was no hanging. The short drop would never break his neck. The rope, pressing hard against his jugular vein, cut off the oxygen to his brain. Within seconds, his face turned pale blue from air hunger. Instinctively, he tried to cheat John out of the pleasure of watching him die from a long painful strangulation. Struggling violently, he used the momentum of his body to swing and jerk against the rope in the hope of ending his agony. Faeces dropped from his anus. John released the rope on the pulley, and he fell to the floor.

In one movement, the monster, bending over, lifted and placed West on the table, facing the ceiling. He could feel the heat from the cooker against the right side of his face. At last, his hands had broken free from the nails pinning them to the back of his skull.

'No treachery will deny me of the death I have prepared for you.'

Something flickered in front of the victim's eye. He could hardly make it out. There it was again, a glint, a sparkle from the flame of the cooker reflecting on metal or glass. The object seemed to be in a hand. Moving his head, following the shape, it looked like a knife or was it a...

John examined the solid steel surgical scalpel. He touched the tip of the triangular blade with his forefinger. The point was razor sharp. Making a brutal, hurried stabbing incision, pausing for effect, John started cutting through the skin from the lower part of the abdomen to the anus to expose the intestines. West could feel the sharp-pointed blade slicing through the skin, muscles, fat, and nerve endings. Undeterred by the continual frantic screams, methodically John hacked away at the long tubular intestine attached to the inner wall of his stomach. Nerve tissues absorbing the pain and the loss of blood induced a state of shock and the victim's heartbeat went spiralling down. The organs in his body were dying.

Exhausted almost to the point of delirium, West tried to look way from the source of his pain. Petrified, his eye stayed transfixed on the surgeon picking up another object from the table. This time it looked like a large scissors with a blunt grip. Horror watched his master inserting the forceps into his stomach. Tweezers grabbed and locked onto his gut. John severed the intestine away from the cavity wall of the abdomen with a scalpel. He pulled on the forceps to remove it. The twisting muscular tube was longer than he expected. He had to resort to wrapping the sausage like tube around his forearm.

'*Suspentsus crepuit medius/et diffusa sunit omnia viscera eius,* hanged he burst open in the middle and all his viscera was spilled.' Holding the bowels above his head for West to see, he moved to the side of the table. '*Il tristo sacco che merda fa di quell che si trangugia,* this is the dire sack which makes the shit of what you swallow. This is the seat of your greed and betrayal. It is the beginning of your damnation in hell.' Still holding the large worm-like tube, droplets of slimy mucus fell from the surface of the wet circular folds and landed on his cheek. He touched the sticky moisture with his fingers and it smelt like salt. In a temper, he threw the intestines onto the ring of the cooker.

The crazy side of a psycho placed a rosary around West's neck and stopped to watch the bowels sizzling, hissing, and popping from the intestinal gases on the cooker.

'The rosary beads are olives from the garden of Gethsemane where Judas betrayed Jesus. They will remind you of your treachery when you walk through the gate of purgatory towards Dante's ninth circle. The beast Lucifer who represents all the dammed, will be waiting to punish you.'

With one eye still closed, West started to lapse into unconsciousness for the last time. Hurrying, no one was going to cheat John out of the finale. 'At the centre of hell you will hang suspended by your legs. Your head will enter one of the mouths of a three-headed monster. His strong teeth will gnaw your bones. Claws will rip your flesh for eternity. *Goxxiava 'l pianto e sanguinosa bava/ da ogne bocca dirompea co' denti/ un peccatore, a guise di maciulla/ sic he ne facea cosi dolente/ a quell dinanzi il morder era nulla,* he wept with all six eyes and the tears fell over his three chins mingled with bloody foam. The teeth of each mouth held a sinner, kept as by a flax rake, thus he held three of them in agony. Before you enter hell, let me pay you thirty pieces of silver for betraying me. Judas received this payment from the priest for betraying Jesus. I think it only fitting I pay you the same for betraying me.' Shocked, the word betrayal banged around inside and sent him into a rage. Using forceps, he picked up two red-hot coins from the hob. With panache, he dropped them into the cavity of his eyes.

'This will feed the greed of your soul through your eyes.'

Fraught, West was not going to cheat him from carrying out the final act. Hastily he dropped the rest of the coins into his mouth and stomach. Time and his life had finally run its course. Outraged at experiencing a brief moment of ecstasy, with the strength of a gorilla, he fractured and snapped off five ribs from the rib cage. Reaching into the cavity with two hands, he ripped out his heart. Sinking to his knees, sobbing uncontrollably, with the heart the size of a fist resting on his knees, emotional incontinence dragged him to a state of hysteria. There was no conscience, no remorse, only unbelievable ecstasy from playing God. From his emotional bag, anger, fear, and regret reared their ugly head. The fear of capture had nothing to do with his condition. It had everything to do with the trepidation of not tasting his perception of mortality again. With blood dripping from his hands onto the floor, John prayed for salvation through the rosary.

'O Virgin, holy and merciful obtain for all who offend the grace of repentance, and graciously accept this poor act of homage from me thy servant, obtaining likewise for me from thy divine son the pardon and remission of all my sins.' The angel of darkness answered his prayer. *'Congratulations on your three strikes. You are now officially a serial killer.'*

★★★

Exasperated, Walsh cradled his head and wished that he had never heard of the name Frank Macleod. The proverbial shit had hit the fan. West's sister reported finding his body in the flat during the early hours of the morning. Tess stepped into the ambulance shaking from a nervous breakdown. For some ridiculous reason she recalled how clean the flat looked. With horror, stabbing a knife straight into her heart, Tess held onto that very thought. It was the only thing resembling reality in the flat. At any moment, the pretend nightmare would end. Then she experienced a flashback, and found herself back in the flat. Using her own key, confronted by the slaughter, vigorously rubbing her eyes, she looked again. That horrible taste on her tongue, that rancid smell of something sizzling on the hob, filled her lungs. It looked like the entrails of a pig hanging in the local butchers shop. Again, that disgusting stench in the room, on her hair, clothes, even her skin, wrapped around her body like a shroud trying to smother her. The unmistakable feeling of going beyond crazy convinced Tess that she was inside a rubber body bag. With every breath, seemingly her last, somehow she knew the bag was open. She stared at the deep open wound exposing his muscles and bones. Her legs gave way to the unreality only an arm's length away. Half-conscious, she slipped back to the insanity of her make-believe reality. The zipper on the body bag started to close. Her eyes were wide open in the dark and the bag tightened. She could feel the rubber pressing hard against her face. Hallucinatory worms started to bore through her skin and eye sockets. Tess could feel all the parasites she could imagine under her scalp eating her brain. From that moment on, obsessed with her living death, self-mutilation, cutting and inflicting injury, seemed the only way to test if she was still alive. A year later, Tess listened carefully to what her reality had to say, and then she bled to death.

After securing the scene, Walsh called for assistance. Neighbouring forces had an agreement to assist each other with serious crime. Within hours of the request, a senior investigating officer, in the guise of Chief Superintendent Clive Jenkins, South Wales Police, and his team had arrived to take over the investigation. Walsh transported Jenkins and his deputy, Chief Inspector David Mears to the scene. With a touch of camaraderie, they told him to piss off back to the station. Jenkins queried if he was capable of answering the phone properly. After all, this crime was a job for real police officers.

The detective sergeant recognised the scrawl on the envelope lying on his desk. It belonged to Macleod. Opening it, the letter read:

*Hope you are mnainagg to cpoe wiuhott me, bcak bferoe you can say pychso. Auixons to takl abuot waht heneppad the oehtr ngiht in the ociffe and ofefr you an elaxpaontin. The trtuh of the matter is taht terhe isn't one. Stmomeies thgins appenh wuothit any lgaicol enlaptaxoin. How mnay teims in the psat six mnhtos hvae you had a gut feenilg or a kont in yuor samotch aoubt smhenotig taht is bnoyed yuor or my unrdtdseinnag. My iuiotitnn aoubt the fuutre is mroe depeovled tahn msot. At tihs meonmt, my itioniutn is tlilneg*

218

*me taht wtih the ancasstsie of Wets our keillr wlil be sitnitg aorscs the inrveeitw tblae and we wlil be in the dvriing saet. Smetomies terhe is no elxaoitnapn to waht hpeanps in yuor mnid, jsut lkie terhe is no eplnxioatan taht I can ofefr to why you hvae eilasy uetnosrdod the cntneot of tihs letter.*

Walsh remembered their conversation before the detective had experienced some sort of self-induced hypnotic trance. Frank mentioned there was a psychopath on the loose. He was also heavily involved with West. At any second, Jenkins and Mears would be asking difficult questions. Only the detective had the answers.

Eventually Frank answered the phone. 'Hello, could I speak to the well-known psycho called Frank who I am going to personally fuck when I get my hands on him.'

'Hang on a second. Frank will you come down from the ceiling one of the hobbits would like to have a word.'

Walsh nearly lost his temper. 'Glad to see you've still got that sarcastic edge. I only phoned to say congratulations on your second prediction.'

'What was that?'

'Remember before you went psycho you predicted that serious shit was going to hit the fan, well congrats because it has.'

'It can't be that bad.'

The frustration in Walsh's voice seethed from his mouth. 'Can't be that bad? At this moment, I'm sitting at my desk with an umbrella above my head because of all the shit falling down on me. You know your buddy West. Well he's really cut up about something, because we found his mutilated body in his flat. But I don't need to tell you about the gruesome details. You've seen it all in your crystal ball.'

'Only superintendents have got crystal balls sarge.'

'And speaking of superintendents, none other than Clive Jenkins from South Wales is trampling around middle earth giving everyone a bollocking. Amongst all the chaos, he told me to piss off. That's what he thinks of my investigative skills.'

'Sarge West was trying to get the evidence to hang John out to dry. The bastard must have found out what we were up to. Someone else is involved, Gregory, the shit lives on the Morse Estate.'

'I'll get Jenkins on it straight away.'

The prolonged ache in his muscles and sedatives to kill the pain

# CHAPTER 23

# MOSES AND THE
# COMMANDMENTS ON PATHOLOGY

Hanson glanced at the long thin features of his boss in the rear view mirror. The symptoms were unmistakable. Despite his blonde albino hair continually disappearing into a deluge of paperwork, the signs were there. His flush face and swelling around his mouth were a dead give-away. 'Atishoo', a burst of air carrying whatever had tickled his noise, splattered against the broad athletic shoulders of the driver.

'Fa Christ's sake, Gesundheit boss.' A strange sounding apology came from a passenger pinching the bridge of his nose. The aerosol shower had finally confirmed his suspicions. After twelve months, Hanson considered himself an expert. He had a three to one chance of guessing what triggered this one off. Could it be pollen, no, pets, maybe? No, it had to be food.

'Trouble with tha old allergy again boss?'

'Afraid so Jace, if I tell you I had French toast by mistake for breakfast this morning will you kindly allow me to get back to my work?'

'Sure, you're tha boss.'

Hanson homed in on the cause of the problem. It must have been the egg in the toast.

'One more thing boss, you're losing your American accent.'

'Thank you for the observation. The good news is that yours is still music to my ears. At this moment I would appreciate it if you would kindly turn down the volume.'

Originally, from Bridgend, his parents were both medical practitioners. It came as no surprise when Moses Black also took up the age-old profession. From the off, holding each other close in an attempt to stand up together, he and his twin sister Sally were inseparable. Sally had literally collided into her future husband at a legal exchange seminar. Married at the ripe old age of twenty-eight, she immigrated to California. Again, it came as no surprise when Moses decided to join them.

The years that followed were the most progressive in both careers. Sally had reached the position of assistant district attorney working out of Berkeley, Moses lectured in medicine at the University of California. At this point, he became interested in forensic criminology. Sally kindled that interest and involved him in several cases. The rest is history. In 1962, he played a fundamental role in opening the first School of Criminology at the University. Two years later, Black published the, *Journal of Forensic Science*. A year after that came his most prestigious critique, *Crime Investigation,* focusing on the physical evidence at crime scenes. His later dissertation on blood pattern analysis established standards of best practice throughout America.

In 1965, at thirty-five, Sally died in a car crash with her husband and six-year-old son. Black would never forget the moment when the police chief called him to give his farewell address. An uncanny silence held his hand as he walked towards the stage. The walls disintegrated into a thousand pieces from the rapturous applause from the crowd. Everyone in the auditorium wanted to show their gratitude to the person who had changed working practices. Black could only live in the country where his sister was buried. Only Wales would satisfy that need. Boarding the airplane with her coffin, he returned to the 'Land of my Fathers'.

America's loss was certainly the homeland gain. His reputation as a forensic pathologist had preceded him. The Royal College of Pathologists formed in 1962, offered him a consultancy. To improve service standards, Black subsequently wrote the codes of practice regarding the integrity of evidence found at a crime scene. He accepted the post on the understanding he could spend weekends at Bridgend to look after his sister's grave. He also volunteered his services as the on-call pathologist responsible for crime scene examination. It gave him the opportunity to gauge existing police practice at the sharp end.

The forensic pathologist glanced up from his paperwork as they passed the turn off to Westgate. Within half an hour, they would arrive at their destination. As usual, Hanson, driving above the speed limit, was indispensable.

Instinctively the American knew what he was looking for. 'They're in tha bottom of tha right-hand door compartment in tissue paper.'

Moreover, they were his tie and comb. 'How did you know I was going to forget my tie?'

'Da bears shit in tha park?'

They had little problem in finding the victim's flat, two police cars were parked outside. Optimism for the day ahead gained momentum when Black noticed the flat and road cordoned off. He introduced himself and handed his identity card issued by the medical council to the officer at the outer cordon.

Black invariably treated everyone with courtesy. 'Would you be kind enough to inform Chief Superintendent Jenkins that I would like to speak to him.'

'I'm sorry, but he's been called away with Chief Inspector Mears to another crime scene.'

'Who is inside the flat?'

'Two detectives.'

'Please ask them to join me immediately.'

The detective briefing, Black broke the news. Jenkins was about to return to the original crime scene.

'Thank you. Two points, no one is to enter the house unless I authorise it. Would you inform the superintendent that he is not to return here under any circumstances? Ask him to remain in his car and I will liaise with him at the end of the drive, sorry road in ten minutes.' After examining a logbook containing the details of everyone attending the homicide, Black established the extent of scene recognition and any provisional search that had already taken place. They moved back to the outer cordon.

Hanson clocked a black limousine pulling up at the far end of the street, and signalled to his boss. Parking on the opposite side of the road, Black approached the limousine. He could see the burley, dishevelled figure of Jenkins sitting in the rear passenger seat.

'Stay in your vehicle. I would prefer it if we had our conversation at a safe distance.'

The low harsh *Kaddiff* pitch of the next accent originated from Cardiff. 'You must be Black. What's this cloak and dagger stuff all about? I'm the bloody senior investigating officer in this murder. I give the orders around here.'

Black sneezed into his handkerchief. He noticed the combination of dandruff and fag ash on the officer's suit. 'As SIO, you should have been at the scene to brief me.'

'I was busy cleaning up this sorry mess. When you were tucked up in your bed, I dealt with the hanging of a local shit that killed West.'

The disappointment on the pathologist's face suggested wrongdoing. 'Are you saying there is a connection between the victim of a hanging and the initial homicide?'

'I've already said so, you can go back to bed, the things cleared up.'

'I hope for your sake you are right. Your management of both crime scenes is disappointing. Can I remind you, that everyone at crime scenes deposit trace evidence? When they leave, they take evidence away. Have you heard of cross-contamination, superintendent? That is exactly what you have achieved. Before I examine any scene I would like to know the circumstances of the case.'

'I've already said it's an open and shut case. Gregory killed West, and then topped himself.'

'Superintendent, as a pathologist, I deal with facts not assumptions. I examined the log at the scene. It should have contained the details of everyone attending the scene. Whilst I was pleased that DS Walsh identified, isolated, and secured the scene. When he left, there is a gap of two hours in the log before it starts again. Tell me superintendent, how can I take elimination fingerprints if I am not aware of who attended the scene?'

The worm called Jenkins wriggled off the hook. 'That's down to Mears, I can't do everything around here.'

'There are other issues but they can wait. Tell me about West and Gregory. Include all the key evidential issues, their respective deaths, association, primary and secondary factors. Furthermore, why you think both scenes are connected? What is the designated approach to the body?'

Jenkins's jaw, always on the lookout for a little extra cash, started to shine his shoes. In disbelief, he looked at Mears sitting next to him. Black had already started a comprehensive record. He added the briefing to his notes.

A detective had already taken photographs of the scene. No one had moved the body. With the absence of any forced entry, the pathologist concluded West or someone else had let the offender in. Did he know the caller, were the premises insecure? He changed into protective clothing. A surgical mask would stop him touching his mouth and nose. Showering the scene with robotic sneezing also had drawbacks. How many prints would he find belonging to police officers?

Extensive footprints at the agreed approach near the front door, begged the question. Why did the police use the same access as the one probably used by the offender? Forensically, a police band marching through the scene with hobnail boots would have caused less of a problem. He placed a covering sheet over the footprints. Hanson would carry out the examination. Standing at the entrance to the room, he surveyed the scene. From the description of the injuries, Black expected to see extensive projected and cast-off blood spatter on the walls and ceiling. A closer examination, a squirt of luminal spray, would reveal minute traces of blood. That would say a great deal about the movement of the offender before and after shedding blood. From the deluge of cigarette butts on the carpet, using a clinical 'Holmes' approach, he deduced that Woodbine had sponsored the band. He also acknowledged the charitable donation of spittle left by the trombone section.

The body was lying on the kitchen table. From his position, Black noted the passive blood spatter and drip patterns on the legs of the table and the floor. The patterns should be consistent with blood dripping from the table, victim, murder weapon or the assailant's hands. Using a flashlight, scanning the floor in front of him, he took photographs of his approach to the table. When he encountered possible trace particles, with patience and care, he gently dabbed them with tape. Standing adjacent to the table, at different angles, the pathologist clicked away with his 35mm Nikon to capture the proximity of the body to the furniture and cooker. Black provisionally daubed the naked body for any trace of fibre, hair, or bodily fluid. After photographing West, he examined and measured the open wound running from the abdomen to the rectum. A deep incision travelling from right to left, had cut through the cavity wall of the stomach. Visible cuts inside the gut also travelled in the same direction. From the location, extensibility, angle of the vertical incision, the offender appeared to be standing at the table near the victim's legs. Why did the offender(s) take that position in preference to the obvious, adjacent to the victim? The answer made his stomach churn. The offender, left handed, must have chosen that spot to see the full effect of the debauchery on the victim's face.

Shining a flashlight at the side of the body and then onto the floor, something had interfered with the blood flow from the point of origin. The extent of blood on the floor bore little resemblance to what he had expected. Razor-like patterns of blood where the body touched the table confirmed his suspicions. Black turned off his flashlight. Standing motionless near the table, he tried to take in the scene. Why did someone place a sheet under the body to prevent blood dripping onto the floor? It made no sense at all. Was this part of some amateur plan to impede or hinder his examination? Where was the sheet? Did the offender use it to scatter blood and other critical evidence in order to lay a false trail? Total lunacy. On reflection, did the offender deserve amateur status? If the deceit continued, at some stage the perpetrator would destroy or distort key evidence. The offender also seemed to be taunting, laughing, by playing silly games with the scene. An inverted V-shaped bruise around the victim's neck appeared to be clear of any straight line bruising caused from ligature strangulation. Even without a post mortem, in addition to the other injuries, he was dealing with a hanging.

He changed to his Polaroid Swinger. The instant camera was a birthday present from Sally. Black had devoted a chapter on ligature marks caused by strangulation or hanging. It stressed the shape, size, and pattern in the skin furrow left around the neck, would be identical to the pronounced weave of the rope that caused it. Before leaving Berkeley, detectives used Polaroid instant photographs as a search tool to trace the offending rope at crime scenes, and other investigative sites. Looking through the viewfinder, the word YES appeared in the window. He wondered if Hanson would ever say YES to him. Through the small pimples of his latex rubber gloves, he felt two puncture wounds and broken skin on a bump around the occipital bone at the base of the victim's skull.

Despite the skulduggery and incompetence, an accurate reconstruction of what had taken place started to emerge. Moving on, he labelled and jarred tape samples taken from the exposed areas around the wound, eyes and hands to find physical evidence. Running two combs through the victim's hair, and another through his pubic hair, he dropped them into separate secure bags. Black knew the significance of properly handling and packaging evidence. The pathologist covered the victim's hands with brown paper bags. Any further examination, including scraping underneath the fingernails and cutting the nails, could wait until post mortem.

Visually, the smooth surface of the table looked promising. Using a fine brush to distribute a small amount of white powder, brushing in the direction of the friction ridges, impressions started to form on the surface. Taking care, stacking the powder onto the ridges, three latent prints reached the clarity he required. After photographing them, Black lifted the prints from the surface using tape. Through a magnifying glass, the majority lacked definition. He dispensed with the brush. Gently he blew the powder across the surface onto the impression. Still lacking definition, with one last attempt, he poured the powder onto a mark. Blowing the excess away the mark confirmed his suspicions. The offender had worn gloves.

Dispensing with his rubber gloves in a paper bag, filling in the label, putting on a new pair, he approached the cooker.

'Atishoo, Atishoo'. Bursts of bacteria cannoned against the inside of the surgical mask. Latex gloves were all part of an allergy problem. This time Black would try something different. He dipped cotton into the powder and gently sprinkled the fine particles over the surface of the cooker. Oily sweat, deposited by the skin ridges on the top of the finger, started to form a pattern. There were at least two prints of sufficient definition to create interest and another twenty or so glove impressions. Was there a distinctive mark, cut, or unusual blemish on the fingers of the glove? Examining his options, a mark at the base of the cooker seemed to be the best of the worst. Changing to a darker powder to improve mark definition on the light surface, he positioned two hand lamps either side of the mark. Looking at the image through a camera, he adjusted the light to get a better angle of illumination.

The pathologist's methodical approach to collecting evidence had reached the 'what has been left behind or taken away stage'. Holding a brown bag in one hand, using forceps, he retrieved a coin from the lower abdomen. Through the handle, he could feel the tip of the forceps touching other objects. Any further exploratory examination could take place at the autopsy. Why would anyone cut out the intestines and then drop coins into the stomach? The beads, did they belong to the victim or the offender? Changing gloves yet again, he removed the rosary and placed it in a bag. The American accent of a tutor interfered with his train of thought. 'Don't forget to leave tha best until last, limey.' The 'best till last' culminated in the enviable task of placing a thermometer into the anus to measure deep body temperature. Black would have difficulty in assessing the time of death because of the open wound and other injuries to the genitalia. The degree and fixation of rigor mortis in the muscles at post mortem would provide a more accurate estimate. With the noticeable absence of discoloured green on the neck, shoulder, or abdomen, he was confident that death had occurred within the last thirty-six hours. The stomach content, taking time to digest, would also provide a more accurate timescale.

Fading light slipped behind the clouds and gave way to the magical 'Blue Hour' in the sky. He placed a bag over the victim's head. Any further examination or search could wait. After supervising the undertaker, he updated his notes in the police mobile trailer. The pathologist deliberated about the type of offender capable of subjecting another human being to such atrocities. He also thought about the significance of a new fingerprint database and the crime scene templates he intended to introduce.

Hanson was already on his way to take him back to the hotel. After a shower, scrub up, complete change of clothing, shoes and new protective kit, Black would go through it all again. This time he also had the additional criterion of finding common features relating to both crime scenes. Closing his eyelids, he could still see random dust particles seemingly responding to a signal from the gods. Drifting away between wakefulness and sleep, Morpheus closed his weary eyes. Muscles, sporadically twitching in his leg, brought back that sinking feeling of how much he missed Sally. Her affectionate smile always seemed to push up through her high cheeks into her mysterious crinkly eyes. Black desperately longed to hear her 'hot chocolate' voice again. Did life have any meaning without his sister?

*Sally looked out from the light of the other world into the window of his* heart. *My brother, death lasted just for a moment. I know how much you love me but please do not grieve any more, there is no need, my soul is home. My physicality has changed, but we are still the same brother and sister. It is true, love transcends all boundaries including death. It does not recognise the difference in worlds, that is why it is called undying love. There was a long pause. Excuse me, but are you saying my voice sounds 'THICK AND HEAVY' like European hot chocolate?*

*No, on the contrary my impetuous sister, I was thinking of the States, sweet, much thinner version with marshmallows and whipped cream.*

# CHAPTER 24

# WHY IS A RAVEN LIKE A WALKING STICK?

Taking another two painkillers, at last the latent pain in his muscles started to subside. Could he unravel the vague one-liner posed by Walsh before he slammed down the phone? What the hell was he driving at when he said, 'Get your arse in this office now or I'll come and drag you out of bed?' He poured another cup of coffee, why did Walsh talk in riddles. The crowd in the station foyer, charging around in all directions, reminded the detective of Cardiff Railway Station on international day. As the DC entered the office, a pale weary Walsh managed to raise his head.

They were engaged in their usual sarcastic banter when the burly tall figure of Chief Superintendent Jenkins barged into the office. His gravelly sarcastic voice rebounded off the smooth surface of the desk. 'You must be the low life Macleod, the so called hero of this tin pot police force.'

Frank glared at the new arrival. 'Who are you?'

'I'm your worst fucking nightmare, that's who I am lad.'

'Sorry, wankers full of their own fucking importance don't scare me at all.'

Jenkins dusted the ash off his lapels. 'One more remark like that and you'll be suspended, that should tell you who I am. I'm fed up to the back teeth of hearing your name, Macleod. Graham, that moron Roberts, *The Police Gazette*, even my assistant chief constable, all I hear is you're name.'

The detective clenched his fist, he was about to go on the offensive then Walsh intervened. 'Sir, can I remind you DC Macleod was the one who put Gregory's name forward in the first place.'

'And can I remind you, as SIO, I'm the one responsible for bringing this enquiry to an end. If it wasn't for me you lot would still be running around like headless chickens.'

Walsh glanced at his partner. 'The superintendent found

Gregory hanging at his home. He thinks Gregory is responsible for killing West.'

Jenkins was in his usual belligerent mood. 'Walsh, for pity sake, call yourself a sergeant, brief your staff properly. I DON'T think Gregory killed West, I KNOW he did. Listen and listen carefully, I don't want you lot interfering in my enquiries. I won't have amateurs dabbling in my investigation. As I told that useless apology for a pathologist, apart from dotting the i's and crossing the t's it's a done deal.'

The detective, pissed off with 'beer breath', glared out of the window and waved *au revoir* to bullshit.

'I don't know if you're aware of it superintendent, but there isn't a letter i or t in the phrase 'load of bollocks'. I'm telling you now you've got the wrong guy.'

'Macleod, know your place, if I want your advice, I'll ask for it.'

'Whether you want it or not, I'm telling you Samuel John killed West. He's also killed Gregory and two schoolgirls.'

'Who the hell is John?'

Walsh winced and looked around for the transporter beam. He knew what was coming next.

Frank seized the opportunity. 'Glad you asked, John is the son of your assistant chief constable.'

Jenkins's cue to burst out laughing, potted an excellent black in the middle pocket, 'Macleod they told me that you're as mad as a 'March Hare', you've just confirmed it.'

It was time for Jenkins to face the truth. 'If you had looked into Alice Worrell's case properly, we wouldn't be in this bloody mess.'

'What are you on about, until you start talking sense, stay on the sick?'

Frank was about to hit a home run. 'Alice Worrell is the young girl John terrorised in the park. You covered up for him didn't you?'

'Be careful Macleod or I'll put you on a charge.'

'Message understood. I'm not going to say another word.'

The detective retrieved the Worrell file from his tray and placed it on the desk in front of Jenkins. The senior officer recognised his handwriting on the file.

'I haven't got time to listen to this crap, you two, twelve thirty in the gymnasium. If you don't believe me, hear it from Dumbo the pathologist.' Jenkins ambled towards the office door. He was

231

somewhat surprised when the courteous detective opened the door.

'Sorry we got off on the wrong foot sir. Would you like me to make an entry in the lost property register?'

'Lost property, what for?'

'It looks as if you've lost your fucking credibility and your crystal balls. Good morning.' Frank slammed the office door.

The investigative team occupied most of the seats in the gymnasium. The new arrivals could feel the buzz of a job well done circulating around the room. Leadership takes on many facets, Jenkins believed in leading from the front. That included every public house, but not the post mortem. That task had the name Mears written all over it. Black sat at the table on a raised platform, Jenkins and Mears were either side. The SIO looked around and banged the table. 'Right, settle down you lot, I know you're anxious to get out of this hellhole.'

Sporadic sound bites rang out from the team.

The SIO continued. 'I said quiet, any more noise and the person responsible will be transferred to, what do you call yourself now, the 'Gwent Police Farce'? The pathologist at both scenes is here to update you. A small team will stay to finish off. The rest can piss off to Cardiff and carry on with the celebrations.' He sat down to a round of applause.

Black studied his notes. The day had started in typical Black fashion, he had left his notes back at the hotel. Again, his chauffeur came to the rescue. Moreover, in the station, his glasses spring-boarded from his pocket and he accidentally stepped on them. Hanson used a plaster from the first aid-kit to hold the broken plastic frame together. With his glasses delicately balancing on his nose, he smiled at the sea of faces sitting in the front row. Hanson waited for the inevitable. He was not disappointed. The spectacles parachuted onto the table. Hanson repaired the frame with a plaster. At the same time, he introduced the SIO to an intimidating glare.

Standing, a subtle professional voice addressed the audience.

'Good afternoon, can I say what a privilege it is for me to be visiting this part of Wales. I assume you have read my report regarding the unfortunate death of West.'

An early interruption from Jenkins. 'I thought you told me you only deal with facts, not assumptions.' Jenkins gave an excellent impression of the 'Cheshire cat' in *Alice in Wonderland*.

Black undaunted, continued. 'Quite, however there are a number of aspects I would like to emphasise. The rope, and weapon used to cause the injuries together with the victims clothing has not been found. This should tell you a great deal about the offender's intent. Even with my experience, I was surprised at the predatory aggression used. This is the most dominant feature of the crime scene. The extent of violence used should provide an insight into the character of the offender. The assailant is an extremely confident individual with primary egotistic traits of self-preoccupation, and self-admiration. And yet this is balanced with excellent organisational skills. The predator is a psychopath who has no moral issues about inflicting unbelievable suffering. He does not see the world as you and I see it and considers himself far superior to mere mortals. I say this in order to re-enforce the category of offender capable of this heinous crime. He fulfils his fantasy by torturing the victim to death.

The pathologist homed in on critical aspects of the scene. 'I would also like to draw your attention to what was left at the scene. Namely, the thirty-shilling coins found in his stomach and eye cavity together with a rosary around the victim's neck. His psychotic behaviour left the offender with no alternative other than to leave, what he considers to be his calling card. The reason for this is twofold. Firstly, the offender is taunting you. It is his way of saying he is far too intelligent to be caught. Secondly, the coins, rosary and the way in which he killed West, have a huge significance in this homicide.'

Jenkins listened intently and started to feel edgy. Why bother with a profile when he had already found the killer dangling from the end of a rope?

Frank caught the lecturer's eye. 'The religious part of the rosary could tie in with the thirty pieces of silver that Judas had from a priest for betraying Jesus?'

'Thank you. This is exactly the reasoning that will move the investigation forward.' Jenkins's impression of a Cheshire cat must be contagious.

'I would, if I may, like to move onto the crime scene of Gregory. Conclusive evidence shows both crime scenes are connected. Gregory was found in his dwelling suspended from a banister with a rope tied around his neck, and an upright kitchen chair in close proximity to his feet. Hanging is the third most commonly used method to commit suicide. The unfortunate victim generally uses a chair or ladder and slowly chokes to death. This appears to be the case in respect of Mr Gregory.' A self-righteous smirk broke across the SIO face. At last, his moment of triumph.

'Homicidal hanging is a rare breed of animal and seldom occurs. If someone used this method by pushing someone off a chair, even the British police would have a difficult task in proving anything else other than suicide.'

'Gregory was fully clothed and wearing shoes. He had a blood transfer on the left side of his jumper, inches below his neck. A transfer occurs when someone wipes their bloody hands on their clothing. Gregory had blood on his right hand. Blood classification AB+ on the jumper is a rare group type, and matches that of the victim, West.' The SIO was not the only one smoking a suspicious substance from a hookah water pipe. Jubilation amongst the team reached a high and they chanted, 'For he's a jolly good fellow.'

Jenkins standing showed his authority. 'Let the man finish, will you, or we'll be here all day.' Silence reigned supreme.

'Thank you superintendent, the rope used in the Gregory hanging has no uncommon feature. It is made of hemp with three strands twisted or braided together. A slipknot was used in preference to the more common fixed knot used in a suicide. This kind of knot is extremely efficient at compressing the airways and blood vessels in the neck because the noose tightens quickly under the weight of the body. Rope identical to the fibre used in the hanging was found in the victim's garden shed. Bruising around the neck, under the chin and directly behind the ear was clearly evident. This bruising or rope burn formed an inverted V pointing away from gravity. The shape and the location described are totally consistent with hanging. The vertical mark did not go around the entire circumference of the neck. When the noose meets the vertical part of the rope, the suspended weight of the body pulls the rope away from the neck and does not leave a mark. I would like to emphasise this point; there was no mark at the back of his neck.'

The S.I.O drummed the table with his fingers. He started to feel decidedly uncomfortable.

Black homed in on the post mortem. 'A further examination of the neck in the presence of Chief Inspector Mears revealed further bruising and a furrow mark entirely separate from the V-shaped mark. This ligature mark was below the thyroid cartilage, commonly known as the Adam's apple.'

Hanson passed around photographs showing the marks on the neck.

'For those of you looking at a photograph of the bruising below the Adams Apple, you can see that the mark consists of a straight line extending horizontally to the back of the neck. Photograph two shows that this mark does not extend around the entire circumference of the neck. There is no mark on the back of the neck. The fibre pattern of the rope visible in this new mark is NOT identical to the weave rope used in the hanging.'

Bad vibes from the horizontal mark switched on alarm bells in the SIO's head. Clearing his throat, standing, leaning forward, Jenkins placed both hands on the table and eyeballed the pathologist.

'Black, all this clever stuff may be well and good, but my team is used to plain speaking. Let me interpret what you said so that criminal catchers and not you so-called academics can understand. The marks on Gregory's neck were caused by hanging. V- shape, straight lines, are all very well, but it all boils down to the same thing. The bastard committed suicide.' Jenkins waited for a reply and glared at his adversary. He used the silence to be offensive, threatening, to mean danger but most of all hatred for the clever bastard standing next to him. Black waited to take his turn, quietly turning a page, he politely signalled to the officer to sit down. To the uncouth, the bully, that response signalled victory. His backside had almost touched the seat when Black continued.

'As I was about to say, unfortunately this is not the case. The horizontal line of bruising below the Adams Apple is critical to your investigation. It is consistent with another rope drawn once around the neck and pulled tight until he lost consciousness. The break in the horizontal ligature at the back of the neck shows the position of the assailant's hands. The offender, standing behind Gregory, tied the rope around his neck and used enormous strength to tighten it. The victim lost consciousness in ten to fifteen seconds. Still alive, but unconscious, the offender lifted Gregory up onto the chair. He placed his neck in the noose, took the chair away and he hung suspended from the banister. I hope this clarifies the situation for you, superintendent?'

Black glanced down. Holding the frame of the glasses with his finger, he waited for the impact to take effect. He did not have to wait long. *Off with his fucking head.*

An infuriated Jenkins again went on the offensive. 'Isn't this a lot of guesswork on your part? I live in the real world of investigation. Two can play at your game. Gregory could have attempted to strangle himself with a piece of rope. When he failed, he climbed on the chair and topped himself.'

'Let me answer your query. A victim of strangulation goes through three stages, severe pain, unconsciousness, and death. It is impossible for someone to commit suicide using self-induced force by placing a ligature around the neck and tightening it. Remember, in the case of Gregory, the ligature was tightened from behind. If he was going to use this extreme method to kill himself, I suggest he would have done so by using a method that left a mark around the entire circumference of the neck. Gregory would have crossed over the ends of the rope around his neck at the front, and applied force by pulling both ends of the ligature away from his neck. Only eleven pounds of pressure is required for ten seconds to the carotid arteries for the victim to lose consciousness. In your scenario, the self-induced pressure would have been released when he lost consciousness. Within thirty seconds, his alertness and response would have returned to normal. To cause life-threatening harm by strangulation, at least three times that pressure must be applied to the windpipe. This is exactly what Gregory was subjected to. Brain death will then occur in about five minutes if strangulation continues. Internal injuries confirm extreme force to his neck using the horizontal ligature. The hyoid bone in the neck, shaped like a horseshoe, that supports the base of the tongue, had fractured. This injury does not occur in suicide by hanging. Neither does excessive bleeding, damage to the voice box or fracture to the thyroid cartilage, all found during post mortem. Mass haemorrhaging in the form of a blood clot and swelling in the brain were evident. These injuries show that Gregory was unconscious at the start of his hanging. Skin bleeding, found in the ligature mark, supports the fact he was unconscious but still alive. Superintendent, in answer to the question you pose, how could Gregory have climbed onto the chair in his unconscious state?'

Pausing, Hanson handed Black a glass of water. 'In my opinion, based on the evidence, you are dealing with a murder cleverly masquerading as a suicide. One ligature mark below the Adam's apple suggests that the assailant did not have to adjust or alter his grip. That, together with the absence of facial injuries or scratch marks on the victim's hands, speaks volumes of the strength used by the offender.'

Hanson handed him a note. 'Sincere apologies, it appears during my presentation I may have used the grammatical masculine word, 'He' when referring to the suspect or offender. Whilst there is strong evidence to suggest that this is the case, it was remiss of me to do so, thank you Hanson. The time of death is between 1.00 a.m. and 4.00 a.m. This is approximately two hours after the estimated time of death of West. The cause of death was cerebral ischemia, and asphyxiation.'

'One or two points and I will leave you in the capable hands of the superintendent. The rope used to strangle Gregory has not been found. I will leave you with a Polaroid photograph of the fibre pattern and weave in the ligature rope you should be looking for. The post mortem on West revealed that the offender is left handed. Nicotine stains on Gregory's fingers, the toughened areas of skin on his hand, suggest he is right handed. The weapon used on West has a fine sharp edge, probably a surgical knife.'

The SIO could not contain himself any longer. He spoke in a whisper. 'Anyone thinking about going home had better think again. Why is everything down to me? You lot go around with your eyes shut. Mears, sort out their work. I'll sort the lot of you out if you don't come up with a lock-up in the next forty-eight hours.'

Hanson looked in the direction of his boss and mimicked a silent round of applause. *If he only knew about the way I fantasise about him, he would be waving goodbye.*

'Would you like me to go through my findings regarding the examination of Gregory's shoes and the passive drip patterns at the crime scene of West?'

'Put it in your damn report, I've got a killer to catch. Walsh and you, whatever your name is, I want a little word in your ear.' He stormed out of the gymnasium.

'Well gentlemen, I wish you the best of luck. If I am unable to attend the funeral would you be kind enough to pass on my condolences to the family.'

Hanson leaned over and whispered in his ear. 'Of course, my colleague has quite rightly pointed out. At some stage I will meet them at the inquest.'

Mears stood up with his head bowed. 'On behalf of the team, thank you, it's appreciated.'

★★★

There were too many questions banging around in his head. Lying on his bed, the pathologist stared out of the hotel window into the darkness. What had he missed, there is always something. He intended to discuss the case with his mentor Rick Land in Berkeley.

*Ever the 'Gentiluomo' my gentle brother. Your kindly way, not raising your voice or losing your temper. But most of all you respect the prejudice in man even though his name happens to be Jenkins. Do you remember the plaque on the wall above your bed that read, 'A gentlemen is someone who never hurts anyone unintentionally? Well that reminds me of your newfound colleague. By the way, who was responsible for the quote?*

*You know who it was, sister, it was Oscar Wilde.*

*Or,on the other hand, to give the intellectual his full title, Oscar Fingal O'Flahertie Wills Wilde. My, you have so much in common with the great man don't you.*

*Sally, how did you arrive at that conclusion?*

*Because I know everything there is to know about you. Whatever your sexual preference, it makes no difference at all in the light beyond, why should it in your world. By the way, don't you think Hanson looks a bit like Dorian Gray? The one thing I am certain about is that you are one gentleman who will never end up with a lady.*

*Thank you for coming back, bless your soul.*

*Remind me Moses to talk to you about the 'bless your soul' comment. You see, things are not what you expect them to be when you go into the light. In any case, I should be thanking you, I am so proud of you. There is no Dorian Gray trait in you, always be true to who you are. Although on that score, I think you may need a little help along the way.*

Black closed his eyes, he drifted off to the land of illusory dreams. Nothing could hurt him again. His world had changed with his sister back in his life.

# CHAPTER 25

# THE INNOCENCE OF MATA HARI

Jenkins continued *to* ride roughshod over the investigation. Yet again, he had failed to recognise the importance of strategic leadership. He excluded local officers from the inquiry. Consequently, the absence of crucial local experience had a dramatic effect, *vis-à-vis,* key evidence. Mears, at his self-indulgent best, issued instructions to his team to piss all over the local community. Between them, they had succeeded in re-writing the *Homicide Investigation Manual.* Profit, the assistant chief constable operations, had already homed in on the investigative skills of Jenkins. Eloquently, he summed up the SIO on his last appraisal when he wrote, 'Missed opportunities were evident. The appraisee failed to recognise or appreciate the significance of gathering key information during the early part of an investigation.' The hardnosed transferee from the Met pointed out that failing to follow basic guidelines, would impede any investigation.

*Why am I thinking about that bastard?* Sitting on the toilet seat, Jenkins leaned forward and locked the door to shut out the memory of his favourite peeler. Rank puddles of sweat under his armpits splashed through his shirt. It had nothing to do with alcohol. Some local numskull must have turned up the central heating. Even the soles of his feet were wet. He hardly noticed the pungent whiff of fungous wafting up his flaring nostrils. The wisdom of Profit, this time disguised as the onion bargee he was thinking about, slipped under his radar. With considerable pain, he recalled the ACC's golden rule on investigation. 'Never give the offender an opportunity to dispose of incriminating evidence or impede your investigation.' *What a clever bastard he is. He doesn't know his prick from his thumb except there's a nail on the one.* Haemorrhoids, particularly transferees, played hell with his bowels. A nice greasy bacon sandwich with brown sauce would put that right. He looked around for the toilet roll. Some bastard had stolen it, another undetected crime. His trousers trailed around his ankles as he waddled to the next cubicle in search of the elusive toilet roll. *The thieving bastards.* As loose bowel movement dripped onto the smooth polished surface, Jenkins wondered if there was a 'G' in resign.

★★★

John on the other hand was off to a flying start. Strategic planning had given him the edge he needed. The extent of evidence from the botched investigation seemed virtually non-existent. He intended to keep it that way. Although he had not expected Black to turn up, the local police would still take an age before they realised that they were dealing with a fake suicide. John intended to utilise that time to tie up any loose ends. He had already briefed Carla, if at some stage they had to account for their movements. Probably out of sheer desperation more than anything else, he expected the police to knock on his door. What evidence could they put to him? Very little, he looked forward to the confrontation. A contemptuous sneer summed up his attitude towards the bungling police. It turned into a smidgen of a cracked smile. Absolutely, without a shadow of a doubt, Carla would have made an excellent police officer.

★★★

The investigation had reached desperation point. Jenkins reluctantly agreed to use the two local traffic wardens, Walsh and Macleod. Their brief, put pressure on the local informants, log the information, and forward it to Mears.

Frank witnessed a mouth-watering experience when he entered the CID office. A voluptuous female, standing near his desk, was in the process of lifting her long shapely leg onto the seat of his chair. Smoothing the front of her black nylon stocking, tracing the seam, she seemed oblivious of the man standing in the doorway. Tantalising the spectator, she leaned forward. Long rich-auburn hair tumbled around her sculpted face. Her leg was exposed way above the knee. Both hands were busy under her black skirt near the apex of her thighs straightening the seam. From his vantage point, Frank could see heavy taunting breasts pushing against the buttons on her

240

police shirt. Gravity pulled on the forbidden fruit. The shape of two perky russet pebbles appeared through her cotton shirt. The odour of carnal craving tingled and danced on her skin. He recognised the distinct oriental smell of perfume playing sex with his nostrils. The new arrival had that compelling sense of familiarity about her. Definitely not their first encounter, for some inexplicable reason he tried to remember her name. It was nearly on the tip of his tongue. She definitely spoke with a West Wales 'sing along' accent.

Motionless, standing in the doorway, he was still mesmerised by the shape of her breasts. She suddenly realised that someone was watching and her elegant frame turned to face him. It should have registered with the observer, apparently not. His eyes still followed the black straps from the cup of the bra to her shoulder. Glancing yet again, her cleavage suggested they were firm, close together, and, hat trick, naturally lifted. Frank read the label on her bra it said, 'sexually frustrated'.

She confronted the gawker. 'Do you always stare at a woman's breasts like that?'

'Sorry, I gave blood this morning, there's not enough to go round. My penis is using it instead of my brain. Have we met somewhere before?'

The notorious middle finger gesture accompanied by a teapot stance gave the misconstrued chat-up line the accolade it deserved. 'You can do better than that love. How do you know we've met before, you haven't bothered to look at my face?'

He dragged his eyes away from her cleavage. Not disappointed, pallid skin gave way to a Cafe-au-lait birthmark high on her right cheekbone below firework-green eyes.

Then that irresistible smouldering gaze took centre stage. Closing his eyes, blinking, opening them, his lungs pushed hard against his rib cage and took his breath away. There was more than a hint of movement in his groin. The fixation of gawking had now transferred to her deliberate study of his groin. Both the rhythm and intonation in her Llanelli accent caught him off guard, still looking at...

'Well love, your chat-up line is crap. Anyway thanks babes for that uplifting experience in your trousers.'

'You know what they say, a hard man is good to find.'

Frank did not attempt to hide his physical turn on. She made no attempt to ignore it. Wallowing in the imminent anticipation of sex, flirting with their eyes, she knew exactly what he was thinking.

The lecherous tone in her voice kissed his groin. 'Now that I've got your attention instead of my boobs, I'd better introduce myself. I'm Junia Browne. Jenkins wants me to act as liaison officer with the local CID.'

A broad roguish grin introduced a poor attempt to redeem lost ground. 'That's strange, I thought we had the same surname?'

'Unless your name is Browne love, you're heading for another finger sign.'

Was that a judgemental tone in her voice? 'It's not Browne, it's Macleod.'

Junia decided to join in with his drivel. 'Go on, I'll buy your pick up line, but only if you promise me that it's long and sticky?'

'Can I carry on, or are you going to totally PISS ON what I was going to say?' His frustrated pitch attempted to push her into listener mode.

Her eyes reflected a 'boys will be boys' attitude. An ill-advised tantrum, shouted at 'frustration' to piss off. 'Bloody hell, what's the point now.'

A mischievous Llanelli accent pulled on the hook in his mouth. 'Carry on babes. I was going to take my bra off to adjust my strap in front of you, but I'll listen to your intellectual conversation instead.'

Doggedness popped its head around the door to rescue the DC. 'Right, Mata Hari was a spy. Her real name was Margareta Macleod.'

Junia seemed undecided if his so-called chat-up line or the last appalling attempt had pissed her off the most. 'For God's sake love, get the blood circulating back to your brain, you're talking in riddles. HANG ON, so you think I'm a spy do you?'

Franks next lunge also missed the target. 'I hope so, she was also an erotic dancer.'

Senseless banter fizzled out like a damp squib. They looked into each other's eyes and wanted the same thing. It had nothing to do with small talk, romance, self-esteem, emotion, or conquest. It had everything to do with the physical need to experience a good old-fashioned shag. A compelling force to satisfy that need, gaining momentum, was now unstoppable.

The anticipation of reciprocating lust pulled into the shunting yard when Walsh walked into the office. 'Morning, hope you have introduced yourselves. Has Junia told you why she is joining us?'

'Yes Sarge, she's kept me fully abreast of why she's here.'

'Right, give Junia a quick tour of the station and then we'll discuss what the SIO wants us to do.'

Hurriedly, they tumbled down the staircase towards the custody area. Frank prayed that the cells were empty. An email from God confirmed his booking. As they entered the cellblock, his heart paused to check his pulse. He pushed the cell door. Their eyes smiled at the single steel bunk anchored to the floor on the wall in front of them. Grabbing hold of Junia by the arm, he pulled her towards him, but Junia took the initiative. Taste buds on her tongue flicked his lower lip before entering his mouth. Almost at the stage of implosion, frantically, he undid the buttons on her shirt. The top button popped and bounced off the concrete floor.

*For fuck's sake what am I playing at, it's push and then pull!*

Vigorously, he again tugged on a fastener and her bra finally surrendered. The sight of heart throbbing bare breasts grabbed his testicles. With his eyes transfixed on the eighth and ninth wonder of the world, unzipping his fly, Junia slipped her hand inside his trousers.

Animalistic to the point of aggression, with a count down from Cape Canaveral banging in his head, he turned her around to face the bed. Junia was familiar with the next move. She lifted her left leg onto the mattress and peeled off her blouse. On the crazy side of passion, he pulled his trousers down and she could feel his hard aching shaft pressing against the groove of her buttocks. The excitement, anticipation of the custody sergeant catching them, only fuelled her sexual appetite. Knickers and tights gave way to a yanking, tugging against her thighs. They fell to her ankles. With her knees slightly bent, Junia moved her leg on the floor away from the mattress as his teeth gently nipped her shoulder. Firmly placing his right arm around her waist, he entered her with one deep thrust. Frank pulled her backwards and touched the dampness between her legs.

'Fuck me as hard as you can love.'

This time Junia pushed backwards and deliberately brushed her back against his hairy muscular chest. Sinking into her again and again, he brought her to a climax. She was now almost upright. Holding the back of both her upper arms, a euphoric sensation of unrelenting pleasure hammered inside his chest. He closed his eyes. Sex had passed the visual and touching stage. With his testicles tightening, he climaxed. The sensation rushed through his legs to his toes. Frank thought he could feel the floor vibrating.

That gentle musky smell of sex tickled his tonsils. The bra was just a glitch. The next poor bastard had no chance of living up to that performance. Yes, time to post a 'job well done' card through her psychological letterbox.

She turned around to face Frank, and he looked into her dusty yellow green eyes. The pupils of his favourite gaming machine registered a jackpot. Was that a smudge, just an inkling of a sparkle? No way, surely he had posted all that sexual hunger first class through her letterbox. The realisation of that oomph kicked him in the backside. That bloody dog libido must have chewed up the card. It had never landed on her mat.

The yearning to continue was still very much alive and living in the land of nymphomania. An uncontrollable longing, pumping, hurried through her veins. Junia grabbed his shirt and whispered in his ear.

'Fuck me again, this time I want to see your face. Look, I'll give you what you really want, you do the same for me love.'

Junia sat on the bunk in front of him and placed his penis between the cleavage of her brazenly exposed breasts. Gently, she caressed and rolled her breasts against his shaft.

'This is what you wanted me to do to you in the office. This is what you really wanted. Go on, push it hard between my breasts.' He responded to her appetite and pulled her to the edge of the mattress. She opened her legs and readily accepted all he had to give her. Face on, painting a zigzag on her lips with his tongue, she wrapped her legs around his waist. Deep nail rasping on taut buttocks, seemingly, made contact with his penis. She moved back onto the mattress and placed her legs together. Frank pushed them back into her waist.

Uncontrollable lust exploded in firework-green eyes. 'Come on, now give me what I want.' Temporary madness triggered off a sudden burst of energy that simultaneously vibrated through their frame.

Despite the lack of support from her bra, the detective managed to get both legs inside his trousers.

Why was there a serious expression on Junia's face? 'Give or take a quid or two I make it about nine quid.'

Her sombre mood reflected in his eyes. 'What the hell. Are you charging me for sex?'

'No perish the thought babes, but you're going to pay for new knickers and a bra.'

Walking somewhat gingerly towards the cell door, he stopped and faced Junia. Raising his eyebrows, he gently kissed her with his eyes and put his arms around her. She responded with a smouldering gaze. Affectionately, they held each other in the middle of the cell. Strangely, the moment created a sensation that had little to do with sex. He remembered the last occasion when he had that feeling with Marian. Soft skin touched and brushed against the side of his face. The sensation brought out goose pimples on every hair on his arms. Kissing her on the forehead, with a feather-like touch, he placed both hands at the back of her neck.

'Bloody hell Frank, that's not a bad cuddle.' She sounded genuine.

'Sorry, I didn't catch that.'

Not for the first time Junia glanced up at the ceiling. 'Well that smirk on your face says you did.'

He seemed determined to be the recipient of more praise. 'Tell me, was that the…'

'Frank will you stop fishing for compliments. I am sorry I said anything now?'

Intuitively he tried again. 'You can say it again if you want to.'

'It is like being with a schoolboy. If I say it again it won't end there will it? Oh no, you will just go on and on.'

With his eyes as wide as saucers, and a child-like expression reminiscent of seeing a Christmas stocking, he was about to continue when Junia placed her hand over his mouth.

'What crèche did you escape from love, stop your nonsense. Look it was a lovely cuddle.'

Frank was no longer lost in the wilderness. What might have been had changed to what could be.

★★★

245

With the sex drive of the Gwent Police Force satisfied. On the other side of town, a far more sinister impulse crawled out of Pandora's Box. The world recognised it as the drive towards death and the urge to destroy. This time, John's death drive had taken him to the parameter of Bingham Colliery. As the car approached the entrance, he switched off the lights and turned into a side road. His watch clocked 2.00 a.m. According to his calculations, he had at least another hour before the security firm carried out their check on the mine. Without making a sound, the driver scanned the colliery and approach road. There was no light or any movement.

This was his second visit. Twelve months previously, he had a guided tour of the mine and explosives store with a group of sixth formers. The manager gave an uninteresting, if not laborious, presentation aimed at the level of the pupils. John recalled the vacant expression on the simpleton when he used his territorial experience and introduced the subject of TNT, nitrate, and ammonium. His embarrassment triggered off a number of behind the hand conversations amongst the pupils. It came as no surprise, their teacher was the font of all knowledge.

Yes, because of his expertise, the investigation had turned into an unmitigated disaster. Nevertheless, his self-esteem had taken a knock that had culminated in rage. The increase in police activity and Susan's disappearance had brought about this frenzy. All that meticulous planning now seemed a waste of time. Why all the hullabaloo? West and Gregory were pathetic colourless objects. The world was a far more palatable place without them. He should have had the freedom of the town, instead of all the continual delays. Surely, the aspiration of life is death. What meaning would their existence have had without the closure he had so graciously bestowed upon them? At least their destruction now had meaning. Their demise was nothing short of a sacrifice to God. Because of the disruption, he experienced inevitable rage. In saying that, Churchill, Einstein, even Vincent Van Gogh all had their problems, what revelous company.

Again, he had managed to turn a negative restraint into a positive opportunity. With the police pre-occupied in chasing their tail, he would help himself to explosives in preparation for the secrets project. John had spent the day planning the destruction of the centre of hell and its congregation. He fantasised about the extent of genocide and mayhem the explosion would cause. The project would remain just that, a figment of his imagination without explosives. John had every expectation of finding blasting powder and dynamite in the store. Explosives were of little use without safety fuses and blasting caps. Electric fuses, even a blasting machine, would be a real bonus. Any shortfall would not deter him from his primary objective to destroy everyone in the congregation. '*Le temps de la colère de Dieu est arrivé,* the time of God's wrath has arrived.'

Slightly embarrassed by the sound of his voice, at that unearthly hour and with treachery on his mind, John burst out laughing. Was that the first sign of madness? He admitted his behaviour bordered on '*La Folie raisonnante,* insanity without delirium'. He even accepted the rationale behind his personality disorder. Was that a car leaving the main road? He glared in the rear view mirror. No, it was all clear. Adjusting the mirror, he could see his profile.

A time when John continually looked in the mirror somersaulted from the wings and landed in the orchestra pit. He was six and alone in his bedroom. The day started like every other. Father had already left before his mother disappeared at around 8.00 a.m. And that was it until the next and all the other days left alone and unloved. One day, he looked in the mirror and saw the reflection of a small boy. Stepping to one side, his reflection disappeared. Samuel spent hours in front of the mirror making himself disappear and then appear again. In control, in his magical game, it became the focal point of every waking hour. He decided who stayed and who disappeared. His parents had left the matrimonial home, but not the memory of his play.

When did his compulsive neurosis start? Samuel was nearly two. Alex had left him in the cot and for good measure, she had locked the bedroom door. Turning the pages of her magazine, she ignored the cowardly whimper polluting the air. *What an ungrateful little brat. If he thinks for one moment that I have the time or any interest, he is sadly mistaken.* Hysteria gave way when Samuel invented his first repetitive game. The two-year-old tied a cord around his teddy's neck and he threw it out of the cot until it was out of sight. Then, pulling on the cord, Toby appeared from nowhere. Samuel bounced up and down on the mattress and pulled his friend back into the cot. In soiled pyjamas, hanging onto the wooden rails of the cot, he repeated the game again and again and again to compensate for his mother. Toby had taught Samuel how to smile, that touch can heal. After all, Toby was a real caring teddy, his best friend, his only friend. The soft teddy bear with a missing ear always had two paws out to give him a big hug. It felt like a special mother's hug. In the dead of night under the soiled blankets, afraid, hungry and unloved, Toby whispered words of comfort in his ear until finally he fell asleep.

His hands gripped the steering wheel as the image of that heartless bitch came back to haunt him. It came as no surprise to anyone except his parents when John became hostile towards authority, particularly Mater and Pater. On a rare occasion, Pater had graced them with his presence. The seven year old deliberately lost his temper to attract attention. Samuel grabbed the newspaper out of his hands and threw it onto the fire. Rees posed a serious question to Alex in front of their son.

'Are you sure, I have serious doubts that Samuel is my son. Is he a protégée of one of your shags around the back of some seedy toilet?'

Alex detested that matter of fact tilt in his voice. 'Never doubt it husband dear, I remember the exact moment I conceived. In fact it was the last time you fucked me.'

'Don't be ridiculous Alex, that's just typical of you to say something like that. Don't forget I've worked my socks off to get on the career ladder. You've done bugger all, you cannot even discipline that child.'

The next voice had a tinge of sympathy. 'Perhaps I was a teensy-weensy bit hasty to condemn you. Sincere apologies offered, and I hope accepted. Do you mind if I ask you a serious question about your role?'

'If you must, get on with it, I need to phone operations for an update.'

'I know your inspector role is a difficult one at strategic level, co-coordinator, and decision maker. In fact, you were kind enough to remind me a thousand times that responsibility rests on your macho shoulders. I was just wondering about the parameter of your role. Is it mandatory that you shag your operational sergeant Irene Davies to a standstill at every given opportunity? The reason I ask, is that fortunately, Irene has caught Gonorrhoea, or did Gonorrhoea catch her. Anyway, I know you use my vibrator. Whilst I would applaud 'the clap' if it turned your penis gangrene. I would be extremely annoyed if I caught it as well.'

'Alex, how could you stoop so low in front of the boy?'

'I am sorry, aren't you confusing me with your girlfriend. She is the one always stooping to give you a blowjob. In any case, I was only trying to provide the boy with an example of what you mean by working your socks off.'

Rees stormed out of the living room. Samuel, on the other hand, considered the argument as a personal triumph.

Samuel had experienced the longest conversation between his parents in living memory. Most of the exchange was beyond his understanding, but it suggested a new beginning. He could recite the dialogue almost verbatim. He was far more astute at the 'sucker punch' impression of his mother.

In the more progressive years, John saw arson as an obvious choice to gain control through destruction. What started out as a cry for help had triggered the beginning of a destructive impulse that would remain with him for the rest of his life. The seven year old peeped through the steel bars of next door's rabbit hutch. He could see two motionless figures in the dark cowering at the back of the wooden hutch. Running a box of matches along the bars brought a response. Two startled egg-shaped brown rabbits moved without making a sound, and then he heard a hollow grinding noise. His hand trembled as he struck a safety match on the rough edge. The red phosphorus head burst into flames. Grass, poking through the bars, gradually caught alight. Mesmerised, the cherry-red flames engulfed and ignited the wooden hutch. Through the smoke, he watched and waited patiently for the buck and doe to burn.

John took a hip flask from his pocket, ha! real Spanish sherry. Wreathed with an incessant grin, he recalled his favourite high. Was it the smell, heat against his face, the long soft fur alight, or perhaps the final grunting noise? No, at the very end the buck, yes the buck lifted his hind leg and started to thump the bottom of the hatch. The utter stupidity of the animal, acting on instinct, he must have been warning other rabbits to flee from the make-believe warren. Like the buck, any rational behaviour died on the day that chaos developed into lunacy.

The incident had taught him a great deal. Destruction and sadistic cruelty are only different neurotic faces of the same clock. At that point, John crossed the line from reality and he entered the world of 'will to believe' delusion. Subjected to the most destructive type of child abuse, had slowly but surely, turned him into a psychopath.

He stared at his reflection in the rear view mirror. Was there any point in denying the very thing that formed part of his living self, a reality that he had to accept? On the balance of probabilities, John thought he was ill rather than in the wrong, a sexual addict, not a sexual predator. A fine point perhaps, but that was his preference. Could he control and suppress his compulsion to kill? NO? At that very moment, if he had the opportunity to press a magical button to stop his death drive, would he do it, would he press the button and walk away? NO? If he turned his back on the destruction of the objects that deserved it, inevitably, he would turn on himself. The death drive would end with his demise.

Now glaring into the mirror, the moment of truth stared back at him and he turned his head away. In his world of illusory truth, the Machiavellian side of his character asked, *'Who am I?'* The rhetorical question annoyed him intensely. John had no intention of avoiding the question. In the lunacy of total insanity, he had an alliance with Thanatos, the god of death. His quest, no vocation, was to guide the blasphemous souls of the church into purgatory. Nemesis, the goddess of retribution, Phobus, the personification of horror, all walked beside him carrying body bags. No one could stop him, carnage and destruction of the ... John stopped and his head jerked back in the seat from the dagger of truth piercing his heart. Dangling over the edge of insanity, he reached out and grabbed the first cliché that came into his head. Hamlet, damnation not that one, and yet there was no denying Polonius's advice to his son when he said, 'This above all to thine own self be true.' In the dark recess of hopelessness, John finally admitted he was untreatable

Gaining access to the explosive store would not be a problem. Additionally, securing somewhere else to work on the project had also been an easy task. Even Carla had some use. The location of the property brought an unexpected bonus. It was next door to the Catholic Church. He gave serious thought about moving. His disappearance would draw suspicion that would instigate a mass search, and hinder progress. No, John decided to wait for the troop of baboons to knock on his door. He relished the thought of kicking the rough red spot on their peel buttocks. What a challenge and opportunity to show the full extent of their buffoonery. Touching a silver crucifix hanging from his neck, he prayed to his God in hell that he would find explosives in the store. John made his way towards the door leading to purgatory and thought about Toby the teddy. What had happened to his cuddly friend? At that very moment, his inner child would have given anything to make Toby appear again.

# CHAPTER 26

## THE LANGUAGE OF LOVE

Always the perfect gentleman and with no ulterior motive, Frank asked Junia if he could escort her back to her hotel room. The detective gave the offer serious thought. The cell experience had definitely slowed down his libido. From previous sexual encounters, he knew that the 'more the better' theory does not necessarily work. Then that irritating voice super ego had the audacity to question his ability to turn up for the second half. It suggested he would be more comfortable with a nice cup of tea, not too hot, perhaps the Radio Times, and fur lined slippers. What about a gingerly biscuit?

Lying naked on the bed next to Junia, nirvana gently caressed his genitals. As soon as they had entered the hotel room, Junia had pushed him towards the path to enlightenment. Never slow at initiating the first move, he was still holding his athletic spikes when Junia fired his starting pistol. The cooing doves never made it to the loft. She made her move as soon as he closed the door. Literally shoving Frank against the wall in the hallway, Junia lunged at his tonsils with her tongue. Again, taking the initiative, she grabbed his hand and dragged the reluctant gigolo to a chair in the lounge next to a full-length mirror.

'Take off your clothes, and sit on the chair love.'

Shove number two propelled Frank towards the seat. Junia watched his rather juvenile attempt to take off his trousers, as frustration ravished the poor little innocent buttons on her blouse. And who could blame them. The buttons, popping onto the floor, rolled towards the door and made a break for it. Plastic teeth on her skirt sizzled as she brutally yanked the zip fastener down. Using a choice of words that would make a sailor blush, she assisted 'the fucking useless sod' with his shoe stuck halfway up his trouser leg.

Kneeling down in front of his chair, leaning, drawing her tongue over the canvas of his lips, the sensation released butterflies inside his mouth. Sleek long strands of hair whisked over and lightly touched the top of his penis. Frank opened his mouth. The light flicking motion of Junia's tongue explored his as she ran her fingernails up and down the back of his arm. Standing, sexually, teasingly, she rolled down her nylon stocking and took it off. Without an, 'if I may sir', Junia wrapped the stocking around the base of his shaft and tied it reasonably tight with three knots. The temptress knew the stocking would prolong the size and duration of his erection. Gingerly, she lowered herself onto his shaft, and glanced in the mirror. Frank entered her. She waited to feel him deep inside, arching her back Junia sat upright. Then leaning slightly forward, with her arms around his neck, she rolled her hips clockwise, squeezed her thighs, and gyrated in circles. Turning her head, she looked at herself in the mirror. Junia could feel the contractions she usually experienced moments before an orgasm. She stopped and sat upright. Slowly, she picked up the rhythm again. Arching, writhing, in seconds her contractions exploded. Frank was about to climax. She responded again with the enthusiasm of a child trying out her first bouncy castle. Banging, bouncing, euphoria raged through his groin.

Was that the finale, fortunately no. Lying on the bed, Junia put on the most erotic experience of his life. Closing her eyes, appealingly, sensually, she masturbated in front of him. With no hang-up, seemingly the most natural thing, she did not attempt to disguise her pleasure. Utilising the largest sexual organ known to man, Frank compared this latest fantasy with his existing list. Why had it gone straight to number one in the charts? Religiously, he scrutinised the top ten again. Two to nine followed the same theme where he was the focal point to tailor-made sexual imageries. All used to great effect, why were they holding second place to a fantasy where he was just an observer. On a positive note, with love potion number nine cooling his physical engine, he felt relaxed.

In ecstasy, gazing at the ceiling, happy chemicals bombarded his brain with weird and wonderful thoughts. How did he see their relationship? Despite the gourmet of delights, Frank hardly knew her. First impressions, he had certainly liked what he saw in the office that afternoon. Genuinely quirky, when naked, she always had a smile. Her accent was deliciously sexy, and her looks well… On one occasion, he caught Walsh ogling her backside. Something was pushing his favourite emotion, LUST to the edge of a cliff. It had no name, but it felt euphoric, enchanting, and obsessive. Digging deep into his emotional sound bite, the detective found the word he was looking for. Infatuation, brought about by a lack of sexual tension. He preferred it to his usual roll over and snore response after sex. With four love showers in the space of less than ten hours, was he setting the bar a little high?

How long could he literally keep it up? He had experienced a similar problem with Annie. His toes curled up as he recalled his unique master plan to counteract her hyperactive sexuality. Oh so simple, Frank intended to prolong his climax and withdraw moments before he was about to ejaculate. He could still maintain Annie's arousal with his fingers and tongue. What could possibly go wrong? Things were going well. He could feel the sensation of a climax playing 'Tubular Bells' with a hammer on his genitals. In the process of making a strategic withdrawal, from nowhere, 'mister point of no return', sat on his backside and whistled Dixie. What sexual calendar could he live with? He would have to be careful or 'La petite mort, the little death', could end up just that.

Nibbling his ear, she put her arms around his waist.

'What are you thinking about, love?'

Frank showed the rare quality of honesty. 'I'm re-writing my fantasy list, thanks to you.'

Junia decided to follow the leader. 'Did I tell you, I had a fantasy about you?'

'What's new pussycat.'

'Do you want me to tell you about my fantasy?'

Arrogance decided to do a vocal. 'Look, if I had the child allowance for every woman who conceived when they were fantasising about me, I'd be a millionaire.'

*Mr bloody macho wants pulling down a peg or three.* 'You are a shy little bugger aren't you, well is it yes or no?'

The self-professed gigolo introduced smirk number five. 'Ok yes and no.'

Junia treated her face to a sugary smile. 'Well you and I were married. We had a lovely house with three children.' His face changed to a 'pinch me I'm dreaming' look.

'And here's my mind-blowing fantasy, you moved out babes and got a flat of your own.'

'And?'

'And that's my fantasy, it really turned me on.'

'I don't get that?'

'Why don't you ask that inflated opinion inside your head love? It knows everything?'

*Got it, it's called taking the piss.*

She breasts, graciously took on a supporting role to his dropped jaw. 'Don't go all grumpy on me. Look I've got a serious question, are the colour of your eyes different? Let me see, I think one is brown and the right one is blue.'

'The lady wins a prize, why are you asking, are you colour blind.' *If she thinks, I'm going to let her get away with scoring points off me, she can bloody well think again.*

She knew he would extract the urine. 'No, the problem is love, sometimes I see different colours in stupid things and I get it all wrong.'

'I'm all ears Miss Browne, or is it Miss Green?' *Fifteen all, new balls.*

'Frank, please don't laugh, but my senses are sort of mixed up. I can see different colours in letters, words, and even numbers.'

The DC looked at his watch. It was time to take the piss again. 'Walsh has the same problem, he mixes up his senses.'

'Oh my God does he? How do you know that babes, what did he say?'

'Well last summer I caught him wearing a loud shirt. When I told him that I was walking you to your hotel, he was green with envy.' *Right on the line, thirty fifteen.*

'Frank, I'm trying to have a sensible conversation here.'

'Sorry, did you say you see different colours in letters and words?'

Junia considered grabbing his testicles. 'Are you just going to take the piss again?'

Frank toned it down. 'No look, give me a clue. Do you see the same colour in all the letters or different colours in different letters? Hang on a second what about this.' He grabbed his jacket from the chair and retrieved his pocket book with 'Gwent Police' in bold black print on a hard cover.

'Right what colour is the word POLICE?'

Junia joined in with the experiment. 'Well, if I focus on each letter in the word, the letter P is indigo, E is yellow. Some of the letters blend into each other. It all depends who they are standing next to. Now If I focus on the word 'POLICE' as a whole, it's orange.'

'What a load of bollocks.'

Junia scowled at his inevitable response. 'There is no point in trying is there?'

'Hang about Mrs Pout, I said bollocks because you are wrong. The word *POLICE* is tangerine, always has been. Since when has the letter E been yellow?'

She could see the serious glint in his eyes. 'I am telling you now, if this is a wind-up, I will never touch your banana again.'

'Junia, what if I told you the letters and numbers have personalities? Let's see, the letter P is female. She's like you, oversexed and shallow.' *Forty fifteen.* 'The figure 4 is male and can't be trusted, he fades in and out from grey to dark brown.'

Junia screamed so loud he had to put his hands to his ears.

'Satisfied now that I'm not taking the piss?'

She gave in gracefully. 'I just knew it as soon as you walked into the office. I knew there was something different about you.'

Confidently, he tossed the ball into the air and served. 'If you remember I told you that at the time.'

Junia lunged to her right. 'Oh no you bloody well didn't.'

His drop shot at the nets left her standing on the baseline. 'Oh yes I bloody well did, don't you remember me telling you that I smelt a rat.' *Advantage to the guy who has just moved out of the flat.*

An angry adversary glared at her opponent. 'Listen hear love, I'll separate you from your breath if you keep on taking the piss.'

'Sorry, that's the last promise. What do you mean I'm different, do you mean like the letter Z?'

Revenge is sweat. 'No not like him, he's odd always facing the wrong way. No, more like D, he's different. You know, young, cocky, with a head the size of Humpty Dumpty.'

*That was a bloody foot fault.*

At advantage point, he decided to play the waiting game. 'How long have you had this thing?'

Junia gave it serious thought. 'I think I've always had it, what about you?'

'No, it's brought on by something. I get a sort of fit. Days, even weeks later, I see what you're on about and then it goes away.'

He waited for a response but Junia had changed to listening mode. The time had arrived for him to show his superior knowledge. 'Guess what, we're not the only ones who have whatever it's called. Duke Ellington has it as well. In the paper, he said he thinks the wiring in his brain is crossed because his senses blend into each other. If you want my opinion, I think some of the senses fall in love with each other. They sort of blend together so that they can give enjoyment.'

Junia turned towards him and he put his hand on her shoulder. She could not believe the relief of knowing that he experienced the same thing. 'Frank, I've got something else to tell you. When I see the sunset, I get the taste of chocolate in my mouth.'

'Bloody hell that's serious, does Cadbury's know about it?' *Game, set and she is no bloody match for me.* Before he had time to change ends, she seized a pillow and repeatedly hit him over the head.

'Seeing stars now funny guy?'

He responded to the challenge. 'No, but I can go one better than your chocolate stuff. I listened to the radio the other day. They were playing the Beatles, 'Love me do' and I saw a fireworks display, Different colour lines moved on a screen in front of me. The strange thing is, the colours moved in a straight line and came out of the screen. It was like looking at the world though kaleidoscopic eyes.'

'Damn you, I cannot match that.' Junia decided not to tell him about her most unusual experience.

At seventeen, on a glorious summer morning she was sitting on a park bench. Through the hazy steam rising from the lake, Junia could see the ducks foraging under the surface of the water. Then the sunlight danced into her eyes, and then she let go. From a place, that no one can explain, she looked down into the heart of her soul and had flashbacks of the moments in her life. A sense of tranquillity, at one with everything, lasted several minutes before she returned to her physical self. The ducks were still entertaining, when something brushed the side of her cheek. It was probably the silken thread of a spider's web. Wrong. Strong thick dark lines pushed hard against her mouth. Panic gave way to the terror sinking its teeth into her neck. Feeling exposed, Junia wanted to hide in the place where nobody could see her. Somehow, she knew the sickly hue was infectious. Frantically the ducks started running along the surface of the water. Rainbow elliptical wings soared into the air.

Still mesmerised by the outline of the blood-red serrated beaks climbing against the threatening sky, she brushed her face and the feeling of dread disappeared.

Junia decided to wipe the smirk off his face. 'On second thoughts, I think I can beat that.'

Again, he responded. 'Don't tell me, let me guess, you can taste shapes or you've got coloured hearing?'

She seized the opportunity. 'Nice try but no cigar sir. Gosh love, I wish I had a penny for every time someone has said that to you.'

*If she doesn't stop, I'll smash her bloody racket.*

The lady gracefully continued. 'In fairness it has to do with taste. I would like to introduce you to my favourite number, sixty-nine. Does it blow your mind as well?'

'No, I prefer sixty-eight, that's when you give me a blow job and you still owe me one.'

A hint of a smirk disappeared under the duvet. Junia looked forward to tasting her favourite banana. *La petite mort* fluffed his pillow, glanced under the sheets, and gave the thumbs down. Definitely, his last throw of the dice. If he failed to roll a natural and make it last, Junia would again be nibbling at his meat and two veg any time soon.

He looked for inspiration. What would the Queen Mother do in his predicament? From his guru's second cassette, the low-pitch of Blue crackled inside his head. *Lad, making it last longer is easy. All you have to do is to take your mind off the job and think about something else.* Searching his library, he picked out something obscure yet appropriate. *That will do nicely. She'll have lockjaw before she gets me to tip my hat. Now think about it, concentrate, where does tomato blight come from? Good question. Is it in the soil or carried around by bugs?* He clenched his teeth as the sensual touch of her mouth stormed through his torso. *It's a fungus, that's what it is. It's err a good for nothing fungus that attacks the stem. Didn't, BLOODY HELL! concentrate. Didn't Sid say, who, concentrate for Christ's sake it was SID. Didn't he say to look out for early signs of blight? Once it gets going, it's hard, it's VERY hard to!* Sadly blight kissed his ripe cherry-plumb tomatoes and fungus travelled up through his vine. A fine white fungal substance wilted and shrivelled his stem for at least the next twenty-four hours.

# CHAPTER 27

## SAMUEL 2
## OH HOW THE MIGHTY HAVE FALLEN

Mears held the station door for Jenkins to enter the foyer. Slowly they made their way to the canteen, now used as a briefing room. The junior, obligingly, had his dig in first.

'Feeling under the weather, sir?'

'At least I didn't bugger off at the smell of the barman's apron. Mears, you're a lot of things, but a drinker you're not.'

Mears looked into the bloodhound eyes of the SIO and wondered if sensible drinking had ever been a norm. DS Thomas met them at the canteen door. 'Profit's waiting for you in your office, Guv.'

Jenkins glanced over the sergeant's shoulder. He could see the thin lanky frame of Profit sitting behind his desk. 'How long has that man been here?'

The DS had bad news. 'Hours boss, he's gone through everything. He's even gone through the action card index.' Thomas carried out a baton change with his eyes trying to detect the athlete who had the strong smell of alcohol.

'Thomas update me for...' Too late the door opened.

'Morning Clive, don't keep me waiting, I have an urgent appointment to go to.'

Jenkins followed the ACC operations into the office with a stride indicative of someone going to the gallows.

A true professional, Profit concealed his contempt for Jenkins. 'Sit down. Clive I know you and I have had our problems, but I've drawn a line under that. The chief has asked me for an update on the progress on both homicides. That's where you come in.'

Jenkins decided to go on the offensive. 'Don't you think you should have phoned me first?'

'I did, several times. Unfortunately you were out, and by the look of you I don't have to second guess where you were.'

259

Floundering for a crutch to lean on, Jenkins grabbed his cigarettes and lighter from his pocket.

'Sorry, but not on my watch Clive. Let's get under way by starting with the response stage.'

Jenkins flashed his bleary eyes. 'I know what this is all about. You've been talking to that shit-stirrer Black.'

'Well done Clive. Yes, I read his report and phoned him straight away about several queries. He wouldn't discuss them with me. When I pressed him, he said he had already spoken to you. If I wanted to know anything, I should do the same. However, from his report I noticed that you had not briefed him when he arrived at the scene. According to the log you were off visiting Gregory's scene.'

'So?'

'So, aren't you aware about the contamination of a crime scene or, in your case, the cross-contamination of two crime scenes, because that is what you did.'

Jenkins angrily raised his voice. 'For Christ's sake, how many times have I got to answer this damn question? As senior investigating officer, I made a decision to go to Gregory's house. I stand by that decision.'

'As SIO, you are also responsible for securing the scene, not making a mess of it. Which brings me onto my next point, officers attending the scene should have worn gloves?'

This time there was a more confident approach from Jenkins. 'You should get your facts right, gloves were worn.'

'Are you sure?'

'I've just said so haven't I?'

'In that case you and Mears should be under arrest. Both your prints were found in West's living room.'

Jenkins glowered at the ACC and continued his derision. 'I knew Black was behind all this.'

'Clive, you seem to have a fixation with Black. Is he also to blame for not introducing the card index system until some thirty-six hours after you arrived at the scene? Is he responsible for the lack of critical information, charts, spread sheets, maps, photographs, and the like not displayed in this very briefing room?'

Jenkins shrugged his shoulders. 'What did you expect to see?'

'I'll tell you exactly what my expectations are, what about the critical examination of both incidents. For example, information on scene features together with photographs, and maps of the parameters of both crime scenes. Additionally, you should have shown the route and link to both scenes. Also, where is the mapping of possible search zones, or areas identified for house-to-house enquiries? Last but not least, what about a detailed offender board. Have I made that clear enough for you?'

Jenkins seemed determined to shot himself in the foot. 'You've jumped the gun. We haven't got an offender yet.'

'The board Clive is used to build up a profile of the offender. Can I remind you that you have two victims? They should have been on the board. Do we know of any motive behind the killings?'

The assistant chief constable clocked a figure lurking outside the door. 'Come on in and join us Chief Inspector Mears.' Mears shuffled into the office with his head bowed. Reluctantly, he sat down next to Jenkins. 'Well, I am still waiting for an answer.'

Continually subjected to ridicule from Jenkins, the last thing Mears wanted was the same treatment from Profit. Pursing his lips, he decided to impress the senior officer. 'Well you can discount theft and robbery, the violence was extreme. It looks as if the offender enjoyed butchering one of his victims. He even left a calling card.'

Profit decided to test their knowledge. 'What do we know about the offender?'

Jenkins glanced at Mears and nodded to suggest that it was his turn again. 'The offender is male, very strong, left handed, and a psychopath who enjoys torturing people until they crock.'

'Mears, is there anything else?'

'No sir, that's about it.'

Profit leaned forward in his chair. 'Isn't the offender also well organised. In addition, what about the high degree of planning and a thousand other things that Black brought to your attention? The offender also tried to disguise the second killing as a suicide?'

A psychological thump on the door echoed the arrival of an uneasy silence. A shaking hand grabbed a paper slip from the desk and started to straighten it.

'Why isn't all this and more on the offender's board? If that was the case chief inspector, you would not have needed my prompting.'

Jenkins crossed his legs and pointed at the subordinate with a paper clip. 'The briefing room is down to Mears.'

'Gentlemen, let's move on to the managerial and strategy stage. How many fast track actions were instigated during the first twenty-four hours chief superintendent in order to progress the investigation?'

'We don't use Metropolitan slang around here.'

'What's the matter with you Clive. Fast tracking action is a term used in the guidelines. To put it mildly, I'm concerned about your lack of knowledge. It refers to any action you should have identified that needs to be carried out by your team as a matter of urgency to progress the investigation. For example, identifying witnesses, and the offender, or house to house enquiries.'

The magic paper clip came into play again. 'Mears should have sorted all that out.'

'When did you start house to house enquiries, chief inspector?'

'The following day, I had a team doing the houses around the scene of both murders.'

'Mears, are you telling me that residents in the immediate vicinity of both killings were not approached until the following day?'

'I didn't have the manpower.'

Profit glared at Jenkins. 'Superintendent, the offender could have been in one of the nearby houses dripping with blood. One of the neighbours could have seen the suspect or his car. All of which could have concluded your investigation. YOU DIDN'T even bother with house to house enquiries until the following day. How many local officers did you employ?'

Jenkins gave Mears the nod to answer the question. The chief inspector had no intention of picking up that hot potato. Jenkins cleared his throat, he could see the direction in which the conversation was heading, 'We didn't use any local officers.'

Profit recognised another felony. 'Correct me if I'm wrong, but local police officers must be used as house co-coordinators because of their local knowledge?'

Beads of sweat trickled down the senior officer's face. A smell of alcohol consumed the room. 'I've already said that was down to Mears.'

The ACC rejected his abdication. 'As THE DECISION

MAKER of this investigation what instructions did you give him?'

'What do you mean what instructions did I give him? I told him to bloody well sort out the house enquiries, isn't that clear enough.'

Professional guidance prompted the next question. 'No it's not, as SIO you should be the one who decides exactly what the team should be focusing on. Your instructions were meaningless, you left him to carry out the enquiries as he saw fit. Let me remind you. You're the one running this show, and you should have established clear objectives, not Mears or his team. If we all followed your strategy, everybody would be doing their own thing. You cannot abdicate your responsibility. Do I make myself clear chief superintendent? Just one more thing, I noticed that the officers on HTH did not use the correct questionnaire. More importantly what have you done about the suspect, John?'

'I was going to…'

Profit interrupted Jenkins. 'Listen to the question, what action have you already carried out, I did not ask you what you intended to do. My information is that the local officer who led you to Gregory also put forward John's name as a critical suspect.'

'You don't expect me to take that man seriously do you, John is…'

Another interruption by Profit. 'I know who John is, what you have done about him? By your silence, it looks as if you have done precisely nothing. Let me summarise the briefing I intend to give to the chief constable. The 'Response Stage' was abysmal. Additionally the 'Management Stage', use of resources and the instigation of critical actions were diabolical. Last and by no means least, your leadership was atrocious and unprofessional. Clive, let me ask you, your work as a senior officer isn't interfering with the amount of time that you can spend going on the piss is it?'

Jenkins acknowledged the travesty of his position. 'Look, there is nothing that can't be turned around.'

'Well said Clive. One last favour from you before I phone the chief constable.'

The relief on Jenkins's face popped into the pub next door to celebrate. 'Fire away anything you just name it.'

'When I leave this office, clear out your drawer, go back to your hotel, pack your suitcase and catch the next train home. If I find you anywhere near your car, I will arrest you for driving whilst unfit through drink or drugs. You are suspended from duty to take immediate effect. Leave your warrant card on the desk. I am not in the habit of giving advice, but in your case, I'll make an exception. Leave an envelope on your desk with your resignation inside. I suggest you resign while you still have your pension to look forward to.' Standing, the ACC waited for a response.

Jenkins tried to defend the indefensible. 'You can't fucking do this to me. All my years in the force, don't they count for anything?'

'I already have Mr Jenkins. The public deserves to be protected. They certainly deserve a more professional response to a DOUBLE HOMICIDE than the one you gave them. I intend to FAST TRACK your suspension. It is in the public interest to do so. If you had taken that procedure on board then maybe the public would be sleeping soundly in their bed instead of worrying about a maniac still on the loose.'

Mears meticulously examined the floor, was he next?

'I intend taking over the role of SIO. If it wasn't for the fact that this investigation requires continuity and stability at senior level, I can assure you Mears, you would also be walking through the door. However be warned, you have exactly two weeks to impress. Now excuse me whilst I get some fresh air. I think I've had enough of stale alcohol fumes down my lungs for one day.'

A briefing from the new SIO to his team focused on the objectives of the investigation. Information and enquires carried out prior to him taking charge were still relevant. In retrospect, he intended to start afresh. The ACC stressed that the public were in grave danger from the predator(s) whose identity still had to be determined. He emphasised the significance of the offender profile and victim notice board. Profit made no excuse for reading the content aloud. No one would leave the room without writing the details in their pocket books. Apart from those responsible for updating the card index with information generated through enquiries, Profit split the rest of the staff into three operational teams, each led by a detective sergeant.

Their collective objective, work as a team and concentrate on the critical elements of a homicide namely location, victim, and association with the offender. The 'Location Team' using a ripple effect, would work outwards from both crime scenes. That team was also responsible for any search, together with house to house enquires. Using standard questionnaires, the usual interview and eliminate system would be employed to categorise and identify residents and any suspects. Profit emphasised the difference in the credibility of an alibi given by someone's family or friend as opposed to one from an independent source. Written reports on the features of each crime scene, the selection of the location, offender travel, and scene proximity to local housing estates, must be available on debrief. 'Someone must have seen something. Find the vehicle, the weapon, the suspect's home address and work place, or place used to plan the homicide.' A second group, the 'Victim Team', would concentrate on the victims' lifestyle, their association with each other, and any suspect. Initially they would focus on the routine activities and critically their whereabouts for the previous forty-eight hours before their demise. The last group, the 'Suspect/Offender Team', had a clear objective to build on the existing offender profile. They would also carry out the arrest of any suspects and interview them.

Profit glanced in the direction of Walsh and Macleod. 'Both of you have put forward Samuel John, a local schoolteacher, as a suspect. We know that the offender is a psychopath and will undoubtedly kill again. Having listened carefully to you and with the safety of the public uppermost in my mind, I intend to take out warrants to search John's house, his caravan, and school. The searches will take place as soon as Mears returns to the station and John is safely behind bars. At the moment there is little evidence we can put to him in interview. Your investigation and search of his premises will alter that. For the time being, he will remain in custody. If later we have to bail him, I will authorise twenty- four hour surveillance. All of you have experience. Let me know your ideas to progress the investigation. On my part, I intend involving you in the decision-making. Just one more point, never compromise the safety of the public or our relationship with them.'

An untimely knock on the front door interrupted an interesting conversation on the European Economic Community between the resident and his solicitor. Carla had already made her way to Cardiff. Mears showed his warrant card to an expectant audience. Using the balls of his feet as a fixed point and leaning forward, John mimed a theatrical applause. It had the desired effect. The senior officer cautioned him and made an arrest earlier than he had anticipated.

'Congratulations Mears, your chief constable will be proud of you. Like all the other buffoons, you have successfully executed a gross divergence in practice. Alternatively, in words that you can understand, mate you have just cocked up the caution. It should have been what you say MAY *not WILL be given in evidence.*'

Mears, miming someone really pissed off, moved forward with his handcuffs.

John continued with his ridicule. 'As a matter of interest, although I doubt you have any interest other than buffoonery. Your surname Mears is of Anglo-Saxon origin. It means someone who lives near a pond. In fact, I once had a tadpole named after you.'

That ended the conversation. John placed both hands behind his back. Lifting his right leg, he religiously polished the top of the shoe on the back of the trousers.

Mears constantly glared at the prisoner in the back of the car to see if there were any emotional clues or stress. Taking the scenic route, Mears continually hurled insults and threats at John who seemed oblivious to it all.

The CID car pulled up in close proximity to the custody unit. After switching off the ignition, to unsettle John, the good guys in blue initiated that well-rehearsed 'all stay in the car' ploy. With the minutes ticking away, the glare from Mears became more hostile and aggressive. Indifference looked at the back of the driver's head. Mears leaned over and pressed his forehead hard against the side of the prisoner's face, still no response. Tilting his head back slightly, then forward, the top of his forehead collided with the right side of the prisoner's cheekbone. Numbness, tingling, spots before his eyes, rattled his frame. John sat upright and looked straight ahead.

'I'm going to enjoy kicking the living shit out of you. You'll shit yourself when you hear my footsteps outside. I'm going to fuck you with my fist.'

There was still no reaction from the prisoner. More abuse penetrated his ears before the officer finally relented and alighted from the car,

Mears deliberately left the door open. 'Get out under your own steam. If you don't, I'll drag you out.'

John still handcuffed, wriggled towards the edge of the seat. With difficulty, leaning forward, he placed one foot outside the vehicle, ducked, and his forehead collided with the doorframe. Still reeling from the blow, with blood trickling from his temple, he pulled himself upright. The contours of his mouth decided to squeeze out a sarcastic grin. John glanced at his shoes and polished his left shoe on the back of the trousers.

Leaning against the wall at the end of the corridor leading from the custody unit, Frank waited for a presence beyond evil to open the door. Only moments before, he was sitting at his desk, when a mass of multi-coloured zigzag lines materialised in front of his eyes. Bouncing, sliding off the walls, the silhouette shapes headed towards the door. They seemed to be luring him down the stairs to the custody unit.

The detective fumbled in his pockets for a cigarette. Suddenly, he could feel heavy breathing on his face. Icy cold ether crawled into his mouth. The acidic taste of sulphur ambushed the back of his throat. Wheezing, his lungs started to freeze. Filling his lungs with air, hands shaking, he tried to control muscle spasms. Instinctively, he pressed both index fingers against his thumbs and made a rolling movement. Without any warning, a galaxy of searchlight laser beams passed straight through the custody steel door. The beams ricocheted against the walls and disintegrated into thousands of spectra light. A symphony of violet grey suspended in every thunder flash, charged down the corridor towards him. Frank closed his eyes and saw the mental image of the prisoner standing in the corridor. Slowly he opened them, John and the escort were now walking towards him. He could see the prominent colours of grey and black surrounding the prisoner's torso turning to a rich black around his head. The aura reflected the core essence of his being. It represented the heart of his black heart. Looking into the core of the black aura, he could see an endless void reaching into his charcoal soul. A familiar voice rattled through his frame. *Can you not see the truth even though it is in front of you? Do you not know that when a body dies the soul lives on. The new is continuous with the old. The soul of this man called John will pass to another body.*

John knew what Frank was looking at. Like a man with his soul laid bare, he glared at the detective. 'You must be Macleod, if I were you I would be very careful. If you look into the abyss for too long, the abyss will start looking back at you.'

The detective tried to catch him off guard. 'Tell me, why do you wear a clown's mask when you abuse children?'

Subtle cues of a nervous twitch lasted only a moment before John reverted to his sardonic self. 'I have no idea what you are referring to, nevertheless an interesting question. If you want my opinion on clowns, it matters not if you are referring to the famous Fratellini, or Chaplin, I think they ALL get away with murder.'

A contrived smile deliberately glared into the nucleus of John's black heart. The next involuntary language and intonation coming from his mouth spoke in the Gallic tongue.

'Ní féidir liom eagla duine ar bith ar féidir leo a mharú an comhlacht ach nach bhfuil in ann a mharú an anam, I do not fear those who can kill the body, but not the soul. It is you who should fear those who can destroy your soul.'

A sharp biting boom echoed from the teacher's voice. 'What does a barbaric heathen like you know about the soul, or anything else for that matter?' The spirit of the living was speaking in tongues, and yet the prisoner seemed to understand.

That prickly feeling in the language centre of his brain started to take physical control. Why were both his arms extending out in front of him? Grabbing John's shirt, pushing him against the wall, a piercing roar exploded against the ceiling, and the floor started to shake. 'Tá tú ag an duine olc a dhaoradh chun siúl eternity… you are the evil one who is condemned to walk eternity. My blood welcomed the son of God to this shore. My blood shared the blessing with Saint Joseph of Armathia, and touched the plate of the Holy Grail that caught the blood from the Cross. My people built Glastonbury Abbey and took the sign of Christianity. No, it is you who does not speak wisdom.'

John snarled and used considerable upper body strength trying to break free. 'I have been given absolution by the oldest institution in the world. I doubt if you even know what that is.'

Pragmatic voices clashed and hung in the corridor.

'We, who founded Christianity before Rome and lived for centuries before close to the earth and close to God, speak the truth. Your soul is dammed and is condemned to wander the earth with your evil spirit.'

The spirit faded from his tongue and the DC released his hold on the prisoner. Mears violently grabbed John and pushed him towards the cells. 'You're all mine now you bastard, there's no absolution for you in here.'

The detective reached the top of the stairs. He could hear the thump of bare knuckles against flesh and bone. There was no scream, only a dull thud.

A team from Cardiff visited the home of the ACC admin to interview Carla. Again, a fully briefed solicitor waited patiently in the lounge for them to arrive. The alibi sounded both creditable and comprehensive. Carla and her brother were home at the relevant time. After consuming two glasses of sherry, listening to Walter Allen, the novelist, on the radio, they retired for the evening. Apparently, John had a cold. He went to bed with two aspirins and a cup of hot chocolate. After further probing Carla elaborated, the programme contained an interesting synopsis about Britain in the thirties. The producer, Cleverdon, had created a marvellous contribution to the night's entertainment. Before retiring, Carla recalled having a short conversation with Samuel about John Betjeman. The surgery confirmed dealing with a prescription in the name of S John on the day following the homicide. Allen's broadcast, on the third programme, started at 10.00 p.m. sharp. Which was fortuitous to any listener who had missed the original broadcast some three months earlier? The alibi looked watertight.

Glory be to the Father. Frank looked toward the heavens when he read the action sheet, his brief included re-visiting Father Graham. Beforehand, he examined a copy of the priest's bank statement and the one relating to the Catholic Church. Apart from the usual monthly contribution, there were two substantial cheques drawn on John's account to the church, each for a thousand pounds. The first, dated three months after his arrival, and the second, only days before his arrest. During their confrontation, John mentioned he had received absolution from the church, absolution from what. He must have confessed his mortal sin to Graham. The priest had no alternative other than to accept the confession to save his miserable soul from damnation. It looked as if John had also shown repentance for his sins by making a significant contribution to the church. The detective decided to improve his knowledge base about confessions. He looked forward to the next encounter. The feeling was not mutual.

Probing, the detective wanted to see if Graham could throw any light on a prominent member of his flock. Cautious and somewhat withdrawn, curiously the priest never questioned why the police were interested. 'Is this going to take all day lad because I seem to be getting the feeling you enjoy wasting my time?'

'No Father it isn't, you're a busy man.'

'Right let's get it over and done with, as you say I have work to do.'

'Father, when was the last time you saw Samuel John?'

The priest looked unperturbed. 'Let me see, he was not in church the other day. It must have been the week before.'

'Did you talk to him?'

'There was little in the way of conversation as I recall. Like all my parishioners, I thanked him for attending the service and that was possibly the end of it.'

The interviewer decided to be liberal with the truth. 'Father I hope you don't mind, can I jog your memory, John's already said he spoke to you in confession.' The look on the reverend's face suggested there was no need to remind him about the conversation.

'As you well know Macleod, that conversation is between John, I and Jesus Christ.'

'Father he's under arrest for two murders. Don't you think your conversation concerns us all?'

'Quite frankly Macleod I don't, Canon law tells us it is, 'Nefas, absolutely wrong', for a priest to betray anyone who confesses his sins and is truly repentant for any reason whatsoever, whether by word or, in any other way.'

'We've got a serial killer here molesting children. How can he be truly repentant for what he's done if he's keeps on doing it?'

The head above the collar raised his eyebrows and scanned the ceiling for the loss of his patience. 'The sacrament of the confession is invincible and cannot be broken, now if...'

With a barefaced interruption, Frank decided to join in the search for the lost art. 'You and I know no-one's safe in this town. No one was safe when you took his first confession. The first time he told you that he'd killed a little girl, he must have said he was repentant, and now he's killed again. If we don't put him away for good, God knows what he'll do next.'

Graham looked in the direction of a stain glass window. 'Officer it is my duty to save souls. It is your duty to prove the crime and arrest him.'

Anger, foul humour, surliness all decided to join in the search with the DC now on the verge of losing his temper. 'I put it to you Father, you've failed to carry out your duty as a priest, and you bloody well know it.'

The priest was somewhat taken by surprise. 'Be careful lad or it will be my duty to report you to your supervisor.'

The detective had his teeth in the Priest's backside and he refused to let go. 'Hear me out, John killed a girl and you heard his confession. He kills again, and you do the same thing again. You cannot give absolution to a person who does not genuinely intend to stop or isn't truly sorry for what he has done. You know John's a psycho and yet you took his confession. You helped him to commit another sin, sacrilege.'

'I can see that you have done your homework detective, but let me put you right. Confession is not about preventing further sins, it is about forgiving sins.' Reluctant to continue, Graham broke eye contact.

Frank still refused to let go. 'I'm not asking what the purpose of confession is. I'm saying you shouldn't have taken his bloody confession in the first place. Question: why didn't you tell him to go to the police?'

'That is not my concern. I was acting as an agent of God.'

'Isn't one of the commandments, Thou shall not kill? Why didn't you accompany him to the station?'

Graham decided to end the conversation. 'I have no intention of listening to what you have to say, I have…'

Barefaced interruption again. 'I'm telling you now, you either listen or I'll take you down the station. Question: why didn't you go with him to the station?'

'Because I didn't think, I didn't honestly think it was my business to do so.'

'You must be the only priest on the planet that thinks you're not in the business of saving lives. We know it's only a matter of time before he strikes again. Question: why haven't you made an anonymous phone call to the police station?' Graham made no reply. *Is he hiding something, or protecting the so-called sanctity of confession?* 'There's something I'm not quite getting here isn't there? Answer me this one, what did he say to you about the murders and his abuse of children outside his confession. You are not under any obligation to keep that a secret?'

'Look lad, I cannot, I just cannot and that is all there is to it.'

Anger spewed from the detective's mouth. 'I'm asking you to repeat what he said to you out of confession and all you can bloody well say is you can't. Why are you protecting him Father, has he got something on you?' The interview was now an interrogation. Frank had two options, either to go full steam ahead or report the matter to Profit and make further enquiries.

His judgemental approach had severed any rapport with the witness.

'If I answer the question, will you leave me be?'

Ghostlike, his heart raced to a point where his muscles ached inside. Frank nodded.

'I am not concerned with myself, but you must understand, it is the credibility of the church that is in jeopardy. The last thing I want is for people to turn away from God.'

The DC gave it one more try. 'For one last time Father, please help us stop any more killing. For John's sake, come back to the station and persuade him to tell us what he's done.'

'I would rather die first.'

Any further questioning seemed pointless. 'Just one more thing and I'll leave you with your conscience. Tell me who is going to hear your confession, who is going to save your soul? Speaking of confessions, here's mine. If he kills again, priest or no fucking priest, I'll be back and I'll shove your rosary right up where the sun doesn't shine.' The detective took a purposeful step forward and eyeballed the priest standing only inches away. 'By the way Father, are you looking after yourself? You're looking a little peaky around the collar.'

The DC fast tracked the action and suggested a senior officer should interview the priest. In the meantime, the SIO could apply for two search warrants for the vicarage and the church.

★★★

Sitting in the front passenger's seat, the driver watched the hem of her black skirt hovering delicately just above the knee and cursed her for it. If she had ignored smoothing the skirt under her buttocks, it would have been at least two inches higher. Frank concluded that Junia was skirt flirting. She could feel two eyes running up her thighs and disappearing down her knickers. The same eyes went into lunar orbit then she pulled the edge of the skirt over the hem of the petticoat. Barely tolerating the mouth-watering sight of her knees together, Junia torpedoed his battleship with the sensuous sound of silk stockings rubbing against the nylon fabric of her petticoat. With a sense of self-control beyond the call of duty, the detective delayed the launch of his distress signal on the clear understanding that every man would do his duty before sunset.

Straining his ears to the point of bursting an eardrum, he moved his head slightly to the left, to pick up the yummy sound of silk stockings.

'Frank, would you do me a favour love and stop the car.'

*Bloody hell what does she want now. I bet I can guess.* He slammed on the brakes and stopped the car in the middle of the road. The time had arrived to expose his second best smouldering look.

'Babes, would you mind if we made our way back to the hotel?'

*She just can't wait can she, act the innocent.* 'What have you forgotten this time?'

'I haven't forgotten anything babes. Did you see the disgruntled look on that elderly gent's face on the pedestrian crossing when you narrowly missed him by about an inch or so? Look love, I can't have that, don't go disappointing the public. Go back and run the bastard over.'

'Message understood.'

'Hope so babes because if I catch you looking at my legs again with your eyes playing peek-a-boo down my knickers instead of watching the road. I'm going to drive my stiletto heel right into your bollocks.'

Junia, not in uniform, seemed edgy and apprehensive. Although proficient at interviewing children, she had an uneasy feeling about the responsibility resting on her shoulders. Every child abuse interview has a unique quality. This one would throw up even more challenges with no complaint and no real key evidence to suggest wrongdoing. Other circumstances beyond her control could also affect the interview. What rapport would she have with Susan Rees and her parents? Junia was well aware of the significance of assessing the schoolgirl's emotional cues. How would Susan react during the interview? The paper-thin case could stand or fall on the outcome of the interview. Religiously going through her notes again, reading the interview plan, the officer felt as if it was her first interview.

Could she gain Susan's trust? That would take time. Nancy answered the door and escorted them into the kitchen. After the usual cordial exchange, she had good news. Under the guise of a health check, a local doctor had examined Susan. He had found her hymen intact. There was also an absence of bruising to suggest interference.

*Should I tell her that this does not rule out wrongdoing?*

Nancy had made every effort. However, it had yet to reach a stage where her daughter would feel confident in confiding anything untoward.

Susan joined Junia and Nancy in the living room. The detective remained in the kitchen taking no part in the interview. Thanks to that smouldering look, within a short space of time, Junia and Susan were getting on like a house on fire. The schoolgirl, mesmerised by Junia's West Wales accent, had a surprise in how much they had in common. The icebreaker was a real success. Junia now wanted to move the conversation on to a stage where Susan could talk freely without interruption. She decided to have a practice interview.

Junia remembered her notes. *Select a neutral topic and then start with open-ended questions.* 'Susan would you like to tell me about the best day of your life?

Eyes sparkled at the memory. 'Oh that one is easy Junia, it was two Christmas's ago.'

*Don't attempt to fill in the silence with another question. Let her carry on until she feels comfortable about talking in front of me.*

The officer's warm smile settled in Susan's stomach, her expression and body language said, please tell me more. 'I came downstairs in the morning and Daddy was hugging Mummy.' An infectious giggle suggested Susan was starting to feel comfortable. 'I think they were kissing each other. When they saw me, they both put their arms around me and gave me a hug.' Susan's angelic gaze fell on the person sitting next to her. 'You remember don't you Mummy, I had a new bike but best of all no quarrelling or rows or anything.'

Magic fireflies danced in her eyes. Susan told them that this year she expected a similar Christmas. The interviewer decided to tell Susan about her make-believe worst day. She was playing tennis in the back garden when the ball accidentally smashed the kitchen window. When her father arrived home, she denied having anything to do with the damage.

'What do you think about that Susan?'

'Not a lot really.'

'Why is that?'

'Well you lied to your Father. You should have said the truth. Mummy has always told me to say the truth haven't you Mummy. She says if you lie, the truth will find you out.'

Having explored her understanding of the difference between the truth and a lie, Junia moved onto the next phase of getting Susan to talk freely about John. 'Susan, as I said love, I'm a police lady. I would like to think I'm your friend as well. You are not in any trouble or anything like that. The thing is I need your help. We were talking the other day and low and behold, the name of one of your teachers, Mr John came up. I was just wondering, love, if you could tell me something about him?'

Fidgeting, sitting almost rigid, Susan tightened her grip on the arms of the chair. A pinkish tinge in her cheeks did not attempt to conceal her reaction to his name. A concerning Junia anxiously studied Susan. The schoolgirl seemed embarrassed, scared, and even anxious about the change in their conversation. Pausing, smiling and deliberately loosening any tension in her shoulders, Junia made every effort not to show any anxiety. Under the circumstances, her notes pointed out that it was inadvisable to ask the same question again. If Susan continued to remain silent, the interview could be in jeopardy.

Begrudgingly, Susan started the conversation. 'Why are you asking me about Sam, is he in any trouble?'

*Thank God, she's showing concern, even using his first name.* 'I'm going to be honest with you, he may be, we will have to wait and see.' *Honest reply, it should make her curious. I hope she goes on the defensive rather than not saying anything.*

The honesty in Susan's voice echoed above the clicking in her dry mouth. 'But he's so kind to everyone, especially to me. When Mummy and Daddy were quarrelling all the time, Sam was the one who helped me. He's a good, good teacher. He even gives up his time after school with the plays and things. And he goes to our church, doesn't he Mummy, and he reads the sermon.' Fervently she defended the schoolteacher. Junia could feel the sweat running into her bra strap. The strong bond with John appeared more than an attachment. That strong fixation might well require a more systematic approach, perhaps over several sessions.

As a last resort, she decided to take Susan to a more comfortable place in her mind before trauma ended the interview. 'It sounds to me that you and Sam are the best of friends.'

'We are, he's always doing nice things for me.'

'Has he ever bought you something nice?'

'Of course he has. Chocolates, drinks he even bought me this.' Susan opened the top of her blouse and proudly showed them a silver crucifix hanging from a chain around her neck.

Junia reacted favourably. 'You're a lucky girl, I wish I had someone like Sam to buy me something like that. The crucifix is beautiful, and you could wear that silver chain on its own or with another piece of jewellery.'

This time Susan had a more upbeat attitude. 'Gosh you're right, I didn't think of that.'

The officer decided to probe. 'I was looking for a chain like that the other day. I wonder if there's any more in the shop where Sam bought it. How long ago did he give it to you?'

'I've had it ages, I can't remember.'

'Was it before or after half-term love?'

'I think it was after half-term.'

Junia was determined to find the answer. 'Was it near someone's birthday, maybe one of your school friends?'

Susan looked surprised. 'Yes, how did you know that? It was the day before Anna's birthday, she is in my class and I remember showing it to her.'

*Check the date out when you interview.* 'You know what boys are like, I don't suppose he bothered to wrap it up properly or put it in a box?'

'Of course he did silly. He wrapped it in silver-blue paper, my favourite colour, and it was in a lovely blue box as well.'

'You lucky girl, I hope you tidied up your room and didn't make a mess leaving the paper and box around?' *Be careful, you are starting to sound pedantic. Watch your teacher/pupil style of approach and keep it friendly.*

'Mummy has always said that cleanliness is next to godliness. I put the paper and the box in the rubbish bin.'

Junia wanted something tangible that would implicate John. 'I love gift tags, did you get one?' Her expressive face etched disappointment, 'No, it doesn't matter. Where did Sam buy it from Susan?'

'I don't know he never said. I think it could be on the inside of the box.' Nancy mimed to Junia, she had not seen the crucifix before.

'What do you think of the crucifix Mummy?'

Nancy continued her supportive role. 'It's beautiful darling, if I had known I would have bought you a jewellery box.'

'So Mummy didn't know you were given a lovely present. Why was that love?' *Be careful, don't use the word WHY in a question, it could imply blame or guilt.*

'Because Sam said it is best not to.'

'What did he say babe?' *Back on track. Don't forget to keep using what instead of WHY.*

'Well he said it was our little secret of what we mean to each other. It's okay isn't it Mummy? I told Sam I would never tell you a lie, but he said keeping a secret is not lying.'

Nancy tried hard to come up smiling. 'You have nothing to worry about darling. I can't wait to hear what else he has bought you.'

Susan seemed more than happy to share the information. 'Well there was a flower, and my lipstick.'

*Don't jump in with both feet and ask about the lipstick, play it down. Ask about the flower first.* 'I knew it, I was going to say he's bought you flowers.'

'See you're wrong again Junia, I DID NOT say flowers, I SAID flower.'

*Why the snappy remark, she is oversensitive about something.* 'Do you know the name of the flower?'

'Yes if you must know, it's a blue larkspur. I keep it in my art book in my desk. In any case it's a dried flower, that's where it belongs.'

'It's an unusual flower, why did Sam choose it?'

Reluctantly, Susan answered the question. 'Because that's why, you probably don't even know what the name of the flower means.'

'Well I think I do clever clogs, it means happiness.'

'Oh no it doesn't, it stands for *FIRST LOVE*.'

Susan blurted out the answer before realising what she had said.

'Well Susan, Mummy and I would love to see it. Why do you keep it at school?'

'Because Sam said so, and he's right.'

'Why is that Susan?' *God I have used that word again.*

Again, Susan had the answer. 'When he takes our class I hold the flower in my hand and I feel close to him just like he said.'

The officer moved on to the crucial gift. 'Do you like the colour of my lipstick, it's pink ice?'

'It's ok, but I like mine the best, it's dark red.'

*Assume John bought the colour for a reason and phrase it in the question. Watch it, you are falling into the trap of asking too many leading questions, keep them open.* 'Let me tell you a secret because we're getting on so well. The detective in the other room bought me my lipstick because it's his favourite colour. Is Sam's favourite colour dark red?'

Susan looked at her mother to see if there was any negativity about the subject. 'Yes, it is but it's mine as well. He likes me to wear it because it makes me look older.'

'Frank, that's my friend, he's very kind. He's even helped me to choose this skirt. What does Sam like you to wear?'

Sharing information had gone beyond the boundary where Susan wanted to go. 'I'm not supposed to tell anyone, and I mean anyone about our secrets.'

'I told you my secret, can't you tell me yours?' *You are pushing her too hard, hold back.*

'I'm not telling so there.'

'Susan all relationships have secrets. I had a secret, and because you're my friend I shared it with you.'

'Well I can't say, and that's that.'

*Obstinate missy, should I leave it or risk it, will I get this* chance *again. Profit is relying on me.*

The difficult decision cog in her brain decided not to risk it, and then she thought about Frank. *He's not the only one with balls.* 'I think I know what your secret is. I keep my relationship with Frank a secret because we are both police officers. The truth is love, our boss wouldn't understand. I think Sam has told you not to say anything because no one would understand.' Junia had hit a nerve and Susan reacted angrily.

'Will you stop calling him Sam? I am the only one that can call him that, he is my Sam not yours.' Junia apologised and waited before moving the conversation on. Curiosity prompted Susan. 'How did you know that Junia?'

'Well love, I'm a bit older than you. Anyway, I'm glad I told you my secret, I've been dying to tell someone. I bet you feel the same way about you and Samuel John.'

Susan's innocent blush answered the question. 'Gosh Junia, sometimes you are clever. I have wanted to ever since he has been my…' Leaning over, Susan whispered 'boyfriend' in the officer's ear.

'What do you think will happen if you tell us your secret?'

'Sam said everyone would be against us. They will try to split us up, and I'm not having it.'

*Support and encourage her again but no physical contact.* 'I'm your friend Susan, why would I want to do a thing like that?' *Why, why, oh bloody why.*

'Just because that's why. Sam said people will be jealous, they would not like it because he is older. I don't know now, I'm a bit confused. Why can't you all be like Father Graham? He said we could do whatever we want.'

*Engage again, but slow the pace down.* 'I know Father Graham, he's a nice man. When did he say that to you?'

'I can see what you are up to Junia, you think I am making this up don't you. Well I am not so there. It was the other day in the vestry.'

*Concentrate, you let the wrong non-verbal slip and she noticed.* 'Susan, Mummy told me and so did you how honest you are. I am interested that's all. Can you remember what day it was?'

Susan gave it some thought. 'It wasn't last Sunday, it was two weeks ago. He even took a photograph of us so there, to show there was nothing wrong.'

'What were you doing in the photograph love?'

'It was just like some of the other ones Sam showed me so I could see there is nothing wrong about us.'

'What was in the photographs he showed you?'

'Well if you must know, they were photographs of girls like me and older men like Sam doing nice things together.'

'What was in your photograph?'

'I sat on Sam's lap, just like Mummy does with daddy and he…' Silence.

'He what love?'

'You know.'

★★★

Frank nearly took the front door off its hinges. Within seconds, the CID car hurtled passed the window.

'What did Samuel do?'

'He kissed me, that's what, so there.'

'What did Father Graham do?'

'It was hot in the vestry, so he took off my blouse and skirt.'

*Do not get upset watch how and what you say.* 'Were you wearing anything else?'

'No I just said, Father Graham took off my blouse.'

'What happened then?'

Innocent eyes again glanced at her mother. 'Well Sam said we were lucky to have a friend like Father Graham. I said yes, so Sam said that it would be nice if I could sit on our friend's lap.'

'Did you sit on his lap, love?'

'Course I did, Sam said to. I even waited for him to take, what's it called Mammy, is it a robe? He was hot as well.'

Nancy wanted to scream at the violation of her daughter. Unable to control her emotion, she burst into tears.

'Susan, I am so proud of you darling, I really am. Would you please go upstairs for a couple of minutes? I just want to speak to Junia.'

Susan looked confused. 'Everything is all right isn't it Mummy. I haven't done anything wrong have I?'

'No darling, you have nothing to worry about, just let me have a word with Junia.'

The schoolgirl reluctantly made her way up to her bedroom.

An incensed and dejected parent turned towards the officer. 'I'm sorry Junia but this is all a little too much for me to take in. Of all people, Father Graham. What happens now?'

'It looks as if the detective is already on his way to talk to Father Graham. I know this is hard for you Nancy, I really do, but I'd like to continue with Susan. We've come so far, I would like her to make a statement.' Nancy rejected the idea. After discussing it with her husband and with his consent, she had no objection to Susan making a statement.

The CID car nearly collided with a stationary vehicle parked outside the Catholic Church. Climbing the steps to the entrance, the detective had one thought on his mind. Graham's feet would not touch the ground. Any bullshit could wait until he occupied the next cell to John.

The priest, conspicuous in his cassock, silk sash and skullcap, was leaning over the altar. Walking briskly, hurrying down the aisle, when he was within striking distance, he intended giving the priest a 'bloody good dig'. Graham failed to acknowledge his presence. Only a stride or two away, the detective noticed something trickling down the steps of the altar. Moving closer, he could distinctly make out at least two different shades of red in a pool of blood at the front of the steps. The priest's upper torso was leaning face down on the marble table of the alter. The detective noticed the right sleeve of his woollen cassock rolled up above his elbow. Frank could see the gory muscle tissue of a deep wound from the elbow to his wrist on the back of his right forearm. It appeared to be following the line of the vein and arteries. Despite the absence of blood dripping from his forearm, droplets still splashed into a massive pool on the floor. From the side, looking along the surface of the marble, the priest's hands were gripping the handle of a dagger. The blade had gone straight through his throat with the steel tip protruding out of the back of his neck. Strangely, the handle was resting against a small block of marble about eight inches square on the surface of the alter. Someone had carved the etching of a cross on the side of the block. Graham must have used bodily pressure against the block to force the blade through his neck.

A holy book of the Gospels, unleavened bread, and a chalice were on the table. Frank noticed an incense burner hanging down by the side of the victim. Why was the handle of the dagger resting against the small marble block instead of the surface of the alter?

Graham had made a sacrifice of himself at his last mass. This was more than a dutiful suicide. Through the ritual of the mass, the priest had turned bleeding to death into the miracle of martyrdom. A small hollow compartment, cut out of the edge of the table, matched the shape and size of the marble block. With his two fingers inside the hole, carefully, he retrieved a small parchment made of lead foil. Wrapped inside, he found the tiny bone fragments of a catholic martyr buried beneath the altar.

In despair, sitting head down in the pew, Frank tried to take in another death in the name of Christianity. In the auditory cortex of his brain, he could hear the voice of the seer. *Look and see what is real. The seat that is holding you is from the ancient temples of Rome. The shape of this church in a cross is not of God, but that of the long ago pagan temples with wings facing north, south, east and west. As you saw with your eyes the black heart of evil, now look at the heart of sacrifice that is the alter. Is it not the same as the one used by pagans for human sacrifice, is not the chalice the same that caught the spilled blood from a human throat of the sacrifice. Look to the candle and incense, are they not used in all of the witchcraft born to man. Do not lose hope my blood. It is not what I, dryw (Seer), spoke to on the shore of our land, named Jesus from Nazareth. The demon will kill again and so must you if you are called to do so.*

Unable to move, shooting pains travelled down his spine and paralysed his nervous system.

# CHAPTER 28

# WHORE SPIDER

The General Post Office came up with a number of interesting telephone calls. John received two calls on the night of the homicide from a telephone kiosk. Gregory phoned West from home at 9.50 p.m. the same evening. The pigeon fancier had also received a call from a telephone kiosk a short distance away from the teacher's home just prior to phoning West. The team thoroughly searched all the likely venues, including the suspect's home and found nothing. West's neighbour reported seeing a Bentley parked in the street during the early hours of the night in question. There was nothing distinctive or suspicious about the car. John's Bentley was now missing.

Totally committed, the team moved methodically through the phases of the investigation and the approach seemed promising. In reality, there was little evidence to connect the prisoner or anyone else to the murders. The positive sighting of the suspect talking to Gregory outside his house connected the offender to the victim. In his statement, West had also implicated John in child abuse. Whether the ACC liked it or not, at some stage, he would have to interview the suspect.

Examining all the evidence and intelligence again, Profit revisited both crime scenes as part of his interview plan. Any statement by Susan would add impetus to the investigation and subsequent interview. At least that would have been the case if her parents had allowed her to make one. During his visit, the ACC emphasised the criticality of the case. He managed to persuade Nancy, but Robert remained steadfast. It was not in his daughter's interest to be involved in the case. Junia made a transcript of the interview with Susan. Without her corroborative evidence, it had little value.

Mears told Profit about the strange confrontation that had taken place between the suspect and Macleod shortly after his arrest. Their verbal exchange had genuinely upset the prisoner. The detective could sit in on the interview as a watching brief. Profit would ask the questions.

Someone had mysteriously hired Sir Kenneth Wood Johnson QC, with chambers in London, to represent the prisoner. He had taken silk some five years earlier after spending the previous twelve as a barrister. Johnson had a formidable reputation on behalf of the Crown. A junior barrister would probably represent John at interview. Surprisingly, the athletic suntanned grey-haired frame of the eminent QC presented himself at the front desk at 1.00 p.m. He demanded to see his client to progress the defence prior to interview.

Standing in the middle of the room, John showed little concern about the impending interview. Pupil dilation, heart rate, adrenaline and nervous system, were all under control. With the same cold-blooded attitude he used towards his victims, he reluctantly sat down at the table next to his barrister. With an air of superiority, John looked straight through the detective. Profit introduced himself to the suspect now diligently listening to a banging noise emanating from a radiator.

Respective pocket books to take notes were on the table. The teacher sneered at Profit sitting across the table, and took the initiative. 'Assistant chief constable, can I pre-empt your opening questions designed to get me talking. Yes, I was offered what can loosely be described as food. I smoke occasionally, and yes I am comfortable as one could imagine in that rat infested hovel you call a cell.'

Profit looked confident. 'Thank you Samuel that will save time.'

John had his own agenda. 'In my anxiety to help, I seem to have taken control of your interview? I appear to be doing it again by pointing out your shortcoming of not asking how I would prefer to be addressed. You will refer to me as Mr John, and I will refer to you as cannon fodder. You can now move onto the next stage, which if my memory serves me right, is the open question stage followed by the direct question phase in your interview plan.'

Profit remained calm. 'Again, thank you Mr John for reminding me. Can we now get on with the interview?'

John seemed to be enjoying himself. 'One last observation, can you hear the hot air trapped in the radiator? As a senior officer, you must be familiar with hot air?' Wrinkling his brow, the horizontal lines across the bridge of his nose showed the utter contempt he had for Profit. 'The solution is obvious. You BLEED it until all the hot air drains away and you hear a HISSING NOISE. I would only be too happy to offer my BLEEDING service. As someone born within the sound of Bow bells, I know linguistically, you love the word 'BLEEDING', so do I. It is now your turn to expound hot air. I will desist and allow you to make a fool of yourself.'

The interviewer started with a standard question designed to clarity John's understanding of his situation. 'Can you tell me why you have been arrested and detained at this station?'

Wood Johnson placed his hand on the prisoner's shoulder. 'If you say one more word Mr John, I will dispense with my services.' The barrister opened his briefcase and placed a document on the table. 'My client wishes to hand in a prepared statement. It adequately covers his innocence in the matters you wish to put to him. The alibi provided by his sister demonstrates that it was impossible for him to commit the crime of murder. Any other outrageous accusations are frankly in the realms of fantasy and are not sustainable at all. Before my client will even consider answering questions, I expect to see all the key witness statements and relevant evidence. If amongst them there are accusations of impropriety with children, I demand they are supported by medical statements from the doctor examining the so-called victims.'

Profit still had his professional hat on. 'Being uncooperative is not going to get us anywhere. All we are trying to do is to seek the truth, nothing more, and nothing less.'

Wood Johnson continued to stamp his authority. 'If it is the truth you're after, what about the truth that my client has been assaulted by DS Thomas during his detention. And what about the Gestapo tactics used on my client by your staff that has resulted in sleep deprivation?'

'I am willing to hear any complaint, can we get on? It is in the interests of justice to continue with the interview.'

'I will be making a formal complaint about the matters raised.'

A spider, diligently working on a web in the far corner of the room, captured the prisoner's attention. Wood Johnson's cufflinks and pearl-effect tiepin were not the only things attributing to his sparkling performance. 'In the meantime, I have no intention of letting my client take part, in what can only be described as a fishing expedition.'

'Can we continue with the interview? Your client has a right to know the accusations against him. He also has the right to reply.'

The barrister bowled a yorker. 'Mr Profit, there is little evidence to implicate my client to the accusations you have conjured up. Let me remind you that my client has the right of silence, and that is what I have advised him to do.'

Profit adjourned the interview. The barrister followed him into a side room to examine the feasibility of continuing the interview. Wood Johnson started the exchange.

'Benjamin, sorry about that, the last time I saw you was at our meeting just before you decided to take up residence in South Wales.'

A more assured look had replaced the anxiety on Profit's face. 'Still in the fraternity?'

'Yes at the Muses, excellent progress on that score. Let me put my cards on the table Benjamin. As Queen's Counsel, my work is concerned with the prosecution. Although I have to say, I am also one of only five QCs with a license to act on behalf of the defence. The truth is I have taken this case as a favour to my client's father. At the same time, I am obligated to tell you that someone is leaking information from your team. I am aware the only statement you have is from the deceased West, and he is hardly going to give evidence to support that statement. With my QC hat on, the investigation went badly from the start. Through your effort, things have turned around somewhat. The truth is you are still not in a position to put significant evidence my client's way. I suggest you release him, continue with your enquiries and obtain the evidence. By that time I will have abandoned ship.'

'Kenneth, sorry, but I am unable to do that.'

A more authoritative barrister continued. 'The reality is you have no choice in this matter.' Wood Johnson handed the officer a writ. 'That is a summons for the chief constable of Gwent to appear at court to secure the release of John. In my opinion, you have unlawfully detained my client. *Habeas Corpus ad sub jiciendum*, you shall have the body, is an ancient writ from the court. It will be for the court to decide if you have the right to detain my client in police custody. I warn you, when the court decides in my favour, petition will be made against the police for civil damages, unlawful arrest, and trespass.'

It was time for Profit to even the score. 'Can I remind you, your loyalty as a brother is to me, Kenneth, and not the prisoner?'

Shaking the right hand of the barrister, using a secret password, Profit pressed his thumb between Johnson's first and second knuckle joint. 'Shibboleth', Johnson responded and repeated the word.

Profit started the formal exchange. 'What is the fraternity?'

'A peculiar system of morality veiled in allegory and illustrated by symbols.'

The interviewer continued. 'Name the grand principles on which the fraternity is founded?'

'Truth, love and belief.'

'Have you anything to tell me?'

Wood Johnson answered the question with the formal response. 'Do you likewise pledge yourself, under the promises of all your obligations that you will conceal what I shall now impart to you with the same strict caution as the other secrets?'

'I do.'

The barrister now took the lead. 'Having been kept for a considerable time in a state of darkness, what is your present condition? What is the predominant wish of your heart?'

The SIO anxiously blurted out the word. 'Light.'

'Then, I have information which you may want me to depart.'

It was Profit's turn again to ask the questions. 'Who is leaking information from my team?'

'Detective Sergeant Ryan Thomas, the so-called complaint against him was fabricated to put you off the scent.'

'Who is the information being leaked to?'

Wood Johnson gave the authoritative reply in order to protect another brother. 'I cannot say, I will not injure him myself or knowingly suffer it to be done by others.'

A concerned Profit asked the next critical question. 'Will your so-called Habeas Corpus writ succeed?'

'Yes, the learned Judge is a brother.'

'Kenneth, what can you tell me about the guilt of your client?'

'John trusts no one, he has not confided in me, except he

appears well informed. I am not aware where he is getting information. He knows nothing about Thomas.'

'What else can you say to assist my case?'

Wood Johnson had no alternative other than to tell all. 'It may be something trivial, Bernard Jones a headmaster, has given a character reference to support the Habeas Corpus. I find that strange, why would he get involved with someone suspected of murder and child abuse. The comprehensive post mortem report came as no surprise. I am aware of the credibility of Moses Black. However, I am surprised that you did not call on his services when you searched my client's house and caravan. He is possibly the best in his field. I suggest you remember that.'

A tinge of irony slipped from Profit's tongue. 'Is there anything you don't know about the investigation? You seem to know everything.'

Wood Johnson continued to assist the SIO. 'One more thing, refrain from asking questions, he is going to say nothing. You will be showing what little evidence we may not be aware of.'

'Will you stop representing John if he is released?'

The barrister looked relieved. 'Yes, my obligation is at an end, I've no intention of assisting him again. Of course, you could bail John on the understanding that he stays with his father in Cardiff. Even though this condition is not legally enforceable prior to charge, it might assist you in some way. You could keep him under surveillance.'

A dejected Profit acknowledged the inevitable. 'It sounds to me that I've little choice. As a brother will you keep me informed?'

Wood Johnson placed the palm of his right hand on his left breast and extended a thumb upwards in the form of a square. 'This is an illusion to the penalty of our obligation implying that as a man of honour and a fellow brother, I would rather have my heart torn from my breast, than improperly disregard the duty you have entrusted in me.'

John continued to take an interest in the spider spinning its web in the corner of the ceiling. He watched as the spider ejected a sticky silk thread to form a strong bridge line to hang the web. Creating Y shapes, it started to make spirals from the centre. With the snare finished, the arthropod sat in the centre of the web, and waited.

Frank decided that a conversation with John was more

preferable to boredom. 'What makes you so interested in spiders?'

The sound of the detective's voice brought John back from his daydreaming. 'Fascinating creatures are they not. Do you think my so-called barrister would have any objection if I educated your ignorant and rather lonely intellect?'

'I'm already hanging by a thread on your every word.' Hypocritical eyes rattled the detective's bones.

The prisoner relished the sound of his own voice. 'In Catholicism the spider also represents the devil. Both are demonic creatures that set an elaborate trap to capture their prey. Just as the spider ensnares the fly, so does a devil traitor. Judas is a prime example. He embraced Christ in the garden of Gethsemane before betraying him.' A softer tone expressed authenticity. 'Of course, there are different species of spider, the one I loathe the most is the whore spider. My mother was a whore spider. She enticed and lured promiscuous insects into her web to engage in sexual intercourse. The spider reminded me of the time when, as a boy, I watched someone like you, McLeod, fucking my mother and I suppose, in essence, fucking any chance I had to have anything like a normal life.' His boyish persona slowly raised his eyes and looked across the table. It seemed to be conveying a message of regret, sadness, acceptance, and a glint of self-pity. 'And this is what you see before you today.'

For a brief moment, Frank could see emotional honesty and hopelessness in his eyes. The magic of remembering searched the soul of the prisoner for that one day, just that one day, when as a child, he woke up and opened his eyes to a mysterious colourful world. Where there was no evil intent or false sense of knowing, only a childlike wonder. Then the trust he had in everything disintegrated. With his innocence defiled, the child in his eyes was lost forever.

John had let his mask slip. He recognized the sincerity in his voice. Adjusting his psychological mask, again insanity took control of his death drive. 'Let me attempt to explain to an ignoramus like you the one thing I admire most about the spider. This arthropod utilises a well-planned hunting technique. It lies in wait at the centre of the web. When the quarry is stuck in the web, like a vampire, the spider carefully injects poison and slowly sucks the life out of it until it dies.'

Could the detective unsettle the teacher again? 'Is that what you did to West, did you suck the life out of him because he betrayed you?'

'It is your job to untangle the web of lies and deceit surrounding the investigation. It is my good fortune to look from the side lines and laugh at your incompetence.'

The DC went for the jugular. 'Speaking of deceit, didn't you tell Graham you were repentant and that you would never kill again? Isn't that a bloody good EXAMPLE of deceit?'

'McLeod, you have no idea what you are talking about.'

'I know one thing, you can't deceive God. If you think your sins are forgiven, you're only deceiving yourself.'

Angrily, the prisoner pushed back his chair. With both hands on the table, he leaned towards the detective. 'It is the divine will of God that people die. Who am I to turn my back on Jehovah?'

A long agonising cry bawled throughout the station. 'Thy will be done on earth as it is in heaven, YOU PATHETIC EXCUSE FOR A HUMAN BEING. Behold the day of the Lord is coming with fury and BURNING with anger. He will through his servant EXTERMINATE sinners.'

This time the officer launched himself and pushed his face directly in front of the prisoner. 'I won't allow you to take any more lives. I'll end your MISERABLE LIFE and bury you in the ground.'

John grabbed his shirt as Profit and Wood Johnson entered the room. The prisoner refused to let go. It took Profit and another police officer to separate them. Wood Johnson made a complaint about the treatment of his client. Profit defended the detective he looked the innocent agent. Nevertheless, Profit still had words of advice. 'I know tempers are running high, but I heard you threatening the prisoner, you could be in trouble.'

Morale took a downturn when the SIO informed his team that he had no alternative other than to release the prisoner on bail into the custody of his father.

# CHAPTER 29

## EURIPIDES – EVERY DOG HAS HIS DAY

A somewhat maudlin Rees John drummed his fingers on the steering wheel to the tune 'Cry me a River'. The police authority knew about the circumstances. Even if the accusations were unfounded, they remained on file. Bulging grimacing muscles tightened around his eyes. All the years of service, even the sufferance of his family, were all now irrelevant. He had tended his resignation. Samuel John opened the rear door of the MGB GT parked outside the station. Even with his sense of superiority, he knew his place. There were no words or even an acknowledgement. The only sound throughout the journey came from the engine. John glared at the back of the drivers head, and he tried to recall any meaningful conversation between them. The recollection amounted to one word, 'SShhh', accompanied by the well-known finger gesture to the lips. '*Por que no te callas*, why don't you shut up' would have been preferable than total rejection.

Boredom, the lack of conversation and the tiresome journey, brought about the reverie of daydreaming. His resourceful imagination would more than compensate for boring company. John glanced out of the window. Why did it always rain in the valley? Tracing the rain crawling down the window, he remembered Bridie's play *Mr Bolfry*. It aptly described his father's ability to initiate humdrum. Bolfry's observation that, 'boredom is a sign of satisfied ignorance, blunted apprehension, crass sympathies, dull understanding, feeble powers of attention, and irreclaimable weakness of character' personified Pater. The recollection brought about a discerning smile. How apt, in the play, Bolfry introduced himself as the devil. Another well-informed smirk sashayed onto his mouth. Of all the accusations levelled against him, being a bore was not one of them. In fact, the majority of his well-rehearsed ad-libs were THE highlights of many a social gathering.

Voltaire's infamous, '*Sept Discours en vers sur l'Homme*, the secret to being a bore is to TELL everything', spring-boarded and balanced rather precariously on his psychological beam. He had more than an inclination to tell Pater everything, particularly the gruesome details. His insatiable appetite consumed and digested the overwhelming thought. Hurriedly, he pressed the restraint button, and, with a full turn, he dismounted from the beam. It was time to think about something else.

Though the darkness beyond insanity, John's repetitive projector flickered the image of his family under the cherry blossom tree with Nettles the Labrador dog. He could see the source of his constant rejection taking a photograph. A small boy tried to reach out to his father through the lens for unconditional love. Surely, Pater had taken the picture to capture his vulnerability, his moment of need. When he looked at the photograph, surely he would recognise that in his son. The chilly intimacy of the picture started to fade. He could still feel the pain of emotional neglect abounding on that hot sunny day. Why was that day so relevant? Resting his head against the window, after all the years of wondering, John realized the significance of it all. When his father looked at him through the camera, they must have made eye contact. Rees John walked from behind the camera, patted the dog on the head and walked briskly passed without acknowledging his existence. At least Nettles seemed at one with the world. After all, he was the one leading a dog's life.

John still rested his head against the car window. If only he could have changed places with Nettles that day. The more he thought about it the more appealing it became. Moreover, dogs are incapable of reading negative energy. They only live for the moment of the day, not in the past or the future. Indubitably, canines are also pack orientated. Voluntarily, they turn their head to avoid eye contact to allow the master to be the leader. But most of all, he liked their aggression to anyone trying to take anything away from them. Surely, Pater's rejection to GIVE him what he craved for derived from the same paradoxical box as TAKING something away from a dog. Give and take may be antonyms, but they both usually end in tragedy. For some insidious reason John could not let go of that thought. Looking out of the window, through the drizzling rain, he could see the sign '*Cardiff 9 Miles*'. Soon he would be in his own back yard. Soon it would be time for this dog to have his day.

# CHAPTER 30

# BARKING MAD

Black zipped up the body bag. The task ended his exploration of the crime scene. Although somewhat unprofessional, he did not intend to apologise to anyone for running from the garage and being gorily sick on the driveway. The scene resembled an abattoir. The pathologist had rarely witnessed the extent of blood on the floor and walls. Rees John was lying almost naked on his back in front of his car. He could see multiple bites extending from the torso to his head. Taking a closer look, dried blood in close proximity to the ears and mouth confirmed haemorrhaging. Both the victim's eyes were also punctured.

John's windpipe, jugular vein, and main artery all torn away from his neck had resulted in total blood loss. Moving in with his camera, he took photographs of the blood splatter on the wall that had spurted out in an arch from the jugular vein. A further examination would describe the movement of both victim and perpetrator before, during, and after the attack. Although an atheist, Black prayed to any supreme being that the victim had lost consciousness before the relentless onslaught.

Black was only one of a handful of pathologists with experience in forensic dentistry. During the early part of his career, he wrote a dissertation on Ralph Keith, the dentistry lead on the Doyle incident in Texas. This case revolutionised the acceptance of forensic dentistry in court. Using his own technique, Keith matched the teeth marks found on a piece of cheese left at the scene to Doyle. Later, Keith became famous when he matched Ted Bundy's unusual dental pattern to a bite mark on the victim's buttock.

His experience also included dealing with a number of vicious attacks carried out by dogs. This had the hallmarks of a canine attack. The sheer depth of the puncture wounds, the ferocious jagged edges left on the skin, gave every indication a vicious animal had caused the injuries. Extreme strength, shaking its head, had succeeded in tearing masses of flesh away from the body. He knew that canine power, from closing the upper and lower jaw, had the capability of transferring far more strength than any human bite. Goring of the skin must have been caused by the two upper and lower large fangs located at the front of the jaw.

As he moved through the blood towards the body, Black could see cluster bites on the forehead that had torn most of the scalp away from the skull. Thick coagulated blood had replaced his right cheek. Yes, it definitely had the ferocity of a canine attack. He used a magnifying glass to examine a mark directly underneath the heart, and another prominent pattern on the bridge of his nose. Impressions from the edges of the teeth on the skin underneath the heart were well defined. The overall appearance of this mark looked more sadistic or sexual in comparison to other aggressive wounds. The mark on his nose comprised of four incisor teeth in the midline of the bite arch. The shape of the bite was almost circular. The teeth were smaller than he expected.

How could the mark be circular? Not infallible, he must have made a mistake. Black expected to see six long, curved, incisor teeth, the characteristics of an animal bite. Although he had not dealt with an attack like this for some time he knew that canine marks formed a U shape. The trauma of the scene must have taken the edge off his concentration. Methodically going through the injuries again, his finding confirmed what he already knew. *God does not exist this is no canine homicide.* A double, almost 3D bite mark, on his stomach from the skin slipping from the teeth after initial contact and then biting again, satisfied his diagnosis. Drag marks from the teeth sliding through the blood were human. He turned the victim onto his side. John had his hands tied behind his back with barbed wire.

With his noiseless world spinning around, unsteady on his feet, dizzy, Black refused to accept that a human being was responsible for this abhorrent attack. The sorrowful truth, particularly the denial of 'what is', rattled inside his skull. Stomach cramp moved up to a new level and he ran from the building. Black pushed aside the investigating team. In the driveway, the green yellow sickly content of his stomach, exploded in his throat and gushed from his mouth and nose. A minute or so of retching, without bringing anything up, hinted at his physical acceptance to acknowledge pure evil.

With a little help from his friend, he revisited the scene. Moving on, the pathologist placed a flash camera on a tripod at a ninety-degree angle to photograph the bite marks. To prevent distortion, he positioned another light source at a perpendicular angle to each bite. Using a colour filter, his technique had to be exact if he wanted to make an accurate match with a suspect's dental profile. Finally, placing an L-shaped ruler at the site of each bite, he measured the curvature, shape, and size of the injury. Improvising, he used cotton tips and cigarette papers to collect the saliva and fluid left in the teeth marks.

His challenge came where the bite marks overlapped each other. This made it difficult for the pathologist to carry out an independent analysis of each site. Reddish bruised arch bites also failed to show any distinctive marks. Black noticed a vertical line of similar bites running from the groin to the neck below the site of his missing right cheek. The marks on the neck, were they love bites. The offender must have been taunting the victim by placing the skin in his mouth, and sucking it, before finally savaging the right side of his face. After photographing the injuries, he concentrated on the more defined impressions. Carefully dusting the incision and shape of the bites with black powder, using finger tape, he transferred the indentation onto sheets of acetate. Taking great care, the pathologist made a plaster cast of two prolific wounds made by the teeth. Another significant injury consisted of a straight-line bruise around the neck.

The pathologist spent the next hour logging and recording the location, shape, colour, size, and type of injury of each mark. With his chin almost touching his chest, he forced air into the lungs to try and take in the sheer depth of the bites penetrating the skin. The extent of the injury must have resulted in nerve and muscle damage.

Exhibit MB/67/IJ looked unusual. Sharp edges had crushed the bone at the top of the index finger of his right hand. The pathologist could just make out a vertical line of letters on the side of the finger, probably made with a needle. The letters, 'SShhh' must have some significance it meant nothing to him.

For the second time in his career, Black modelled a plaster cast of the upper and lower dentations of the offender. From photographs, acetates, and castings, he made an accurate representation of a dental profile. Key features in the dentistry were encouraging. Both lateral incisors at the front of the lower jaw were twisted and rotated. He focused in on the blank space between the first and third right molar on the upper jaw. The overall result, including the width and thickness of the teeth, evidentially, looked promising. The cast was only part of the puzzle. Hopefully at some stage he would be able to obtain wax impressions, bite samples, from a suspect and compare them with the cast.

In the meantime, for elimination purposes, Black acquired the dental records of Samuel John. The information on record was both adequate and reliable. Seven features from the dental records matched the master cast. Additionally, records showed gaps in his profile identical to the marks found on the body. After making a risk assessment, the extent of evidence had reached a stage that would allow him in a court of law to classify the match as 'unusually rare if not unique'. Any further analysis of the suspect's features could move the evidential qualification on to allow him to say it was a 'perfect match'. From the demographic and position of the bites, most of them were delivered by the offender face on with his head tilting slightly upwards looking at the victim.

★★★

Black sat behind a desk and pulled down the blinds. His calendar registered the sixth day of systematically going through all the evidence. Sadly, the post-mortem revealed that the victim had regained conscious recognition prior to his fatal attack. He closed his eyes to the scattering of starlight and dark shadows filtering into the room. The pathologist was still trying to rationalise the incident. How could anyone maul his father like a savage animal? *Non compos mentis* must have taken him to a place way beyond insanity. The pathologist took comfort in the fact that he had a devoted family. Sally had been the icing on the dynasty cake. Their relationship epitomised the intimate bond only twins can understand. Sharing experiences at the same point in their emotional and physical life created an inimitable attachment. Some considered they were freakish, with an interdependent identity. It had never entered his mind at all. The bonding exuded a passionate intensity until the tragic accident severed their emotional cord.

Moses recalled a quizzical teacher who insisted on an explanation regarding the extent of their emotional connection. He told a lie saying the bond was too difficult to describe. How could he attempt to rationalise the incident when Sally fell in the play yard, and miles away he felt excruciating pain to his knee? Yes, their attachment went way beyond the five senses.

*Isn't it just like you to remember something that puts me at a disadvantage? If you are going to take that line, what about all the times you had dental treatment and I was the one who felt the pain.*

*I think the lady doth protest too much. In my defence, your pain was nothing in comparison to what I had to endure when you gave birth.*

*Moses, the most hilarious thing was you continually phoning me to complain about morning sickness!*

Moses smiled as Sally's laughter echoed around his soul. *Sally, I hope you do not mind me asking, but am I dreaming or am I going insane?*

*Brother dear, you are not dreaming, but as I suspect, as they say in our adopted country, you are definitely an olive short of a pizza. It is hard to explain, my consciousness is piercing through your physical self. You are awake, everything you hear is inside your head.*

*Sally can you see me?*

Sally was enjoying the interchange because she had all the answers. *I can do better than that. Since my experience of going through the light, not only can I see you, I know everything you have ever done in your life. I instantly know what you are thinking.*

Black posed another question. *What do you mean, 'Going through the light?'*

*The first thing I remember after the car crash was looking down at my body still in the car. It was strange seeing me for the first time in three-dimensional form. I then had the feeling of being drawn into a stream of light. For some reason I knew the light was beyond visible light. There was no light absorption, colour, or reflection. The intensity of it was so bright it looked as if infinity was lit up with a million fluorescent tubes. When the energy absorbed me, somehow I became aware that the light knew all about me, just as I know everything about you. But there was something more hypnotic. The light embraced me like, like the warm hands of a loving parent, I felt pure emotion. The only explanation I can give is that something was giving me all the love I could possibly take in. I could distinctly feel something inviting me into the second light, where I knew I would experience a kind of love beyond description. The most amazing feeling of belonging brushed my* consciousness. I knew that once I embraced the second light I could not return. I could yield to it any time, but once I accepted it, I could not return. Silence.

Moses seemed apprehensive. *What did you decide to do, Sally?*

*Moses as they say, I decided to take a rain check.*

*Why?*

*I could ask you the same question. Why do you think I knew about the non-return clause? I think it was a reciprocal statement to a pre-ordained decision. The choice I had really was no choice at all. The funny thing was I knew I was going to turn it down even before the asking.*

Black reflected on her explanation. *Unfortunately sister, your explanation does not answer my question.*

*What about this, my clever brother. I believe, and so do, you that everything happens for a purpose. My death, my rejection to move on, has happened for a purpose. I know there is no devil or purgatory waiting on the other side. At least I have never experienced it. All you feel is the profound love of an omnipotent God with no strings attached and no hidden agenda.*

Moses thought about asking a question. Sally knew what it was before he opened his mouth. *Please let me finish Moses, I will answer the question you want to ask later. From the boot camp that you call earth, I have seen the evil inherent in those who want to harm, maim, and debase their fellow human being. Your world is full of monsters that for whatever reason, take pleasure in raping an innocent child walking home from school, or literally blowing away anyone unfortunate to be in the wrong place at the wrong time. And there are people like you who are destined to walk with the spirit on earth to bring sanity to a world that cries out for justice. You have a gift. As someone in a past life involved in the system, I was gobsmacked when, for the first time, I saw my brother using fingerprint methodology to transfer the marks of a bite onto acetate. I do not have to tell you the contribution you have and will continue to make to forensic science. Moses, remember when you and I sat an essay exam. We gave exactly the same answer, and the headmaster accused us of cheating. In order to save our secret you took the blame and had to re-sit the exam. You were always there for me when I needed a hand, well now it is my turn. I know you cannot let go, you are still holding on to the memories of what we were. I also know you were silly enough to contemplate suicide. To be honest with you Moses, I seriously doubt if you can survive without my help. I also have doubts that I can face whatever happens to me without you.*

*To answer the question you were about to ask when I mentioned the word God. Does such a thing exist? I can tell you now, your atheist belief is not* wrong, but you are certainly not right either. From my limited experience, the beyond is more personalised and less formal than religion. What I can say to you is love and not religion is important. There is meaning beyond the universe. The important thing for you to accept is that it IS the how and why I will deal with later. The next thing you will be asking is how many angels' heads can you balance on a pinhead. The upside is now I know everything and I MEAN everything about you. Thanks to you, I can answer the other impossible question, 'what does a one handclap sound like'.

Instinctively, Black cleared his throat. *I am aware of the so-called mystical question, but I do not see how your all-knowing of me has answered that question.*

*Then let me enlighten you Moses. Every time you masturbate under the duvet, the angels hear the sound of a one-hand clap. Would you like me to tell you how many times in your life you have orchestrated the one handclap?*

His complexion changed to a blush pink. *Please stop it Sally, you are embarrassing me.*

*Just one last thing and then I will let you off the hook. Can you tell me what was unique about the handclap you demonstrated on the 11th February 1946?*

*How do I switch you off Sally?*

*I already know you cannot answer. When you masturbated, you fantasised about women.*

The all-seeing experience must have been contagious. Moses knew she was right.

*By the way, brother I have good news for you on that score. The light is only concerned with what is within your heart, and not your sexual preference. We are all connected together and we are all the same. It is natural not a sin. The only reason why some think of it as a sin is that they have to hate or shame somebody. Unfortunately, homosexuality is the bitter pill of the generation you are living in.*

Moses was more than interested in his next query. *Will the attitude towards homosexuals ever change?*

*I honestly do not know, you live in the present, I died in the past and the future belongs to the future. The strange thing is in this dimension there is no such thing as time or space. However, I can tell you that you are running out of time, if you do not put John behind bars any time soon, he will continue with his killing spree. Can I add a PS and then I promise to leave you in peace?*

*Go ahead my all-seeing sister.*

# CHAPTER 31

# DROCHFHOULA

John turned off the A48 and headed north along the 'Heads of the Valley' road towards Abergavenny. Checking the speedometer, travelling at a reasonable speed, the last thing he wanted was to draw attention. At that moment, apart from his perfect choice in hiring a Ford Transit, he had grave reservations about everything, including his state of depression. A feeling of guilt, even regret for behaving like a zombie towards Pater, had dragged his soul to a very dark and lonely place. The flesh-eating vile act had even curtailed the euphoric high he usually experienced after a kill. How could he have done such a thing? With tears running down the cheeks, he tried to rationalise his behaviour. This killing was personal. For the first time, uncontrollable rage and hatred to the exclusion of anything else had motivated this dogfight.

Impulsive, unrestrained killing had no place in his portfolio. John gloried in the fact that his belligerence was nothing short of a model in goal orientation. He had lost count of the number of times he had fantasised about killing Father. When the time came to make the fantasy a reality, *tasteless* unsavoury behaviour spoilt the essence of the day. Something elbowed the laugh centre in his brain. The urge to burst out laughing at his own critique surged into his mouth. He was not going to let that happen. Clenching his jaws and biting his tongue would do the trick. Muscles like marbles, formed at the corners of the mouth. John could still taste the urge fizzing on his tongue, like champagne. Was it entirely appropriate to describe the mouth-watering experience as 'tasteless'? Snorting gave way to a shrill whinnying noise. Holding his nose, at the same time, he covered his mouth. He could hear the footsteps of idioms and metaphors all forming an orderly queue. The giggle twins, 'biting off more than you can chew' and 'making a meal of it', sliding down the yardarm, took the wind out of his sails. He started to howl like a prostitute that had just found a wallet under her bed.

Gripping the steering wheel, he pulled into the nearest lay-by. The whammy, 'life has a tendency to come back and bite you in the arse' caught him off guard with a sucker punch under the armpit. Rolling around, gripping the car seat and holding his breath, he skipped through a multiplication table. However, to no avail, idioms continued to snog his brain. SH- SH- surely, he started to shake. Surely, it was in the 'best possible taste'. Initially he had no intention of biting 'the hand that feeds you'. In fact, the whole incident had left *a* 'bad taste in his mouth'. The tower bells of Notre Dame, ringing out to celebrate the arrival of lunacy, imploded in his brain.

Several minutes passed before the pain finally subsided in his stomach muscles. He found the revelry quite bizarre. The very thing that brought about his sorry state had ended up making him laugh. Wiping the mucous streaming from his nose, hysterical depression stepped out of the spotlight to give way to the ridicule of the creatures inhabiting this planet. Yes, he and he alone had single-handedly taken up the challenge against the evil inherent within mankind, including the Catholic Church. Metaphors, even idioms, were all entertaining, but quotations had far more substance particularly from the mouth of George Orwell. Orwell described his predicament when he said, 'People sleep peaceably in their beds at night only because rough men stand ready to do violence on their behalf.' He whole-heartedly agreed with the sanctity of the statement.

And sanctity was certainly the next thing on the agenda. Tomorrow, the 50th anniversary of Fatima would finally arrive to fulfil his destiny as a true disciple ordained to 'enlighten the world'. Glancing in the rear view mirror, he could see all the sacks of ammonium nitrate fertiliser lying on the floor and the steel drums containing liquid nitro methane. The late night escapade at the colliery had also secured blasting powder, delay caps, fuse wire, dynamite, and a two-wire blasting machine. Yes, he had more than enough explosives to send the congregation attending the funeral to hell and back. John regretted Graham taking his own life. He would have been more than happy to undertake that task.

The trailing edge of the sun, disappearing below the horizon, left a smear of vibrant orange lava on the skyline. The last light, reflecting on the clouds, scattered a tint of amber across the entire sky. Looking west towards the sunset, he could see a Kermit-green flash, almost like a dot, directly above the sun as it fell below the horizon. Then the dark blue band of the earth's shadow hovered in the sky and his jaw dropped. Would he ever experience a magical sunset again? They would have found Pater's body by now. Even the police had enough grey matter to realise who the culprit was. John switched on the ignition and engaged the gears. The van slowly left the lay-by to continue his death drive. Wiping the condensation off the windscreen, rationalising, his life could have been so different. That made him angry. It annoyed him to think he was capable of spontaneous wistfulness.

Darkness tumbled down the mountains on either side of the road only, the headlights provided a glimmer of hope in the valley of impending gloom. In the distance, he could see light filtering from the hillside on both sides of the road. It seemed more confined and intense than a grass fire. Taking a series of left turns, John had a clear view of the light from the mountainside on the offside of the road. It looked like a bonfire. He could clearly see a whorl of flames rising into the air. Blood red flames, emanating from the base of the fire, reached into the sky. They should have been white. Slowing down to a crawl, he saw the fire swirling, climbing in the shape of a spiral. The intensity of the blaze remained constant and yet no one seemed to be attending the bonfire. A similar bonfire to his left came into view. The road was now straightening. In the distance, he could see a series of bonfires on either side of the road leading through the valley. Their location at the top of the hillside suggested they were a signal, like the bonfires that signalled the approach of the Spanish Armada.

THUD, he ducked, something landed on the roof of the van. He could hear a tapping noise above his head and then a high-pitched shrill. It was probably a bird. Suddenly, he felt pins and needles in both hands and feet. Initially John put it down to muscular cramp or poor circulation brought on by the journey. The sharp pinging noise of the bird's beak against the steel roof started to get progressively louder. Within seconds, the noise vibrating against the inside of the van pierced his eardrum. It sounded like Morse code. He looked at his hands, he could feel insects crawling, biting under his skin. They were also crawling around inside his brain and anus. Then, he experienced the feeling of a red-hot poker under his skin. The pain increased with the intensity of the noise.

He thought about pulling into a lay-by. A slight differential in the on/off tapping on the roof transmitted short and long indentations to his brain. The right side of his cortex interpreted the message. *Turn back before it is too late. The time to destroy the immortality of your evil soul and all that you are is soon. Your soul is soured, it will not live on in your grave. You will join the world of the evil dead.* Instinctively, he banged on the roof with his fist and a black raven flew away. John could make out a raven hovering against the red sky light. He knew the bird was following him.

★★★

The death of one of the most powerful officers in Wales had instigated a manhunt involving all the forces in the principality. By that time, the killer had already reached the two-storey house next to the church and garaged his van under the watchful eye of a Raven.

Because of the conversation with Wood Johnson, Profit had introduced two actions into the investigation. Find the mole tipping off the suspect and widen the scope of the investigation to include Bernard Jones, the headmaster. The SIO decided to take Walsh and Macleod into his confidence. They came up with the same name, PC Dan Archer. The officer's association with John and his more than passing interest in the enquiry made him the obvious choice. Of the two, Jones seemed the more preferable option to progress the case. At this stage, leaning heavily on a police officer with nothing more than a hunch, would probably lead nowhere. On the other hand, drip-feeding Archer with bullshit could work to an advantage.

Frank rummaged through his drawer for a clean tie. Curry stains down the front would hardly create a favourable impression with the headmaster. How handy is that? Ties, pants, stockings, shirts, even a historical pepperoni sandwich all conveniently at hand in the same drawer. Mr Hygiene moved a small box resting on top of the refuse tip to get at his pepperoni. At least he thought it was his. Using his most prominent characteristic, 'without thinking', he opened the box containing two Celtic rings. His mind wondered back to the only time he had worn the rings and the disastrous consequences that ensued. Curiosity whispered in his ear, and the rings balanced on the tip of each little finger. Photons of light from the spiral ring travelled in a straight line and penetrated his eyes. He experienced what seemed like an arc flash. Both of his hands looked like a black and white photograph. Both rings were now resting at the base of each little finger.

★★★

The detective kicked his heels against the wall waiting for someone, anyone, to answer the door. Frank had no qualms about not bothering to tell the head teacher he was calling. The element of surprise should unsettle the resident. His only other plan had to do with lady luck treating him kindly. Frank's dogged misguided confidence worked on the premise that he could make his own luck. Although unorthodox, sometimes it paid dividends. *Are they ever going to open this door?* Brass gleaming from the number thirteen on the door lifted his eyelids. The devil's number, unlucky for some, thirteen steps to the gallows, and the number of turns in the hangman's noose. He hoped they all applied to the resident. Knuckles rattled the door a third time. *This is really starting to piss me off two can play that game.*

A buxom middle-aged woman wearing a pinafore opened the door and introduced herself as the cleaner. Grudgingly, he showed his warrant card. 'Apologies for disturbing your catnap but could I have the forwarding address of the Jones family?'

The fuzz above her top lip moved sideways. 'Whatever do you mean? Forwarding address, they still live here.'

'Are you sure, by the time it took you to answer the door they could have moved to Australia?' She read the tattoo scrawled on his tongue. It said *bollocks to you and Christmas.*

'Less of your cheek lad, I am a busy woman. I don't sit on my arse like you all day drinking coffee.'

'With respect, you're talking through your trunk because I've just solved another crime.'

The cleaner glared in disbelief. 'Crime? For goodness sake, what crime?'

His deliberate glare settled on the midriff of the obese figure standing in front of him. 'Well I now know who ate all the pies stolen from the baker's shop.'

The DC had deliberately started the argument. There was nothing more unsettling than raised voices on the doorstep, particularly on your day off. The commotion had reached the ears of the headmaster in the back garden. With the door slightly ajar, the visitor could see Jones charging along the hallway. Less than a step or two from the front door, the detective changed the mood and substance of the conversation.

'I've already said, I appreciate it is his day off, but will you please tell him I'm concerned about his safety.'

The slim intellectual frame and receding hairline of Jones, now standing behind the cleaner, heard his remark.

Confused, the cleaner went on the offensive. 'You might be a policeman but you have a screw loose. What the blooming heck are you on about, one minute you are ...'

Jones interrupted. 'That is quite enough Flora. Can I remind you as cleaner you are not employed to insult people.'

'There you are Mr Jones, thank goodness, you will not believe what this so-called policeman said to me I have...'

The look over the headmaster's glasses suggested he had trodden in dog shit. 'Flora, I have heard all I want to hear from you. Would you kindly carry on with your work? I will deal with this matter.'

'Mr Jones you don't understand he...'

Sweat under the armpits oozed through his shirt. 'I do not intend to repeat myself, either you go back to work, or you can put your coat on and leave.'

Flora reluctantly hauled her 'I'll get you for that you bastard' expression inside and left them on the doorstep.

Reluctantly, Jones escorted his uninvited guest to the conservatory. Sitting comfortably in reclining chairs, the headmaster initiated the conversation.

'Well so much for heeding to the advice of my doctor. Avoiding anxiety is something I am not very good at.'

'Is there anything I can get you Mr Jones, you look pale?' Although his non-verbal told another story, inside he was ecstatic.

'Say what you have to say and then I would be grateful if you would be on your way.'

*Get straight to the point.* 'Samuel John was released from custody yesterday. He's continued his killing spree. We found what was left of his father at his home in Cardiff. No one's safe; he could be in our area.'

Same expression, different dog shit. 'Be careful of the accusations you make against my colleague, it could come back to haunt you.'

Frank was more than happy to take advantage of that remark. 'The thing that's going to haunt me for the rest of my life, Mr Jones, is the gruesome murder of his last two victims. West had his stomach cut open. Can you imagine the poor bastard with his guts hanging out and his intestines burning on a cooker?' *Go on try, it'll upset you.*

Jones seemed determined not to react to the gory scene. However, he failed miserably to show that in his dry mouth and shaky right hand.

'Let me get you a drink of water.' Without waiting for a response, the detective returned from the kitchen with a glass of water and placed it on the table in front of Jones. 'The boss would like me to assure you that a car will patrol this area day and night'. He picked up the glass of water and handed it to Jones.

Both simultaneously touched the glass. An electric charge vibrated through the detective's body into his hand holding the glass. Within seconds, the water bubbling, almost reached boiling point. Current passing through the teacher's arm connected to his brain. The link induced sensory neutrons to receive and send simultaneous pictures. At the front of the forebrain, they both saw the image of Jones sitting in the garden shed looking at a porno photograph of a child. The officer recognised Susan, the naked girl in the picture. With his hand inside his trousers, the teacher mesmerised by the photo, rigorously masturbated. When the grave scene ended, Jones wearing garden gloves hid the photographs under a loose floorboard in the shed. The image faded by focusing on a calendar partially hidden behind a pair of overalls on the back door.

Steam on the patio window obscured the view of the garden shed. An uneasy silence settled in the room. Frank, sickened by the scene, looked away and ignored the person sitting opposite. Instead of tasting victory, he had a nasty taste in the mouth. The DC had no desire to land a knockout punch. With an overwhelming revulsion for his fellow human being, he had difficulty taking in the abhorrent scene. The act of cancerous deviancy continued to play and he wondered why this insane asylum called earth, tolerated the unforgivable. What about Jones, did he fall into the category of a 'contented Paedophile' that had temporarily satisfied his sexual appetite? Would his malignant fantasies incite him to move on to something even more repulsive in the real world? Had he already stepped over that line?

Jones sat motionless in the chair and grieved for the inevitable loss of his freedom. He gave little thought about the shame to his family. *How could anyone expect me to resist the ingenuous smooth touch of my pupils?* Furthermore, could he expect any redemption or empathy for his predicament? Of the limited options available, hiding behind the pretend mask of depression seemed the more preferable choice. Given time, surely some bleeding heart would intervene, understand, and forgive the indefensible.

The only definition of silence that interested the DC was the one that implied consent. Springing out of the chair, closing in and leaning over, he glowered at Jones like an executioner waiting for a prisoner to finish his last meal.

'Move and I'll fucking kill you.'

Head bowed he dragged his feet along the path to face the manipulation of the unspeakable. Wearing gloves, he entered the shed, loosened the floorboard, and examined several photographs of sexual abuse. Five photographs contained gross images of penetrative and oral sex with adults. The last two photographs showed schoolgirls in an erotic pose. Susan was sitting naked on someone's knee smiling an innocent crooked grin into the camera.

Then, the detective with an addictive personality, the one constantly in someone's face, always taking the piss, experienced a lump in his throat. Fervently denying whatever was running down his cheeks into his mouth, a rage of unmitigated helplessness and anger exploded in his head. Catching hold of a workbench, he wrenched it from the wall before putting his fist through the window.

The exorcism of anger triggered his determination to nail the bastard. Did the calendar behind the door have any significance? Against a range of dates in each month, someone had written the letters A, J, and M. Walsh had described paedophiles as compulsive when it came to collecting porn. The search team would no doubt uncover a deluge of photographs.

Jones stared into space as the detective placed the pictures and the calendar on the coffee table in front of him. 'You have two minutes to pick up the photographs and leave your fingerprints on them.'

Jones turned his head away.

'The choice is yours. You either touch them or I'll break your fucking wrist and say it was done when you resisted arrest.'

The detective started counting. 'One hundred and fucking sixteen.' He jumped out of his chair, Jones could see the hatred in his eyes dragging him to hell. Leaning over the table, the teacher touched the pictures.

The DC was less than pleased. 'Do it properly you bastard, pick them up and look at them.'

Reluctantly, Jones picked up the photographs.

*His collection should be a good indication to what he's up to, or what he'd like to do. Most of the pictures are serious stuff, is he a child molester?*

Frank pushed the calendar towards Jones. 'What's this all about?'

The eyelids on his poker face flickered. Jones pretended to be in a state of shock.

'There are letters against certain dates, what do they stand for?'

Eyelids again, this time with raised eyebrows. Jones licked his lips. No answer.

'If you don't look at me, so help me God I'll rip your head off your shoulders.' His aggressive tone and violent move towards the suspect had the desired effect.

Jones turned towards the detective fearful of catching his eye.

The detective sprinted around the table, placed his hands on either side of Jones's thin face, and shouted in his eardrum. 'YOU'RE FUCKING ABOUT WITH THE WRONG GUY.' Then a softer tone. 'I am going to ask you one more time, what's the significance of the letters A, J and M on the calendar?'

Jones paused, looked down at the floor and cleared his throat. 'If I tell you will you promise not to hurt me?'

Frank released his grip.

'The letters represent girls in the fifth form.'

'Question: why are the letters written against nearly the same dates of every month?'

Jones looked in the direction of the garden. 'They represent their monthly period.'

'Question: who is A J and M?'

Jones was too petrified to withhold the information. 'Ann Roberts, Jackie Williams, and Marian Willis.'

'Question: have you sexually abused them?'

'Yes, I only touched them.'

'Where and when?'

'In my office after school.'

'Question: was anyone else there?'

'John was there. He took photographs of the girls sitting on my lap.'

'Question: what else have you been doing to them?'

'Nothing else, I have told you everything.'

Frank thought about reminding Jones that he owned the trademark for bullshit. 'And I'm supposed to accept that am I? So you keep a record of the monthly period of three schoolgirls on a calendar in your shed, so that John can take photographs of them sitting on your knee in your office. As a headmaster with a degree, does that make sense to you, because to me it makes no sense at all? Question: how do you know when their periods are?'

The query jarred the teacher. His nervous system started spiralling down.

The intense dark red flush on the detective's face indicated that he was about to explode. 'Headmaster, trying to get you to answer is like pulling teeth. I saw pliers in your shed. The next time you keep your mouth shut, I'm going to open your mouth and pull your bastard teeth out one at a time.'

A dull ache in Jones's chest cried out for help. 'If I tell you, will you get my tablets, they are on the kitchen table?'

'If you don't tell me I'll spread that nose you've been trying to grow into all over your face.'

With persuasion, Jones made his confession. John selected girls that were suitable for extracurricular activity at the headmaster's home. Most of them were reluctant to engage in sex until John persuaded them otherwise. Jackie Williams had taken an overdose because of his persuasive tongue. Jones stated that he had a minor role in comparison to his colleague. John had dragged him into a paedophile ring. There was no get-out clause.

Was this going to be the basis of his defence? The detective's learning curve of occasionally doing the right thing seemed to be in the ascendency. He decided to phone Walsh to update him.

Eventually Walsh picked up the phone. 'Junia's looking for you, I think she's after your body.'

'The only body I'm interested in is the one I've just lifted in possession of porn.'

'Frank, I'm the only one here, the governor has gone to Graham's funeral.'

'What time is the funeral?'

Walsh picked up the service sheet and held the telephone with his other hand. 'It starts in about ten minutes.'

Frank could feel an electric buzz moving through his hand holding the telephone. It imploded in his head. Electrons seemed to be coming from the bi-directional path of the phone. The energy source opened up a connection to the otherworld.

Through a portal of quantum immortality, at the front of his brain, he could see the Catholic Church. This time the majestic building had a malevolent sense of foreboding about it. The sharp stone masonry of the spire reaching into the sky played host to a flock of ravens. A sea of black feathers obliterated the outline of the tower against an ominous sky. They were waiting to guide the souls of the newly departed to the afterlife. A raven perched at the top of the needle spire with a curved bill and a white patch on the neck, stood out against a hostile background. Soaring into the sky, the raven made a harsh nasal croak. In answer to the bird's call, the flock soared into the air. Playing with the wind, they gained height as the cold clammy whisper of darkness descended on the church.

A Ford van white in colour, partially blocked the front entrance to the church. The detective could just see a stone rose window at the top of the pointed archway just above the roof of the van. Suddenly, a gigantic ignition of heat, light, and compressed gas, lifted the vehicle into the air and it exploded. The release of energy triggered off a shock wave travelling at supersonic speed towards the church. With overwhelming force, the leading edge of the blast ripped through the structure of the building shattering the walls. Intensity from the blast, several times greater than an impacting earthquake, pushed against the front exterior walls. Within seconds, the structure at the front of the building collapsed and brought down part of the roof. Blast waves continued the journey through the outer porch, shattering the inner glass door. Two stain glass windows on either side of the building imploded. In no time, the front of the church looked like a rock field. The building had turned into a grave of dreams. At the speed of sound, glass and other debris carried by the air blast entered the main body of the church.

Before anyone could realise what was happening, projectiles collided with the congregation sitting in the back aisles from behind. Toxic gas and dust particles hung in the musty air as the image faded. The detective found himself back in the hallway.

Still holding the phone, Walsh's erratic voice pierced his eardrum. 'Frank, what the hell is going on, are you pissed or what?'

With the potent noise and sting of the explosion still buzzing, he tried to drag himself back to reality. 'Listen sarge, that bastard is going to blow up the church. Get a message to Profit to evacuate the place.'

Walsh swallowed his Adam's apple. 'Don't do another one on me. How many funerals have you been to and you've left your radio on? You're minutes away, make your way there, I'll see what I can do this end.'

Jones handcuffed to a radiator, heard the CID car screeching out of the driveway. His chest tightened, he felt excruciating pain in both arms and his jaw. Moments before, Frank had sat motionless watching the disease called paedophilia clutching his chest. Jones pleaded with him to get his tablets. The headmaster burst into tears when Llewellyn's pink elephant sat on his chest. Irregular heartbeats sent fatal messages to his brain. The chances of meeting any bleeding heart in this world, just like his heart muscles, were dying.

Within minutes, the CID car was flying along Canal Terrace. In the distance, he could see the van parked against the entrance to the church. Frank thought of ramming the car into the back of the van to push it away from the door. *Bugger off, that will cause an explosion.* With no one in the vicinity, he parked his car on the opposite side of the road and ran towards the van gripping his truncheon. As the detective approached, he could hear the faint sound of organ music giving way to the congregation.

Frantically trying all the doors, to no avail, he smashed in the driver's window with his truncheon. Releasing the catch, climbing in behind the wheel, he looked under the dash. *I'll bet that bastard has wired the ignition to trigger an explosion.*

Under the steering column, the detective crossed two red wires to turn on the fuel pump and engine. He touched them against the ignition wire and the van started. Pulling out into the road at speed, in the rear mirror, he could see the barrels containing ammonium nitrate mixed with liquid nitro methane, petrol, and black blasting powder. He failed to notice the safety fuse and blasting caps attached to the sticks of dynamite wrapped around the barrels.

Hurtling down the road, a continual hissing noise coming from the heat burning through the textile overlaps of the fuse, started to sap his sanity. The flame, travelling along the safety fuse towards the dynamite, had been primed to take sixty seconds to burn through every thirty centimetres of fuse.

The slap and pull base rhythm of his heartbeat thumped hard against his ribs. Would the safety fuse be long enough for him to reach safety before the heat detonated the blasting caps? Frank was terrified to the point of losing control. *I don't believe it. Someone is taking the piss.* He could hear a high-pitched voice coming from somewhere inside the van. The detective glared in the mirror, no one. He checked under the dashboard. *Fuck me no one.* His thumb brushed against the lower lip, his mouth was definitely moving. He continued to recite the Lord's Prayer.

Travelling a thousand yards or so, braking hard, taking a sharp left, he turned into the car park of an abandoned furniture store. Accelerating, breaking through the wooden barrier, the vehicle headed straight for the entrance of the store. Without slowing down, he crashed through the front glass panel, and it shattered into a crystal shower of thousands of jagged shards. Literally screaming, hurtling along the shop floor, the van skidded to a grinding halt at the far end of the building. He knew enough to realise that the further you are from an explosion the better are the chances of survival.

As he started to sprint towards the entrance, an announcement on the factory loud speaker dissolved his sanity. 'On behalf of all the management and staff, thank you for your custom and welcome to the race of your fucking life.' Every tick of the second hand gave him an edge to cheat death. He tried to make a deal with his maker. *Spare my life I'm begging, I don't deserve it. I'll change, give me one more bloody chance.* In his infinite wisdom, the Supreme Being had turned off the prayer channel to focus on playing golf. A huge explosion ruptured the air obliterating everything in close proximity to the detonation. Shaped like an iron fist, the pressure pulse from the blast wave surged through the trunk of the explosion, expanding in all directions. The front of the blast charged down the shop floor closing in for the kill.

He had almost reached the entrance to the store when the van exploded into the air. Diving through the shattered glass panel, he hid behind a wall as the blast wave destroyed everything in its path. Transient pressure, like a cyclonic windstorm, crunched against the bottom of the wall he was hiding behind. Holding momentarily at the base, it gave way and crumbled.

Through the black smoke, the framework of the roof started to collapse. In desperation, he looked around. There was nowhere else to hide. Steel frames, an avalanche of bricks, tiles, even the sky rained down. Crouching, he covered his head and waited for his inevitable fate. God must have birdied the seventeenth and finished with a hole in one on the eighteenth. Through the clouds of dust and rubble, he managed to stand. Apart from the cuts on his arms, face and torso, as far as he could tell he had crossed the finishing line unscathed.

Frank tried to convince himself that he was still alive. Had he cheated Abaddon, the angel of the abyss and survived? Occasionally in life, an unbelievable warm feeling can ooze from the most bizarre places. Eureka, it was only when the detective realised he had pissed himself that his survival became a reality. Sitting amongst the rubble, the muffled sound in his ears popped from adrenalin as euphoria replaced excitement. An overwhelming sense of achievement took him way, way, beyond happiness. Strong emotion changing to high energy pumped through his veins. In the madness of self-expression, he got to his feet and kicked out at the rubble as if it had no right to be there. Out of the corner of his eye, he could see the church in the distance, still playing host to the birds on the high tower. The guides of the souls were again waiting to escort the newly departed to the afterlife. *What newly departed*? He had cheated the ravens of their duty.

Then, drifting gently on the wind, he heard the sickening thud of a second explosion from the church. High explosives, hidden away in the anteroom at the side of the pulpit, had been primed to detonate ten minutes after the initial explosion. John wanted to catch the congregation in a crossfire to kill as many as possible. With the primary blast at the entrance to the church cutting off any escape, the blast wave would have driven the survivors into the secondary blast. Moreover, when the overpressure from the primary blast had reached its peak, the secondary blast would detonate and cause unsustainable pressure on the interior walls. More fatalities would have ensued from the building collapsing than the bomb blast.

Profit and two other officers were organising an evacuation near the pulpit only seconds before the explosion. As Profit turned around to face the anteroom to his left, a past dimension from a parallel universe encroached into the present. He could see time slowing down. It felt as if he was living inside a clock that needed re-winding. Speed and motion slowed to the extent that everything appeared to be flat lining. In slow motion, the wall of the anteroom disintegrated from the blast. Sound waves from the explosion oscillated on nearly the same frequency. A flash burn at the front of the blast crawled towards him. In a time frame of repeatedly watching a snapshot in almost the same instant, the flash burn started to melt exposed skin on his face, one layer at a time. With his eyes open, the pressure from the blast gradually dissolved the rest of his muscles. Seemingly, taking forever, turning, he looked down to watch laser-like pressure from the wave cutting through and amputating both legs. His skeleton carcass floated into the air.

The wave stormed into the main building. An elderly couple standing by the high altar waiting their turn to walk down the aisle were the first casualties. The blast penetrated their human frame with such force it caused total disruption. The shock wave literally blew them away. Nancy only had time to lift Susan up in her arms before the blast cut through her neck like a chainsaw. Glass, travelling through the main building, took on a tumbling effect that increased the cutting capability to anything in its path.

This time, with the sound of souls crying inside, the DC ran the race towards death. When he arrived, survivors were falling, crawling out of the main entrance. Moments later with no one else exiting the building, fire officers, medics, and the DC entered the church. Through the dust of broken fragments, Frank could see the structure at the south end of the church collapsing. Searching through the rubble for any sign of life, he stumbled across Nancy and Susan huddled together on the floor in the aisle. He took his jacket off and placed it over their bodies. An aching, nauseating guilt settled in the pit of his stomach. Something warm wrenched into his mouth. The diversion of the first blast away from the church must have saved lives. Should he have considered an alternative? Glancing around the sea of carnage, it looked like a war zone and he felt responsible.

From the audio part of his brain, he heard the voice of John's ridicule.

*Tremble, earth and you who make profession of serving Jesus Christ and who on the inside adore yourselves. Tremble, for God is going to deliver you over to his enemy because the holy places are in corruption.*

He clenched his fists and looked around. With no sight of John, angrily, frustrated, he bawled out, 'You can hide John, but it's not over by a long way you bastard. I swear if it's the last thing I do I'll bury you alive in the same way you buried these poor souls.'

Rob Thomas, a local practitioner, was lying on his back near the steps to the alter holding onto a teenager with his leg trapped under the weight of marble stone. 'I'm sorry but I don't have time to listen to your shit. If you want to do something useful, come over here?' Thomas had no option other than to amputate the limb in order to stop the boy from bleeding to death. Frank recognised the boy and his heart sank. It was Andrew Nichols, his soul mate from his first arrest. Gripping Andrew's upper torso, holding on, he watched the doctor sawing through the bone and healthy tissue of his thigh above the knee. His body flaccid, Andrew lost consciousness. The sound of steel teeth grinding through the bone echoed against the fragmented walls of the church. Still unconscious, lifting him onto a stretcher, the doctor continued to dress the open stump as the medics carried him to the ambulance.

John watched the result of his handiwork from the safety of a crowd gathered on the opposite side of the road. The self-fulfilled sinner's head almost spun off his shoulders with delirium from the taste and smell of burning flesh. After all those years of planning, all the disappointment, he had finally reached nirvana. In the rubble and falling masonry at the south end the DC found another victim, Dan Archer. He had no visible injuries only frothy blood secreted around the mouth. His lungs and internal organs had imploded from the pressure exerted by the blast wave.

That day on the anniversary of the blessed Mary's apparition at Fatima, nineteen of the congregation walked through the light to an everlasting peace.

★★★

Walsh had finally managed to persuade his partner to leave the scene. He turned down any visit to the hospital. The electric charge in his nervous system had caused a sensory overload, gradually his body was closing down. He managed to get to his bedroom before his eyes failed to respond to the light. A sustained burst of pain from the muscular spasms in his spinal column ravaged every cell. Losing consciousness, he knew in his heart that it could be fatal.

Somewhere between reality and dreaming, the neurons in his brain became active. Was he awake or asleep? Warm Celtic rays of brilliant sunlight filtering through the air, touched his skin and washed through the pain. The nucleus in the sunlight seemed to move between two instants in time. Every atom, every molecule, throbbed to the energy vibrating through his frame. He could hear the voice of the seer travelling down a coupling beam.

*My blood, it is time for you to follow the way of your ancestors. Your bodily soul is in grave danger, you must heal or you will join the other world. Your destiny is the same as those who have gone before. It is to prevent the evil amongst you. Like the warrior Cuchulainn, who showed courage in battle when he tied himself to a stone to die on his feet, so to must you show courage.*

A smell of paraffin wax entered his nostrils. Feeling a waft of cool air, someone seemingly passing the side of his bed came into focus.

*What you see is the procession of the dead. It is the intrusion into our world of those who died in the church.*

Through the light, Frank could see Susan, the last person in the procession. He could just make out her small frame. Her entire body was saturated with water. Susan walked towards the keeper of the souls, leaving pools of water on the floor.

*Your friend is wet from the tears shed for her in your world after the death of her body. Her torment and the grief of her family will change when the evil one is no more. You must be willing to sacrifice yourself in order to stop the suffering. You must destroy v fear na DROCHFHOULA, the man of* bad blood as I tell you or his evil soul will live on elsewhere. Know now the soul is immortal, and can live again in others until it is delivered to the keeper. Since the beginning when God first gave Adam breath, your ancestors have known that within man there is another self, it is the self-soul. Look at the spiral of life on the ring, it represents the cycle of life, death, and rebirth. Death is not the end, the soul is immortal and it resides in the heart. It is the heart of your heart. The soul of this man is damned forever. It will never be delivered to the keeper. He is condemned to wander your world for eternity. If you do not follow closely what I say, he will rise from the grave like Drochfhoula before him and he will steal the body of another while it is asleep. His soul will live on and pass to that body. You must strike him in the heart with a stake made from the Rowan tree. When you do so, close your left hand into a fist and place your thumb between the index and little finger as the announcer of death. Cut the arteries and bleed him to his death. This is so because the blood is the very self-soul. Let the blood flow away until there is no more.

When you have done, Morrigan, the goddess of death will come to you as a raven and settle on his evil soul. The raven will show you to him if you recover, this will take time. I do not know if your injuries have gone too far. You must tie a wicker band around his ankle, bury him upside down, and surround the grave with bright rowanberries. The bonfires of Beltane lit by the spirits of nature to heal you will burn a little longer to drive away the demons and then return to the other world. Other demon souls will come to the aid of the evil one, but they will not pass. Only Baal, prince of the underworld, can breach the power of the purification of the ritual of Beltane. The magic of the bonfire made by the druids to heal your bodily self will last for a short time to allow darkness, falsehood, and death to give to the light. This is not the end. It is only the beginning. There is more for you to do in your world against evil. You are the ancestor of the seventh son of the seventh son, born on Shamain. The champion you possess is second sight. You have yet to receive the knowledge of all things. When this is done, you will have the power to confront all that is evil. If you fall before Baal, show the courage of Cuchulainn and Arthur. Do not give way, never surrender. Remember my ancestor who you are can never change. If you have to lose your earthly body do so as a Celt, if you cannot be saved so be it.

The voice gave way to a raven tapping its beak against the bedroom window. Would the detective fulfil his destiny?

He glanced around the bedroom. Frank was definitely back in the world of the living. Even dream messages from the gods could not emulate his untidy room. For a brief moment, his subconscious suppressed the trauma that would one day snap his brain like a twig. There appeared to be an absence of pain. A loud bang on the front door pierced his eardrums. They could 'foxtrot oscar'. The thumping, rhythmic sound of bare knuckles brought back the memory of a leapfrog experience with Junia. A baton-like shape in the bedclothes orchestrated by his erect penis, suggested he was not the only one thinking about her.

Turning the lecherous moment over in his mind, he recalled apologising for the slight bump on her forehead caused by an overzealous climax. Junia's response would stay etched on his bedpost forever.

'And so you should be love, four minutes and twenty-five seconds is nothing to a girl like me.' Was that an ever so sly dig about his sexual prowess?

Gradually, the dramatic trauma of the explosion flooded his brain and stuck in his throat. Frank was about to fight for his sanity when he heard the crack of the doorframe taken off its hinges. Mears entered the bedroom followed by Walsh.

His partner seemed annoyed. 'For Christ's sake Frank, why didn't you answer the door?'

Confused, he sat up in bed trying to focus on his two guests.

Mears approached the bed. 'I can answer that one; he's like every other warped sadistic bastard who won't open the door. He's as guilty as shit.'

Walsh moved forward to rescue the DC. 'Let me have a word with him.'

Raised eyebrows from Mears. 'You will do nothing of the sort, I agreed for you to come along, but that's all this is my show.'

Through the haze, even Frank realised they were not there to enquire about his health.

The senior officer continued his derision. 'Listen to me you grotesque piece of shit. Admit it was you, plead insanity, or you will go down in history as the last person to get his neck stretched.'

The detective decided to choose his words carefully. The stupidity of his next remark even surprised him. 'It's John, he's dead, you're here because of him?'

'Well done Macleod, how did you know that? Look, try these on for size.' Mears threw his handcuffs on the bed.

One of the forensic team moved forward and handed him a protective suit. 'Wear that, and before you ask, you can't go to the bathroom for a shower.'

Walsh looked at the sorry state of his colleague. 'Come on Frank I'll give you a hand.'

Mears again raised his voice. 'Are you hard of hearing what is it you don't understand about the phrase 'fuck off'.'

The detective sergeant stretched to his full height, but no one seemed to notice. 'If anyone is going to arrest him it's me. He's my partner and my responsibility.'

'Walsh grow up, I don't care who arrests him but I want him in the cell now, is that understood? And here's another thing you had better understand sharpish. If you visit your so-called psycho partner in the cell or contact him in any way, I'll arrest you for conspiring to pervert the course of justice.'

★★★

Sergeant Bosom watched from behind the counter in the custody suite as they wheeled the prisoner in.

'This shit has been arrested for the murder of Samuel John under common law. Book him in, and throw him in the cells.'

Bosom ignored Mears and looked at the prisoner. Behind his gaunt business-like expression, the detective could see a tinge of empathy. 'What evidence have we got to hold him?'

Mears looked straight through the sergeant. 'He's killed John in cold blood that's all you need to know.'

The sergeant continued with his demand. 'I need to know more than that if I am going to deprive him of his liberty.'

'That's where you are wrong sergeant, you don't need to know fuck all. Hand me the keys, there's a good boy, and I'll tuck him into bed for you.'

Bosom walked from around the counter. 'Don't play silly buggers with me chief inspector. As a custody sergeant, under the judge's rules governing the treatment of suspects, I need to be informed about your investigation. Your bullying tactics won't cut any ice with me.'

Mears played his ace. 'Then this will, book him in or you will be relieved of your duties. If you want to save your pension, do as you're told.'

The custody sergeant had clearly made his point. He still had no intention of backing down. The prisoner stepped forward.

'Sarge, I think he could be onto something. I want to be treated fairly when I'm in here, I'll get that from you.'

He cautioned the prisoner, informed him of the rights and filled in the charge sheet.

The temporary SIO examined the sheet. 'Bosom get a grip will you, you've forgotten to write down what he just said on the charge sheet.'

'You may be the investigating officer, but I'm the custody sergeant. He made that comment before I cautioned him. That's why it's not on the sheet.'

The smirk on Mears's face suggested he was about to deliver a knockout punch. 'Then in that case, you and I will put what looks like a confession in our pocket books.'

Bosom locked the cell door and placed the key on his belt. There would only be authorised visits on his watch.

***

Black placed the last of the prisoner's clothing in a nylon bag and secured it with sellotape. After a thorough examination of the detective's flat, he checked his mental list. Only one more task, after a shower and change of clothing, he could call it a day.

Bosom opened the cell and introduced the forensic pathologist to the prisoner.

The pathologist started the interaction. 'When did you last have a shower detective?'

'Yesterday.'

Black probed further. 'By yesterday you mean Monday?'

'You're wrong, yesterday was Sunday.'

'Officer today is Tuesday so you must be referring to Monday.' The pathologist could see the confusion. He ended any further questions to allow the prisoner to take in the disparity.

Treating his body like a walk-in crime scene, the examiner concentrated on finding physical evidence or pattern injury to link the detective to the scene or the victim. Standing naked on a sheet of brown paper in the cell, the detective watched the methodical way in which the pathologist went about his business. After ascertaining how the suspect had sustained the injuries, Black took photographs before systematically applying swabs to the skin to capture any dried liquid or foreign matter on his body. Clinically he obtained specimens of blood, saliva, and hair samples. They were carefully labelled and bagged. The pathologist had difficulty when he attempted to take samples from under his short nails. Gently scraping under the nail plate, he reverted to swabbing the surface of his fingers. Finally, pinhead swabs were dabbed between the folds of the outer skin around each nail plate.

Bosom's failure to remove the prisoner's rings was somewhat fortuitous for Black. He had every expectation of finding particles under the band or inside the mounted head. The nylon fibres of his brush touched the outer surface of the spiral ring. An electric shock moved through the examiner's hand. A warm jolt in his head gave out a whooshy noise. At a point between his eyebrows, he could see Sally. Her dreamy smile, cute bug eyes, etched features and short black curly hair, looked resplendent against a background of full bright sunlight. Black felt the sensation of undying love. Looking closer, he could see a white bio-electromagnetic aura around the shape of her head looking like a halo. An energy charge from the aura had processed her spiritual soul into physical matter. Although unable to hear what she said, the message was unmistakable. 'I love you brother dear.' Sally held her arms out to give him an imaginary hug and the image faded. Back in the cell, his legs gave way. He sat on the edge of the steel bed and studied the floor. Several minutes passed before Black raised his head to look at the prisoner.

'Seeing my sister again means more to me than you will ever know. Thank you.'

Frank thought of telling Black that he had no control over the process. 'Can I ask a favour?'

The pathologist reverted to his norm. 'It depends on what it is. If it is anything to do with the case, I am afraid I cannot help you.'

'The truth is I don't remember killing John although if I'm honest I bloody well wanted to. I know you've visited the crime scene and examined his body, that's why you're here. Without giving anything away, what are the chances of you proving it was me?'

Black hesitated. Facing the cell door, he rang the bell on the wall. Bosom opened the door. They were about to leave when Black stopped. 'The answer to your question is if you are responsible, forensically, I will have no problem in proving it.'

★★★

Since his rapid temporary promotion to senior investigating officer, Mears had carried out everything by the book. He instigated an inner and outer cordon to prevent access to a major incident. Furthermore, he obtained forensic and cross border support. Even setting up a temporary mortuary and casualty bureau, were all decisions out of the manual. As far as Mears was concerned, the so-called manual faded into obscurity in comparison with the latest development that had promotion written all over it. Because of his intervention, not only had he brought a closure to horrendous crimes, he could now announce the arrest of someone implicated in the enquiry. Would the detective be gullible enough to admit something in interview? Forensic would come up with the critical evidence, anything else gleaned from an interview would be a bonus.

The suspect sat down at the table and glared at Mears entering the interview room. The first salvo from Mears was a deliberate attempt to make the detective lose his temper. 'Tell me Macleod, what is an evil sadistic bastard like you doing in this job?'

The interviewee decided not to comment. He could feel the blood pumping into his hands His plan lasted sixty seconds. 'Well I try my best to make ignorant shits like you look good.'

'Detective, did you make me look good when you failed to prevent the death of poor innocent members of your community?'

'Do you know Mears, you are so full of bullshit one of these days you're going to explode.'

Mears saw an opening and went for it. 'You're right there lad, when you used the word explode. I suppose you were shagging or fitting somebody up when John nicked the explosives from Bingham Colliery. To make matters worse what enquiries did you carry out FUCK ALL?'

'You can't lay that one on me you bastard and you know it.'

The grimace on the detective's face encouraged Mears to continue. 'All I know is you're the local dick. How many incidents have you dealt with where explosives were nicked? Why didn't you make it a priority, even a brain dead like you should have linked that to John?'

An incensed detective glared at his adversary. 'You're a liar, we handed that onto your team for action. It was down to you and that other piece of guzzling shit to make certain enquiries were carried out.'

'Well this is not the way I see it nor will the press when I tell them that if the local cops had done their job loss of life could have been averted. How do you like that hero, or should I call you zero?'

Something imploded in the DC's head. 'I know what you're playing at, you're trying to rattle me. Well guess what, you've succeeded. Now put me back in that cell or I'll be responsible for another fucking death.'

Raising his eyebrows and nicotine lips, the SIO showed his yellow teeth. 'That sounds like another confession to me. At least that is how it's going to read in my pocket book. Listen to this, zero. I saw you threatening and assaulting John in this station. You also threatened to kill him in front of Profit. I have two statements saying that shortly after the explosion you shouted that you were going to 'bury him alive'. As well, you're up to your eyeballs in this case with creepy things going on. You even said you could have done it. Walsh is protecting you, but not for long. What have you got to say about that?'

'Except for go fuck yourself nothing really.'

It was only at this point that Mears decided to revert to standard questioning. 'Where were you between 9.00 p.m. on Saturday night and Tuesday morning when we picked you up?'

Frank wondered if he could make Mears lose his temper. 'No problem I have a cast-iron alibi, I was shagging your mother. By the way, did you know she likes it up the arse?'

Mears could feel his anger rising, the glare he gave his target smarted of violence. 'The next time I interview you Macleod, I'll have all the forensic I need to hang you. I can tell you now you're creepy torture nonsense don't cut any ice with me. I've seen some things but I've never seen anything like that.'

The interviewer looked at the prisoner to see if there were any well-known clues. He expected to see concealed signs of guilt in his eyes or body language. He only saw someone looking confused.

Both of them gave serious thought of how to continue. The SIO broke the uneasy silence. 'Look, this is getting us nowhere. Either make a statement or I'm going to stick you back in the cell and you can rot until I decide to have another go at you.'

Frank decided to play ball. 'Can't we come to some sort of arrangement? I'll make a statement if you answer one or two questions?'

Mears nodded. 'Go ahead, I've got nothing to lose.'

'Where did you find his body?'

'Where you left it Macleod, in the house next door to the church.'

'Was there a stake through his heart?'

'What sort of crazy question is that? In saying that, it's going to look good in my pocket book'

'How did he die?'

Mears decided to end the interview. 'You're starting to piss me off, are you going to make a statement or what?'

Frank's iconic grin bounced off the smooth surface of the table straight into the interviewer's face. 'Yes, I'll make a statement. As usual, you've got the wrong guy. I'm innocent and you know it. You just want a body in the cell so that you can say you've made an arrest, and I'm the patsy.'

'Got it in one detective, well done.'

Frank took on the interviewer role. 'Tell me one shred of evidence you've got against me?'

'The only thing I'm going to tell you is I'm banging you up for the night, that will loosen your tongue.'

For the first time, the prisoner had reservations that he was responsible for killing John. He had to have another dig. 'It must run in the family your mothers got a fetish about my tongue.'

Both acknowledged the futility of the interview by standing and glaring at each other.

Frank was still determined to have one last pop. 'Would you do me one last favour sir? I get lonely in that cell. I was wondering if you'd visit me and try to pull the same stunt that you did with John, or are you a fucking coward?'

The interviewer tried not to lose his temper. Frank turned the slurs and innuendo up a notch. 'Look tell your mother I'm out of condoms. There's no way I'm shagging that slag without protection.'

Restraint popped a button on the SIO waistcoat.

The next verbal was way below the belt. 'Did you know your mother and father are brother and sister?'

Mears threw a round-arm punch and missed the target. A small fracture to his right cheekbone was a painful reminder not to tangle with a crazy. The detective had landed a lucky punch. It took three officers to break up the brawl. They were all holding the prisoner. Mears put another entry in his pocket book, this time for assault.

Without any encouragement, Christine Walsh decided to take on the role of caterer and the prisoner received three square meals a day. Apart from the occasional confrontation with Mears, Frank was left to rot in his cell. After three nights in the cell, he started to blur the perception of reality with his dreamlike experience. He had no recollection of killing the teacher, and yet he distinctly remembered the instructions of how to carry it out. Had he used some other method to kill John? Was that the reason why the inveterate seer had remained silent since his arrest?

Staring at the light bulb in the ceiling, something was playing tricks with his incoherent mind. It started when he heard the steel cell door slam and the double turn of the key grinding against the lock. That was it, he felt trapped. Frank had grave reservations about the lack of air in the cell. He placed one foot in front of the other to measure the confined space. *The cell is so small you can't even swing a cat around in it. Clasaustrum,* a shut in place, turned the next page of his phobia to escape routes. *Not one, go on tell me where they are. What if there's a fire, why the fuck are the walls closing in, even the ceiling.* Hallucinating, he could feel his body caged with wires. They seemed to be tightening by the minute. *Sweaty bloody palm, that bastard is turning up the ventilation.* Short of breath and with panic setting in, he climbed onto the bunk and marked the point where the ceiling met the walls. In his imagining, the cell had now turned into a coffin. In the darkness, he could feel long thick worms feeding, living inside his corpse. Then, the hallucinatory sensation of bristle hairs and a sticky substance on the cylinder tube of the worms crawled out of his mouth and nose. He convinced himself, *other people* suffered from the phobia.

# CHAPTER 32

# THE YEAR OF THE RAT

At the tender age of seven, showing a sense of maturity beyond his years, Samuel John decided to keep his mother's sexual encounter with the gardener a secret. For that, Alex decided to punish him. The thought of sexual intercourse in front of her son had initially turned her on. However teaching him a lesson he would never forget had safeguards. One day the wretched boy would say something out of turn. About to look for that something special in the form of punishment, fate took a hand.

Rats had infested the barn. Samuel ran out screaming his head off at the mere glimpse of his long-tailed friend. That gave Alex the cue she wanted. What sort of macho behaviour was that, it had no place in manliness? Her utter disappointment of giving birth to a sissy turned to revulsion when Samuel experienced, what she could only describe as a panic attack. Alex gave instructions to the rat catcher to capture the parasites because she wanted them as pets. His rat catching ability only took second place to his phenomenal knowledge on the rodent. Yes, she knew the rats were probably from the nearby sewer. She also found it mildly interesting when her 'Pied Piper' explained the difference in cultural attitude towards her new hairy pet. 'In the West, rats are unclean parasites that spread disease. In the East, they are sacred.'

How informative. Alex listened intently to the story about the rats of Karni Mata Temple. She was dumbfounded when the parasite told her that the species were the reincarnation of holy men. The subject was certainly interesting enough to pass on to her flea-infested mother-in-law. The story about the priests feeding milk and grain to the rats took on an appeal when he explained that pilgrims regularly join the rats in the feast. Any self-doubt about the wisdom of eating food touched by rats fell away when her storyteller explained the obvious. 'The privilege of eating with the teeth-grinding rodent is a blessing.'

Of course it is. Good old mother-in-law regularly fed Samuel with bullshit about Christianity, now it was her turn.

Alex, enthused with the adventure, fumbled with the key to unlock the garden shed. What a yummy treat, not one or two but three large black rats were peering out of a steel trap on the bench. What a pleasant surprise, their tails were longer than their body. What an even bigger surprise, one of them looked like a small cat. Her well-informed rat catcher explained that this particular species carried the fleas on their back that had caused the pandemic 'Black Death', killing twenty-five million people.

Nothing, absolutely nothing was too good for her son. Alex placed a nutritious small bowl of milk and grain inside the shed door. She intended to entice her 'peeping tom' into the shed under the pretext he had a special gift waiting inside to unwrap. The feast was hardly enough to feed a mouse let alone three burly handsome black rats. She had every confidence they would appreciate the minuscule meal after their diet of fresh air for the past week.

Timing was of the essence if Alex intended to derive the maximum pleasure from her innocent prank. Samuel stumbled on the step as he entered the shed blindfolded followed by the alluring glare of his mother. 'Stay where you are darling, almost ready.'

Wearing gloves, her favourite pair with a daisy design, she approached the trap covered in birthday paper on the bench. Quietly opening the trap door, taking a deep breath, she removed the blindfold and gently nudged her son towards his present surprise.

'Thank you my darling for looking after Mummy's interest. It is only something small, but you will remember my little treat for the rest of your life.'

Samuel moved towards the parcel while Alex tiptoed out of the shed and locked the door. Looking through the window, the observer waited for the fun to begin.

Eagerly, the small boy started to unwrap the paper as one of the rats left the steel trap. Within seconds, all three were out sashaying on the table. Samuel's jaw dropped. Too frightened to scream, standing in front of the bench, he confronted his worst nightmare. The rats, smelling the food, scampered past the boy who could only watch too terrified to move. He heard a commotion behind. The huge dominant rat was asserting its authority over the other two.

Charging, the burly guardian chased them away from the milk.

Samuel could hear a hissing sound. A rat darted up the side of the shed to the ceiling. Another rat on the bench watched his every move. His only chance of escape lay behind. He could hear his heartbeat, skipping, stopping, as the muscles in his legs tightened. Covering his face with both hands, Samuel turned around. Showing the sort of courage that tilts the world on its axis, the small boy forced open his eyes. The sight of the coarse fur and long tail of the rat filled him with revulsion. He watched in horror as the dominant rat, again lunging, biting one of its own, pinned it against the door. With its mouth full of fur, the rodent stared directly into the face of a boy too petrified to close his eyes. Samuel glared into large pink beads. The rat made a boorish chirping noise. Laughing, it was actually laughing at him.

His nose started to run. Instinctively he wiped it. His fingers were dripping with blood. Trauma had ruptured a vessel at the back of his nose. Blood streaming through his nostrils splashed onto the floor. Dirt or an eyelash was now irritating his lower eyelid. Rubbing his eyes, blood leaking into his tear duct, started to fall from his eye and trickle down his face. Digging in, with his brain twisting like a corkscrew, his world containing three rats went spiralling out of control. He could feel the muscles in his legs jerking, twitching. Paralysed, they gave way. Moments before he collapsed Samuel experienced hysterical blindness. In that pitch-black corner behind bloody eyes, hallucinatory images rattled his will to survive. This time he could smell a rat right under his nose. This time he could taste the rat's furry head in his mouth.

Alex decided to leave him in the shed until the following day. That was more than enough time for him to be acquainted with his new friends. Eventually she opened the shed door. Samuel was still lying on the floor. His clothes reeked of urine and he had faeces in his hair. A purple rash visible around the open sore of the bites on his bare legs, indicated that rat fever had already entered his blood stream.

John distinctly remembered walking in the direction of the kitchen and experiencing an adrenalin rush. Playing through the reel again, he hit the pause button at the point where they carried the body bags from the church. Then, he felt a dull thump at the back of his skull. Regaining consciousness, he was lying naked face up on the cellar floor with both his arms spread-eagled and tied to two brick columns on either side. He pulled against the taut manacle around his right wrist and the wire cut through his skin to the bone. Glancing down, his legs were free. What sort of amateur had dared to lock horns with him? In this sorry predicament, even his face had not expected the revival of a confident smirk. Applying his mind to the undemanding challenge, with his legs free, he could easily stand. That would give enough slack in the wire to untie his hands. Before making any move, John listened intently to hear 'l'amateur' moving around or breathing. All clear, he tried to stand but something was horribly wrong. He attempted to move his legs, no response, again, nothing.

'You are wasting your time. The tendons at the back of your knees are severed.'

The voice seemed to trigger off an acute rasping pain in the hollow at the back of his knees. He could also feel a sting like ache running up both sides of his face from the edges of his mouth to his earlobes. With his tongue, he touched the deep cuts on either side of the mouth and traced the lines on his face made with a Stanley knife.

'I see you've found your smile.'

A sweet musky scent filled his nostrils. His eyes homed in on the smell. Was that a can of tar on the floor near his left leg?

'What's your worst nightmare? You tell me yours and I'll tell you mine? When you are faced with it, you will scream so loud, your smile will explode all over your face. You can tell me after this.' A creaking noise on the hardwood floor approached from behind. He had a dull muted awareness of hands moving around on the top of his head. There seemed to be an absence of fingers prodding and touching his skull. In his unconscious state, someone had pressed a rag heavily smeared with hot tar on the top of his skull. It had now cooled and hardened. He was wearing a makeshift version of a pitch cap. Someone slowly, violently pulled the rag cloth away from his skull tearing unyielding chunks of flesh and hair with it. Unbearable pain from the raw endings of his almost skinless skull rushed through his body, like an express train. Sharp agonising pain cut his nervous system to shreds. Biting hard, he dug his teeth into his bottom lip.

Every instinct and reason encouraged John to beg for mercy.

He had no intention of doing that. The best he could hope for was the quick release of death. In order to do that he would have to admit to his most compelling fear. Even the word brought profound terror cutting into the gut. John waited for the grave-racking pain to subside. His head, torso, and limbs, felt as if they were alight with petrol. He weighed up the sufferance and the hurt of unbearable pain. *There is no hurt in death. O death where is thy victory. O death where is thy sting.* John knew that soon he would be incapable of rational thought, only interminable grief. In desperation, he filled his lungs and he shouted, 'RATS.' With his pulse ranting, rasping, the top of his skull, the cellar door closed. Gradually he lost consciousness and the pain in his world lifted from his gaze.

★★★

Through an obscure blur, the bleak cellar came into focus. This time a weight was resting on his stomach. Partially closing his eyes, he squinted to concentrate on the object. For some ridiculous reason it looked like a birdcage. They always do. What else had changed? He looked down, his legs spread-eagled, were tied to two columns. Why? To what purpose? Something itched, tickled and crawled on his stomach. Straining his neck, he looked into the cage again. The unmistakable shape of two brown rats stirred to the irritation on his stomach. There was no bottom to the birdcage. With one last throw of the dice, John tried to move his torso. His guardian had hammered nails through the contour muscles on either side of his shoulder. His hipbones had also splintered from the nails securing them to the wooden floor. The pain from trying to achieve the impossible sapped what little strength he had left. That musky stink filled his nostrils again. He recognised another smell. Black powder. He closed his eyes, the sight of curved pointy claws touching his stomach was driving him to delirium. The rats seemed to be walking about on tiptoe. John filled his lungs with air. A bellowing screech could be fatal. The loss of blood from his face exploding would induce unconsciousness. Then a liquid substance of tar mixed with black powder, fell onto and soaked his penis, testicles and lower abdomen.

'Your catholic friends were caught like rats in a barrel. Now it's your turn.'

The sound of a match striking held centre stage. He could just make out the outline of a small flame. The tar below his scrotum ignited, very slowly the flames moved towards the birdcage. Blue flames burning through the layers of his skin under the tar started to breakdown the last of his nerve endings. The rats, petrified by the intensity of the heat against their fur, scampered around the cage trying to find an escape route. This time John could taste and smell his pain, alight in the flames. Excruciating, unbearable agony had a minor role to the trauma of the rats running around on his stomach. John glared at the only thing in the world that petrified him. He tried to move every muscle, any muscle, and failed.

Terrified beyond the point of fear, panicking, the rats started to gnaw and bite through the fleshy part of his stomach below his breastbone. He could hear the grinding noise of their teeth making contact. The upper incisors held onto his muscle and skin as the lower teeth cut against it and opened up puncture wounds. The intensity of the heat, drawing ever nearer, encouraged the rats on to make their escape. Vigorously, purposely using their claws, the rats were now burrowing down into his chest cavity. As the front claws wrenched out flesh and fat from his stomach, the hind feet kicked it backwards. Through the bars of the birdcage, he watched the rats tunnelling through into his stomach fat, muscles, and intestines. However, most of all, he experienced the horror of the rodent's long sharp teeth biting, gnawing at his ribcage. Hysterical, trying to endure the intolerable, he had to take control. The once small boy, who wanted to believe, clenched his teeth, forced his tongue against his bottom jaw, and screamed his bloody face off. Then the last silent pause. His voice, like of a child whispering, hung in the cell.

'Doo evil, yoo will reap evil. I will be waiting for yoo in…'

The drone of terror from the other side crashed against his soul, and his smile finally exploded. After some time, John felt totally numb, paralysed, in retrospect a corpse. Through the pitch-black darkness, somehow he knew he had stopped breathing. To his frantic horror, he also knew that his soul was trapped inside his body. Still capable of reasoning, he experienced an outlandish nightmare where his mask of sanity had vanished to expose the monster that he is. The reality of an invisible claw scraping, rasped his skin at the back of his right wrist. Drawing blood, it left three deep vertical scratch marks. A horizontal red brand, like a burn from a hot poker, appeared at the base under the scars. The 'devil's mark' represented his allegiance to Satan. He could hear a 'devil to pay' voice. He listened intently to what the hissing maniacal laughter had to say. John could not believe his luck. If he had a face he would have smiled, it really was the year of the rat.

# CHAPTER 33

## THE END OF THE BEGINNING

The temporary SIO had no interest in anyone else. Macleod had to prove his innocence. Until then he could hallucinate and rot in the cells. The detective needed a good seeing to. That would happen as soon as, err, his fracture had healed. He strongly believed in the virtues of physical pain, it had a strong influence in obtaining a confession. Just a couple of hours with that cocky bastard and Macleod would only be too eager to make a statement. His wife Vera had her first slap on their wedding night. As far as he could tell, they never looked back. He literally counted down the days when he could finally return home to Cardiff.

There was nothing more gratifying than a good hard spanking from Dot. Mears, a slave to sadomasochism, regarded Dot as the best. Usually he wore motorcycle chaps exposing his bare backside. Bending over a 'spanking horse' his 'whipping love' usually started to inflict pain with a soft blow on his bare bottom. Gradually, Dot increased the strength of the hand slap before resorting to a riding crop. First, a controlled delicate flick, then a sharp turn of her wrist that made the leather tongue crack hard against his afterglow. Then the climax, the welt, lash, finally the sting, and intense pain from the crop's stiff shaft cutting through his skin. Moreover, he experienced the helplessness, relief, and therapeutic escape from life.

After studying the content of a Danish magazine, Mears concluded that spankers in the UK had a raw deal. If only every country could replicate Latvia on a Palm Sunday. Traditionally on that day, all the guys had their bare buttocks whipped with a pussy willow. And what, yes what, about the Chinese? At the start of the New Year, the male population were encouraged to visit the temple. Through the ritual of purging bad luck, they had the spanking of their life. A smile the size of Dot showed his teeth. Surely, there was nothing more satisfying than starting the New Year with a set of cherry red buttocks.

Someone had the audacity to interrupt his daydreaming. The mail had arrived. He noticed a Jiffy bag on top of the mail in his tray. The stamp mark had yesterday's date posted in Cardiff. Cutting the top of the Jiffy bag, he emptied the contents onto the desk. Mears recognised the severed little finger straight away. The jury was still out regarding the small black particles. The bitter tang of rotten eggs attacked his palate with a karate kick before sorting out the rest of his taste buds. That smell had hung around for days after visiting John's crime scene. The charcoal like flecks looked like tissue paper. The foreman read out the unanimous verdict, the charred flecks were definitely skin and muscle. Opening a letter inside it read:

*'Congratulations on arresting the wrong one so I can kill again. PS, If you are looking for John's other little finger, call off the dogs. I have posted it to the chief constable of Gwent together with a rundown of how I killed that evil bastard. Rats all for now.'*

He scrutinised the typing. Find the typewriter and you will find Macleod's accomplice, the ruse would not put him off the scent. Mears had confidence in Black. The pathologist would have little problem in finding latent fingerprints on the paper. Hell, he could probably identify the model. When it came to forensic identification, typed notes, the fabric, ribbon, type design, and other individual characteristics from misuse and wear, all were unique.

Rummaging through the rest of the mail, searchlight eyes focused on an envelope marked, 'Royal College of Pathology'. At last, the pathologist had submitted his report. He scanned the first two pages dealing with the examination of the scene. The part that interested him the most started on page eight, the pathologist's examination of Macleod.

The section listed thirteen specimens found on the suspect's clothing and body from both explosions. Physical evidence, textile fibre transfer, and the specimens were all broken down and itemised. Mears homed in on the summary:

*'Interpretation linking the suspect, victim, and crime scene. All samples and specimens were re-examined. There is no physical or biological evidence to link or connect Macleod with the victim or the crime scene.'*

Even if he managed to obtain a confession, the report would cast serious doubt on its credibility. Nervously, Mears turned the pages back to the face sheet. The circulation also included the South

Wales chief constable. If he wanted to sustain his chances of promotion, he would have to act quickly. Releasing Macleod from custody seemed an obvious step in the right direction. A make-believe phone call from Vera stating that all hell had broken loose, could also be the order of the day. With deep regret, he would have no choice other than to return to Cardiff. If anyone deserved a good spanking with a 'Cat o' nine tails', it was Mears.

★★★

Frank dangled his legs over the metal bunk bed and listened to the world yawning outside his cell window. Checking the mythical cards in his hand, he was more than happy to exchange the 'joker' for a 'get out of jail' card. He was thinking about his good fortune when a sunbeam filtered through the cell window and penetrated his eyes. Electro particles connected with his sensory receptors to form images at the front of his skull. Frank could see a long winding gravel path beyond a wrought iron gate leading to a detached old redbrick mansion. Two large solid oak windows complimented the classic Gothic design of the front door. The image faded without revealing the significance of the image.

Only a step away from his newfound freedom, he opened the station door and the DC came face to face with Moses Black. Both were slightly embarrassed about literally bumping into each other.

A rejuvenated detective started the interchange. 'Don't tell me, let me guess, Mears wants to see you about your report?'

'Sorry officer, but I cannot discuss my report in detail.'

A sly smile from the detective hinted he accepted the standoff. What intrigued him was the quizzical look on the pathologists face. 'If you've got something to say go ahead, I've got too much respect for you to be offended.'

Black squeezed his nose. The detective opened a side door to the waiting room and the pathologist followed.

The pathologist appeared to be wrestling with a crisis. 'Can I apologise? Nevertheless, I have to ask you detective, how did you manage to do it. How did you manage to kill Samuel John?'

'Why do you think it was me?'

Black gave some thought of how to continue. 'Because every instinct I have about the case is telling me it was you.'

The DC looked surprised. 'I thought you only dealt with evidence.'

'That may be so, but I also believe that intuitive power is always the secret witness at every crime. The truth of the matter is there is something singularly unusual about this case. I can see you have guessed my report. In any case, the circumstances speak for themselves. If my report implicated you in any way, you would still be in custody. Detective, if I was a betting man I would give odds that you are the one responsible.'

Frank struggled with the next line. 'What do you want me to say? I don't know and that's the truth.'

'Tell me; are you capable of killing someone without leaving any physical or chemical trace?' Black paused in anticipation.

The detective cleared his throat. 'I'm not going to feed you bullshit, how do you expect me to answer that.'

'Our experience in the cell with my sister, is that typical?'

The DC thought he was stating the obvious. 'Everyone has quirky stuff going on?'

'I am afraid not detective.'

Frank raised his voice. 'It looks as if you've got all the answers. Explain you're so called gut feeling?'

'In America they call it the 'I know' signal from the brain. In my case, the faculty of knowing is based on strong judgment using my knowledge and experience as a pathologist. When we started this conversation, I asked you how you did it, not if you were responsible. You were honest with me so I will reciprocate. My mental matching of who and what you are, my heightened observation of this crime, above all my 'emotional thinking', brings me to the conclusion you killed John. I know you are the culprit detective. One day you will tell me how you committed the perfect crime.'

The DC started to get annoyed. 'You can think what you like, being different does not make me a killer. I'm one move ahead, that's all.'

'The phenomenon power to perceive things that are not apparent to the senses can hardly be described as one move ahead.'

Reluctant to continue, the hesitancy showed in Black's voice. 'In the cells you said you had no recollection of killing John but there was intent on your part. Let me tell you what my colleague said about you. Emotional intent, an overwhelming compulsion to kill, has the propensity to give rise to that behaviour. The fact that you cannot remember could be down to your psychological rejection to recall the incident. This could be self-induced or by another party through hypnotism. Make no comment to what I am about to say. Your extraordinary sensory ability could be susceptible to strange dreams or hallucinations. When you are in a state of hypnosis, pattern-matching programmes with an emotionally driven agenda could be downloaded from your dream into your brain. Again, my colleague explains, at some stage when you are awake, the emotional side of the brain is capable of hijacking your conscious mind. In the driving seat, 'emotion' precedes 'reasoning' and that motivates you to carry out the act without any conscious recollection.'

The puzzled grimace of the detective had a tinge of horror about it. 'Are you saying what I think your saying?'

'Afraid so, there is a possibility that something is programming you to kill.' A forced smile broke out across Black's intuitive face. 'I seem to have touched a nerve. This may be the time to leave the subject. On a positive note, many a relationship has started with a gut feeling. Perhaps in the future our paths will cross again.'

Frank opened the door for the pathologist. A ball of light inside his head, activating energy, transferred to his hand on Black's shoulder. The DC expected an image to form, not so. Looking at Black, the expression of horror on his face told a different story. With his mouth wide open, he covered his eyes in an attempt to shelter from the graphic gore and repulsion of his waking nightmare. Frank removed his hand. Black collapsed into the nearest chair and he sat motionless holding his head for several minutes.

'Unfortunately officer it looks as if our paths will cross again. May your God have mercy on our soul.'

The journey to Roach took on a new significance when the DC picked up David Worrell. A cordial handshake ended the brief conversation between them. Frank did not attempt to explain the purpose of the visit. Worrell never asked. The unspoken word of a grieving father who never had the opportunity to say goodbye to his daughter tugged at his heartstrings. Her touch, naivety, and passion for life, even honesty, all paid homage to the unspoken word. As the car approached a roundabout at the end of the terrace, light filtered through the windscreen. A sunbeam entered his eyes and created a tingling sensation at the front of his skull. Audible cues downloaded the direction of travel to their destination. During the journey, Frank tried to fathom out the extent of control he had over the vehicle. Gently turning the steering wheel to the left, the car moved to the nearside. Still, the detective had that distinct feeling he was on autopilot.

After half an hour, taking a sharp right, entering a narrow lane, ahead in the distance he could see a wrought iron gate leading to a mansion. With the gate padlocked, they entered the ground through a side gate.

Like a magnet, something seemed to be drawing the detective to the rear of the mansion. He opened the gate leading to the back garden. Simultaneously, in a magical second, the travellers experienced an intense feeling of love. They held onto that feeling for some time before an emotional wave touched their heart. Worrell could feel the warm soft touch of his daughter reaching, stretching into the hole in his bleeding soul. He experienced the all-powering emotion of how much Alice meant to him. There was no pain or grieving for her loss, only the raw feeling of happiness. Ahead, he could see a lawn with a vegetable patch at the rear. Like shadows from the past, a shaft of light bursting onto the surface near the fence focused on something planted in the soil. Worrell, walking then running along the path to take a closer look, stopped. His heart crawled into his mouth. At a point where the light kissed the soil, he could see a cluster of purple tulips. Alice's favourite flower, they were also his. Leaving the path, he slowly made his way towards the tulips. Dark green stems proudly holding the petals reached into the sky towards the other world. Bending down to take a closer look, something brushed against his cheek, and again. He smiled the reflective love of a father. Alice was home at last, it could have been an insect, but he knew differently, he just knew. Worrell jogged back along the path. Without saying anything, he hugged the DC. This time the unspoken word came from his heart. When Worrell looked back, he regarded this experience as the most meaningful conversation. There would be no tomorrow with Alice. However, today would last forever.

***

Another kind of love was waiting on the platform to board the train to Cardiff. Junia had difficulty in deciding what frustrated her the most, a late train, or her partner's premature ejaculation. It was too hard to call. A rumbling noise vibrated along the track as a train approached the station. The locomotive made a chuffing sound and bellowed out hot air onto the platform. A jet of steam, gently pressing against the front of her lemon silk dress, flaunted the outline of sensually toned thighs. Why did everything remind her of Frank?

Usually the epitome of sociability, on this occasion, Junia would be more than content with a compartment to herself. Without any distraction or small talk, she could think about the future. To her surprise, the jolting train and the sound of the wheels grinding against the track started to turn her on. Butterfly tingles between her legs turned her nipples rock hard. She crossed her legs, naughty call, nylon stockings brushing against the outline of her knickers only made matters worse. Everything seemed to be changing daily. Junia wondered if every pregnant woman had to endure this frustration. Only three months into the pregnancy, and her body had experienced most of the telltale symptoms. Even Walsh congratulated her on the number of times she visited the toilet. Eight in one shift, was she turning into one of those donkeys on Barry Island sands?

Holding that idyllic thought in her mind, it gave way to someone else reminiscent of a donkey. God only knows how she had managed to keep the secret from Frank. Junia yearned for the moment when she could break the dramatic news that she was going to be a proud mother, and he was going to be Frank. It seemed logical to break the news before punching his teeth down his throat. All the arrangements would be her responsibility. Frank even had difficulty in blinking properly. Excitement about the impending wedding kidnapped her every thought. A diary appeared from a handbag, yes, three weeks on Friday had a familiar ring about it. Of course, there were bound to be complications. Junia winced at the thought of having to invite Frank.

At some stage, that pleasurable experience between her legs would require attention. Junia thought about the most suitable way to respond. With at least two luscious options in the inspirational bubble above her head, the door of the compartment slid open. Of all people, it had to be a man of the cloth.

'Would you mind awfully if I join you?' The carnal desire to say 'no piss off' nearly ballooned from her mouth. Then Junia realised that her reaction to the new arrival was again symptomatic of her pregnancy.

Shrinking pupils hid behind thick eyebrows as a fake smile gestured to the man to take a seat. For some reason he looked vaguely familiar.

The new arrival started polite conversation. 'Awfully nice day for a train ride, don't you think?'

'Yes love, it looks as if we could be in for a decent summer.' *Hallelujah,* unexpectedly, heavenly bliss descended on the carriage. The time had arrived to consider the merit or otherwise of the prospective husband. Did he have the potential to be a perfect partner? NO. In fact, that was definitely a NO GO. Would he turn out to be a decent father? The word NO started to get that weary, dizzy feeling.

*Apart from being pregnant, why the bloody hell am I marrying him.* Her guardian angel came to the rescue and whispered in her ear. *It's because he's a bloody good shag babes.*

She glanced at the middle-aged companion still growing into his third chin obviously deep in thought about something. She hoped that thought would last for the remainder of the journey. Laugh lines and southbound man boobs suggested better days. Blast, their eyes met.

'Sorry to bother you, but I think I know you from many years ago. You're George's little girl aren't you. One moment it's on the tip of my tongue. Your name is, got it, Charlotte.'

The sharp pain in her gut had nothing to do with her pregnancy. 'And you are?'

'The minister of Saint Michaels. Many moons ago I undertook the burial service of your dear mother's funeral, who I believe was called Rose if I'm not mistaken.'

Her mood changed dramatically. A pickaxe scratched the inside of her brain and brought on a migraine.

*You bastard.* 'Small world isn't it.'

'It certainly is, when I saw you on the platform I thought you looked vaguely familiar. I pride myself on never forgetting a face. I also pride myself in having a photographic memory. In those distant days I believe your hair was blonde, and now I can clearly see you are a brunette.'

The conductor must have turned up the heating in the compartment. The female passenger was now decidedly uncomfortable and angry.

'And what are you doing these days, Charlotte?'

The name triggered off a response that turned revulsion into outrage. Junia had to gain the higher ground. 'Being addressed by my Christian name, which by the way, is Junia.'

'I do apologise, why do I distinctly remember you as Charlotte?'

The dart named Charlotte rebounded off the wire of the bull and stabbed her remembering. 'A long time ago everyone called me by that name. When my brother, Charles, died my parents decided that I would lose my identity. It started when they changed my name to Charlotte. As you probably know, because it looks as if you know everything, Charlotte is the female equivalent of Charles.'

The minister seemed genuinely concerned. 'Why would they do a thing like that?'

'Did you know my father, George the local bank manager?'

This time there was a more informative approach from the man of the cloth. 'I certainly did, in fact I'm proud to say we actually went to the same grammar school. Not in the same year, in fact…'

Rude interruption, 'Well my father had many qualities including violent sex with me. By the way, I hope you're not letting the school tie down with a normal sex life. Anyway, he was also a man of vision. He knew, one day I would be sitting opposite some little shit on a train asking silly questions that would make me lose my FUCKING temper.'

Junia flashed her piecing green eyes to emphasise the point. His embarrassment changed to fright. 'Obviously I have touched a nerve, and for that I apologise.'

The officer thought that sarcasm was entirely in accord with the situation. 'Perish the thought love. How could you have touched a nerve by reminding me that my own father fucked me when I was a child? As a matter of interest, did you shag your daughter or were you content to bugger your choirboys?'

Even with divine help, he could not drag his gaze away from

her perverse glare. The intensity of dark green in her eyes reflecting in the light split her iris into several smaller opal lenses. That sullen look had anger with a capital D.

Junia imagined what it would be like to hurt him 'really badly'. Lately she appeared to be making her way through the learned professions. Was the belligerent upstart going to be her second victim within a matter of weeks? The harsh grinding noise of the carriage wheel against the track reminded her of the yell of her last victim. In the drama of remembering, Junia forgot about the annoying passenger, the wedding, even her pregnancy. Her thoughts drifted to a more comfortable place when she would kill again. The destruction of 'whatever, in at the kill', was far more preferable than giving birth. George had taught her that, she did not intend to let all that insanity go to waste.

'Reverend, did you read about the poor bastard who was pushed from a train?'

Stuttering, he attempted to say something. The scary cat seemed to have his head in a vice.

Frank finally, reluctantly, made his way to the pulpit after spending the early waking hour rehearsing the psalm Worrell had asked him to read at the funeral. Junia's critique at the breakfast table on his final rehearsal definitely had that hint of optimism. Apparently, he had started abysmally in pitch, inflection, and then things sort of fell away from there.

Dragging his bruised ego, he aimlessly made his way back to his seat. How did he acquire a stammer halfway through the reading?

Frank looked for an answer at the back of the church. His eyes settled on a stranger standing in the last pew. The silhouette of the visitor moved stealthily towards the exit. Swallowing hard, suddenly petrified to the point of implosion, the DC could not believe his eyes. He did a double take. The thin luminous grey and black aura around the shape of the figure was unmistakable. It represented his worst nightmare. With his brain sizzling, he refused to admit where he had seen it before. The detective even rejected the taste of sulphur at the back of his throat. Gasping for breath, with horror freezing his brain and blood in the veins, the previous sickening encounter ravished his sanity. It had taken place in the corridor leading from the custody suite to the cells.

Junia had no idea that Frank had left the pulpit. In ecstasy, she was still wallowing in self-adulation about her new word, *'Junaphobia'*, the fear of being pushed from a train. That was until Frank sank to his knees in the aisle, and shouted out a deluge of obscene language. The church door slammed. Everyone turned around to listen to the plucking steel teeth of a ballerina jewellery box playing the theme from Swan Lake.

The end of the beginning

## Commentarii de Bello Gallico
## Commentaries about the Gallic Wars 52 BC

'The principal point of their doctrine is that the soul does not die and that after death it passes from one body into another. With regard to their actual course of studies. The main object of all education is, in their opinion, to imbue their scholars with a firm belief in the indestructibility of the human soul. Which according to their belief, merely passes at death from one tenement to another? For by such doctrine alone, they say, which robs death of all its terrors, can the highest form of human courage be developed. Subsidiary to the teachings of this main principle, they hold various lectures and discussions on astronomy, on the different branches of natural philosophy, and on many problems connected with religion.'

*Julius Caesar, 'De Bello Gallico', VI, 13*

# EPILOGUE

An epilogue is usually a short chapter that normally brings a closure. Can I apologise to any reader for thinking that this it is a stand-alone novel. A trilogy follows the main protagonist to a conclusion.

Also used to tie up any loose ends and, with your permission, I would like to dedicate this novel to Brian. After all these years, I miss you. Additionally, I dedicate it to Blue, Dylan the Poet and everyone else that has given purpose to life, particularly my colleagues during forty-four years in the police force. Although somewhat remiss to single out two, but heartfelt thanks to my tutor constable. An apology may be in order for the chicken shit prank. Again, thank you to the dearly departed Sergeant Paine for his support on my first day in the police force that could have been my last.

Finally and emphatically, I dedicate my life to Joanne. I love you dearly.